"A compelling, life-affirming story of a man's endurance and will to live under the most brutal of circumstances. If this was pure fiction, no-one would believe it." HELEN FITZGERALD

"Moving, thrilling and rousing ... A magnificent piece of work." DOUGLAS SKELTON

PRAISE FOR MICHAEL J. MALONE'S PREVIOUS BOOKS:

"Blasts onto the scene like a bullet... my debut of the year." TONY BLACK

"Taut and expertly detailed with blistering prose... an explosively cool and riveting novel." SAM MILLAR, novelist and reviewer for *The New York Journal of Books*.

"This book had me gripped by the throat from first page to last. An absolute stunner." IAN AYRIS

"An addictive thriller that has more twists, turns and blind alleys than a labyrinth. ... A bold and dazzling debut." CRIMESQUAD.COM

"Urgent, pacy prose and sharp dialogue shot through with gallows humour." EVA DOLAN

"A remarkably assured debut novel... The writing is expressive and taut, and the plot unfolds at a relentless pace." ROB KITCHIN

"A superb piece of writing." KEN BRUEN

"An outstanding novel and a must-read." – UNDISCOVERED SCOTLAND

"Quite simply, one of the best novels I've read in the last ten years." CARO RAMSAY

"Effortless prose and the piercing insight that creates characters you not only believe in but actually feel for... Deeply disturbing and emotionally charged... a must read for fans of psychological crime fiction." EVA DOLAN

"An expert storyteller." SARAH WARD, CRIMEPIECES

Also by Michael J. Malone

Fiction

Blood Tears

A Taste for Malice

Non-Fiction

Carnegie's Call

THE

GUILLOTINE CHOICE

Michael J. Malone

and

Bashir Saoudi

CONTRABAND

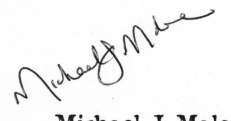

Contraband is an imprint of Saraband

Published by Saraband
Suite 202, 98 Woodlands Road Glasgow
G3 6HB, Scotland
www.saraband.net

ISBN: 9781908643407
ebook: 9781908643445

Printed in the EU on sustainably sourced paper.

Editor: Craig Hillsley
Text design: Laura Jones

1 3 5 7 9 10 8 6 4 2

I would like to dedicate this book to all the members of my family: to my siblings, Tahar, Chérif, Abderahman and Zahra; my wife, Samia; and my children, Tamlan, Lias and Nathan. I also dedicate it to my aunty, Nana Messaouda, for her hours of hard work in providing so much missing information to help make this story complete.

To the entire population of M'chedallah, the people our father loved and served during his time as Secrétaire Général. We are all richer for having him live and work among us. Thank you for your interest and support in the telling of his story.

To every member of the family Saoudi, in the hope that this book will remind us of our father's last fervent wish before his death, to stay united.

To all the people who fight for freedom and justice in our world.

To my loving 93-year-old mother, who was our father's dearest companion.

Finally, I would like to dedicate this book to our father, whom I got to know better after thirty years of research. His life is an inspiration and serves as an education to all of our children. This book is a way to thank him and to say what I should have told him in the living years, that is: DAD, I LOVE YOU.

BASHIR SAOUDI

PROLOGUE

Bashir's Story

I flew first class with Air France from Boston to Algiers via Paris. Paid for and arranged by my American employer. The cabin was quiet. The stewardess read my reserve and only interrupted my thoughts in order to offer me some food and alcohol. I shook my head at both offers.

'Some water, perhaps?' she asked, her face long with concern, and for the first time I realised I had been crying.

I nodded, forced a smile and wiped a tear from my cheek.

Water might do me good. My mouth was as parched as my thoughts. They kept going back to that last time before the news came through. The last time I saw my father alive.

He stood at the door of his house while my cousin drove me back to the airport. In the wing mirror I could see that he stayed to watch until the car shrank into the distance.

We hugged before I left.

We gathered a lifetime of hugs in that month.

His skin lined, his frame shrunk, his eyes were framed in an expression of loss. From the distance of time I can read that expression.

He knew.

Fathers and sons... Was it every man's experience to go back home, take part in the funeral service, and question what his father was really like and wonder what might have been?

I closed my eyes tight against the feelings that threatened to swamp me. I had to keep control, until the ceremony at least.

A cough intruded on my thoughts. The stewardess with my water. She pointed towards the table on the back of the seat in front of me. Another weak smile. I released the table so she could place the small bottle and glass in front of me.

'Can I get you anything else, sir?' she asked.

'No. Thank you,' I answered. All I could manage was a whisper; my throat was so tight with emotion.

I scanned my memory for my father. Things he had done and said. He was remarkable, by any man's measure, but how well did I really know him? How well does any son know his father? And does the fault for this lack lie with the son? Or the father?

Resolve tightened in my gut, worked at the muscles of my jaw. I should know more about my dad. I should speak with the old ones. His generation. I should record what they have to say about him. I should write it all down and make sure the world knows.

I thought about the days ahead. The funeral. The turnout was going to be huge. My chest tightened with pride at this thought. Hundreds of people would be there and many of them would travel for miles, such was his influence and reputation.

He was special, and this is not just a bereft son's belief. What made a man from such a humble beginning become such a force in a huge region of Algeria?

* * *

A memory. My father's voice, low and without judgement. Telling the tale of his favourite dog and what he witnessed that day as a child. How many other boys would have grown to manhood and demanded retribution against a conquering nation, instead of seeking rapprochement?

Much of his story he kept to himself, but this was one episode he was happy to repeat. In fact, I heard the story so many times as a boy it almost feels like the memory is mine.

As if I was actually there...

PART ONE

ALGERIA

ONE

The Harvest, 1913

The dog was chained at the boy's feet. A question in the angle of his head and in his large brown eyes. Kaci bent down and hugged him, taking warmth from the animal. Its tail brushed back and forth across the grey dust of the earth. Smiling, Kaci rubbed the dog's head, just in that spot he loved so much; between the ears and the top of his skull. The dog's eyes all but closed in pleasure as the boy's small knuckles did their work.

'You like that, don't you, Lion?'

Lion was not the biggest dog in the village, but he had the biggest heart and the loudest, most persistent bark. Bear and boar dare not enter his territory and he had even chased a leopard away from the field where the olives grew. Or perhaps Papa had pretended about that one. He was always laughing and teasing.

Kaci stood up and looked in towards the olive trees. Small as he was, he still had a job to do at harvest, picking olives from the sacking that lay beneath the trees, while his uncles, brothers and older cousins climbed up and shook them loose. It was also his task to watch over Lion as he guarded the increasing pile of harvested olives in front of the family home. Although he was only six years old, Kaci already knew that other village children would be paid pocket money for any stray olives that managed to work their way under their *gandora*, the loose, thin shift they wore in all seasons. He also knew that every olive gathered would improve his family's financial position.

The Saoudi family, unlike most, still owned some land. That it had not been taken over by some French *colon* was a tribute to their hard work and persistence. It did, however, cause some jealousy among some of the extended family and neighbours. Kaci had heard his father, Hadj Yahia, argue at the last village meeting that this was all part of the Frenchman's plan. If the *indigènes* fight among themselves, he stressed, the French can go on stealing what remains of their land. He had even offered to share what he could with the poorest families of the area in an effort to stem the flow of resentment that surfaced every year around harvest time.

'Have I not also suffered under the French?'

Kaci remembered his father's expression, dark with suppressed anger as he faced down some of the louder voices. This had brought silence and everyone looked over at Kaci as they remembered his mother. Perhaps if there had been a doctor nearby and money to pay him, she might have survived. He was only two when she died in labour. The lack of healthcare for the *indigènes* was acute, and the blood loss was too much for the local woman who acted as midwife to try and repair.

Kaci had pretended to examine the small wooden carving he was playing with, the image of his father standing tall in the room strong in his mind. He felt he might burst with pride at his father's bearing, and his kindness. He too would be a son who would help his fellow Algerians. He would grow into a wise man. One day, he would be such a man to make his father proud.

Back in the present, the dog stiffened under his fingers. His ears up: his snout and body pointing in one direction. He issued a low growl.

Kaci looked where the dog was aiming his warning and could see nothing but a speck in the distance.

The speck grew larger. The dog grew fiercer.

Kaci felt a tremble in his thighs and worry churn in his gut. He put a hand out to soothe the dog and spoke sharply, ordering him to sit.

The shape moved closer still.

The dog's anger surged to fury and he jumped to the end of his chain with such madness that he choked off his bark, his body aimed like an arrow at a large shape moving closer with each second.

A man on a large horse. Closer.

Still the dog barked.

And on the man rode, unmoved by the dog's fury.

'Quiet, Lion, please be quiet,' Kaci pleaded, and reached for the dog's collar, thankful for the chain. Without it, Lion would surely be lunging at the horse's flanks, and would just as surely receive a hard kick. With all of his strength he held on, willing the dog to be still.

Kaci struggled to keep his feet and still the dog tried to throw himself at the figure making its unhurried way up the dirt road to the house. He was close enough now for Kaci to make out the uniform of a *Garde Champêtre*, one of the hated French field police.

The guard was wearing his hat low over his face and all Kaci could see was the line of his nose and thin lips angled in mild irritation. He must have been a tall man, for he seemed like a giant on top of his dun-coloured horse. The horse snorted its concern over the closeness of the angry animal on the chain, but the guard simply pulled at the bridle and drew nearer.

The Frenchman reached a spot that he seemed to consider safe enough for his horse. He jumped from its back and walked towards the boy and the dog, his focus never wavering from them, his expression not altering.

Still the dog lunged and barked.

'Please stop, Lion, please!' Kaci shouted as loudly as he could, fighting to hide his own fear.

The guard came closer.

And still the dog barked. And jumped. An electrifying bundle of hair and muscle.

With one fluid movement, the guard reached for the pistol at his side, pointed it at the dog and fired from point blank range down the animal's exposed throat.

Dog and boy collapsed to the ground, like puppets whose strings had been severed. All that energy and fury cut off with the roar of a gun. Kaci held on to the dog's neck, fingers entwined in his fur.

'No. No. No. Lion!' he screamed. 'You killed Lion.' His ears rang with the report from the weapon.

The sound of the gun brought the men running from the field.

Kaci wouldn't, couldn't, let go and his cousin Hana Addidi was there, prising his fingers from the fur.

His father picked him up and held him tight against his chest. Kaci screamed and twisted; kicked and punched at his father.

'He killed Lion.'

'Be quiet, Mohand.' Normally the use of his formal name was enough to stop Kaci in his tracks, but he couldn't stop. It was as if the fury from the dog had been transferred to him. He landed a blow on his father's nose, and in surprise his father dropped him. Kaci lunged for the blood-matted dog lying lifeless on the ground.

The Frenchman spoke for the first time. 'Who owns this sack of fur?'

'Chouchou,' Hana Addidi whispered. 'Please. Let go.'

Kaci looked up at the guard through eyes thick with tears. The man's expression had altered only slightly; he looked as if he had found enough energy to move beyond bored. Kaci's little body was shaking with emotion, yet part of his mind was watching events with detachment. Some instinct told him there was still danger here and he had to be alert to it. The guard had murdered his favourite creature with less thought than he might stub out a cigarette. What might he do to his people?

'I do,' Hadj Yahia answered, chin high.

'Then you have committed a crime. You are charged with owning a dangerous animal and you will pay sixteen francs.'

There was a loud gasp from the adults gathered nearby. Few of them spoke sufficient French to know exactly what the guard had said, but they all understood the sum of money he was talking about. It was enough to feed a family for a month.

Everyone there had been touched by the case of a local man who had forgotten to register his son's birth: another of the man's children had died just days earlier in a house fire and he had been distracted by grief. For that he had been sent to jail for six years.

What if his father was sent to prison, too? If Hadj Yahia did not find the money, would he have to sell off more land to meet the fine, as many of his countrymen had done in the past? If he did so, how would the loss of revenue from the olives affect the family's wellbeing?

Kaci had not let go of the dog's coat, his body still heaving as he sobbed. How could this foreigner come here and do this to his people? How could Allah allow this to happen? How could this man of flesh and blood and bone treat Lion, his best friend in the whole world, in such a manner?

'I will pay your fine, Frenchman,' said Hadj Yahia, muttering a Berber curse under his breath. His eyes never wavered from the guard's face. But Kaci read something in them. Had he the words at that young age to describe what he saw, he would have been torn between 'defiance' and 'acceptance'. It was as if somewhere deep inside, his father was staring at some terrible truth.

Kaci swore that one day he would understand. He would watch. He would study and he would learn everything about the French, so that he and his kind would show that they were worth more; that they too were of flesh and blood and bone.

One day he would grow up to be a man worthy of respect, from everyone.

TWO

The Orphan and the Moon, 1924

A teenage Kaci sat under a tree, his belly full after an evening meal of couscous, watching the setting sun paint the ridge of the distant mountain gold and red. Wood doves called to each other in the olive groves around him to the accompaniment of children's feet scuffing the dusty earth as they chased and fought and played.

One of the children broke away from the group. His little body was rigid with anger as he stamped across to the trees.

'Baby!' one child shouted after him. 'Zaki is a baby.'

Head down, Zaki tried to ignore the taunts until he was safely under the shelter of an olive tree. From Kaci's vantage point he could see that once he was out of sight of the other children, the boy slumped on the ground and gave in to his feelings, sobbing into his sleeve.

Kaci jumped to his feet and, as if the child was a wild animal, approached him with care. Once he was sure the boy wouldn't run off he crouched down beside him.

'Zaki is a very wonderful name,' Kaci said softly. The boy turned away from him, his face in his hands.

'A powerful name.' Kaci placed his hand on the boy's bony shoulder. 'Do you know what it means?'

Zaki lifted his head from his hands, curiosity stilling his emotion. He nodded. 'It means "clever".'

'Oh, it is so much more than that, Zaki,' Kaci said with a large smile. 'It means the owner is so smart he could rule the world one day.'

The boy's eyes widened as if struggling to contain such a notion.

'The world?' he asked.

'A boy with this name is so smart he can understand every story his wise uncle could tell him.'

'You are going to tell me a story?' Zaki swivelled on his little bottom until he was facing Kaci. All Berber children loved to hear a story and the word hung in the air above Kaci's head as if pinned their by Zaki's excitement. Like butterflies to the sweetest scented flower, the other children gathered around Kaci's feet with a clamour of bare feet and dust.

Looking around at the small faces tuned in to hear his words, Kaci told them his favourite fable. The very story his own father told him the day after the Frenchman had shot his dog.

'Many years ago there was an orphan child wandering about upon the earth. He was very sad as he had no father and no mother. Nobody would talk to him, or pay him any attention. Nobody cared why he was so sad. Despite his anguish, the boy was unable to weep as tears had not yet entered the world.'

Ten little faces each formed a pout of consideration as they assessed this news.

'There were no tears?' Zaki asked.

Kaci nodded. 'No tears. This night, the moon noticed the distraught orphan boy and felt great compassion towards him. The moon left the heavens, slid down from the sky and came to lie upon the earth before the orphaned child. He addressed the boy: "Weep, sad child! But you cannot let the tears drop to the earth, as it would make it unclean for people who get their food from it. Rather, let your tears fall onto me. I will then carry them back with me up into the sky." The orphan child obeyed. For who could ignore the moon? The oceans can't. The wolves can't. So he began to weep. The first tears ever to fall, rolled down his cheeks and dropped onto the moon.

'The moon gave the lonely child a blessing, saying: "From now on, every person shall love you." When the child could weep no more, the moon returned to the heavens. Thereafter the orphan became happy and people would give him all that he needed and all that would make him rejoice. Every time you look at the moon's face, you will be able to see the stains left by the tears of the orphan child, the first tears ever shed.'

The children gasped in concert and as one they all craned their necks up to look at the great silver ball in the sky.

'Uncle Kaci?' asked Zaki. 'Does that mean that it is always okay to cry? If the little boy in the story was given permission to cry by the moon, then how can it be wrong?'

'Zaki, you are a very clever boy to work this out.' Kaci reached out and patted the boy on the shoulder. Zaki beamed a smile, whirled to the side and ran away whooping with joy. He was quickly followed by a whirlwind of children that formed and swooped around him.

Kaci could only laugh as he watched them all begin a new game. He settled down under the tree and allowed his eyes to roam around the area as he regarded his clan at rest. This was his favourite time of the day. Everyone in the family was relaxed after a hard day's work and they could look forward to some chat and music before nightfall and a well-earned sleep.

He was feeling good about his efforts on behalf of the family. He had recently been given work at the mayor's office as an administrator and as such was one of the few men in the family who was bringing in hard currency. At his young age this was a major achievement, but one that he wore with humility. He was in a unique position because of the gifts Allah had given him. Why should he not take advantage of them? And why should he allow this to make him feel better than anyone else? He had a duty to his tribe and the only pride he would allow himself was that he carried this duty out to the best of his abilities.

Thoughts of his family had him turn and look over his shoulder towards the houses. There were four buildings, low to the ground, made of mud and stone and thatched roofs. Homes where his father, his uncles and aunts and all their twenty-two offspring thrived despite the best efforts of the French.

He heard the footfall of an adult, turned to the other side to see the squat and muscular shape of his cousin Arab. Kaci couldn't help but be flattered by the attentions of the man. He was more than twice his age, yet he sought out the words of an inexperienced youth like himself.

His father had warned him about Arab. Muttered something about 'not to be trusted' and 'a danger to us all'. There had been an argument. Threats were issued. And then everything died down. After all, thought Kaci, we are Berbers. We are family. Nothing is more sacred to Berbers than family. And loud voices were nothing new. His was a boisterous family and always the loud voices were talked down from their position of anger with humour, and soon there were grins all around the room.

He watched Arab as he folded his legs and sat beside him.

'You treat them too soft, boy.' Arab's eyes were black in the moonlight, picking up only the tiniest glint from the distant fire. 'Life is difficult for an Algerian. We must toughen them up. Not tell them fanciful tales.'

'Ach, you are a hard man, Arab. We should let the children be children for as long as we can. Life will be difficult soon enough.'

Arab's answering laugh was loud and harsh. A sound that could often clear a room.

'Mohand OuYahia, Saoudi the Sage,' Arab said, his voice dripping with mockery. 'How old are you, boy?'

'Old enough.' Kaci bristled. He would not be bowed by this man.

'Yes, I heard that my young cousin was to become a man.' Arab's teeth were displayed in a smile. His voice was softer now. The change was so abrupt that it threw Kaci from his defensive tone.

'Yes,' he said, a little more relaxed, warmed by the thought and yet nervous of his impending marriage. 'Seventeen is a good age to take a wife, don't you think?'

'A wife is good for a man,' Arab said, patting him on the shoulder. 'Helps to keep his blood cool.'

Kaci fought to control his blush. Although he was a virgin, he had some experience with girls and he had overheard men talk.

* * *

The task of finding a wife was normally the role of a mother, but for Kaci and his brother Amar it had fallen to his father and Hana Addidi. Hana was the Berber word for 'dearest' and this lady that Kaci would love to his dying day had adopted the maternal role after his own mother died. She had eight children of her own, but it was clear to anyone who had a pair of eyes in their head that she favoured Kaci above her own.

And now he was to be married. In the absence of a mother, Hana Addidi was given the task of finding both of the young Saoudis a bride. Eventually, for Kaci, she suggested a girl from her extended family. She was thirteen years and six months old. Hana Addidi assured him that she was dark and she was lovely and she had a sweet temperament. Such was his trust for this kindest of women, that her words were good enough for him.

The process of agreeing this match took almost as long as the prospecting. For the girl to qualify as being worthy of this position as his wife, his father had to make enquiries into the status of her family. If the family were of the same status as theirs, they would approach them and a dowry would be agreed.

The boy and girl would not see each other before the night of the wedding. They were young. What did they know about picking a mate for life?

Amar was marrying a cousin from a branch of the family that lived nearby. Kaci's future wife was called Saada and Amar's was called Messaouda. A double celebration was prepared.

* * *

Kaci and Amar fought to out-do the other as they both struggled to appear cool and unaffected by the preparations for the big event. They alternated between elbowing each other in the ribs and then staring with inscrutable expressions into the distance. Then they would fall into giggles, excited by the attention of those around them and the thought that they would soon become men.

Kaci was as pleased for Amar as he was for himself. Life had been difficult for his older brother and it was wonderful to see something good happen to him. It had happened too long ago for him to remember much, and he was only a child himself at the time, but he remembers mucus streaming from one of Amar's eyes. An extended stay in bed. Lots of moaning. Some screaming and then silence. Eventually his brother emerged, with one glass eye. Which was endlessly fascinating to Kaci as a child. Amar was also in a much weaker state, tired easily and never seemed to grow into his shoulders the way other boys did.

The soon-to-be men were given time out from their normal duties and, unsure what to do with all this free time, they loitered around the house, listening to the chatter and songs of the women.

Amar soon tired of the women's talk and wanted to go walking in the mountains. Kaci was torn between performing a more manly pursuit and eavesdropping on the women's conversation. He stood at the door, leaning on the frame, eyes focused on the trees outside while his ears strained to hear.

'Let's go.' Amar pulled at his sleeve.

'Sssh,' Kaci hissed at him. 'We are about to have wives, shouldn't we try to learn something about women?'

'Why?' asked Amar, straining for understanding, looking into Kaci's eyes as if his brother's body had been taken over by a mad stranger.

The women were talking about the 'Night of the Henna'. They were saying that the girls were changing their status from children in their father's house to wife and potential mother in their husband's. They would be praying for an abundant life. Henna was used to stave off the 'evil eye'.

Drought, disease and barrenness were ever-present threats to the Algerian people at that time. What the women prayed for was prosperity, health and growing families. Henna painted on to the feet and hands of the new wives would avert the *djinns* that might bring withered crops, bodies and hopes.

Kaci learned that good quality henna was mixed with lemon juice to help set the mixture. Black tea was added to strengthen the henna stains.

He was open-mouthed when he heard that the application of the henna pattern was performed in a ritual that took up to three hours. And once painted, the bride-to-be couldn't disturb the painted area. She must cover it with cloth and let it set overnight.

Eeee, thought Kaci, how is it possible to sit still for all that time while someone paints your hands and feet? Then the same again while the pattern stained deep into the skin.

'People would have to bring you food and drink,' he whispered to Amar. 'But who would do all your chores?'

'And how would you take a piss?' asked Amar.

Their giggles drew the attention of the women. Their aunt drew them a glare.

'What are you boys doing hanging around the women?' she demanded.

'Perhaps they would like some henna painted on their hands,' another woman said. Yet another said that they should be out hunting, eating fresh meat. They had duties to perform soon as new husbands. They should put some fire in their bellies beforehand. Then they all laughed. Blushing, the young men were chased from the house by cat-calls and ribald comments that questioned their manliness.

* * *

Those relatives who lived nearest started arriving early to help with the preparation and soon donkeys, mules and horses were attached to fig trees everywhere around the house. Most of the men were dressed in clean, traditional Berber clothing: a white baggy trouser, with a long piece of cloth hanging between the legs; a white shirt; a waistcoat and a turban made from a long white cloth, which tradition dictates must be wound around the head thirty-three times. They were also wearing a *burnous*.

This is something that every Berber man should own, but not everyone could because of the cost. It is a hooded cloak made from camel wool, not usually worn during the summer months, but the status it conveys means that it should be worn at weddings. Most of the men also carried a rifle, with its strap over their shoulders, for it is said that in Berber culture, two things must not be lent out: the wife and the gun.

The first day was reserved mainly for the close family to celebrate together and prepare for the big wedding the next day. That evening, after a lavish dinner of couscous flavoured with herbs and chunks of melt-in-the-mouth lamb, a small group of selected members of the family visited the bride's home. There they took part in the Night of the Henna and joined in the celebrations with music and dance. Early next morning, the women started cooking the wedding feast.

By midday, two horses for the brides were prepared with colourful ribbons and halters. A group was formed to collect Saada with one horse and Messaouda with the other. A time and a place was arranged where they should meet before forming a procession to the home of their waiting grooms.

When they met, Hamadache, the uncle of both grooms, was so excited about the future prosperity such a pair of unions might bring to his family that he fired his gun in the air. The loud noise caused Saada's horse to panic. It reared and she fought to hold onto the reins before she fell to the ground. Once the horse recovered from its fright, everyone could see that poor Saada was trembling.

Another uncle remonstrated with Hamadache: 'You old fool. The poor girl is terrified. How is she supposed to go to her groom in such a state?'

'Put both girls on Messaouda's horse. It's more even-tempered,' another said, with a glare aimed at Hamadache. 'Then we should be able to get them to the wedding safely.'

Hamadache simply grinned. Nothing could spoil his good humour on this most special of days. He simply bided his time and once the house was in sight he aimed his rifle into the clear blue sky and set off a volley of bullets.

The call of his rifle was answered by those relatives waiting outside the house: the air was filled with the smell of cordite, and eardrums were rattled by gunfire.

Rifles were fired in the air for a good ten minutes and then a mixture of sweets and nuts were thrown to the crowd. All you could see was the cloud of dust, smoke from the guns and the bare heels of children running after the sweets. The air was ripe with joy.

These were hard times, thought Hamadache, and a reason for celebration was welcome by everyone.

The two grooms were nowhere to be seen. A crowd of people

waited with Hadj Yahia before the house. It was his duty, as father of the grooms, to welcome the two brides to his family. As the horse approached, Hamadache stopped it with a great meaty hand. With as little effort as a shepherd picking up newly born lambs, he plucked the girls from their seat on the horse and, turning with a girl in each arm, he walked toward Hadj Yahia.

'Brother, here are your two daughters.'

The brides were fully covered with the traditional colourful Berber material and with many small mirrors, which were thought to turn evil away, sewn in to bright red headdresses that all but obscured their vision. It was Hana Addidi's job to guide the girls towards the house, to a room that had been specially prepared for them.

By now, invited guests were arriving in good numbers. They were all fed while sitting on brightly coloured, handmade Berber carpets under the huge tree in front of the house. Laughter and happy shouts filled the air. Men celebrated together outside with some traditional games like 'ring under the cups', cards or dominoes, while the women were inside, where they sang and danced all night.

* * *

On the third day of feasting, people started to leave. The young people would now get a chance to be together. As was customary, the mother would not sleep that night until she witnessed the blood on the sheets to prove the girl was a virgin. This was a crucial test of a girl's honour, and the power and respectability of her family.

On this occasion, Hana Addidi took the role of the boys' mother. In the morning she waved the two sheets in the air, each stained with hymenal blood, and with the support of the brides' mothers they made a loud Berber noise, *Asliloui,* an ululation that filled the air so that everyone could hear that the marriages were consummated successfully.

As Hana sang this ancient song, she looked to the heavens, trying to hide the pride that swelled her heart. In the eyes of the world, her boy was now a man.

THREE

A Gun

Some months after the wedding, Hadj Yahia was approached in town by a *colon* called Henri Lapoque. He was an industrialist in wood and properties who owned many hectares of land stolen from the *indigènes*. 'Theft' wasn't the word that Lapoque would have applied to the re-appropriation of land formerly owned by native Algerians. For him, the colonists were simply improving on the historic and, quite frankly, outdated practices of the natives. That the French had to take the land over to do so was absolutely necessary.

He wanted to cultivate wheat or barley on different parcels of his land. Hadj Yahia was a man that Lapoque admired. A man who knew the land and the people. A man who could get the job done.

Yahia did as he was bid. He organised everything and completed the job effectively and on time as requested by the *colon*.

On the allotted day he rode to Lapoque's farmhouse on his mule to collect his dues. He rode past field upon field ripe with potatoes and beans, and orchards of apples, pears and apricots, while the heat from the sun pushed against his head and shoulders. Hadj Yahia stifled his feelings about the bounty that surrounded him. All of this produce would be shipped across to France, while many families around him were only able to eat a poor mash of barley, flavoured with dried beans and chilli powder.

When he arrived at the farm door he was kept waiting by a servant, who vanished into the cool interior of the building, leaving Hadj Yahia standing in the sun. A fellow Berber would never have behaved in this way. One of his own people would have ushered him in to the home or would have taken him to a seat under the shelter of a tree and offered a cooling drink.

As he waited he looked around himself at the gardens that surrounded the large, white house. Grass, flowers and low, box hedges in an arrangement that, Lapoque informed him during a previous visit, was modelled on a king's garden in France.

He ground his teeth against his resentment and ruefully considered that he would soon have no teeth left. He had, however, managed to look after his family better than most. Earlier in his life he had worked for the French in the construction of the railways. One day he stole a piece of railway track. He hid the stretch of metal in some bushes and at the end of his shift, loaded it on to a mule and travelled to the far side of the Djurdjura mountains, where there would be fewer questions asked. He had sold the metal in the market for a more handsome sum than he hoped for.

With a rising pulse, he had realised that this capital could help him start up as a trader. He began to travel far and wide throughout the Kabylie region, selling and buying. He would fill the panniers on his mule with olive oil and figs and head towards the Arabs in the south, nearer the Sahara. From there he would load his mule with wheat, barley and salt and head north towards the cities of Tizi Ouzou and Bejaia.

All his travel meant he was away from his family for four to six days at a time. He joked to his wife she shouldn't worry about him while he was away. He was sleeping in the hotel of a thousand stars. He had Mother Earth for a bed and a bright, night sky for his roof.

Over the years he built up a reputation for fairness and quality, and whenever he arrived at a market people would argue among themselves who should get first pick of his fine goods. At times these arguments even resulted in fights.

The money from these ventures enabled him to buy land in his valley and whenever the French forced the sale of an *indigène's* land he would do what he could to buy it before a Frenchman did. His aim: to keep as much Algerian land for Algeria as he could.

The downside was that it brought him into the orbit of people like Henri Lapoque, who was bustling to his door; fat on the bounty of colonialism. Hadj Yahia swallowed his anger and waited for the offer of recompense he was due. He forced his features into a neutral expression and faced the *colon*.

'I am pleased with your work,' said Lapoque. 'So much so that I would like to offer you this good hunting gun as payment.' He held out a rifle. 'This is better than money, *non*? You can hunt with this. Feed your family.'

Hadj Yahia stood braced with his feet on the earth, showing nothing of the thoughts that were racing through his mind. He was no idiot; he knew that this patronising offer was made to save the Frenchman some cash. But Lapoque hadn't become this successful just from hard work and conniving against the locals. He was a dangerous man, with a mouth close to the ears of the local officials. The wrong word in the right place could cost his family greatly and Hadj Yahia knew that he had to handle this transaction with care.

His stomach churned with the effort of restraining his true response. He could see his fingers close around Lapoque's fat throat, squeezing the life from him. But there was only two ways that episode would finish: the guillotine or Devil's Island.

He asked to reflect on it for a couple of days before making his decision and as he rode away from the farm he was chill under the cloud of his resentment.

After almost a hundred years of French rule, his people were all but destitute in their own country. This situation was outlined to him by Caid Mezaine one day over a sweet coffee in a cafe in Maillot.

The Caids were Algerians placed in a position of power over their brothers by the French. Many Caids were corrupted by this power and used it to stuff their own pockets at the expense of their neighbours.

This had the effect of making Algerians focus a good deal of their anger and frustration onto one of their own rather than the real architect of their misery: the *colons*.

Caid Mezaine, however, was a man above such greed. He played the game with sufficient attention only to keep himself on the right side of the French. As best he could, he used his authority to help his neighbours.

 Literary

'When the French arrived,' Caid Mezaine had explained to Hadj Yahia between sips, 'literacy levels in Algeria were the same as those in France. Now however, it is thought that only four per cent of Algerians can read and write.

'The French even have a term for what they have done to us.' Caid Mezaine clasped his hands in front of him and swallowed as if the word he was about to utter might burn on the way out. '*Clochardisation.* They have effectively turned us into a nation of beggars.'

* * *

All the way home and all through that evening's meal, Hadj Yahia considered what he should do. He knew that if he forced the issue, Lapoque would find a way to hurt him. It would be no difficult task for him to find some minor transgression; complain to the magistrates and before Hadj Yahia knew it he would have a huge fine to pay. A fine that he could only pay if he were to sell some of his precious land.

On the other hand he was struggling to contain his frustration at yet again being taken advantage of by the French. There was only so much a proud man could take. He looked around the menfolk of his tribe, crossed-legged on the carpet under the tree. They were all absorbed, discussing the issues of the day, while the air cooled and the sun coloured the mountain peaks amber. This was not something he could throw into the open forum. Some of them might be drawn into doing something dangerous. Who should he speak to? He watched his sons as they spoke to the group. Dahmane or Amar, as per the Berber customs, should be sounded out. They were old enough to offer counsel.

Then his eyes lit on his youngest, Kaci. He couldn't ask him, could he? People would scoff that a man such as he should seek words of advice from a boy who had barely grown a beard. Kaci faced him, aware of his scrutiny and raised an eyebrow in question. Hadj Yahia was struck by the maturity of the gesture and the intellect sparking in his youngest son's eyes, for there was no doubting Kaci's intelligence. Who else in the family could read and write perfect French?

He remembered the boy of eleven and his excitement that his

time for schooling had begun. One of the Frenchman's ways of ensuring the subjugation of his people was to limit their exposure to education. Only one child from each family was allowed to go to school at any one time, and even then they were restricted to the basic *certificat d'études primaires.* Of course in a nation comprised of large families, this often meant that many Algerians were adults before their turn came round. By which time their assistance in the fields was essential for the survival of the family unit.

Luckily for Kaci, his elder brothers didn't take to schooling so his turn came sooner than might be expected, and he welcomed the opportunity it presented with open hands and a voracious mind. Summer or winter, sunshine or snow, Kaci would walk up to twenty kilometres a day to and from the nearest school, crossing a river on foot. Shoes were a luxury to his people and this was to be done on bare feet. He would arrive home exhausted, eat his only meal of the day and go straight to bed. Only to get back up in the dark of the early morning and, on an empty stomach, trudge the same distance all over again.

He remembered Kaci's complaints that he had lost a year's teaching because Monsieur Aslan, who was a nice man, by the way, was such a terrible teacher. How many boys would make such an observation?

How could he, Hadj Yahia, put his problem to anyone else?

* * *

It was a Tuesday at the end of the market day.

'What would you recommend I do?' Hadj Yahia absently stroked the gun.

Kaci held his hand out to take the rifle from his father. As Hadj Yahia continued speaking, Kaci held the weapon to his cheek and looked along the sight. Then he stroked the butt that had been burnished to a deep walnut. He felt the weight of it in his hands and considered the food he could bring to the family meals.

'This is a beautiful gun, Vava,' he said. 'I would love to keep it for myself.'

Understanding coursed between father and son. Although the

main bulk of Kaci's wage went directly to his father, he was allowed to keep a small amount of coin for himself, which he had no doubt been saving with painstaking patience until it amounted to something.

'I have some money, Vava. I'll buy the gun from you. This means you get good coin. I get a weapon.' His father saw instantly that this was the perfect solution and did not hesitate. He patted his youngest child on the shoulder.

'You make me proud, my son.'

They sealed the transaction with a hug and parted; the father to consider the man he had raised, and the son to dream of long days in the hills with nothing between him and his prey but the brush and silence.

That night, during the evening meal, Hadj Yahia informed the family of recent events. With people living so closely together, the family cell was a vital component of Berber life, and decisions were normally only made after lengthy debate. However, not one dissenting voice was raised that evening. Everyone understood the importance of Kaci to the clan, how deserving he was of this honour and, more importantly, how unspoilt he was. And even if this tacit understanding wasn't part of the family make-up, such was the delivery of the decision that no one dared question that the gun was given to the youngest in the family.

* * *

Immediately, Kaci embarked on this exciting newfound hobby and started practising with his new gun. He became an excellent shot within a very short space of time, and soon he was able to save from his earnings and buy a new, better gun from Algiers. This he registered in his father's name with all the administrative formalities required at that time. The old gun he passed on to his eldest brother, Dahmane, who accepted it with pleasure.

Every spare moment he had, Kaci was afoot in the mountains, sighting hare, dove and boar down the barrel of his rifle.

A passion developed in him for hunting that would eventually lead to the murder of an innocent man and the threat of the guillotine.

FOUR

Infighting

Hadj Yahia and his brothers, Hamadache and OuHamou, along with their wives and children, lived within a very small space. Their numbers totalled twenty-nine. Hadj Yahia often looked over the masses of people crammed in of an evening and wondered how they managed. What other choice did they have? He was the head of the family since his two elder brothers and his father were dead. Hamadache's children, Ali and Arab, were both in their late thirties. Everyone contributed to the family by working on the land that Hadj Yahia invested in. As leader of the family, he took great care to ensure their survival. And land became the focus of this intent. Whenever and wherever he could, he saved and saved to ensure that there was enough coin in the family coffers to buy up any land that became available.

His control over this was absolute until the family owned most of the land that surrounded Maillot. The price, however, was high and the cost was that the family lived and worked for the most part on an empty stomach.

Water from the well was all that was drunk in the morning; there was no way that coffee would be allowed. Lunch was a basic dish called *aamouch*, which was a paste of barley flour mixed with olive oil. Figs were plentiful so they were permitted as a form of dessert. Dinner in the evenings was always couscous, but it was composed of barley mixed with acorns and served with a sauce made from dried beans and chilli powder.

The family had another house further up in the mountains, where some of them might go in the heat of the summer with the livestock for cool, fresh grazing. This was an even more basic construction. Just one room to house the family and those animals that were too precious to risk against the hunger of the jackals roaming those parts.

With so many people under the one roof, it was inevitable that tensions would ferment. That was why the family council, a *djamaa*, was so important. Then complaints could be aired. Everyone would have their say, and the wiser members of the family could propose a solution. If a solution couldn't be reached, friends from nearby families who were known for their sage counsel could be called upon to settle matters. It was a system that had worked well for generations. For the Saoudi clan, however, it was about to be put to the strongest test, and found wanting.

Ali was the first to cause problems. The rule was that everything was shared among the family. In the interest of fairness there could be no exceptions. However, he demanded that the war pension he received be ignored by the family. As far as he was concerned this was his, he had earned it the hardest way possible and no one was receiving a sous.

Ali's brother, Arab, was the next one to cause an issue. He had been married twice before and on his third marriage he chose a cousin from a part of the family with which there were problems. His uncle Hadj Yahia and other members of the family did not approve and tried to persuade him to choose someone else. Arab was resolute. She was the girl he wanted and the one he would have.

From the moment she arrived, Saadia was trouble. She ignored the efforts of the family council, bickered constantly with the women and generally behaved only as she wanted. The men brought their wives' issues to Arab, but he was so besotted with his new wife he would only shrug his shoulders and carry on with whatever task he was performing.

Further problems arose when Dahmane married within the house to Arab's daughter, Fatima, whom he loved to distraction. Hadj Yahia saw his chance to punish Ali and Arab's lack of respect, and he applied pressure to Dahmane to divorce his new wife.

Dahmane could not see what the problem was. Fatima was a lovely girl, she behaved impeccably. Besides, she filled his heart with joy; why should he divorce her? With trepidation he ignored his father's order.

So one day, when Dahmane was away from the house, the girl's mother was told a lie: your daughter has been divorced by Dahmane. Ignorant of the truth, the mother started packing her daughter's belongings.

After a hard day in the furthest field from the house, Dahmane was tired. All he could think of was lying with a full belly that night, with his young wife in his arms. His father approached him before he reached the house.

'Before you go into the house, my son, I have something to tell you,' said Hadj Yahia. He placed his hand on his son's shoulder and guided him to a quiet spot among the olive groves. 'Your wife has left the family home, son. You are now divorced.'

Dahmane was stunned into silence.

He shrugged off his father's hand and walked over to another tree, his feet dragging in the dust. Under the shelter of the tree's branches, he considered recent events. What did this mean? What could he do? He knew he had not really divorced his wife. He was also aware of the undercurrents between the different sections of the family. What should he do, he repeated to himself time and time again. He loved his wife. He also loved and respected his father. He chewed on his lip and fought back the tears.

This was impossible. He trusted his father's motives. He knew as well as anyone the disruptive influence that Ali and Arab were on the family. But why should he and Fatima suffer? He moved around the tree so that he was hidden from the house. Here no one could see him and study his reaction. With elbows on his knees and head in his hands he wept. If only Ali shared the family values. If only he wasn't so greedy. If only he had caught a bullet from a German's gun.

He heard the footsteps of a child. The small brown face of Talis peered at him from behind the bark. The boy flashed a smile, eyes wide in the joy of the moment. Dahmane brushed a hand through the air in short sharp movements. Go away, he was trying to signal, without speaking. Talis thrust a pink tongue in his face, turned and ran away.

Dahmane was in an impossible position. He had to choose between the love for his wife and the respect for his father, which in turn meant the extended family. He couldn't begin to imagine how it would feel to have everyone he loved turn against him. He was also acutely aware that whatever decision he made, his ex-wife would soon return home to live with her parents. Everyone under the one roof. Together and apart.

Within days the lie became a truth. There was nothing Dahmane could do to stop events. He could run away, but where to? There was very little work and very little food. The French would see a lone male and assume he was a terrorist. So after a period of adjustment with her maternal grandparents, Fatima returned to her father's home. In the eyes of the world the couple were divorced and Dahmane was resigned to sleeping in the corner with the other single men and boys.

* * *

The family atmosphere continued to worsen. Ali continually ignored Hadj Yahia's requests to share his pension. Everyone else who could earn cash now and again did so and placed it at the disposal of the whole family. Kaci was by now working for the French in the town hall and as such was the only one able to bring in regular money. He always handed it straight over to his father, who had a good eye for how to work these funds for the family, and built up a modest herd of cattle. Kaci was jokingly known as 'the golden boy'. He took this in his stride, for he knew that he was only doing his part. From his point of view the others had the hardest work of all, toiling all day in the sun out in the fields.

Only Ali refused to join in the spirit of the commune. Hadj Yahia tried time and time again to bring him back into line.

'We are a family. We share. It is that simple,' he said one night after dinner, his expression calm, his eyes fixed on Ali's face.

Ali jumped to his feet. 'I fought the Germans for the bastard French. I lay in freezing cold mud waiting for a bomb to blow me to pieces.' As he shouted his hands were punching the air around him. It was true, he had fought in the Great War and on his return home he was awarded a special pension by the authorities; a modest sum of money paid out on a regular basis.

'I slept while rats nibbled at my feet. I lived in a hell, for what? A few coppers. No one is taking that money from me.' He spat on the earth and looked around him. Only Hadj Yahia held his gaze. Everyone else stared at their feet.

Hadj Yahia stood up and stared him down. 'This is the way we do things. There can be no exceptions. This is what keeps us united against the French.' He paused. He knew that nothing he could say would change Ali's mind. After all, they had been having this same conversation for months. His mind had presented him with only one option, but his tongue was unwilling to push out the words.

Eventually he spoke. 'You leave with me no choice.'

There were gasps from the assembly. Everyone suspected what was about to happen but no one had imagined it would actually come to this.

'From now on each man is responsible for his own wives and children. We will meet here again in two days time and we will divide the family assets. Then you are on your own, Ali.'

Hadj Yahia's gaze was cold, but his legs trembled with the importance of the words he was saying. 'You, Ali, I will never forgive for splitting this family.' He resumed his seated position and pulled a pipe from a fold in his trousers. Only the insects around them made any noise. Everyone present was robbed of the gift of speech. Mute, they could only wonder what would happen to the family now.

Ali spat again. Cursed at everyone there and walked away into the night. Arab waited for a couple of beats then, with curses that echoed his brother's, he jumped to his feet and sped off to join him.

* * *

As dictated by Hadj Yahia, two days later the three families met to split the assets. Respected friends were called in to help them divide everything on a fair and equitable basis. All their land, livestock, tools, cloth, stored grains; anything of value was detailed and discussed.

The fathers – Hadj Yahia, Hamadache and OuHamou – sat in three camps with their sons and grandsons. Hadj Yahia's heart ached as they worked out who should get what. He never ever thought he would be party to a decision that would split the tribe. Every now and again he looked over at Ali and Arab, trying to take a measure of their expressions. If he was feeling sick at the thought of this happening, how could Ali look so accepting? And greedy. His eyes shone with the need to possess, while he slowly stroked his moustache at every gain.

Hadj Yahia expected trouble during the debate. After all, a vulture has to obey the dictates of its nature. It was shameful that he should consider his nephew in such a way, but Ali's actions left him with a deep sense of distrust. And he was his father's son. Hamadache was a loud, tough man. Quick to laugh and quick to anger, he was brutal with his sons. Even now that they were grown men, he would still strike them if they displeased him. It was a known fact, but never discussed in his presence, that Hamadache had killed a man. An argument with a neighbour over who should have the right to the dung from the cattle grazing on communal land. Hamadache reacted quickly. With a shovel. The neighbour died. Hamadache was never punished by the authorities. An *indigène* killed another *indigène*, why should the French be concerned about that?

How could Arab and Ali have turned out any other way? Although his spirit quailed at the thought of the family split, in a small part of his brain he was grateful. The atmosphere in and around the home had been truly awful these last months. And he was pleased at the thought that Kaci wouldn't be so close to his cousins. Despite his quick mind, he was still at an impressionable age, and there was a certain glamour to his older cousins. Ali had fought in a war. He also had a strength of conviction that any young man inexperienced in the ways of the world might be influenced by. And any influence that

Arab, in particular, might have on anyone couldn't be good.

His reverie was interrupted by Arab's voice getting louder.

'The cattle,' he said. 'You recently bought cattle with the money that Kaci earned. They should be included.'

'Kaci earned that money during a period Ali has been receiving his war pension. Will you share that?'

'You know our answer to that, Uncle.' Arab spoke the title as if it were the worst insult he could imagine.

Hadj Yahia could feel himself reacting to Arab's tone. He had been determined to stay calm and not rise to Arab's baiting, but enough was enough. All the resentment he felt at his nephews' behaviour boiled to the surface. He was on his feet before he realised.

'Not one penny of my son's earnings will be shared. And the last parcel of land I purchased will not be included in the split.'

Everyone started shouting at this. But Hadj Yahia was resolute. He stood with his feet planted shoulder-width apart, his arms crossed and his expression firm. At this moment he was still the head of the family and he had spoken. Most of the voices quietened when they saw how he was standing. From long experience everyone knew that once such a decision was made Hadj Yahia would not back down. The only one still talking was Arab.

His expression was full of venom as he attempted to stare his uncle down. Eventually, in a voice that was almost a whisper, Arab spoke.

'Hadj Yahia, I swear by these moustaches,' he tugged at his facial hair for emphasis, 'I will get you one day. Don't rest. Don't sleep. For when you do, I'll be there.'

FIVE

A New Job

Kaci blessed Allah and his good fortune. He had a good wife, a job, family and, at nineteen, his whole life was in front of him like a promise. Life was calming down after the recent family troubles and here he was in the mountains having time away from his work at the town hall. There was simply nothing he enjoyed more. He stood with his feet shoulder-width apart, fixed the rifle strap on his shoulders and filled his lungs with pine-scented air. His hunting dog, Finette, was ten yards ahead. She stood stock still, her body aimed higher up the mountain, her head swivelled to face him, eyes focused on his, waiting for the next command.

The air still held the cool of the dawn and the animals he hunted would be foraging before the heat of the midday sun sent them scurrying into the dark to sleep and conserve energy. Then later on in the day their search for food would continue, all the while evading the claw of a predator. Such was life among the animals. The search for food was all. Here there was none of the complexities of life among humans.

So much for the addition of the thinking mind, he thought ruefully.

At least the family was beginning to achieve some form of routine. Kaci felt sorry that his earnings would not go to everyone. This would inevitably lead to difficulties for most of them except for Hadj Yahia's family. What could he do? He considered giving his father less and sharing anything saved with his cousins, but his father knew what earnings Kaci consistently brought in and he would question the missing amount.

Arab regularly stopped by with a haunch of meat and some fruit for him, and they would talk. Surely Arab was sorry for his part in the family feud? Why couldn't his father see this? All his father could do was continually warn him about his cousins. Kaci had seen him place his knife under the matting that cushioned him into sleep. His father was normally such a wise man, but he was becoming like an old woman. Arab clearly had his faults, but surely he was not about to harm any of his family.

Kaci looked in the direction Finette was lined towards. From long habit she knew the direction he headed in. Kaci sniffed at the air as if scenting the need for a change. He turned his face so that he was looking towards the south-west. It was indeed time for a different approach. Hunting had become less productive in recent weeks. He should explore new territories. So he headed for the area where they were building the new dam between Ily'thene and Imezdhourare.

* * *

After a few hours of stalking and firing his gun, the success of his strategy was evident in the catch of the day hanging around Kaci's waist: a pair of pheasants and a large rabbit.

With a pleased smile he judged the height of the sun. It was past noon and his stomach was now growling for attention. He ignored it and continued walking. He had heard that the French were constructing a dam in this area. They were apparently planning to harness the power of water and turn it into electricity. This was something he had to see.

Sometime later he heard the deep rumble of conversation and, walking through a copse of pine trees, he encountered a small group of men. They were dressed in the simple robes typical of the Morrocan. They all held a small tin cup in one hand and a chunk of bread in the other. Even these men stopped for lunch. Although the workers were all dirty from their labours, they looked well fed and content with their lot. Apart from the Moroccans he could see a couple of other men who, by their style of dress, could only be French.

Here in the heart of Algeria, in possibly the best source of income in the area, not one Algerian was on the payroll.

This grated on Kaci, but what could he do at this point? He could throw rocks at the men or throw curses at them, but what good would that achieve? They were here at the behest of his oppressors. They were as much victims of French greed as he was. Also, he was well aware that the colonialist regime would not risk employing Algerians. That would go against their attempts to turn his people into beggars. Their North African cousins had proven an easier beast to tame and were shipped into his country in great numbers to work on any project that required the sweat of many men.

Kaci offered a small smile and quick nod in the direction of the seated men. The wise man in this situation would not throw rocks or curses. Is it not true, thought Kaci, that if a man picks up a hot coal to hurl it at his enemy, that he is the first to be burned? He believed that if this was not a time to fight, then it must be a time to learn.

Aiming his voice at the two Frenchmen, Kaci said, '*Bon appétit!*'

One of the men stood, visibly surprised. Few Algerians spoke French and those that did rarely spoke with a perfect accent.

'Welcome to the dam. Would you like to join us for lunch?' The Frenchman took a couple of steps towards him. He was a tall, slim man. His khaki shirt looked freshly laundered, as if he had done nothing more exhausting that day than order a coffee and croissant in a café in Algiers.

'*Merci*,' said Kaci, '*mais non*.' He pointed at the carcasses on his waist.

'I haven't noticed you around here before,' said the Frenchman. 'Do you live nearby?' His expression was open and friendly, his curiosity driven by nothing more than a wish to engage this intriguing young man in conversation.

Kaci felt himself respond to the smile in the man's eyes.

'My family has a small home further up the valley. I come here to hunt. To spend some time on my own in nature.'

'Your French is perfect,' said the man. 'Have you spent some time in France?'

Kaci chuckled at the very thought of it. He'd barely been any further than thirty kilometres in any given direction. A trip to France was well out of his scope, not to mention his pocket.

'*Non,*' he answered. 'I studied with the children of some of the local *colons*. That is, until I was forbidden to go any further.' This was true. He had done so well in the school for the *indigènes* that his teachers had fought for him to go as far in the system as it was possible to in those days. 'I achieved *le certificat*, but because... you know...' Kaci raised an eyebrow, referring silently to the treatment of his people. 'I had to leave school before I sat the *baccalauréat*.'

Kaci added this last part in, not to engage the man's sympathy, but to gauge his response. However the Frenchman reacted would give him the measure of the man.

'*Mon dieu*. What a waste.' The Frenchman examined Kaci. He did not find this probing gaze uncomfortable and was confident that whatever the man was looking for, he would find it.

'How would you like a job?'

Kaci was so surprised he took a step back. 'Excuse me?' This wasn't what he expected. The Frenchman's smile was full of warmth and respect, which was almost as surprising as the job offer. These were qualities that were missing from most interchanges between the two races.

'My name is Samson.' He stepped forward with his arm outstretched. 'I would like you to come and work for me.'

'Thank you, Monsieur Samson, but I already have a job. I work for the town hall.' As he said this, Kaci's mind was processing the information. Although he performed his current position to the best of his abilities, he didn't really enjoy it. How much better it would be to work up here in the mountains, in the fresh air. And this man. There was something that Kaci immediately warmed to.

'Call me Samson. And I can offer you more money than you get at the town hall.'

'And I am Mohand Kaci Saoudi. How much more? And what job must I do to earn all of this money?'

Samson gave a sum that was double his current earnings and went on to describe the job he had in mind. He needed an assistant. Someone who was good with figures. Someone who knew the people and the area. Someone who spoke perfect French.

Kaci fought to keep his emotions under control. He would be able to spend time hunting, he would earn more money for the family and he would be working for a man he could respect.

He smiled and took hold of the hand that had been offered to him.

'Samson,' he smiled. 'You have a new employee.'

* * *

Kaci returned to Maillot, barely able to contain his excitement. Soon everyone knew of Kaci's good fortune and how it would benefit the family. Even Arab and Ali were quick to celebrate with him despite the fact that this new development would not be worth anything for them.

Hadj Yahia, who continued to sleep with a knife by his side, warned Kaci that they might have ulterior motives, but Kaci was so pleased with developments that he refused to take notice of his father's words. Perhaps with the money he earned he could do something about the rift in the family. His improved earning ability may make his father heed his opinion more. He would give it some time. He would use his relationship with the Frenchman to better the lot of his family and then his father couldn't help but listen to him. Soon the family would be together again.

* * *

Like young men the world over, he turned up for work on the first day wearing his best work clothes and carrying lunch lovingly provided by his surrogate mother. Under the soft heat of an autumn sunrise he stepped into the administration offices of the North African Hydro-Electric Company. These offices were located by the side of the main road that crossed the Djurdjura mountains, about three kilometres from his home. The actual construction of the dam was further south, about six kilometres away. His main duties were to assist with the accounts and manage the logistics of the workers' main canteen. This meant his time was split between the office and the dam. Which in his mind made the job perfect. On the way up the mountain he could use the journey wisely to practise his skills as a hunter.

* * *

Monsieur Samson turned out to be the main accountant for the project and in no time his judgement was vindicated. The young Algerian was bright, eager to learn and conscientious. He also opened his eyes to the possibilities of the locals. His countrymen were, in his view, too quick to discount the indigenous population and he would prove it to them. He would take Kaci under his wing and prove that the French were wrong to treat Algeria so cruelly. As victors they had a responsibility to the local people. If they were to continue only to rob them of their livelihood then they were storing up terrible problems for the future.

The time he spent on horseback climbing the mountain between the offices and the dam were some of the best times he'd had since coming to the country. He and Kaci developed a routine on certain days. On occasion, he even allowed himself to go hunting and found he enjoyed the thrill of the hunt, although he doubted he could ever match the shooting skills of his young friend. In fact, most days that they went up the mountain together they managed to get in a little shooting, and his wife began to enjoy cooking the spoils of the hunt. The only day that they couldn't do that was on a Friday. This was the day they carried the wages up to the men working at the dam. It wouldn't do to delay their movement up the mountain road. There never had been a moment while carrying the gold down to the dam that he felt threatened, but he didn't like to tempt fate.

As for his latest employee, he quickly came to admire his quick mind and generous spirit. Most men put in that position would see what was happening and resent the possibilities that had been stolen from their families. Kaci seemed to be above all that, willing to experience everything that life presented to him. This was a huge relief to Samson. For too long he'd had to put up with the sullen attitude of the men below him. Kaci's behaviour was completely contrary to the popular view that Algerians should be not allowed to think for themselves and not receive an education. To have someone with an intellect that matched his own in these lonely hills was, quite literally, like a breath of fresh, mountain air.

Nor had he realised the enforced silence he'd been under since he started with the company. Now that he had a willing listener he found himself detailing the facts of his life. The solitude of the mountain, the silence – save for the footfall of the horses – served almost as a confessional. He talked about the broad tree-lined avenues of his childhood in Paris, his wish to enter the priesthood and his father's refusal. He talked of his decision to marry, his children and his hopes for an integrated Algeria.

He often found himself regarding Kaci as he went about his duties and hoping that his own sons would grow into such a man. Whenever he could he would press a packet of something into his hand along with his wages; goods like coffee, sugar, butter, marmalade and many other things from the French canteen. He invited him back to his home on many occasions and introduced him to his wife, Yvette, and his two sons, Nicolas and François. There he tried to demonstrate that the French had many virtues, knowing that no matter how much he tried, how much he gave, it could never be enough.

SIX

The Possibility of Threat

Nicolas and Francois raced alongside his horse as Kaci made his way back home after an evening meal with the Samsons.

'When are you coming back, Kaci?' Nicolas' small face was turned up to catch Kaci's answer. He was the more serious of the two boys.

'When he feels like it, stupid,' François answered on Kaci's behalf, and aimed a punch at his brother's shoulder. Which was difficult to do when they were both running alongside a walking horse.

'As soon as I can,' answered Kaci. 'Now go back to the house before my horse runs over you both.' He turned in his saddle and waved back at the house where the boys' parents were standing at the doorway of their home watching him ride away. They both waved as if their arms were linked to the same brain signal. Kaci wouldn't have been surprised if they were. Rarely had he seen such a devoted couple.

'Will you bring Finette the next time?' Nicolas stopped running and shouted after him. François, pleased that his brother gave up before him, kept running for several more paces before he too stopped.

'I'll try,' answered Kaci. The truth was that it was not always possible to bring his dog with him, but he knew how fascinated the boys were with her, so evasion was easier on them than the truth.

Soon the boys were only a dot in the distance behind him and he was close to home. He was already anticipating the looks of pleasure on the faces of his family when he shared out the goodies that the Samsons had given him.

Every day he blessed Allah for bringing them into his life. They gave him and his family access to many things that most other Algerians could only dream of during these harsh times.

He was sure that Ali or Arab would be at the house when he got there. The Saoudi mountain home was not out of bounds to them as was the house in Maillot. And here, Kaci could share his newfound wealth without his father's disapproval, while he worked to calm his cousins down and to bring them back into the family fold.

Just as he expected, Arab was hunched by the door as if he'd been waiting there for hours.

'Hello, cousin,' Arab greeted him, teeth flashing in the gloom.

Kaci jumped off the horse, ignored the dog that was clamouring for his attention and pressed a package into his cousin's hand.

'What's this?' Arab asked while pulling at the brown paper. 'Butter.'

Was it Kaci's imagination or did Arab sound disappointed? Most people would have loved the opportunity to have some French butter with their bread.

'Should I give it to someone else?' asked Kaci, holding out his hand as if to retrieve it.

'Oh, no, no, no.' Arab carefully wrapped the package up. He looked at Kaci. 'Although another kind of golden material might be more welcome.'

Kaci tethered the horse to a tree and ruffled the ears of his dog. What could Arab be talking about? The man talked in riddles sometimes.

'Friday is the day you take the gold up to the Moroccans, eh?' Arab was pulling at his moustache.

'What of it?' asked Kaci. In his mind he was already discounting the idea of Arab attempting to steal any of the money.

'Who knows? Maybe one day I'll be there to take it off your Frenchman's hands.'

SEVEN

Gunfire in the Djurdjura

On Saturday 2nd July, 1927, Kaci strode off to work with a huge smile on his face. Even the sun shone brighter this morning, as if sharing in his joy. He was going to be a father.

His own father had woken him that morning.

'Time to go to work, Mohand,' he said. Knuckling sleep from his eyes, Kaci joined his father at the fresh water barrel at the side of the squat building.

'Arab was up and about early this morning,' Hadj Yahia said as he splashed water over his face.

'Mmm,' replied Kaci, struggling to clear his mind of the fog of sleep.

'He must be giving the fig trees some *dokar*.' Hadj Yahia was referring to the Berber practice that was used to encourage a better harvest. It had to be done before the sun rises. There was something about the cool breeze of the pre-dawn that made the treatment more effective.

Before leaving Kaci returned to his wife to kiss her goodbye. His marriage at first had not been promising. He didn't take to her. She was too dark. She didn't talk enough. She talked too much. But now he realised that the enforced change in his lifestyle caused this and he simply had to learn to adjust to the fact that he was a married man.

He gave her the nickname of 'Senegal'. Dark one. And before long he began to court her smiles. Smiles that would flavour his mind as he made his way up the mountain in the morning. His mind conjured up the image of her face and his own response surprised him. He was in love.

That morning he had held her smiling face in his hands and kissed her nose. 'You have made me the happiest man in the world.'

'I will give you such a son that will make you burst with pride,' she whispered. Then she cast her eyes to the floor. Pride was a shameful thing in Islam, but perhaps her whispers would not carry to the ears of the *djinns* that wait to pray on such a careless utterance.

Kaci judged her reaction to her own words and felt his heart swell. Poor thing. He didn't want to leave her side. He could stay here with her and watch as she worked with the other women.

Of course this was impossible. The women would laugh at him. They'd throw comments suggesting that she had hidden his manhood under her pillow. Then there was Samson. It was Saturday. He needed Kaci to ride with him down the mountain.

With a long sigh, he had kissed his wife one more time and with the sensation of her lips pressing against his committed to memory, he left for his day's work.

* * *

As he walked, a shadow formed in a recess of Kaci's mind. As the morning grew around him, so did the shadow. The sights and sounds he knew so well from coming this way each morning seemed muted. Even the birds were silent. What was happening? Just moments ago he had been the happiest he had ever been in his life. Was he worrying that it might all be taken away from him? It was not the lot of his countrymen to find such happiness in their life, was he about to pay a price for his own?

He gave himself a mental shake. He was thinking like an old woman. He was a fortunate man. Allah was smiling on him and nothing could go wrong.

Still, the sense of foreboding continued as he moved on his way to the rendezvous point with Samson. He joined one of the numerous footpaths that criss-crossed the mountain, walking west until he reached the main road, where he continued north for one kilometre.

Arab's voice sounded in his mind. So strong was it that he looked about himself, convinced that his cousin was at his side. Of course, he was alone. If this is what happens when you find love then you can forget it. There was nothing to worry about. Nothing.

Arab's voice persisted. Each night when Kaci returned home he'd change into his more comfortable Berber robes and join the men by the big tree. There they'd chat over the large and little things of life while watching the sky changing from blue ozone to red then to black with billions of stars shining like beacons, as if lighting the way to the possibility of a better life.

Each night Arab would find a way to bring the conversation round to the gold that paid the Moroccans.

'This should be our money, so it really wouldn't count as theft.'

'How much did you say these men are paid each week?'

'It is an insult to the memory of our ancestors that this work goes on each week.'

Just that previous night Arab became more daring than he had ever been.

'I can shoot you in the leg and make it look like a robbery. And then I'll share the money with you.'

Until that moment Kaci had dismissed Arab's talk. He was an angry man who needed to point to other people's failings to cover his own. He needed to make as much noise about others as he could to make himself feel better. This talk of theft and violence was simply an extension of that.

Surely even Arab wouldn't consider stealing from the French? And to throw in the threat of violence? There was only one way that could end. At the guillotine.

Confused and stunned by the outburst, Kaci fell quiet and ignored him.

'I will kill the Frenchman and you will have to throw me the bags if you want to live,' Arab added.

'Enough.' Kaci jumped to his feet. 'Samson has been good to this family. You will not harm a hair on his head.'

'Allah be praised,' laughed Arab as he stood up. 'The pup has teeth.'

'And these teeth will tear out your heart if you harm my friend,' Kaci countered, hoping that no one else could hear his heart hammering at his ribs. He stared down his cousin, knowing that if he looked away it would be seen as a weakness.

Arab merely smiled. 'Maybe the pup will have to die, too.'

Ali laughed from his corner of the carpet. 'No one will die, you miserable pair of jackals.' He called them both such an obscene and improbable insult that everyone laughed and the tension was immediately lifted.

His father had been visiting the mountain home that day to look over his cattle and he had caught the end of the conversation as he came back from his fields. He took Kaci to the side before everyone prepared for sleep.

'Mohand, please be careful,' he said. Kaci knew things were serious when his father called him Mohand.

'It is fine, Father,' Kaci answered, placing his hand on his father's shoulder. 'Arab tells a fine story, but he is nothing but a desert wind. Hot air.'

'And when a desert wind blows it destroys all in its path,' his father countered. 'I might have agreed with you recently. But there is something about his behaviour that has me worried.' He paused. His eyes under the bush of his brows were creased with worry. 'Be careful, son.'

Kaci brushed his father's warning aside, murmuring, 'I know what I am doing, Dad. And Arab wouldn't dare.'

* * *

Kaci arrived at the offices around 5am. Samson greeted him with a strong, black coffee.

'Here,' he smiled, 'this will set you up for the day.'

'Thanks,' grinned Kaci and accepted the cup. His grin withered as his mind returned to the mood that had grown on him the further he had walked from his house.

'Everything okay?' asked Samson.

'Yes.' Kaci gave himself a mental shake and thrust some energy into his answer. '*Bien sûr.*' Then he considered what his friend's response might be when he told him his good news. The grin returned to his face in full force.

'That's better,' said Samson. He tilted his head to the left in that way Kaci noticed he did when something had occurred to him. 'What?' asked the Frenchman.

'What do you mean... what?' asked Kaci, wanting to draw the moment out.

'Your smile. There was something big. No...' He thought for a moment. 'Something profound behind it.'

Kaci thought his face was about to split in two if his smile was to grow any bigger. He looked at his friend, puffed out his chest and told him.

'I am going to be a father.'

Samson whooped with delight. He punched Kaci's arm and then drew him into a bearhug.

'Fantastic news, my young friend. This is fantastic news.'

Kaci warmed to the Frenchman's enthusiasm for his news and compared it to his father's. Hadj Yahia had simply nodded and patted his son on the shoulder. Children were a boon to the Algerians, particularly if it was a healthy boy, but they were also an added pressure. Due to the complete lack of healthcare, mothers and children regularly died during pregnancy and childbirth. As had happened to Kaci's mother. Hadj Yahia could no longer see the glint of promise without it being dulled by the fog of threat.

The Frenchman, by comparison, had simply been caught up in the wonder of the news. In his privileged position, news of progeny was a time to celebrate; time to consider the joy of children and of a brighter future.

'Let's leave the horse this morning,' said Samson. 'A father-to-be needs to build up his fitness if he is to chase a son over these hills.'

Kaci nodded his agreement and hefted a pannier of coin over his shoulder. It was heavy, worth the equivalent of 38,559 French francs. A sum that could keep his family in food for years, but it could have been rocks he was carrying for all he considered it.

Their conversation filled the air as they walked. Samson was full of the possibilities of a future Algeria where Kaci's sons and his sons would play together, grow together and then as adults work together to bring prosperity to all. Kaci, who was almost fifteen years younger, could only smile at the naivety of his boss. As pleasing as the notion was, he was more tuned in to the chasm that lay between the two races. It would take more than a group of childhood friends to heal that.

Soon, they settled into a companionable silence. The sun was bright, its heat softened by the breeze this high up. There was not another human within miles of them and the only sound apart from their breathing and the crunch of their footsteps on the scree underfoot was the occasional call of a bird.

They were about half a kilometre from the dam offices when a loud noise broke the deep silence. The echo of this sound seemed to bounce across the mountains. Kaci's brain was trying to relay the information to him. Confused, he followed the echo, trying to work out what had caused a noise that seemed to go on forever. His mind then separated the noise from the gasp that sounded behind him. A gasp and a grunt that sounded mere seconds after the gunfire.

Gunfire.

He turned just as Samson collapsed to the ground clutching his chest.

A gun. The noise was gunshot. Kaci instinctively fell to a crouch in order to make a smaller target. The gold. That was the real target.

Samson.

Unmindful of the gold, he threw it from his shoulder and went to his friend.

Scrambling to his knees, he placed Samson's head on his lap.

'Don't die,' he ordered. 'I'll get help. Please don't die.' Raising his voice he shouted for help. Surely the report from the gun would reach the dam offices and the workers' camp. Surely people would come running to investigate.

'Help me!' he screamed against the echo of the gunfire that still rang in his ears.

Blood from his friend's wound was soaking his trousers and his hands. There was so much blood. How could a body contain so much?

Only then did he realise that he himself might be in danger.

He sensed movement behind him. A shadow was moving quickly from one bush to the next as it moved closer to the bag of money. The man was dressed in black, his face covered with rags. Only a pair of eyes were visible. All it took was one glance and Kaci knew who was responsible.

Arab.

'What have you done?' he screamed. 'What have you done?' The response of the French would be rapid and brutal. They would not stop until the perpetrators were caught and punished.

He should go. He should run.

Now.

If the police caught him like this, drenched in the blood of a Frenchman, they would march him straight up the steps of the guillotine. He'd never see his father, or his brothers, or Hana Addidi again. Or his wife.

His son. He'd never see his son.

He should run. Run for miles and never stop, but his legs betrayed him. They didn't move. Couldn't move. Trapped under the weight of his dying friend.

How could he talk of running while his friend's blood was draining from his veins? Samson's eyes fluttered open.

'Don't die, Samson,' Kaci wept. 'You have everything to live for. You have two strong sons.'

'What... will happen... to my boys, Kaci?' Samson struggled to speak.

The anguish from his friend was palpable. He was near death, yet he was mourning the loss of seeing his sons grow into their futures.

'Ssssh,' Kaci spoke through his tears. 'Don't talk of these things. You will live to see your boys grow up to be strong men.'

Just then Arab reached the bag and lifted it on to his shoulder. With a look of hate, he glanced at Kaci and the dying Frenchman and then turned and ran into the bushes.

'What have you done?' Kaci screamed as the figure quickly grew smaller in the distance. 'What have you done?'

Samson coughed and looked up at Kaci.

‘You know him, don’t you?’ he asked, his voice weak with pain.

‘I… I…’ Kaci didn’t know how to answer. ‘Help. Help,’ he shouted, fighting to distract Samson from an answer he could never give.

The look of betrayal that formed in his friend’s face was more than he could bear. He continued to shout himself hoarse rather than face it.

EIGHT

Under Guard

The sound of the gun and Kaci's calls for help attracted people from nearby and some co-workers carried Samson back to the offices and called the authorities. When the *gendarmes* arrived on the scene they found the Frenchman still had a pulse.

While they tended to Samson's wounds as best they could, preparing to take him down the mountain to the hospital, they argued among themselves.

'We should just make him as comfortable as we can,' said one. 'His wounds are too great.'

'Nonsense,' said another. 'He's as tough as old boots. He'll be fine.'

While they argued, a pair of them stood over Kaci, their rifles aimed at his head. They had already decided on his guilt. He was an *indigène*. He was present when a Frenchman's blood had been spilled. His guilt was as evident as the blood that stained his trousers.

'Take him to the hospital. You must save him,' argued Kaci, his voice hoarse from shouting.

Pain bloomed in the side of his head. His reward for speaking was a rifle butt to the temple.

'Silence, Algerian dog, or we'll kill you where you lie.'

Kaci groaned and fought to ignore the pain. This was nothing to what his friend was going through. As if he could read his thoughts, Samson groaned. His chest rose with a series of shallow grunts as he struggled to fill his lungs. Blood frothed at the corner of his mouth.

A young soldier crouched down to speak to Samson. Since they arrived he was the one Kaci had been most worried about. While the others spoke he simply stared at Kaci as if his eyes were claws, and looks were able to tear out his heart. Muscles twitched in the line of the young soldier's jaw. He pulled off his hat and rubbed at the thatch of blond hair on his head.

'Monsieur Samson, tell us this man shot you and we will pull his intestines out of his belly and leave him for the birds.'

A tall soldier behind him, with legs like sticks, laughed. 'Pull his intestines out of his belly? You've been reading too many cheap novels, Meric.'

'Shut your mouth, Grosjean.' As he spoke, Meric's eyes never left Kaci's face. 'Monsieur Samson, did this man shoot you?'

Samson managed to move his head from side to side. 'Kaci... couldn't. There was...' He groaned louder, the effort of speech was draining what energy he had.

Couldn't anyone see that his friend needed a doctor? He needed help or he would die.

'A doctor,' Kaci shouted. He didn't care if it earned him another bruise. 'My friend is dying. He needs a doctor.'

Meric jumped to his feet and with one step he was close enough to strike. His boot lashed out, catching Kaci on the chin.

'See how he tries to distract Monsieur Samson from speaking,' Meric roared. He aimed another kick at Kaci, catching him on the side.

'Enough.' Grosjean stepped over and with a bored expression on his face gave Meric a shove. The blond fell to the ground. 'Idiot. Was there not enough air in Brittany when you grew up? Or does all the blood get diverted from your brain to try and feed that puny little prick of yours? We need the young Algerian to stand trial. We need to set a public example.'

Kaci shuddered. He knew what they were talking about. A public beheading.

'I have killed no one. I am innocent.'

Grosjean shrugged a 'whatever'. 'You were here. That is enough.'

The next words froze on Kaci's tongue. He could understand

Meric's fury. He was covered in Samson's blood, after all. If the positions were changed he might feel the same, but Grosjean's indifference chilled him to the marrow. He watched the taller man as he chewed on a hangnail. If it suited him, he could stamp on Kaci's head until it was nothing but mush, then return to his cigarette. He could pluck out his eyes with as much thought as a child might pull the legs from a spider.

'Monsieur Samson…' Meric said as he scrambled over to the injured man. A nod and he would place a bullet between the Algerian's eyes. 'Did this man shoot you?'

Samson managed to shake his head once more. 'Not… him.' He coughed. 'There is no way he would… but he…' Samson coughed some more.

Kaci cringed with the harshness of the cough. He could hear a rattling sound.

'Blood in the lungs.' Grosjean shrugged again. 'All we can do now is make him comfortable and wait.'

A solitary tear slid down Kaci's face, making a track through the dirt and dust. They were waiting for his friend to die.

NINE

The First Prison Cell

Kaci's eyes were so swollen from the beating he'd received from the soldiers that he couldn't make out his surroundings. The last thing he could remember was kicks and punches raining down on him before he mercifully blacked out. He tried to move and groaned from the pain. It seemed that every part of his body was bruised. He moved his arms. His legs. He groaned at the pain. At least he had some movement. At least they weren't broken. He ran fingers over his jaw. Swollen. *Ahhh, painful.* He opened his mouth slightly. Not broken. He shivered.

Samson.

What kind of man are you, Mohand, he asked himself? Complaining about a few aches and pains when he had no idea if his friend was alive or dead. He extended his other senses to try and make out where he was. He could feel cold, hard concrete against his naked back and legs.

He could hear... nothing. Complete silence. Wait. What was that? A cough echoed in the distance. As if coming from the end of a long corridor.

'Hello,' he croaked. He tried again. Louder this time. 'Hello?' He felt shame at the fear evident in the tremble of his voice. Just in those two short syllables. He ran his fingers over his eyelids. He had to find out where he was. He had to see. His eyes were badly swollen and crusted with something he guessed could only be blood. Cuts in the skin round his eyes must have bled into his lashes, which were glued together. With thumb and index finger he tried to prise them apart, but with little success. Then he picked at the larger clumps. Eventually he was able open his eyes a little more and he could see…

Total darkness.

Panic surged through him. Acid churned violently in his gut.

'Guards,' he shouted. 'Guards.'

A cackle sounded in the distance. '"Guards," he shouts. Rule number one of prison, my friend. Don't shout for the guards.'

Prison. He was in prison.

'Who are you? Where am I? What is happening here?'

Another cackle. 'Rule number two of prison. Don't ask any questions.'

Another voice. Deeper this time. Sounded like it was closer. 'Would you two fucking shut up? Silence is the rule here or the guards will…'

'Sorry, silence is rule number one,' the first voice interrupted. He chuckled. 'All these rules. How is a poor man to remember them all?'

Kaci leaned against a cold wall and instinctively crouched, making himself a smaller target. He had never known fear like this. His whole body trembled with it. What was going to happen to him? Samson was surely dead. There was no way he could have survived those terrible wounds. The French authorities need look no further than he. Discovered by the body of a dying Frenchman, drenched in his blood.

What about his family? He had heard tales of reprisals from the French where whole families had been slaughtered in revenge. His father. Would his father know what happened to him? His wife. His 'Senegal'. Saada. What would happen to the child growing in her womb?

It was too much. A scream formed in his throat and flowed out. Tears coursed down his face. He rocked himself back and forward, panting now against the pain in his chest. He was going to die. He would never see his family again. Samson, his friend, was dead.

Footsteps sounded in the dark. Strong, booted footsteps. Two men were marching in his direction.

His door banged open. Strong daylight flowed in, outlining the broad shoulders of two men.

'Shut it,' a voice roared in French.

Kaci cowered as far into the corner as he could. One of the guards made a short, sharp movement and cold water drenched him.

'We demand silence in these cells. Silence. Does your puny little Arab mind not know the meaning of the word?'

'So this is the Berber bastard that murdered one of ours?' the other man said.

Even as Kaci shivered at the cold and shrank against their insults, part of his mind mocked their ignorance. Arab or Berber. These idiots didn't know the difference. Nor did they care.

One moved closer to him. 'They breed their murderers young, eh?' He cuffed the side of Kaci's head. Kaci lost his balance and fell to the floor. He curled himself into a ball fearful that he was about to experience even more violence.

The other guard laughed. A thin, hollow sound. 'Look at the little fucker. They've really done him over. There's not a bit of him that's not bruised.'

'Can you bruise a bruise, I wonder?' A boot connected with his buttock.

'Probably better to let the bruising and swelling settle. Gives you something to aim for, eh?' one man said with a quizzical tone to his voice.

'I like the way your mind works, Dubois.'

Kaci stayed exactly where he was. Any movement from him would only entice more action from the men towering over him.

Another boot connected with his spine. Kaci moaned at this fresh assault. He clenched his jaw against the pain. Grinding his teeth to ensure he wouldn't cry out. He would not give these bullies the satisfaction. But he didn't know if he could take much more.

'Silence is the rule in here, prisoner. Any talking, whispering, screaming… any noise whatsoever and we'll come back again. But next time we'll really hurt you. Understand?'

'Don't know why you're bothering explaining, Leblanc. These savages can't understand a word of the mother tongue.' With that, he moved his face into Kaci's line of sight and placed his index finger in front of his pursed lips. Then he mimicked the movement of a knife across his throat with a smile that suggested he would happily wield the knife.

Kaci was too uncoordinated in his thoughts to tell them he could understand every word they said. He simply nodded. He was numb with fear, cold and uncertainty. What was waiting for him at the end of all this? A lifetime in prison? The guillotine?

As if the guards could read his mind, one of them spoke.

'A knife across his throat isn't much of a threat, man. Surely he knows he's headed for the guillotine anyway.'

With a smile and shrug the other guard moved back from Kaci and they left the cell, banging the door behind them.

He was once again locked in darkness so complete he might have been blind, with nothing but his own fear for company.

* * *

Kaci entered a strange world between sleep and waking, never sure at any one time which was his true state. Both were cold and dark. In both, his body trembled violently and words issued in his mind.

Murderer.
Your child will grow up without a father.
The French will rape your wife before slitting her throat.

He lost all sense of time, having nothing to measure it with, save his own shallow breath. It could have been days or moments before the door opened again and some striped cotton was thrown at him. Darkness. And then time crawled and sprinted again until the door opened and a bowl of something was slid across the floor towards him.

Once the door closed he couldn't see where the bowl had gone. On his knees, he guessed where it might be and moved slowly in that direction, sweeping the ground with his fingers. They touched something and he picked up the bowl and held it to his mouth. The contents were tasteless. Water with small lumps, which may have been rice. Something knocked against his teeth. Bread. He tried to break a chunk off. It was solid. He used his teeth and just managed to tear a corner off. He used the water and his saliva to soften it a little before swallowing. In this careful manner he eventually managed to work his way through his meal.

This repeated action was enough to still his mind. It allowed him to focus on something else other than the real fear that his life might end. His trembling limbs now had a meagre covering and the fact he had something in his belly added some heat to his bones.

The guard's voice replayed in his head. He called him a murderer. He claimed he was headed for the guillotine. That could only mean one thing. Samson had died.

He wept again. Mourning his friend. And the loss of his own future.

What about his family? They relied on him to provide for them. He was the only one with an education. The only one who could come close to dealing with the French on their own terms.

Who are you kidding, Saoudi? He laughed at the movement of his thoughts. On terms with the French? He was in prison, surely awaiting trial for murder. There were no terms. It was only master and slave.

No. He shook his head. He would not allow this thread of thought to continue. The French would never know from him that they were the masters.

For the first time he thought of Arab. What had happened to him? Where had he gone with all that money? An *indigène* with so much wealth could not escape the attention of the authorities.

Kaci was surprised to realise that thoughts of Arab were not consumed with revenge. Why might this be? Surely he should be denouncing him to the French and demanding he stand trial for the killing?

What would that achieve? Yet another Algerian rotting in a French jail. Arab had simply played the part that was offered to him by the colonialists. Divide and conquer. They'd followed the conqueror's maxim as old as the Roman Empire itself. And most of his poor countrymen were too full of thoughts of revenge; their minds full of the lack of anything meaningful in their lives. Yet there was something of importance that the French could not rid them of. There was surely something of meaning in their existence. Family. The Berber way was all about family and throughout any amount of torture and suffering, he, Mohand Kaci Saoudi, would hold that thought to his heart.

* * *

Prison life passed in its own rhythm. A rhythm that Kaci had no control over. A rhythm that centred around the movement of the guards and the shuffle of the prisoners. Hearing the beating that was administered to Kaci, there was no further noise from any of the other inmates. He had no way of knowing what day it was, let alone what time of day. Equally he couldn't know how many more men shared this section of the jail. Who they were or why they were here. Were they as innocent as him, or had they committed real crimes? He spent fruitless hours in such conjecture, as thinking was all he had to pass the time. That or waiting for the next excuse for a meal to be passed to him and then tracking the movement of that meal as it passed through his body and out into the bucket that sat in a far corner of his cell.

Each morning a man would trundle a large bucket along the corridor outside and pause at each door, calling for the inhabitant to pass their waste through the hole at the bottom of the door. The stench that surrounded this man was too much for Kaci to bear and he almost thought he would prefer a clean death under the blade of the guillotine to a life of swilling out other men's excrement.

His mind then moved back to his family, his wife. Did they believe him guilty of such an act? Surely they would suspect Arab straight away? An image of Samson's wife and her two boys imposed itself on Kaci's mind. Did they think he was capable of such a traitorous act? He had been in their home, treated as a trusted member of the family. How they must regret ever allowing him into their home.

Round and round and round his head such thoughts would go, hour after hour after hour.

Until he was pulled from his cell and pushed towards another part of the jail.

He blinked furiously, trying to adjust to the painful daylight, and followed the direction of his guard, while another walked behind him. As he walked his mind was crowded with a fresh set of questions. Questions he dare not ask as he well knew the violence that would result in. All he could do was determine that he would accept the abrupt change in his situation and face whatever came his way with as much dignity as he could muster. He would show these poor excuses for men who guarded him that here at least was one *indigène* they could not discount as an animal.

He lost track of his passage through the jail as he turned one corner after another. He walked across a courtyard. Here he would have given anything to stop and feel the breeze ruffle his hair, the sunlight on his skin, but when he paused the guard behind him shoved him so hard he fell to the ground.

'No dawdling, prisoner,' the guard roared.

Kaci showed no reaction. He climbed back up on to his feet and carried on walking. Eventually he came to a door just like any other door he had passed. This was opened and he was pushed through.

The room was unfurnished. A window was set high up on the far wall, near the line of the ceiling. It was small and the glass was so dirty that the sunlight coming through was as thin as rags. The walls were bare apart from what looked like a butcher's hook high on one side and a pair of steel rings on the other. Stains ran off them like a warning of their gruesome purpose. For a moment Kaci imagined that the room rang with the sounds of the muted screams of the tortured.

There were more guards inside and two men standing in the far right corner.

One of the men stumbled towards him as soon as he saw him.

'Mohand?'

He recognised the voice but not the man who spoke. He was old. His face lined and grey. His once proud and strong frame now stooped and slight.

'Father?' Kaci asked. 'Father, what have they done to you?'

'What have they done to you, my son?' A tear tracked down the coarse grain of his father's cheek.

As they moved to embrace, a guard stepped in between them and wordlessly indicated that they should not touch.

'We are here to help you, Mohand.' The man with his father spoke for the first time. He was dressed in the traditional Berber robes, but robes of a finer quality than any he had ever seen. This was one of the Caids; a group of specially chosen Algerians who were used by the French to sow discord among the natives in order to distract them from the real enemy, the *colons* themselves.

'Caid Mezaine is a good man, son. You must listen to him.' As his father spoke, he wrung his hands in distress. Kaci stared. His mind struggled to keep up with the notion that this shadow of a man was his father. He recognised the voice, but his sight warned him that this man was a stranger.

While he stared, his father looked back at him anguish large in his expression. 'Are they feeding you, son?' He stretched an arm out, trying to touch his son's face. 'Bruises. Such bruises,' he whispered.

'How long have I been here?' Kaci asked. The pain in his father's expression was too much for him to bear. He couldn't show weakness. He couldn't allow the guards to see what the impact of their actions was. He had to be strong.

'What have they done to you, son?' His father traced his figure with his eyes. It was clear that he would willingly switch positions. His pride and joy was in danger and he would do anything to save him. That he was powerless to do so was evident in every line on his face.

'Three weeks,' answered the Caid.

In only three weeks his father had been reduced to this? Kaci reached out to touch his father and the guard growled.

'We only have brief moments, Mohand, so you must listen and answer my question,' said the Caid. 'Your father has gone to great lengths to arrange this meeting. He has sold nearly everything he owns to give you a chance at freedom, young man, and I suggest you grasp it with both hands.' As he spoke, Hadj Yahia simply nodded his agreement, his eyes fixed on his son's face. Imploring him.

Kaci couldn't stand the pain in them and turned away to look at the other man.

'What is your… what do you want from me?'

'The authorities arrested Ali weeks ago. And knowing how close the two brothers are, they are waiting for an excuse to arrest Arab. They are certain one of them murdered the Frenchman, but they can't prove who it was.'

As Kaci listened, he understood with clarity beyond his years what was being asked of him. While the words filled his ears, his mind traced the actions of the last few months, his friendship with Samson and the behaviour of his cousin.

'We need you to tell us who fired the weapon.'

'Kaci, you must tell us. They say they will let you go free.' His father shuffled closer to him. 'They will let you go free. You can come home to your wife and your family.' Hope that this might happen seemed to add strength to his curved spine.

'But what if I don't know?' Kaci asked.

'Then you don't know... and you will be charged with complicity in this murder,' answered the Caid. 'Monsieur Samson's last words were quite damning. Witnesses say he said you knew the man who shot him. The authorities claim that this is enough to lock you up for the rest of your life.' His eyes looked deep into Kaci's, trying to impress on him the severity of the situation. 'They are talking about Cayenne.'

Kaci's heart lurched. He heard his father gasp. Cayenne was the destination that every Algerian feared. It was the pride of the French penal system. It meant almost certain death in the worst prison on the planet: Devil's Island.

'Kaci tell us. Which of your cousins killed that man? Whoever it was is worthless scum and deserves the blade. You are young. Twenty years old with all of your life before you. You are more precious than ten men like him.'

While his father pleaded and the Caid detailed the charges against him, Kaci measured his options with a calm that surprised him. The French wanted blood. They wanted a public spectacle they could use to frighten his people. He was surprised that they didn't just go ahead and execute all three of them; after all, who was there to stop them? Presumably they were keen to be at least seen to be doing the right thing. And that meant certainty.

It occurred to him that the French view might be that if all three of them were executed, there would be danger that they would become martyrs to the cause of Algeria. Whereas if one of them was accused and proven to have committed a cold-blooded murder that involved the theft of a great deal of money, then the lustre of martyrdom would not apply.

He had a choice. On the one hand, he could name his cousin as the guilty party and go free. He would then see his son being born and work for the prosperity of his extended family. If he did give Arab's name, his cousin would be taken to the place of public execution and guillotined; his head removed from his neck and France would win another battle in an ongoing war.

If Kaci didn't name his cousin, he would never be allowed to leave prison; whether that be in Algeria or Cayenne.

'Who did it, son? Arab or Ali?' His father's voice grew stronger with the certainty that his son would choose death for his cousin and a life of freedom for himself.

Kaci was mute. His mind cartwheeled between his choices. Spend the rest of his life in prison, or send his cousin to the guillotine?

TEN

The Arrest of Ali

Arab ran like a man possessed. His mind had already moved from the killing of the Frenchman to avoiding capture and ensuring the money would remain his. To throw off the scent of any potential pursuers he traced a detour. He first headed north up the mountain then, after some distance, he changed direction south towards his house.

He stopped at a spring to get his breath back and to rest his exhausted limbs. He washed his face, removed the scarf and hid the gun in a cloth. Then he continued south, where he met a shepherd. His expression was one of surprise. It was not a regular occurrence to see a mature man running in the mountains at the early hours of the morning.

Arab simply waved and smiled and carried on his way. When he arrived home, he went straight to the *asaghour*, the storage building to the right of the main house where hay was kept for the animals. This has a round platform with the pole in the middle, used for grinding wheat and barley. There he had earlier hidden a pile of clothing. He changed his clothes and hid the money and the gun under the hay. From there, breathing now back to normal, he walked over to the house and pulled his wife outside. There he spoke quietly to her. She nodded, fully understanding his instructions. Without another word he turned on his heels and ran down the hills towards Maillot.

His wife, Saadia, moved quickly to follow his instructions. She built a small fire and fed it with the clothes her husband had been wearing. The gun she moved inside their home and hid under their bedding. Then she went about her normal duties – cleaning out the animals before feeding them, preparing couscous for the evening meal – biding her time before completing her next set of instructions.

***

Under the scorching heat of the midday sun, while everyone was asleep, Saadia crept from the house to the *asaghour*. Rummaging under the hay she located the money, just as Arab described it to her. She moved it into her husband's *gandora* and buried everything in a safe place in the courtyard.

So quickly did she move that she missed a two-franc note in a bottom corner of the bag.

Just as her heartbeat was getting back to normal she realised that if ever the *gendarmes* were to search her house, they would find the gun with ease. She looked around her, wondering where was the best place to hide it. There, under that tree. So she crept back into the house, wrapped it in some old cloths and buried it in the spot she had chosen.

***

On hearing of Samson's death, the French action was swift. Reinforcements were sent from the nearest large town, Bouira, and the investigation began. When they arrived in the mountains they started questioning everyone they could find. No one was safe from their questions. The French tactics of sowing discord among the *indigènes* had been so successful over the years that people were always willing to inform on their enemies. However, in times like this, it became counterproductive. Locals used this crime to even old scores and fingered the wrong people. As a result many people who had absolutely nothing to do with the shooting were taken away for further questioning.

A group of *gendarmes* was sent to the scene. They had with them an Algerian traitor used as an interpreter, and one who was more than happy to do their dirty work. These people were given the worst name you could give an Algerian: *Harki*. On their way up the hill they met Arab walking at speed through Saharidj, a village about ten miles from Maillot. The *Harki* was a local, from a family that was jealous of the Saoudi's relative success, and he recognised Arab as being a relative of their only suspect thus far.

'You there, Saoudi!' he shouted. 'Where are you going?'

Arab was relaxed and confident. He entered the part of a humble farmer out working for his family, allowing a little fake humility to leak into his act so that his questioners wouldn't suspect him.

A *gendarme* spoke. The *Harki* translated. They took details of his movements. While they spoke Arab fought to remember the man's name. Once this was all over he would make sure he would rue the day he collaborated against a Saoudi. He picked out a word among the stream of French. Minouche.

'I've just left my home to go into town on an errand. My wife can verify this if you want.' He shrugged as if it didn't matter to him one way or the other.

'Is this errand so important that you have to rush?' asked Minouche.

'A farmer's life is a busy one.' Arab allowed his humility to slip a little. 'As you would know if you weren't so busy kissing French arses.' He knew he was taking a risk by speaking like this, but if he didn't show the customary hate that the typical Algerian felt for traitors then the *Harki* would know something was wrong.

Minouche spat at Arab's feet. Arab clenched a fist and then regarded the *gendarmes* that surrounded him.

'Can I carry on with my work, or do you have other reasons to pester a poor farmer?' he asked.

The *Harki* translated for the French. They spoke in turn.

'Take us to your home. We will check out your story.'

Arab could do nothing but comply.

When they reached his house in Boufanzar they told Arab to call the family out of the house. This he did and all the family was lined up along the wall at gunpoint.

The Algerian fired questions at the family. He started with Arab's wife.

'Did your husband stay the night with you?'

'What was he doing this morning?'

'What time did he leave for Maillot?'

Her answers succeeded in moving suspicion from Arab so he continued with the rest of the family for some time.

After taking all the details, the *gendarmes* entered the house. They threw everything out into the courtyard while the family could do nothing but watch and allow their resentment to burn in the quiet storm of their minds. After an hour of searching they found the soldiers had found nothing.

The family were still lined up against the wall. The collaborator walked along them as if searching their faces for a clue.

'Someone is missing.' He paused and smiled with wicked intent. 'Correction. Two people are missing. Mohand we have in custody. He was found covered in the Frenchman's blood.' His eyes sought those of Hadj Yahia, all but crowing at the worry he found there. 'A guilty man if ever there was one. But one more of you miserable Saoudis is missing. Where is Ali?'

They were told that Ali and his wife were in the grazing area with their animals. They mentioned the name of the place and the traitor nodded. He knew of this place and he could guide the *gendarmes*. He hawked up some phlegm and aimed at the feet of Hadj Yahia.

'I knew you Saoudis were no good.' He looked over at Arab, who appeared unconcerned and was crouched against the wall picking at the dirt in his fingernails with a small blade.

'Don't think you are in the clear, Arab. The French think that there's no way you could have made that distance in time to shoot the man, steal the gold and return home in time for us to meet you.'

Steadily, Arab met his gaze as if challenging him.

'I'm not so sure,' Minouche continued. 'I will pick a fast man to run that way and we'll see.'

The *gendarmes* left the house and headed towards the grazing area. When they arrived in front of the platform where many huts were erected, the *Harki* began shouting.

'Ali OulHadj show yourself.'

His wife come out from one of the huts and, seeing the group of grim-faced soldiers all bearing arms, she almost collapsed with fear.

'What do you want with my husband?' she managed to ask.

'Where is he?' demanded Minouche.

She could only point and with a shaking voice tell them that her husband had been out all night protecting the herd from jackals. He was now fast asleep on the big rock just a hundred yards away. Without another word the soldiers marched over to him and prodded him awake with their guns.

Ali awoke with a start. His brain struggled to make sense of the fact that he was surrounded by some very angry looking French soldiers, all carrying rifles that were pointed at him.

'What… who?' He sat up wild-haired and bleary-eyed. He rubbed at his face.

'What is going on? What have I done wrong?'

Minouche moved to the front of the *gendarmes* and asked him, 'Did you visit Kaci at the dam the other day?'

'Yes, I did, as always. Why?' Aware that everyone was towering over him he leapt to his feet.

'Why did you visit Kaci?'

'I took him some fresh sour milk and butter.' He rubbed at his head trying to work out where this was all going.

'What else did you do?'

'Nothing… I did nothing. What is this all about?'

Ali's wife was standing to the side, holding her baby. When the French turn up with guns and start asking questions, this is a time to worry. She was shaking from fear and rocking the baby in an attempt to keep herself calm.

'Have you done something, Ali?' she asked. 'What does the enemy of God want this time?'

Minouche, trying to calm her, said, 'Nothing to worry about, it is just a routine check.'

A couple of *gendarmes* were sent to search inside their hut. Their meagre belongings began to sail out the door and onto the ground in front of them. Only minutes later, one of them come out shouting,

'I found it.'

He was holding a gun in the air.

This was not a registered weapon and Ali's wife, weak with worry, sank to her knees thinking that this was the reason for this visit.

'I told you to take the gun to the town hall. Why didn't you register it, Ali? You are getting into trouble for something that is so stupid. Why, Ali? Why?'

Ali, however, could see from the reaction of the French that the gun was a bonus. It was unexpected. He whispered to her, 'This is not about the gun. These enemies of God are after my head for some reason.'

As the *gendarme* looked over the gun Ali gave them a reason for his failure to register it.

'I'm busy up here in the hills with my animals. If I'm not here to look after them, the jackals will eat them. I don't have time to run down to Maillot and register it.' This was all true, but nonetheless it was not a reason the authorities would accept.

A *gendarme* sniffed at the barrel. He opened it and looked over at the traitor and said something. He indicated Ali with a violent nod of his head. Ali looked around him. The atmosphere had suddenly changed. The *gendarmes* all brought their weapons to bear on him.

Ali fell to his knees in fear. 'What is going on? What is wrong?'

'This gun has been fired recently. What did you use the gun for?' The collaborator translated.

'I had to kill a jackal that came for my herd.'

Many more questions were fired in anger. Then they turned to Ali's wife and started questioning her. She looked her husband in the face and whispered, 'What shall I tell them now?'

He replied softly, 'Just tell them what they want to know, I have no idea of what is going on.'

'We are taking the gun for tests. We need to prove that this is the weapon that killed him,' said Minouche.

'Weapon? Killed? Killed who?' Ali demanded. 'What are you talking about? I have killed no one. I fired at a jackal.' In his panic he was shouting. Something terrible had happened and he was caught up in it. 'Tell me what is going on.'

The traitor was delighted with this outcome. He knew the Saoudis were involved in this up to their armpits and now he had proof. It didn't matter if this gun was used to fire the lethal shot. It was a gun. It was in the hands of a suspect and the courts would see that was enough.

With delight he aimed a blow at Ali's head. 'You are under arrest.'

'What did I do? What am I guilty of? Protecting my herd? This is ridiculous.'

His stream of questions was cut off with a blow to his stomach with the butt of a rifle. He fell to his knees coughing.

Minouche smiled. 'I can tell you nothing. All I can say is that the authorities want you.' He got hold of Ali's hands and pulled some handcuffs from a pocket in his robes.

'At least let me get some clothes on and my sandals.'

The traitor was enjoying himself too much to allow Ali any comfort. He shouted into his face. 'No need, we will take you just as you are.'

They dragged him half-naked down the hill like an animal to the slaughter while his wife, powerless, stood watching. There was her provider, the father of her children shrinking, then vanishing in the distance. The thought occurred to her with cold certainty, that this was the last time she would see him alive.

* * *

Hadj Yahia was reeling from the news. This was the worst day in the family's history. His favoured son was in prison, about to be tried for a murder he had nothing to do with, and the man who he was certain had fired the gun was walking about as if all this commotion to the family was the most natural thing in the world.

He couldn't go to the authorities with his suspicions, based on nothing but gossip. Yes, Arab had talked about nothing else for the last few weeks leading up to the murder, but the *gendarmes* would never believe what he was saying based on their nightly *djamaa* meetings.

His mind was consumed with thoughts of revenge. He could knife Arab while he slept. He could tie him up and drag him out into the fields. There they could cover him in honey and leave him for the ants. Only when he was crying from the torture of being eaten alive would he relent and admit to his sins. Then they could see about freeing Mohand.

This, of course, was utter folly. Arab was too cunning by far to allow himself to fall prey to such actions.

He stumbled about in a daze. He was a man of action. A man who built this family up to great success despite everything and now it was all as worthless as the dust at his feet.

A proud man, Hadj Yahia resorted to begging.

'You have to give yourself up, Arab. You are leaving an innocent boy to rot in jail. And what about your brother, Ali? Can you really allow your brother to be tried for a crime that you committed?'

Arab merely looked Hadj Yahia over, his expression full of scorn. His face read of his contempt for the once powerful ruler of his family.

'Look at you. You are... nothing. A weak man. An embarrassment to this family. Why did we ever think you could make decisions for us?'

* * *

At this time, Arab continued working his land, playing the part of the impoverished farmer, with no sign of wealth in his family. He knew that the minute he spent one sous of the stolen money he would be marched to the steps of the guillotine. So he was prepared to wait. Once matters had died down he could slowly start to spend the money. He would become a man of importance in the region. A man to be reckoned with. In the meantime he would keep his powder dry and wait. He would leave the money in a safe place and control his greed.

There was, however, one thing out of his control and that was the wagging tongues of gossips. No one in the area thought for a minute that Kaci was guilty of such a crime. They all knew that the murdered Frenchman had been a real friend to the young man, and Kaci had impressed everyone with his strength of character. As for Ali, the gossips sang, he was a weak man. Far too pretty by far. No, the real culprit was sure to be Arab. The whispers grew. People spoke behind their hands. Many eyes tracked his movements through the surrounding area. Fingers pointed, but Arab would show them all. He had committed the perfect crime and he would get away with it.

After a couple of weeks, he was sure that the storm of gossip had passed and he visited Maillot during a market day. While doing his shopping he noticed people looking at him and pointing. He gritted his teeth and carried on. He would not be bowed by the small minds of these people. Then he overheard someone speak.

'Here is the killer.'

Arab flew into a rage. Through the mist of his fury he identified the man who spoke and launched himself at him. People scattered. Stalls were overturned. Voices were raised. Arab was oblivious to it all. He kicked and punched his victim, completely unmindful of the damage he was doing. Men tried to intervene and were punched and kicked in turn. No one could stop him. He was always a strong man but the fear of his discovery had built in him to such an extent that now he had an outlet for it, he was like an enraged bull. The *gendarmes* in the vicinity were called and a rifle butt to the back of his head rendered him unconscious.

His victim, a man by the name of Chuma, was taken to hospital where he spent a couple of days in recovery. On his release, he pressed charges. He was furious that a man such as Arab would publicly beat him. Usually, the French were reluctant to use their valuable time on prosecuting violence between the *indigènes*, but for once, the authorities were happy to listen. They were aware who Arab was and his connection to the men already in jail for the murder of Samson.

Arab was arrested, convicted and sentenced to three months in prison at Bouira.

* * *

In prison he was reunited with his brother. Ali had never been a strong man, but Arab was astonished nonetheless at the change a few weeks in prison had made to his brother. This was still not enough for Arab to relent and inform the French of his culpability in the Samson murder. He would keep his mouth shut, keep his head down and get through his sentence.

12 04 AM
Marshall [illegible]

65 pages => 2 hours

120 min ÷ 65 =

1.84 min/page

Remaining =>

375 − 71 = 304

304 x 1.84 => 561 min

÷ 60 = 9.4 hours

ELEVEN

A Hiding Place

The sunshine was relentless. The exercise yard was fully in its glare. In some prisons time spent out in the fresh air was a reward for good behaviour. In Bouira prison it was part of the punishment. The walls were so high there was no breeze and the yard was sited to take the full force of the North African sunshine. Guards patrolled the high walls, rifles lazily slung across their shoulders.

Prisoners gathered in clumps within the confines of the white walls. Listless under the heat, the two brothers crouched in a corner. Such was Arab's reputation that the other prisoners largely left them to their own devices. In only a few weeks he had beaten up several of them to ensure his position in the prison pecking order.

'You have to let them know who's boss,' was how he explained his actions to Ali after he had aimed a kick at the backside of a local man called Ramzi. 'The law of the jungle,' he added with a self-satisfied smile when Ramzi picked himself up and walked away.

Ali simply nodded, knowing that his brother took pleasure in violence. He didn't do it to cement his position. He did it because he could. He did it because he enjoyed hurting others.

'Brother, this is hot. Thanks be to Allah I have only three more weeks,' said Arab.

'You have three weeks. I have the rest of my life, brother,' Ali answered him, colouring the title 'brother' with the bile of bitterness.

Arab refused to rise to the bait. He simply sucked on his teeth and stared his younger brother out.

Ali was resolute. His gaze remained fixed on Arab.

'How many times do we have to have this conversation?' asked Arab. 'Do you think me insane that I would tell the truth? I have no wish to face the blade.'

'You murdered a man. It is no more than you deserve.'

'And yet, here you are.'

Ali shoved his face into Arab's. 'Do you feel no guilt, brother?'

Arab shrugged and with little effort pushed his brother away. 'The strong survive.' He shrugged. 'There is no other way.'

* * *

The next day Ali continued his campaign.

'Arab, you have to help me,' begged Ali. 'I have done nothing. I am an innocent man.'

'There is nothing I have to do, brother. Except breathe and eat. Making more children would also be nice.' He grinned.

'Something I'll never be able to do again, thanks to you, brother,' Ali said and then spat at his brother's feet.

Arab rounded on Ali, his infamous temper getting the better of him once again. He pinned him to the wall with one hand, while pressing the knuckles of his other hand against Ali's jaw.

'If you weren't my brother…' he growled.

'What? You'd what? What else could you possibly do to someone not of your own flesh that could be worse than what you have done to me?' Ali sobbed.

Just then another inmate walked past them.

'I thought you Saoudis were too close to fight,' he joked.

'What do you want, Boudjemaa?' asked Arab. Boudjemaa was a small, handsome light-skinned man, who lived just outside Maillot. He had been locked up for public drunkenness and was due to be released in just a few days.

Boudjemaa looked pointedly upwards at the guards who were now looking down at them, no doubt attracted by the rough voices and Arab's barely stifled anger.

Both brothers thanked Boudjemaa silently with a smile, who

walked away with one hand scratching his head, while the other scratched his arse.

'Your anger is in the wrong place, Ali.' Arab's anger dissipated after Boudjemaa's intervention and he relented at the sight of his weeping sibling. 'It is not me who brought you here.'

There was silence and then both brothers said the same name at the same time.

'Minouche.'

A plan started to gel in their minds. The money was safely hidden, Arab was adamant that nothing would make him give it back. However, it had come in a leather satchel engraved with the name of the hydro-electric company.

'What might the authorities think if that was found close to someone else's home?' Arab thought aloud.

'What if that someone else was someone the French had used to investigate the murder?' Ali continued his line of thought.

Again, they both repeated the same name at the same time.

'Minouche.'

'They would see that you couldn't possibly be the killer and set you free,' Arab cheered and thumped his brother on the back.

* * *

To put their plan into place, Arab had to get in touch with his wife. Permitted visits were rare and, besides, a lone female couldn't travel the distance from Maillot to Bouira. A letter would be the best way to get in touch, but neither Arab nor Ali could write, and they had no idea at that time where Kaci was.

Given that most of the inmates were illiterate, anyone with an education became a very important person in Algeria's prisons. Word went out that Arab required a writer. One was located and given the job of noting down Arab's instructions. The letter detailed that an important item was hidden in a field and that it needed to be moved. A location was suggested. One that would do the most damage to the Minouche family.

Now that the letter was written, the next task was to get it safely into the hands of his wife. To get the letter out of prison, they needed someone who was due for release.

'Of course,' said Ali. 'Boudjemaa is ideal. He is getting out next week and he lives nearby. It would only be a short detour for him to safely pass on the letter.'

Boudjemaa was approached at the next exercise session. It was decided that Ali would ask him, given that no one in the whole establishment had a good word to say about Arab.

The soon-to-be-released Boudjemaa was no fool. He may have been unable to read but it was clear from both Arab and Ali's body language that this was more than an ordinary letter. He himself was a repeat offender and a frequent visitor to the Algerian prison system. Both of his sons had died during a famine some years previously and his subsequent anger was turned inwards. An anger that he tried to drown repeatedly with as much wine as he could get his hands on. A habit that, unfortunately, kept getting him locked up.

A drunken sot he may have been, but he was no idiot. Smuggling a letter out of prison could get him into more trouble than he had ever been in his life. Before he agreed to do this he told the Saoudi brothers that he needed time to think it through.

He thought about it out loud, to the man who slept in the bunk above him, Ramzi. Unfortunately for the success of the plan, this was a man who had been beaten by Arab on too many occasions, and he was ripe for revenge. Ramzi grasped the opportunity he had just been offered by his fellow prisoner.

'What harm could it do?' he said to Boudjemaa while his mind worked out how he could best take advantage of this situation. 'A simple letter to his wife. What man doesn't want to pour out his heart to the woman he loves?'

'Ach, you are right, Ramzi. I am like an old woman. Worrying about nothing.'

The next day, Boudjemaa told the brothers that in the interests of keeping romance alive, he would happily pass on the letter.

At that very moment Ramzi was seeking an audience with the prison warden. He had heard the gossip that flowed around Arab. He was a murderer. He had killed at least five Frenchmen and he had hidden a king's ransom of gold in the mountains. Ramzi knew how gossip grew but he was prepared to believe that some of this was based on fact and, if that was the case, the authorities might be prepared to extend leniency to a man who helped the cause of the French. He guessed that this letter might allow him to curry favour with the prison authorities if it proved to be as important as he thought.

The next morning, the hapless Boudjemaa prepared himself for the search he knew would happen before he was released to his freedom. He had considered the best place to hide the letter about his person and decided upon his chewing tobacco holder. Surely the guards wouldn't think to look inside there?

Boudjemaa was duly stopped just before the prison gates and subjected to his search. An experienced inmate, he knew to simply stand still as a lump of stone and to allow the guards to do their job. It became apparent quickly however that this was no ordinary search. They'd never been quite so thorough with him before. With a sinking heart he watched as they went through every item on his person. The last thing they looked at was his tobacco holder, where they discovered the letter folded and tucked away inside.

* * *

The authorities wasted no time. A huge convoy of *gendarmes* swooped down on Maillot, where they picked up a few Algerian collaborators before continuing toward Boufanzar in the mountains.

When they arrived at the house, they pushed the front door and entered the courtyard. It was early morning and the family was just rousing for the day. They were shocked to find themselves invaded by all these men in uniforms carrying guns on their shoulders.

In a frightening replay of the day of the murder, the family were lined up against a wall and one of the collaborators was told to explain why they were there.

'We have found a letter addressed to your cousin Arab's wife. In this letter he tells her to hide a certain bag. A bag that held the money stolen from the murdered Frenchman.'

Gasps sounded along the wall. Then there was silence. Then everyone clamoured to be heard.

'Ridiculous.'

'What crazy talk is that?'

'Silence,' the captain of the troops roared above them all, brandishing a rifle above his head. 'We have a letter…' As he spoke he was looking at his colleagues with his hand out, asking for one of them to give him the damning evidence.

They all looked at each other, each expecting the other to reach into a pocket and furnish their captain with the missing item. No one moved.

All of the Saoudis looked at each other and stifled smiles behind sleeves.

Clenching his teeth against his administration and its laughable inefficiency, the captain ordered silence once again. Needing to save face, he was about to tear a strip out of his youngest officer when someone remembered that the bag was hidden in a place that started with the name 'Alma'.

So the captain of the *gendarmes* ordered the family to tell them all of the places nearby that began with 'Alma'. Despite the seriousness of the situation, the family again bit down on their smiles. The family allowed that it was not the fault of the stupid French that they did not know that *alma* in Berber means 'green field'. There were many such places throughout the country. It became something of a game as people shouted out place names that began with a green field.

Eventually someone mentioned 'Alma Boughni'. The soldiers recognised this name instantly and demanded to be taken there.

Once they arrived they spread their forces across the area and started searching. The family was made to stay indoors. After a couple of hours without results, the person in charge ordered reinforcements by calling Moroccan workers from the dam. They were duly shipped in and in the middle of the afternoon someone eventually shouted, 'I found it.' The bag was pulled out from under the earth, dusted down and identified.

With this evidence in their hands, Arab was now officially known to be involved in the crime. However, they still did not know which of the three men in custody fired the fatal shot.

TWELVE

A Father's Desperation

Hadj Yahia came to know the route from Maillot to the prison in Bouira like he knew the lines of trees in his olive groves; like he knew the land around his home. He had built this land up over decades, buying as much as he could afford to keep it away from the *Pieds-Noirs*.

Following Kaci's arrest he was thankful for his vision on this issue, for now he had something to sell that he could use to finance his son's legal defence. His son's freedom was now more important to him than his name on the title for a parcel of earth. Piece by piece he began to sell the land in order to afford a French lawyer. He knew that his son was innocent and he would simply not accept that he could lose him.

However, the French lawyer was prohibitively expensive and his land and his money began to run out. In desperation he then turned his mind to the money Arab had stolen from the French. There would surely be a certain irony in using this money in the defence of his kin.

He wasted no time and walked over to Arab's house and approached his wife, Saadia. As he walked he wondered what situation he would find her in. If she looked well fed and as if she was prospering, his suspicions would be aroused immediately. He then berated himself for being so naive. Surely she would be slow to spend any of the money so as not to alert the powers that be? No matter, he told himself, whatever the situation he had no other choice. Money was running out. He needed to find the stolen francs.

He found Saadia crouched in the yard in front of the house. She was on her knees mending a threadbare *gandora,* looking every inch the destitute wife of a suspected criminal. He immediately felt sorry for his suspicions and vowed to take a more gentle tone.

'I need the money, Saadia.' He stood over her. His sympathy for her plight withered before the storm of his fear for his son.

She looked up at him and squinted into the sun.

'Do I look like I have money, Uncle?'

'You must know where your husband hid the money.'

'He never told me,' she replied, casting her eyes to the ground at Hadj Yahia's feet. 'I am merely his wife. Arab only tells me what he thinks I need to know.'

'You expect me to believe that?' Anger added weight to his words.

'Surely you can hear the truth in them? Arab is a difficult man, Uncle.' As Saadia spoke her voice cracked with emotion. 'But as a good wife I know my duty.'

Hadj Yahia looked around himself. He was at a loss as to what to say next. Always a confident man, the plight his family was now in had robbed him of the certainty that tailored his previous actions. Here at his feet was a woman of his family whose husband faced a terrible punishment. This was no crime of hers. And now that she was a woman on her own she was reliant on the other male relatives to provide for her. Life in Algeria was difficult, but for a lone female it was impossible.

His eyes roamed the land around the house. It actually looked well tended. Her sons must be good workers. There were a couple of cattle down by the stream that ran through their land, along with some goats and sheep. He counted them. He couldn't be sure, but he was surprised that Arab had quite so many.

He looked down again at Saadia who, aware of his scrutiny, had her eyes fixed on the cloth in her hands. Could she be lying to him, he wondered. Was this all an act? Then her eyes met his briefly and he could read shame and sorrow in them. Shame that she was reduced to such a state that she was trying to repair a garment which should by rights be thrown out. Sorrow that she was now a woman on her own in a male-dominated society.

'The money will be used to buy their freedom, Saadia. The risks here are great. They could be guillotined in public.' An image of the great blade falling onto his son's neck almost made Hadj Yahia sway on his feet.

'I understand, Uncle. But still I don't know, he never told me, I swear.'

'We both know that Arab did this terrible deed. The money is here somewhere. Do you want me to bring my other sons and search?'

'You must do what you must do, Uncle.' Saadia was every inch the humble Berber wife.

'I do not believe you. If you love your husband, you have to cooperate.'

'I love my husband and I understand what you are saying, but believe me when I tell you that he never shared his secrets with me.'

Hadj Yahia once again looked over the fields at the animals grazing there. He had put Saadia to the test but he had to give it one more try. He owed it to his son.

'In that case I will take you to Lala Khadidja. And there you must swear that you know nothing of the whereabouts of this money.'

Lala Khadidja was a shrine to a Muslim sage. A place of pilgrimage place that people came to visit from miles around. If Saadia swore of her lack of knowledge in such a sacred place then Hadj Yahia would have no option but to believe her.

* * *

The shrine was located in the mountains not far from their house. A distance that could be travelled by mule within an afternoon. Meekly, Saadia allowed herself to be guided there to offer witness.

The shrine was a small, white, dome-shaped building standing in the cool of some pine trees. When they arrived it was empty so they were able to walk in without waiting for other pilgrims to finish their prayers.

Once his eyes adjusted to the gloom of the space, Hadj Yahia could see that in the middle of the single room lay a large coffin laden with piles of colourful sewing material. The custom was that a strip of cloth was payment for guidance. Supplicants would shuffle in and offer prayers and seek wisdom in the presence of the spirit of the holy person.

Hadj Yahia told Saadia to put her hands on the coffin at the end where a head might rest. She complied. As she moved her hands into position Hadj Yahia noticed a slight tremble. He looked into the woman's eyes. She met his gaze and slid her eyes down to the coffin. Hadj Yahia told himself that he was imagining things. Such was his desperation that he was willing to read something into even the smallest gesture. Then again, his instincts were telling him that something was not right here despite this woman acting like the perfect wife and mother.

'Saadia, wife of Arab, to believe that you are telling the truth, I must ask you to swear on the life of your youngest child. Here in the presence of Lala Khadidja.'

Saadia did not hesitate. 'I swear on my son that I don't know anything about the money.'

Hadj Yahia slumped to his knees. The money was lost to him. How was he now to defend his son?

THIRTEEN

A Prisoner's Life

The authorities relaxed now that they were convinced all of the guilty parties were under lock and key. Kaci was moved out of solitary confinement into the general population. No reason for this was given. He was simply pulled from his cell, doused with cold water, given clean clothing and shepherded towards another area of the prison.

Now he had a different routine to get used to. Even before the sun had coloured the sky he was awakened by the clamour of the guards and the clatter of the trolley that went round the cells collecting human waste from the night before.

At least here he could speak without the threat of a beating, and he was allowed out into the yard for his daily bout of exercise. It was here for the first time since the murder that he came face to face with Arab.

Dry-mouthed and almost beaten to his knees by the heat of the sun, he forced himself to stand and stare into the face of his cousin. As he stared his father's words echoed in his mind, reminding him that he had a choice. All he had to do was point a finger and he would be sent home.

'You killed my friend,' he said to Arab.

His cousin stared him down. With his peripheral vision Kaci was aware that everyone in the yard had stopped to watch them. What he wasn't yet aware of was the fear that his cousin was regarded with and subsequently he wouldn't be aware that his stance before his cousin would earn him a great deal of respect among the other men. He was unmindful and uncaring of any of this. All he could think of was that this man had robbed his friend of his life and he himself of his future.

'For a sackful of francs you brought dishonour to your family,' he said and spat at Arab's feet.

Arab simply kept on staring at him, but a small twitch at the corner of his left eye let Kaci know that his words were striking home.

'Your brother and your cousin face the guillotine because of your greed,' Kaci said and moved his face close to his cousins. 'Do you feel no shame?'

Arab's eye continued to twitch, but he stayed where he was.

Kaci ground his teeth together under the force of his anger. All that kept him from lashing out was the thought of the punishment the guards would give him. He had taken enough blows and bruises from his jailers.

Just then he felt a hand on his shoulders and heard a familiar voice.

'Cousin, I see you've met my brother.'

Kaci turned to the side to see Ali standing before him. Ali smiled and spoke in low tones. 'Now is not the time, Kaci. The guards are watching. If you want to do violence to my brother, I won't stop you ...'

Arab voiced a low growl at this.

'You deserve it, brother. But now is not the time,' Ali said.

Kaci nodded and took a step back, but never for a moment did he remove his eyes from Arab's face. 'You are right, Ali. The enemies of our family have enough ammunition.'

He relaxed into a smile and, moving to the side, gathered Ali into a hug. 'How are you, cousin?' he asked. 'Are your spirits strong?'

'Strong enough,' Ali answered, looking Kaci up and down. His expression read of his surprise. This man of confidence was not what he expected from the boy he watched grow up. Sure, he was smart. And before the shooting he had been growing into a life of comparative privilege, but it was obvious from the look in Ali's eyes that he was not expecting such a show of character.

'What do I need to know to survive in this place, cousin?' Kaci asked Ali.

'Avoid the Arabs. They'll only want to play with a boy as cute as you,' he grinned. 'Marton, the chief guard, is a bastard. Any chance he gets he will hurt you. Or if you have anything of value he'll steal it from you.'

Kaci listened carefully and nodded, standing as if braced for whatever his new life could throw at him.

'Whatever the world casts at you, Mohand, you will surely cope.' Ali spoke as if suddenly served with a premonition.

Kaci leaned against the wall and, with his head cocked to the side, considered how Ali had moved from his boyhood name to his more formal one.

'Mohand,' he repeated. This suited the man he was becoming. Kaci was dead, mouldering in a dark silent cell, crying for the comforts of home. Mohand was the man who would help him become what he needed to be.

* * *

For the next few weeks Mohand observed the rituals of prison life and learned from the behaviours of the older inmates. He would adjust, for what other choice did he have? This was a life so removed from his previous experiences that it might as well be happening on the burning surface of the sun.

He learned quickly that men in prison prey on weakness. He noticed a young man of similar height and build to himself who shuffled around the prison as if looking for another inmate to bully him. And of course there were plenty who were more than happy to oblige. He observed how the men integrated with one another. How the men of the same region stuck together. How Berber and Arab spoke mainly among their own kind. Only strength is admired, but his was not the strength of Arab, who had quick fists. His strength was one of will. Strength of dignity and certainty. He deserved respect and, by his quiet manner and quick wit, he would make sure that was what he received. But if that didn't work, then he was more than prepared to bring his fists to bear.

He didn't have long to wait to test this resolve. He was given the position of prison writer and time in a communal cell to work with the other men to scribe letters to their loved ones. A guard stood by the door at all times to ensure that nothing untoward happened. Mohand had just finished with one man and he looked up from a fresh sheet of paper to face his next client.

'Gabir,' the man said. His smile was all teeth and leer. He had deep lines in his face and scraps of grey in his hair. His nose was long and when he opened his mouth he displayed yellow teeth shaped like coffin lids.

Gabir rested one hand on the table and reached over with the other and lightly touched the back of Mohand's hand, which was poised over a fresh sheet of paper.

'Who should I address your letter to, Gabir?' Mohand ignored the tremor in his voice and willed himself not to react to the obvious nature of this man's interest.

'My mother wants to know how her son is coping in this terrible place.' His voice was deep and the tone at odds with his words. Mohand struggled with the sense of it. Threat. Was he reading threat in the man's voice? He looked at Gabir's hands. Long, thick fingers, knuckled with hair. Fingers that were now stretching over the back of his hand into a hard squeeze.

'Tell her that I make friends in here. My friends make my time pass… more quickly.'

Mohand realised that Gabir hadn't taken his eyes from his since he sat down. He could read the danger in the way this man looked at him. Like a farmer might look at a bull before sending it to the butcher. Liquid chilled in his stomach, but he gathered his strength and faced this man down.

'Friends are important.' He risked a glance at the guard who was at that precise moment picking his nose. 'But you have to be sure you have the right friends.'

'Friends let me protect them in this evil place in return for a few… favours,' said Gabir while still squeezing on Mohand's hand.

Ignoring the pain of his bones being compressed, Mohand kept his vision on Gabir. Any weakness and he knew this man would claim him, and his life would be over. He had seen other young men who, in fear for their lives, had given themselves willingly to older, stronger men in the hope that they would receive some protection. But this was not a situation he would ever give himself to.

Mohand moved the pen that was poised over the paper above the hand that was gripping his. It was a small piece of wood with a metal nib that could be dipped time and time again into a small bottle of ink. He pushed the nib onto a bulbous vein on the back of Gabir's hand. Hard.

'The one talent I have, my new friend, is to write letters. If you seek other talents, I suggest you seek another friend.' As he spoke he was careful not to alter his tone in order not to alert the guard, while at the same time exerting more and more pressure with the pen onto the back of Gabir's hand. The only sign that Gabir was in any discomfort was a muscle in his jaw that flexed against the pain.

'Some friends need persuasion, don't you find?' asked Gabir.

'Yes, but the quick minds among us soon realise that their efforts might be better appreciated elsewhere.'

Gabir stopped squeezing on Mohand's hand.

He moved his pen back to the page.

Gabir slowly stood up, his eyes still locked on Mohand's.

'I think my poor mother would be disappointed by any letter I might write her today,' he said, pushing the words out from between clenched teeth. With one last look that suggested this battle was far from over, he turned and walked from the room.

Mohand realised he had been holding his breath and he slowly filled his lungs.

'Next,' he said to the guard, his voice sounding too loud to his own ears. The guard winked and smiled at him, letting him know that he hadn't missed a thing.

* * *

Soon, Mohand was to face another test of this strength. His father visited him in prison. When he arrived he was smiling as if the world couldn't contain his joy.

Mohand was instantly intrigued. Had the authorities decided on his innocence? Had his father managed to buy back some of his precious land?

'Dad, you look very happy today, what happened?'

'My son, I have some very good news for you.'

Mohand was aware of his heart beating heavily in his chest. It must be big to have excited his father so.

'What? Tell me, Father. What could be so good while I am locked away in here?'

'Your wife has delivered this morning.' He reached through the wire and grabbed his son's hand. 'You have a son.'

Mohand stayed silent for several beats while he absorbed the news. As his father watched, his own expression sank until it was matching that of his son.

'Oh Dad, how can I enjoy the birth of my son?' Mohand was close to tears. 'My future is so bleak.'

Hadj Yahia pulled Mohand closer to the wire and rested his forehead against his son's. 'I understand how you feel, my son. May God make it easy for you.' As he did so, he slipped a hand into a pocket of his son's prison tunic. 'Buy yourself a bowl of couscous. They're not feeding you enough.'

Mohand turned as if to walk away.

'Tell Arab his son has died,' his father said. The pause before he said this made Mohand feel that his father had debated telling him this news.

He turned back to face his father, who was staring at some indeterminate point beyond him.

'Tell him that his wife Saadia swore on his son's life that she knew nothing about where the gold had been hidden.' There was a hard light in his eyes that read of grim satisfaction and regret. 'And now the boy is dead.'

* * *

As he returned to his cell, Mohand was so absorbed with what his father had told him, he all but walked into a wall. He stumbled back and then looked up at the man before him.

It was Marton, the chief guard. Mohand hadn't seen him up this close before. He was over six feet tall and as round as the great earthenware barrels they used at home to store food over the winter. His face was puffy with greed and his eyes as sharp as a grabbed opportunity.

'Your visitor passed something to you.' He didn't wait for confirmation, he simply held out his hand. 'Give it to me.'

Still stunned by the news, Mohand could only stare.

'We can't have contraband in my prison, you little pile of dung. Hand it over.'

Mohand opened his mouth to speak when he was suddenly grabbed from behind, his arms pinned behind his back.

'Search him, guards,' Marton ordered.

Hands ran over every inch of him before eventually reaching into his pocket and finding the pathetic little folded note of currency that his father had dropped into it.

'What have we here?' crowed Marton. 'A little smuggler, eh? Take off your clothes, boy.'

'Wha … ?'

Before Mohand could issue another syllable the guards around removed his clothing with brutal efficiency.

Marton's fat cheeks bunched into a smile. 'When someone smuggles into my prison, we have to search them very thoroughly. Open your mouth.'

Mohand opened his mouth, his face burning with the indignity of being naked in front of these men. Fingers were thrust into his mouth, where they probed under his tongue and against the back of his throat, forcing him to gag.

'Lift up your balls,' ordered Marton, looking down at his groin. 'We need to know you have nothing tucked in at your thighs.'

Eyes now screwed shut, Mohand did as he was told. He wanted to scream at this man. He wanted to take his fat face and bash it repeatedly against the wall. But he dare not move because he knew the torture he would receive in punishment would be prolonged and have him begging to die.

'Do you have a "plan", boy?'

'Wha ... ?'

'A "plan". You useless little fucker. A "plan". Don't all of you Arabs have a "plan" tucked up your arses?'

He was talking about a small tube made of metal that prisoners used to hide any wealth they might have. It was then inserted into the most intimate place that only the most thorough search could find.

From his expression, Mohand was sure that Marton wasn't expecting to find a 'plan' about his person so that made his next action all the more humiliating and all the more unforgiveable.

The solder behind him pushed his head forward until he was bent over from the waist. Then his feet were kicked apart and he felt Marton's fingers pull his cheeks apart and then insert themselves into his anus.

Mohand couldn't stop the scream that burst from his mouth. He had never felt pain like this before. 'What are you ... ?'

A fist connected with the side of his head and he fell to the floor. Marton threw his clothes at him.

'Get back to your cell, dungheap, and make sure you don't bring anything else back into my jail.'

Mohand stumbled to his feet, but before he even had time to dress himself, Marton lashed out with his foot and kicked him down the corridor, to the tune of the cruel laughs from his colleagues.

Back in his cell, dressed in his prison uniform and wrapped in his blanket, Mohand's mind was a morass of dark thoughts. If that man ever... how could he treat someone as cruelly as that? What manner of man thinks that form of action is acceptable? The indignity of it was almost more than he could bear. There was surely a black mark that covered his entire body, which only the sandblast of a desert storm could scour from his skin.

For days Mohand spoke to no one. Long after the ache had subsided in that most tender of parts he could still feel the dirty, fat fingers probing.

It was with a start that one night he realised that he had barely given thought to his son. Such was the impact of this man that this most momentous of occasions had been almost forgotten.

What did he look like? Did he have the same dark skin as his wife? Did he keep her up all night, crying for her milk?

With his head in his hands he could feel himself sinking to a new level of despair. What would life be like for a fatherless child in this subjugated Algeria? His family had barely enough food to feed everyone else, let alone another child. He would be nothing more than a bastard.

It would be better for him if he died.

His cellmates tried to cajole him out of his black mood, but he was having none of it. He simply wrapped himself up in his threadbare blanket and turned to stare at the wall. This mood refused to lift itself for weeks. But then one day he noticed that he was shuffling rather than walking. Just like the young man that he himself had labelled as a victim.

Was that what he had become? A victim? If that was the case, he had best find himself a nice high wall and just jump off it. No. He was better than that. He would endure.

He would show Marton that this was one *indigène* he couldn't intimidate.

The very next day he reported to the camp commandant. He was a Frenchman by the name of Arnaud Bettencourt, and he was just reaching retirement. He was clearly taken aback by the calm assurance of the young *indigène* who detailed his complaint against the chief guard. Not only did he calmly recite the detail of the theft and the assault on his person, but he did so most eloquently, in perfect French.

'Am I not a man also?' Mohand said. 'If you prick me, do I not bleed?'

Bettencourt was stumped. An educated Algerian quoting from a great work of literature?

'I will… I will look into this, young Saoudi,' he said fixing his collar. To hell with this godforsaken corner of France, he was thinking. I've seen it all now.

'Be sure you do, sir,' Mohand said. 'The men will be most displeased if you don't.'

'Are you threatening me, young man?' Bettencourt rose to his feet.

'Simply stating facts, sir. With the greatest of respect, the man you have placed in charge here is a bully of the worse kind and the men are close to revolt. I am only warning you in advance of any action they might take.'

Of course, Bettencourt did nothing. Retirement was mere months away and the last thing he wanted was to make any changes to his regime.

* * *

The revolt was subtle at first. Inmates were slow to behave, slow to act on instructions and quick to take offence. The atmosphere in his once calm jail was turning sour.

The number of guards covering the night shift had to be doubled when half of the inmates began to stay up all night singing and banging their tin cups on the prison bars.

Bettencourt was beside himself. This was supposed to be a cushy little number in a provincial prison before he retired to a *gîte* on the coast of Brittany. He called Marton to his office.

'Well?' he asked. 'What do you suggest?'

'Saoudi is the ringleader, sir. You should transfer him to a bigger prison in Algiers. Let them take care of him.'

'Are you telling me you can't take care of slip of a lad, barely out of his teens?' Bettencourt demanded.

'We could request reinforcements, sir.'

Bettencourt sniffed. 'We can barely pay the staff we have now, Marton.' Which is why you and your staff are reduced to thieving from some of the poorest people on the planet, he almost added.

'We've tried threat. The solitary cells are full. If we feed them any less, they'll all starve. We've tried everything, sir. The only thing they say will work is if you sack me.' Marton grinned at the pure cheek of such a thought. Sack him? Then the prison surely would go to the dogs. Bettencourt himself was worse than useless, a Parisian fop who struggled to cope with anything more demanding than trimming his toenails. They needed him and he knew it.

'The best thing would be to transfer the three Saoudis to another jail. Let some other bastard deal with them.'

* * *

They were transferred to Serkadji prison in Algiers within the week and no sooner were they ensconced there than Mohand was ensuring that the inmates were being treated with respect. He had learned a valuable lesson in Bouira prison. Violence against the guards was only met with further violence, but subtle disobedience unnerved the establishment and, when used for the right reason, it could change the whole outlook of the institution and bring about small changes.

He found himself in an isolation cell on no less than twelve separate occasions. This was because he could not keep quiet. Whenever he saw a prisoner being treated inhumanely he was quick to complain, and no number of visits to solitary confinement could still the fire that burned in him at the maltreatment of his countrymen. While he was bound, frozen and naked in these dark cells, he would remind himself of the treatment he suffered under the hands of Marton, which fuelled the cold certainty that he and his people did not deserve to be treated in such a way.

* * *

One such time – where Mohand simply had to speak up – occurred when he realised that barbers were brought in only for the French prisoners. As soon as he noticed this, he asked to see the director immediately.

'Sir, I have noticed that the hairdressers are brought in only for the French prisoners. Are Algerians not humans with hair, beards and moustaches like everyone else?

The director was a Frenchman of Jewish descent by the name of Gabriel Guignard. He was a strict man, but one with a strong core of decency. At times he was forced to look the other way or he would never get through a day, and he consistently felt a pull on his conscience by the demands of his job. He immediately took a liking to the young man standing ramrod straight in his office.

'You have nothing to shave, young man. You are only a baby,' he replied, to see how the prisoner would react.

'Sir, I am talking about all Algerian prisoners, not about myself.'

Guignard drummed his fingers on his desk and considered his next move.

'Please ask only what you claim and want for yourself and I will see that you get it, but leave others out.'

The prisoner before him cocked his head to the side in contemplation. 'Sir, I am not looking for special treatment for myself. All I am asking is that my people be allowed the dignity of a trim appearance.'

From that day on, the hairdressers were brought in for all prisoners.

FOURTEEN

Return to Maillot

It seemed to Mohand and his cousins that the slow grind of the French penal system had passed them by. Surely, they whispered among themselves, such a grievous crime as the one they were suspected of could not be forgotten? But still another day would pass without the call to the courts.

Time donned a cloak of concrete for the three men and they allowed themselves the thought that Madame Guillotine would have to wait a good while longer for a taste of Saoudi blood.

The long hours and days of monotony they endured was at least punctuated for Mohand by his new task of public writer for Serkadji prison. Every evening he was called from his cell to listen to yet another of his countrymen dictate letters to wives, children and parents. In these letters the truth of prison life was given the sheen of normality for relatives who didn't want to hear brutal truths. They wanted to hear that their men were well-fed and well-housed. That the worst thing they faced was boredom. And so the prisoners, with the collusion of the young Saoudi, fed this wish.

Day after day, week after week, Mohand continued this job and sometimes it felt that he was in a bizarre world of ink, paper and the rough voices of his fellow Algerians. Until the day he was called in to the director's office. It was 2nd July, 1928, exactly one year after the murder.

'Monsieur Saoudi.' Guignard motioned for Mohand to come from the corridor and stand before his desk. 'The courts have issued a demand for witnesses to your alleged crime.' He scratched at his cheek with a manicured finger. 'The wheels of the French penal system turn slowly, Mohand. But they do turn. In this…' he considered his next word carefully, 'twilight world we can sometimes forget that.'

Mohand shifted his feet and Guignard read the unspoken comment in that tiny movement. He offered a small smile. 'Forgive my loquaciousness this morning. I don't often have an audience with a vocabulary of more than ten words.' He cleared his throat. 'In any case, you and your cousins are required at Bouira. From there you will go to Maillot and walk the route that the murderer of Samson might have walked. It seems the courts will have its witnesses.' He paused and injected a more serious tone in his next five words. 'One way or the other.'

* * *

They wore heavy chains and were surrounded by armed guards. The place was full of people from the region. They come to see the lost sons of Maillot for the last time. For that was how they were considered. Everyone present believed that, guilty or not, these men were in the maw of the French system and nothing would get them out of it.

All of the Saoudi family were present that day, including Mohand's wife. Saada held her baby high in her hands as if offering him to the heavens, hoping that Mohand would catch a glimpse of him through the crowds. She dreaded the thought of seeing her husband in such a situation but came in the hope that she could give him the gift of seeing his son.

His family were huddled together, offering each other comfort while trying to ignore the looks of pity from the others. Mohand was of course aware of all of this, but his eyes were fixed on his son; the little brown face with its button nose, crowned with a crop of black hair. He ignored as best he could the stares of his enemies. These people were given no choice by the French system. They were so used to being manipulated that they had largely lost the ability to think for themselves. He knew what they were seeing. Just last year he was the envy of most people and now he was one of the most despised, and being treated like a murderer.

He recognised that there was an element of human nature that looked at the downfall and anguish of others and took a certain pleasure in it, an angle of behaviour that the French were willing to manipulate.

Having committed the small face to memory, he tore his eyes from his son and searched for his father. There. He was surrounded by his lawyers, brothers and cousins, looking fifty years older and torn with suffering. Hadj Yahia approached his son, moving slowly through the crowd so as not to draw attention. Mohand could barely look at the pain in his eyes. When Hadj Yahia arrived within earshot he offered words of counsel.

'Be a man, my son. May God protect you.'

Mohand turned around, looked his father in the eyes and offered him his strength and support through a confident smile.

'Do not worry for me, dear father. I am like oil on water. I will always rise to the top of any situation.'

This answer was absorbed by his father. He was bolstered by the apparent serenity of his favourite son and happy to hear such words of wisdom.

'Go, my son, may God facilitate your tasks.' He paused, anxious to convey meaning. 'I am like a man relieved of your suffering.'

Caid Mezaine was standing just behind his father and when his friend had finished he stepped forward and placed a hand on Mohand's shoulder. There was a strange light in his eye when he praised Mohand's courage and offered him support.

'May your prison be like that of Joseph,' Mezaine said, his words in the tone of a blessing. Like Joseph, thought Mohand. What does that mean? But before he could ask, the guards bustled them away on the march up the mountain while they called for witnesses to the murder of the Frenchman by the name of Samson.

* * *

During their first six months in Algiers there had been neither investigation nor judgement, but now it was relentless. They each spent hour after hour being questioned by the various elements of the justice system.

It seemed now that the French had woken up and they demanded the truth. Or, a truth that would serve their purposes best.

Following on from the reconstruction at the murder site, witness reports flowed in to the authorities. It seemed that people were outdoing themselves to offer wild versions of events. Before they committed these fantasies to the court stenographers, they each solicited from the French administration an assurance for their protection before testifying. People tripped over themselves to contradict their neighbours. Mohand shot him. No, it was Ali. It was Ali and Árab holding the gun while Mohand held the Frenchman down. The Saoudis had obviously been leeching from Samson for years, they crowed. How else could they afford all that land? It seemed the family's success had won them many enemies and they were all demanding their day in court.

Now that the wheels were in motion they were all transferred to another prison while awaiting trial. One day in September 1929, they were escorted to the director's office by a group of guards.

He wasted no time in explaining the situation.

'Your files with all details have been returned. The hearing by the judge, Monsieur Truck, is set up to take place by the end of September 1929. Please take a copy of your files.' He pushed a fat, brown folder at them from across his desk.

As soon as they heard the name 'Truck', their faces grew pale. This was a man who was infamous throughout the penal system. They came out from the office shaking and without saying a word they headed straight to the exercise courtyard.

Monsieur Truck was the most feared judge of all. His name caused fear even in the hearts of the French prisoners. He had the firm and unwavering conviction that he had only two verdicts to choose from; the guillotine or forced labour for life on Devil's Island.

His nickname was 'The Butcher'.

In the courtyard, Arab and Ali crowded Mohand with questions.

'What does the file say?'

'What does all that paper mean?'

Mohand shushed them as he flipped through the file, which contained every minute detail of the investigations. This included details of the murder, information extracted from people who had clearly been tortured, and many false statements by the so-called witnesses. The only thing it did not contain was the official reports by the *gendarmes*. With a sinking heart Mohand read out the information to his cousins. Once he finished reading, all three of them slumped against the wall, lost in their own thoughts. Each certain that their time on this planet was about to run out.

* * *

It was a matter of course that when any lawyers worthy of their fees heard that Monsieur Truck would be presiding over their client's hearings, they would advise the defendant to apply for an appeal. The hope was that the appeal would delay the trial, Truck's visit to the colony would come to an end and it would then receive a date when a more lenient court officer was in residence.

Hearing this advice, Mohand applied for his appeal immediately and helped his cousins to do so, too. He claimed that something was missing from their files. How could they possibly be placed in front of the court without a full and proper investigation?

As a result of these appeals, the files were returned to court for further verification. Until they heard further they spent every waking moment in prayer, hoping this would enable them to escape the nightmare of standing in front of The Butcher.

Unfortunately, all of the lawyers with clients awaiting trial had the same idea, and there were no hearings taking place at all during that particular visit of Monsieur Truck. As a result of this, Truck sent a wire to the French authorities in Paris requesting an extension of his residency in the province. They extended his stay by a further three months in order to catch up on the backlog.

Late in November 1929 their appeal was rejected and they were called once again to the director's office to be informed of events. Knowing that he would stand in front of The Butcher after all, Mohand shuffled back to his cell in a daze of worry. He knew very well that his time was running out and that he may never see his loved ones again.

With almost machine-like precision, prisoners started queuing before The Butcher, who, true to his legend, started handing out his usual harsh sentences. The news went around the prison like wildfire. The lowest sentence handed out during this particular session so far was a grim twenty years' forced labour on Devil's Island.

* * *

When their files finally returned, the trial date had been set. On 24th December, 1929, Mohand, Ali and Arab would face the full weight of the French penal system.

FIFTEEN

A Last Intervention

Two days before the hearing, his lawyer came to see Hadj Yahia one last time. His warning was a dire one.

'The whole French system, the judge, the lawyers and the procurer are against them. The outcome is more or less decided. They are guilty even before the hearing. You must speak to your son, Monsieur Saoudi. Mohand must tell the truth. Only then can we be assured of his freedom. We believe your son is innocent and would be freed if only he would tell the truth and point the finger at Arab.'

Feeling in his heart that this had long been a lost cause, Hadj Yahia decided to give this approach one last try. With heavy limbs and the weight of the French system on his shoulders, he made one last journey to the prison before his son was placed on trial.

It was clear that Mohand loved to see his father during his regular visits. Hadj Yahia would always find him in good humour and he in turn always came away buoyed by the strength of his son and his capacity to endure.

On this occasion he carried with him a small packet of couscous with tender lamb, which had been cooked by his wife.

Mohand plucked a small piece of meat and popped it in his mouth. He chewed slowly with his eyes closed tight. He finished chewing, smacked his lips and asked, 'How are my son and my wife?'

'They are well and they send their love. So do not worry about them.' He stopped speaking and searched his son's eyes. Mohand was in the process of popping another piece of lamb into his mouth. He stopped with his fingers just before his lips.

'What?'

'The lawyers tell me that this case is tried before you even step foot in the court. Even before the jury is called you have all been found guilty.' Hadj Yahia closed his eyes and found the energy to ask the question one last time. He allowed a little hope to glitter in his eye as his mouth formed the words.

'You only need tell them the truth. Everyone knows you are innocent. We only need to hear it from your lips and you will be set free.' He fought to keep the pleading tone from his voice as he spoke. 'I spoke with Caid Mezaine before I left the village.' This was a man that he knew his son had come to hold in the highest regard and he hoped that by invoking the name of this sage he could sway his son. 'He told me to tell you that you must do the right thing.'

'Dad, I could never look another man in the eyes', Mohand stared directly into his father's, 'if I let my cousin be guillotined in public in front of our enemies. That, for me, is the right thing.'

'I hear you, my son,' Hadj Yahia said. Was there a slight waver in Mohand's voice? A pause before he answered? He searched Mohand's eyes for something. Anything that might give him hope. 'Your wife needs you, Mohand. Your son needs you.' Emotion tightened his voice. 'Hana Addidi needs you. We all need you.'

Mohand breathed deeply and appeared to consider his father's words. Hadj Yahia imagined what his son's thoughts might be. With the right words of his own, Mohand would be a free man. He would see his son reach adulthood. He would once again hold his wife in his arms, feel a mountain breeze whisper across his face, smell mountain herbs as he…

But.

'Father,' he said. Two syllables laden with apology. He shook his head slowly. He couldn't.

Hadj Yahia grasped Mohand's hands in his own. He looked down at the two pairs of hands. His old skin folded over and between the unlined, firm skin of his child. He knew that he had no choice but to accept the position and decision of the man he was proud to call his son. But in that moment something in him died. The hope and fight that had sustained him through these long, dark months wilted before the glare of his son's certainty.

He left the prison that day knowing with stomach-churning certainty that he had lost his son for good.

SIXTEEN

The Hearing

On the day of the hearing Ali and Arab were taken to the first floor while Mohand was left on the ground floor. The cell he was taken to was full, with seventy prisoners waiting to stand trial. It seemed all seventy turned to stare as he entered. Their eyes fixed on him for only a moment, as if their attention had been torn from their own desperate musings and they were anxious to return there.

Earlier that morning, cleaners had been asked to prepare the death row cells. Word quickly reached the ears of the other prisoners. Everyone was aware that one among them was to be charged with the murder of a Frenchman. Everyone was equally aware that this was a crime the colonial power would not condone.

Perhaps the new man was the one waiting to put his neck on the chopping block? Mohand could hear the whispers and the looks of pity. He felt a tremble in his thighs and prayed to Allah for the strength to endure. He could not allow people to see that he was afraid. It was the unknown, the waiting for someone to decide whether you going to live or die, that he was finding hard to deal with. He would almost rather get it over with; he would prefer to face down this evil judge and take his punishment. He only hoped they would make it quick.

It may have been hours, or only minutes, when the approaching sound of heavy boots filled the cell. The murmurs died down. Seventy men held their breath. In his mind Mohand could see the key inserted in the keyhole and hear it turning from the other side. The door opened and, with the certainty of the condemned, he knew that his name was about to be called.

A rough voice shouted, 'Saoudi Kaci ben Yahia.'

He blinked. Once. Twice. This is it.

'Good luck, son,' someone said in Berber. Several other voices joined in and soon all the prisoners were wishing him good luck. The guard, with not a sign of care on his face, pulled him aside, chained his feet and hands together and dragged him down the corridors towards the courtroom.

Entering the court, he was guided into a securely guarded box where Ali and Arab were waiting. He was unchained and seated while surrounded by a phalanx of guards. He looked across at his cousins. They were both wearing matching expressions, the skin tight on their faces, their jaws set.

Mohand made himself look around at the people in the room. Facing him was a long barrier made from a dark, rich wood. Behind it sat a man on a seat that might have resembled a throne. So this was the infamous Monsieur Truck. He seemed such an insignificant being to hold such a position. He had a small face, centred with a large nose on which was perched a pair of half-moon spectacles. A former teacher of Mohand's wore such a pair of glasses and on him they lent a benevolent air, but with Truck the effect was quite the opposite. It was as if the eyes behind them had shrunk to a black dot and the person peering out from them lost his soul the second he put them on. Befitting his position as one of the men most responsible for sending the *indigènes* to Madame Guillotine, he was dressed in black robes. The only spot of colour was a white collar.

Tearing his eyes away from the judge, Mohand looked to the left and the twelve members of the jury. They were all French. All the lawyers including the defence were French.

What chance of justice, he thought. The only Algerian present in the court, other than the prisoners, was an interpreter, and as most of the proceedings would be carried out in French, Mohand was sure his real job was to translate a one-word verdict decided before he had even entered the room: guilty.

* * *

The hearing started with the declaration of the accused. Then the cousins were called one at a time and questioned by the prosecution lawyers. Arab was his usual surly self and answered with an aggression that bordered on the suicidal. Ali was quiet, diffident and had to be asked on several occasions to speak up.

When it came to Mohand's turn he endeavoured to answer with as much pride as he could muster. He was asked the questions in Berber and that was how he answered them. He knew how the assembled French might see his ability to speak perfect French. He would not give them the satisfaction of thinking that this was one *indigène* who had taken their gift of an education and turned against his 'benefactors'.

Where the judge was a small man, his prosecution lawyer looked like he ate his way through a bakery for breakfast, a patisserie for lunch and the butcher's for dinner. His face was bright red and he kept dabbing at his forehead with a square of white linen. The questions were thrown rapidfire at Mohand and translated by the court worker.

Yes, he worked for the North African Hydro-Electric Company.

Yes, he was taken on and treated like family by Monsieur Samson.

Yes – and here his voice caught in his throat – he was present when the Frenchman was murdered.

No, he did not do it.

No, he was not able to identify the killer.

Here the lawyer paused and took some more time to dab at the area where his jawline melted into his chin.

'Is it not true that you were in collaboration with the killer? You knew there was a great deal of money being transported up the mountain and in your greed weren't you desperate to get your hands on this money,' he paused for dramatic effect, his eyes glinting, 'despite everything Monsieur Samson had done for you?'

Mohand didn't answer. Couldn't answer. Fury trembled in every line of his body and robbed him of coherent speech.

The lawyer persisted.

Mohand continued to choke on the words that he feared would send him to his death.

'In the interests of justice, I insist that you answer my question, young man.'

The storm broke.

'Justice, you say. Justice?' Before he knew what he was doing Mohand was on his feet. Despite his earlier promise to himself not to speak French, Mohand couldn't help himself. 'Nothing about today is to do with justice…'

'Silence,' shouted the judge.

'Your court makes a mockery of justice.'

Gasps sounded from the jury at the sight of this young *indigène* so boldly speaking up in a French court. 'This whole event is a farce that couldn't be bettered by the pen…'

'Silence,' shouted Truck once again, his voice surprisingly loud and wrapped in an unquestionable authority. 'There will be no such insolence in my courtroom, young man. Or you and your fellow accused will feel the full weight of my office.'

A hand reached out to Mohand's shoulder and pushed him roughly to his seat. Ali pulled at his trousers and begged him to calm down with a look full of fear.

Grinding his teeth, Mohand burned with indignation as he listened to the lawyer declaim loudly to the court the arrogance of the *indigènes* and their lack of ability to behave when faced with the might of the French system.

The questions began again.

No, he could not and even if he could, he would not point out the man who shot Monsieur Samson.

Soon the lawyer was finished with Mohand and then followed the questioning of the witnesses. The *indigènes* were easily differentiated from the French in the court by their threadbare clothing and their weatherbeaten faces. At first Mohand listened carefully to everything that was being said, but quickly he came to realise that there was little point.

Most of the people that were speaking before the court were strangers to him and none of them could possibly have witnessed the shooting. However, this didn't deter them: one by one they described a course of events that could only have been planted in their heads by the authorities. The main thrust of events as concocted by the prosecution was that one of the accused, Mohand, had been the guide that led Monsieur Samson to his death and the other accused were both seen in the vicinity of the shooting directly thereafter. The stocky one, Arab, was seen hiding a gun. The slim, tall one was seen carrying a heavy bag.

A long line of people were questioned in order to help the prosecution establish these events as fact in the eyes of the jury. Then they began to call witnesses to testify to the character of the men in the dock. Thieves, bullies, brigands and responsible for surely more than the one death they were facing the charge for – that was the proclamation for the next group of witnesses to testify to. Such was the passion and authority with which witnesses talked about this side of his character that Mohand almost wondered if there was some form of *djinn* wandering the Kabylie masquerading as him.

One of the witnesses called during this time was the director of Serkadji prison. Once he was sworn in and asked about the nature of the men before the court, he talked about Ali and Arab in similar terms to the previous witnesses. Then he allowed all of his frustration at Mohand's behaviour to colour any script he may have been handed.

'In Serkadji prison,' he reported with an indignant tone while pointing at Mohand, 'a certain prisoner knows the law better than the lawyers themselves.'

One prosecution witness refused to follow the script. Dubourouz worked in the administration offices for the North African Hydro-Electric Company, and presumably the prosecution thought it would help their case to have a fellow employee disparage the youngest Saoudi in front of the assembled court. At seventy-six, he could have been forgiven for thinking that he should have an easy life from here on in. He was thin and wiry, and pale at the thought of what he was about to say, but his conscience would not allow any answer other than the truth. The crown of white hair on his head bristled with righteous anger as he spoke.

'During this very sad incident I was in France, so I can't possibly testify to the actual events, but what I can say…' At this point he paused as if working through some internal battle. Once he reached his decision he looked Mohand firmly in the eyes. 'What I can say is that from the knowledge I have of Kaci Saoudi, I am certain that he had nothing whatsoever to do with this evil action.'

At this point the prosecution lawyer realised that this particular witness was not going to plan and he began to hurriedly thank Dubourouz and order him from the stand.

The old man, however, had other plans. Now that he had spoken up he had even more to say.

'Don't worry about the family, Kaci,' he said, unaware of Mohand's thus far inarticulated decision to change his name. 'Yvette is devastated by her husband's death, but she knows it was not you.'

'Enough,' Monsieur Truck shouted above the old man. 'Remove this man from my court,' he ordered. A pair of guards pulled the frail old man from where he was standing and carried him from the court. Above the clamour, Mohand could hear Dubourouz's voice as it grew fainter and fainter, but six words shouted over and over again reached his ears like a prayer.

'She knows it was not you.'

* * *

At the end of the first day, they were chained again and dragged back to their cells. In Mohand's, all was silent as the men inside waited to hear the news. As soon as the door closed behind him, voices clamoured for information.

The cell was almost in darkness, but he could see enough to avoid the bodies that littered the naked floor. As he walked over to his corner, questions were thrown at him. Mohand began to describe the day. But how to encapsulate the otherwordly mixture of monotony and fear? Each answer he gave resulted in further questions and Mohand felt moved by the brotherhood expressed in those questions. They were all suffering under the yoke of the French and even such a small gesture as the concern shown from a fellow prisoner was proof that humanity ran strong in the group of men he was locked up with.

He was easily the youngest man in the room and he was aware that each of the men in that dim cell saw their own sons bound up in his frame. They feared for the future of their sons, but would take strength from the obduracy he was showing in the face of the French.

From his days in the French school he remembered tales from their book of religion. One such story sprang to mind. He would be an Algerian David to the French Goliath and show them that their sons would have the courage and strength to face whatever the colonial power would throw at them.

Then the story of Joseph popped into his head. And the words of Caid Mezaine.

'May your prison be like that of Joseph.'

Of course. Joseph was a prominent figure in both the Bible and the Koran. He was sold into slavery: betrayed by his family, but then rose to prominence. Could this be what Mezaine saw might be in his future?

* * *

The next day was the turn of the defence. Artur Legrand was an experienced lawyer and although Mohand could see that he was trying his best, he could also see that there was a resignation in the shape of his slender frame. In his bones Legrand knew this was a case he could not win, but he would still give it his best efforts.

Late on in the afternoon Mohand understood that part of his lawyer's tactic was to beat down the opposition. He went over and over every piece of testimony from the prosecution, demonstrating the weakness of their argument. This dragged on until 8pm.

When Mohand returned to his cell late that day, his cellmates were in a state of worry: it had taken so long, they could only think of one outcome. As he entered this world of deep silence, every head turned in his direction. With the door still open behind him, he headed towards his spot on the floor. He tried to hide his frustration and terrible disappointment. He refused to drag his feet. He kept his head up and his chest out and chewed on the thought that with his closing statements his lawyer had given up on him.

Usually at this point the prisoners would start talking among themselves, but this time there was a deep silence. Knowing the gravity of his case, they thought that he had come back to get his belongings before being moved to the death row cells. When he reached his place and made himself comfortable, there was a sigh of relief.

'So what happened then?' The man next to him broke into the quiet.

'The case is not finished yet, we have to go back tomorrow.'

Everyone demanded to know what had happened. They all started talking, questioning, sounding like a field of crows.

'Praise be to Allah you are still safe,' he heard one man say.

Mohand cleared his throat. For a moment he couldn't trust himself to speak, so moved was he by the concern shown.

'My defence lawyer went through everything. At first he fought like a lion in that court of the damned French, trying to show that each of the witnesses from the day before spoke nothing but lies.' He paused while he tried to find something positive in the way that the session had ended. But he could find nothing. 'Then he finished … he said that he doubted the role played by the accused … hence he asked for a sentence of forced labour for life at perpetuity in Cayenne.'

His neighbour could only look at him in surprise.

'Is this not good news? Sounds like you won't be sent to the guillotine.'

Mohand turned to the speaker, anger making a mask of his face. 'I am innocent. A man I loved like a brother was killed and I am to be grateful to receive a life sentence of forced labour?'

It was only when he felt a couple of other men pulling at him that he realised his fingers were round his neighbour's throat. He coughed, offered a weak apology and fell into a crouch on the floor.

Forced labour for life. Better that they sent him to the guillotine. Then his life would be over quickly rather than having to face a lifetime suffering a slow death.

He paused in his thoughts. Who was this stranger taking over his mind? He was better than this. But he was in a situation with no hope. There was no way out. He had no will. No choice. No control.

***

The trial ran on for a few more days. On the last afternoon Monsieur Truck was ushered into the court to deliver the outcome of his deliberations.

'A man died,' he said, staring at the accused. 'A god-fearing man. A man with nothing but good in his soul. A man who tried to help the poor *indigène*. And the three of you took this help and spat on it. You deprived two boys of the love and attention of their father. You have deprived a good Christian woman the love of her husband. For this you should each be sent to the guillotine.' He stopped speaking and allowed his last word to echo through the room. 'However…' He allowed his frustration to boil over into this word. 'There is great doubt of the role played by each one of you in this foul murder. Therefore on this day, 29th December, 1929, I sentence each of you to hard labour, doublage and perpetuity.'

With this statement, The Butcher's legend was strengthened. Deprived of the guillotine by a lack of cast-iron proof of the killer's identity, he fell back on to the only other punishment he could tolerate... forced labour on Devil's Island.

As Truck spoke, Mohand fell into a trance-like state. He simply could not take in the enormity of what was going on. Truck mentioned each of them in turn, read out their personal history, the crime of which they were convicted and their sentence. His two cousins were convicted and given a sentence of forced labour for life. Then Truck turned his attention to Mohand.

'Saoudi Kaci ben Yahia, twenty-two years old, born 26th January, 1907, in Mechedallah. For complicity in assassination and theft, 2nd July, 1927, you are sentenced to twenty years of forced labour. Doublage and perpetuity.'

40 pgs
2 hr 15

end
11:15 pm
Sat 3/13

SEVENTEEN

Maison Carrée

Immediately after the sentencing the three men were chained and transported to prison. At first, Mohand railed at the thought he had not been given a chance to say goodbye to the men who shared his cell. In that brief intense time each of them had become like surrogate fathers and he desperately wanted to show some appreciation for their support.

Eeee, it was one loss of dignity after another. How could he and his people bear this? How could they have suffered this for a hundred years?

He screwed his eyes tight against such thoughts. There was nothing he could do. He was but a pimple on the giant French arse. If they wanted to sit on him and squeeze the life from his lungs, all he could do was bear the torture and pray.

Liberty, equality, fraternity. Was this not what the French sang about? How could they promise such ideals and limit them only to their own peoples? Were all humans not brothers? Do they not all share the same need for love, food and shelter?

These people had taken his liberty. They spat on any notion of equality and no Berber would ever treat his brother in such a manner. He ignored the thought that this is exactly what his Berber brothers had done to him. After all, they had colluded in his conviction… but that was only after decades of abuse and manipulation in which his people had lost their vision of themselves.

***

Maison Carrée was to prove to be a prison like no other they had been locked up in. Here the French were determined to make use of the Algerians under their ward, and they were worked like slaves. They were manufacturing all sorts of things for the prison to sell for its own benefit, and for the benefit of the French prisoners. Algerians were given impossible quotas to meet. When these were inevitably not met, the transgressors were punished severely. They were made to run barefoot in the courtyard all weekend, while others were enjoying time off. When they dropped with exhaustion, they were kicked and beaten back on to their feet. When the beatings failed to elicit a response, the bruised and battered man was dragged off to an isolation cell for days, weeks or even months, depending on the severity of the so-called crime.

Most prisoners who entered the walls of Maison Carrée soon found that there was a good chance they would lose their health along with their freedom. Tuberculosis found a home in many victims, who were weakened by the rampant brutality. A favourite method of torture was to revive a battered prisoner by throwing him in a trough of ice-cold water.

Another part of the de-humanisation process was to keep the amount of visitors to a strict minimum and when they were permitted, physical contact of any sort was forbidden.

The prisoner and the visitor were separated by two fences. The fences were spaced a metre apart and a guard was always present in the middle, monitoring the conversation. Twenty minutes was the maximum allowed and the guard would bark out a cough to signal the end of the visit.

Mohand had already learned that one of the most important jobs in the French-Algerian penal system was that of prison writer. It appeared to be a huge contradiction in the way his people were treated. Why torture them, keep them apart from their loved ones, and then allow them contact in this most personal of manner? It didn't make any sense to him. Perhaps their Christian values dictated that the written word was sacrosanct?

Whatever their notions were, this was one situation that Mohand could make use of.

When he first started work for the prison, he was given a job in the shoe manufacturing area. Then, after a few weeks, he became prison writer. The benefits of this promotion were many. He was exempt from hard labour and any punishments that went with it. He was paid three francs per month and given a mattress to sleep on instead of the thin carpet on the floor used by other prisoners.

At first this 'promotion' prayed on his mind. How he could accept this privilege when his fellow countrymen were treated so badly? When he realised that he could use this position to help his family, he was happier to take it on. He could attempt to save some of his pitiful wage and pass it back to his father. Although he was in prison he still had some months before he would be shipped across to Devil's Island. He could save his earnings and do what he could to support his wife and his child.

* * *

Ten months after their arrival in Maison Carrée, on Thursday 30th October, 1930, the director called Arab, Ali and Mohand to his office. When the three men stood before his desk he looked up from his papers, removed the spectacles from the perch on his nose and passed on the verdict of their appeal.

'The court has reviewed your convictions and decided that the original decision was a sound one. You are to be kept here until the next transportation of prisoners can be arranged for French Guiana.'

Arab swore, Ali hid his face in his hands and Mohand stared at an indeterminate space above the director's head. Aware of the profound nature of the words he had just issued, the director then appeared to be at a loss as to what to say next. 'I… eh… I would remind you that you have the right to write home once per week. Thursdays or Sundays only.'

* * *

That evening, Mohand asked for some writing materials and, ignoring the requests of other prisoners to write letters for them, he concentrated on his own family. But what to say? How could he form shapes on to the page from the emotions that churned in his gut or the thoughts that careered around in his head?

The blank paper seemed to mock him. He who had written countless letters for other men could only feel the pen slip on the oil-slick of sweat shining on his fingers. What to say and how to say it?

When he was writing for others the scratch of the pen across the paper was automatic. The words were effective and functional. Perhaps that would be the best way to communicate, to pretend he was writing on another's behalf.

He took a deep breath and wrote two words – *Dear Father* – and then the letter took care of itself.

Dear Father,

It is with a heavy heart that I have just learned our appeal has failed. Your very best efforts and the work of our lawyers have crashed against the brick wall that is the Frenchman's determination to see someone punished for the murder of my good friend.

That we have been spared the guillotine is thanks to your determination to see that the French would not get it all their own way. Although I confess that, in my darkest moments, I crave the fall of the blade instead of the lingering death that waits for me on Devil's Island.

The prisoners talk of little else. It seems I am to be sent to a prison that is the worst man can come up with. Very few who go there survive to complete their sentence, apparently.

Sorry, Father, I shouldn't have written this last part. I'm sure it is an exaggeration. Why would the French go to the trouble of sending prisoners to the furthest shores of their world only to work them to death? They could do that here in Algeria.

Words fill my mind, Father, but when I reach out to grasp them they scatter like rabbits before a hound. I know that I will soon never see you, my brothers, my wife or my son ever again and the importance of that is simply beyond my grasp.

Despite the uncertainty of what lies before me I can see how Allah has smiled on me in the past. To have been given a father such as you. To be given your example of how a man should play his part in the world is a gift beyond any and I humbly thank you and Allah for it.

There are also my brothers, good men both. They are the future of our family and I rest assured that such a future is in capable hands.

Hana. What did I do to deserve such a mother? Many motherless children are cared for by female relatives, but who among them has been as fortunate as I to be favoured and truly loved?

My wife, my Senegal, my Saada. We only had a brief time together. Even now, even here, as I write this I find a smile warms my face. Every man should have such a wife. To feel that I have let her down, let all of you down, is almost more than I can bear.

Please find it in your heart to forgive me for the pain I have caused you. Perhaps you can find peace in the fact that I was true to the man you raised me to be.

God blessed me with a son for which I thank him. However in my absence I fear for a child without its father, better that he had never been born and I therefore pray to God to take back this gift.

* * *

Switching from French to his native tongue, he wrote at the bottom of the letter, '*Sadkaath isithi abdelkader ouldjillali*,' meaning he was offering his son as an omen to Allah.

He read the letter over and over. He considered tearing it up and then ignored this impulse as one born of the fear of displaying his vulnerability. Now was not the time for such a small-minded action. His family deserved more of him. They deserved whatever he could give them by way of an offering of peace.

He folded the thick paper over on itself. Sealed it and pressed it to his lips. He breathed in the smell of the ink and hoped that the love squeezing the air from his chest would find its way on to the page and from there to his father's heart.

* * *

The next day Mohand was working on a machine, making shoes under the watch of one of the guards, an acne-scarred barrel of a man called Gauthier. All the bitterness and despair he had been feeling over the last few months welled up in him and it was all he could do to hold the leather to be stitched.

Before he knew it the guard was in his face.

'Why are you staring at me like that?' Gauthier demanded.

'I… I…' Amazed at the guard's outburst, Mohand couldn't speak. The guard had a hold of his tunic and was pulling him towards his face as if he was about to take a bite out of his nose. Suddenly bitterness and despair changed to barely controlled anger. Go on, thought Mohand. Go on, give me an excuse and I swear I'll tear your heart from your chest. He shook with the force of his fury.

'For your information I have cross-eyes from the Great War.' The guard pushed Mohand away as if cowed by the rage he saw in the younger man's eyes. Then he stood tall and spoke loud enough for everyone in the vicinity to hear. 'If you step out of line one more time, I will make you pay.'

Mohand bent over his workstation, fighting to hide the force of the anger that caused his limbs to tremble. He had been so close to letting the dark beast in his soul loose, and that could have ended in only one way.

The guard, seeing Mohand bent in such a way, thought the prisoner was bowing before him.

'Look at you, you sorry little Berber bastard. Wait until we get you out to Cayenne. Then you'll know what a prison is really like. Pah, we pamper you people here. On Devil's Island they really know how to treat a prisoner. A handsome young boy like you, you'll be some ugly old lifer's whore in no time. Well, that's if you survive the logging camps in the jungle. In the meantime, little Berber boy, just pray that you don't cross me again. For I'll make your life even more miserable.'

* * *

In the letter to his father, Mohand made reference to his fear that he would not last long in Cayenne. He had dismissed it then, but the other prisoners were convinced that it was a real danger. Once all the appeals had been attempted and all of them failed, the prisoners could all get on with the business of debating their sentences and their likelihood of survival.

When passing sentence on him and his cousins, Truck had spoken several words that until now had been a mystery. Terms like 'doublage' and 'perpetuity'. No one had bothered to explain these terms and their implications.

'Are you aware of the doublage?' an older fellow asked while Mohand scribed a letter for him.

'Doublage?' said Mohand. 'Truck mentioned it when he passed sentence.' He shrugged his non-concern, displaying that sanity-saving ability that successful prisoners had to learn: show no weakness.

His friend smiled at Mohand's naivety. 'Doublage? Simple. If you get to the end of your twenty years, you have the additional satisfaction of doing another twenty.' He paused and picked at his teeth. 'However, the French are not complete monsters; they know that almost no one will ever do this. '

'What's the point of this doublage if not many do it? Why don't they do it… and what does perpetuity mean?'

'It is simple, my friend,' he said. 'The French send each fresh batch of prisoners out into the jungle to work in the logging camps. Apparently few survive their first year.' He was silent for a moment to allow the words to sink in. 'And those unlucky few who can manage their doublage, have to face perpetuity in the penal colony. For they are never allowed to leave the island.'

EIGHTEEN

Preparation for the Voyage

Three weeks before the date set for their voyage, Arab, Ali and Mohand were transferred to the 1st Quarter, which was an area of the prison reserved only for those prisoners destined for long sentences. In the 1st Quarter, they benefitted from a few liberties: they were allowed to smoke and spend their savings on things like cigarettes, chocolates, sweets and other foodstuffs they might need.

Naturally, they were suspicious. Why would their guards suddenly decide to treat them like humans? It took some time for the men to relax into this new regime. Little did they know that there was reason behind the authority's apparent madness. They were given meat four times a week and a quart of wine, but this was simply to fatten them up so that they would have enough strength to face the fearsome ocean crossing that was waiting for them.

They were even allowed to talk between themselves during the two daily half-hour promenades in the courtyard. They could also continue to write a letter every Thursday or Sunday and a relative was allowed to visit for twenty minutes, also on Thursday or Sunday.

Mohand was gaining weight and strength from the extra food they were given, but his will was becoming weaker by the day. He could sense that the end approached. There was no hope of a better tomorrow. The guards took grim pleasure in constantly reminding them of what was waiting for them, the living hell at the other side of an ocean.

This was further enforced when he and his fellow inmates were lined up outside a room on the ground floor of the prison. One by one they were each pushed into a small room and forced onto a chair. When it was Mohand's turn, standing before him was a fellow prisoner with a tattoo kit in his hand and a bottle of black ink. A guard pushed up his sleeve and shaved the hair from his forearm. Then the prisoner got to work.

'What ... ?' he tried to ask.

'Silence,' the guard ordered.

A series of numbers began to grow on his skin: 5 ... 1 ... 2 ... 4 ... 0.

When the tattooist finished, Mohand was ordered to stand up.

'You have no name,' the guard said. 'You are now prisoner 51240, nothing but a number.'

Such was the prison's adherence to this system of numbers that when prisoners died before the voyage to Cayenne they were buried in a reserved cemetery. There was no name allowed to mark the man who had just died. If he was a Christian, a simple cross was stuck in the earth. If he was a Muslim, a stone was laid. There was no name inscribed on the cross or the stone.

* * *

Time was approaching for the voyage and his father made his last visit. When a guard called for 51240 to tell him that a visitor was waiting for him, Mohand started walking towards the visitor's area. He knew that it could only be his father and he was not sure if it was a good idea to meet at all. He wanted his father to forget about him quickly. He wanted him to think of Mohand as being dead.

When he entered the visitor's area, he saw him standing, deep in thought on the far side of the fence. A guard was standing between the two fences, monitoring a few visitors at a time.

He looked older again, more stooped, more wrinkled even since their last meeting. Mohand sat on the chair and forced his features into a smile. He put his fingers through the fence while his father did the same. They each imagined the press of the other's fingers on their own. After a long silence, looking at each other through this forbidden fence, Mohand was the first to speak.

'Hello, Dad.'

His father responded with a nod, not able to trust that his voice could work while such strong emotions clogged in his throat and chest.

Kaci needed to hear his father speak and was uncaring of how mundane the conversation might be. 'Have you been waiting long?'

'No, son, I arrived just a few minutes ago.'

'How is everything at home, Dad?'

'Would you believe me if I said it was okay?' His smile was weak. They each fell into silence. Then Hadj Yahia spoke.

'Your little boy…'

'Yes…' Mohand read his father's expression and with a sinking heart knew that what he was about to be told was bad news.

'He became… ill. He didn't suffer. It was only a few days. And then he died.'

Mohand simply nodded. This was Allah being merciful and answering his prayers. A harsh prayer but what life would a boy have in this Algeria without a father?

'Saada. How is she?' Mohand asked. He did not want to dwell on these things. He had made his decision and no amount of debating the issue would change anything.

'She is like any mother. She grieves. For her son… and her husband.'

Silence stretched between them like a dark cloth that bound both their mouths and their minds, forbidding them speech. Words were nothing. Words could do nothing, yet words were all they had.

'Dad, why did you come?' Mohand forced his voice out into the quiet.

'What do you mean, son? Why would I not come? I had news. I wanted to see you. I am sixty-five years old and cannot bear dying without seeing you for the last time.'

'Why are you talking about death, Dad?' Mohand felt the chill of an involuntary shiver.

'Son, I wish death to come every day.'

Mohand observed his father and how dignified he was in his grief. He felt a tear slide down his cheek and, hoping that he father didn't notice, wiped it from his face with his sleeve.

'No, Dad, you can't,' he argued. 'You need to be strong for the others. I am not the only son you have.

'It is not easy. This is killing me slowly.' Hadj Yahia allowed the words to stumble from his mouth. From his expression, Mohand read that he instantly regretted them.

'Oh, Dad, I am sorry for putting you through all this. I wish with all my heart that I could put the clock back, but I cannot.'

'I understand you, my son.' Hadj Yahia's voice grew louder. 'Whatever I'm going through, it must be harder for you. It must be hell for you to go through this. I don't want to…'

'The future scares the hell out of me, Dad,' Mohand interrupted. 'I cannot accept the thought of never returning to my country and never seeing my loved ones again. But I take comfort knowing that you are there to take care of everyone.'

They were both silent for a time. Both allowing the tears to flow freely. Both wishing they could hold the other for one last time.

Mohand gripped the fence as if he could tear it from the earth.

'Son, this is Allah's will, we just have to pray for strength to go through this, everything will work out fine in the end.'

Now Kaci allowed full vent to his emotions. He was sobbing, struggling to breathe and speak at the same time. 'There is no God. He left me the day he put me in this mess.'

'Son, you should not think that. You should have faith and be strong. All the family is praying for you.'

'I am trying, Dad. I just regret putting the family…' Emotion robbed him of the remainder of his sentence.

Hadj Yahia ached at his son's pain. 'Don't blame yourself. You should not worry about anything.'

Mohand's laugh was like a bark of warning. 'Dad, I am about to be sent to hell on the other side of the world with the guarantee that I will never be back and a very slim chance of surviving the first year. Off course I am worried.'

Now it was his father's turn to give vent to his emotions. His eyes flooded with tears, his voice shaking, he spoke: 'Son, I cannot bear losing you. Every night as I fight for sleep, I pray to God to take my life in your place.'

Both men were leaning against their portion of the fence, crying openly. Neither could do anything to change the situation, they could only pray for the courage to endure.

Mohand struggled to find the right words. It was not right that his father should have these thoughts.

'No, Dad, you should not wish that on yourself. This is my doing and I will pay the price by myself. You have the rest of the family to think of.'

For a time the space that separated them was filled with a deep silence. They stood looking at each other, simply allowing the quiet to communicate the depths of their feelings. Kaci wanted to capture this last moment for the remainder of what was left of his life.

The guard coughed and his father's visit was over. Neither of them moved. Neither of them could. They simply stood looking at each other until a guard took hold of Mohand's arm and pulled him away.

As the guard escorted him back to his cell, Mohand's strength almost gave in. His thigh muscles shook with every step, such was the guilt he felt. His family's pain: this was his doing. His decision. Was it too late to approach the court with the name of the killer?

NINETEEN

A Burning

Some days later the prisoners were each supplied with the uniforms used by the convicts in the prison in Cayenne, French Guiana. The cloth was brightly coloured with red and white stripes. Their shoes were of a very basic construction with a wooden base and leather top. Mohand studied his, sure that after only minutes with these on, his feet would be covered in blisters. They were also given a *bonnet*, a pancake-shaped hat that fell down at either side of the head.

All this was an indication that their last day on Algerian soil was upon them and that they were officially convicts rather than prisoners. A subtle but vitally important distinction in the eyes of the French.

A notion went through the prison like fire that the men had nothing to lose and they should give vent to the desperation they were each feeling. One man dragged his mattress to the courtyard and set it alight, and soon every mattress in that part of the prison was on the pyre, sending flames and smoke high in the air. Everything the men could find that could be smashed was flung against a wall; everything that could burn was added to the fire.

The guards could do nothing against this wave of destruction and simply stood by. They knew that these men were about to go to a prison that was reputed to be the worst on the planet. If they suddenly decided to attack a guard, what other punishment could the authorities impose on them? Besides, this was not the first batch of men to be sent to French Guiana who had reacted in such a manner.

The fury of the convicts ran unchecked. They wanted to remember this day. This was a revolt against a system imposed on them by a nation from across the sea, a nation that had taken its men and its resources and raped them. They had taken everything and given nothing in return except for misery.

Once everything they could get their hands on was destroyed, the convicts looted the food and drink supplies. They would eat, drink and perhaps find some joy at the bottom of a wine barrel. This was their last day, their longest day. They did not want it to end and they each determined that they would stay awake all night, drinking and reminiscing about their loved ones and savouring their last moments on Algerian soil.

Mohand took pleasure in the release such violent action could bring. He joined in the destruction with relish. Everything he owned was thrown onto the pyre in the courtyard, even his cherished writing material, and for the first time in his young life he sought release in alcohol.

Again he considered his decision to remain silent. After his father's last visit he had come close to seeking an audience with the prison authorities. The pain in Hadj Yahia's eyes was there because of him and he could take it all away by uttering one word: Arab.

And the word remained still on his tongue.

He spotted a man who was about to throw a bottle of wine over the courtyard wall.

'That's good wine, my friend. Don't let it go to waste.'

'Ha, but it might hit some French bastard on the head,' the man replied, his face wild with the expectation that he might be able to hurt one of the hated French. He leaned back, his arm behind his head; he overbalanced but managed to right himself before he fell. Mohand leaned forward and plucked the bottle from the man's hands.

'You little bastard,' he roared, his face twisted with fury, and he swung at Mohand's head. He dodged the blow easily and, with his foot, pushed the fellow on to his arse. 'You little ...'

'Get some sleep, granddad,' Mohand offered. 'If you manage to do any more damage this night, it will only be to yourself.'

'I'll get ... you little fucker ... just you ...'

Mohand shrugged the man's anger off and moved around the courtyard, looking for a spot where he could sit and rest with his wine. Men were in disarray everywhere he looked. Some slept where they fell, some hung around in clumps, and pairs of men hid in the darkest corners seeking warmth and any form of comfort they could find. Mohand shuddered. This kind of love between men was anathema to the Berbers, and despite more than a few demonstrations of it since he had entered the prison system, it was something he could never quite get used to.

One man, having burned everything he possessed, even his new uniform, danced naked before the still-burning fire. He bent over every now and again, aimed his backside at the guards, and shouted, 'Kiss my arse!'

Mohand found Arab and Ali with a couple of men from a neighbouring village. They hailed him over and he sat down beside them.

'Ah, you have wine, cousin,' said Arab, getting up from his crouch and stretching his arm out. 'Stolen from Zaydane, I see.'

'And it's all for me,' said Mohand with a dark expression that said, *go on try and take it from me and you will suffer*. Arab read Mohand's expression and decided it was not worth the effort.

Ali winked at Mohand. 'Good for you. He deserves nothing.' Mohand smiled and then pulled the cork from the bottle with his teeth. He had always been brought up to respect the effect that alcohol might have on a man, but now he was past caring about any of that. If it could make him forget everything that he was about to lose, even for a moment, then it was fine by him.

He drank determinedly from the wine until it was finished. Then he pitched the empty bottle into the fire, with a roar.

'Bastards!'

The few men around him who still had any energy joined him in the chorus, all of them shouting the same word.

Mohand slumped to the ground and lay spread out, arms and legs wide, looking up at the bright night sky. As the wine took effect, the stars spun and wheeled across the sky on a drunken axis. The moon was a thin sliver of silver fingernail and Mohand remembered the story he had told his little cousins. Would the moon weep for him, he wondered? Or would it feel that he deserved everything he got?

Again, he questioned his actions. He was innocent. Another innocent man died and he could have ensured that his killer received the ultimate punishment. All he needed to do was tell the truth, and his father would have his son back, his wife would have her husband, his son might have lived.

Could he do it?

He looked across at Arab, who chose that moment to take a swallow of wine.

He could get his life back. Or was it too late? He felt a drop of wine on his cheek and wiped it with a sleeve.

Then the Berber code that fortified his veins stirred and his mind showed him an image of Arab kneeling under the blade of the guillotine. His neck bare and ready to be severed with the silent rush of sharp steel. He imagined the crowd. Faces naked with the need for blood. The flash of the blade. A gasp and celebratory cheer.

This he could not allow to happen. He had been handed a role in the story of Samson's murder and he could have played no other part. In truth, it would have been easier for the moon to come down to the Earth and mop up the tears of every child made orphan by the actions of the French colonial power.

TWENTY

The Day of Departure

At 4am on 5th May, 1932, the bell rang and men began to stir. The guards, knowing that their charges were exhausted and hungover, were no longer worried about maintaining control. Shouts filled the air as the convicts were harassed and bullied back into line. This was the day that they would be taken on the voyage to their new home and the guards were on a strict schedule in order to make the men prepare and pack.

They were given meat, cheese and a length of baguette for breakfast. Then they were stripped of all their belongings. Small personal items like jewellery were catalogued and would follow the convict to his destination. It was too risky to allow them to travel with small portable valuables on their person, for many men had been murdered during the crossing for the tiniest piece of gold. The authorities knew of the convict habit of keeping some cash or even gold in a 'plan', which would then be inserted in the anus.

Other items belonging to the convicts were placed in a store and would remain there for a period of one year to allow the convicted man's family to claim them back. After a year, anything not claimed was destroyed. This was an issue mainly for the French prisoners, most of the Algerians were as poor as the day they were born and had nothing that their families might wish to claim.

After breakfast the convicts were provided with special items. These would be their only belongings from now on. They had already been given uniforms, and a pair of shoes; to this was added a haversack, or *musette,* containing a mess tin, a tin quart for their drinks, a fork, a spoon and a cloth.

Those who were fortunate to have some cash were allowed to stock up with supplies for the lengthy voyage. These lucky ones filled their bags with things like olives, cakes, chocolate and cigarettes.

After washing and changing into their new uniforms, they were called out by number. Then they were aligned in the courtyard and chained into groups of four prisoners. Four of these groups were then chained together again, forming a big group of sixteen prisoners, with four columns and four rows.

The chains were locked and assembled with cold efficiency. Hands and feet tied together in all directions, making it impossible for any one individual to free themselves from the group. They were given just enough slack in the chains to enable them to walk.

For further security, four *gendarmes* were placed at the four corners of each group of sixteen prisoners.

Mohand, being the youngest, was offered the chance to be chained with his cousins Ali and Arab, and another Berber. He tried not to show any of the fear that coursed through his veins when, with an awful finality, his chains were locked together.

His limbs trembled, his heart raced, his stomach threatened to throw up every scrap of his breakfast. He felt himself weaken, stumble and almost fall until a firm hand righted him. He looked up to see Arab reaching out to gain a hold of him. The expression on Arab's face revealed a riot of emotion. Yes, the old anger was there, but etched into the deep lines of his face was fear, trepidation … and sorrow. In the only way he knew how, Arab was finally admitting that his actions had rid his cousin of his future, and he was filled with remorse.

Mohand shaped his mouth into an attempt at a smile. His muscles were frozen and wouldn't obey the message he sent from his brain. He managed to make his head move on his neck, which was more of a wobble than a nod. A movement meant to convey understanding. Arab nodded back and slid his hand under Mohand's arm, helping him to meet the rhythm of the other condemned men.

With their shoes made of wood and canvas it was almost impossible to walk without pain, blisters formed on the feet of every man seemingly within moments. And so with a slow, forced shuffle, the men followed the direction of their guards and moved towards their fate.

The convicts were forced to march from the prison to the railway station. Pairs of armed soldiers were positioned every twenty metres along the route, one on each side of the road. These soldiers had the darkest faces of any men Mohand had ever seen.

'Senegalese,' Arab whispered to him. 'See how the French use other slaves to keep us in line.'

This display of force wasn't really to stop people escaping, for who could free themselves from such an arrangement of men and chains? It was, in fact, to demonstrate the power that the French held over the Algerians. Such a potent symbol of dominance by the French army helped them maintain their position as it intimidated Algerians into thinking that any uprising against the oppressor would be assuredly doomed to failure.

When the gates of the prison opened, the convicts could see that many people were waiting to see them off. Silence was imposed on the convicts and, strangely, this seemed to carry itself across to the watching relatives. At first. When the men started walking, the only noise was the stamp of many feet and the clanking of their chains.

To allow the convoy of convicts to pass, the roads were cleared of traffic. People stood on the pavement waiting for the train of doomed men to pass by.

The event was advertised well in advance. People were encouraged to come and support France's effort to subjugate the Algerians and, with a tragic complicity, the *indigènes* submitted. Locals were paid or bullied to witness the march; brainwashed or forced by the enemy, they soon started screaming at the men in chains.

'Murderers.'

'Animals.'

'Bastards.'

Fierce insults were thrown at them by their own people, and the prisoners could do nothing other than endure this abuse.

There were also people who stood quietly, allowing the silent flow of tears to do their shouting for them. From time to time the insults were threaded through with words of support.

'Animals are treated better than these poor souls.'

'This is not justice.'

'May God go with you.'

Mohand allowed nothing of the fear that filled his mind to show on his expression. He was more terrified at that moment than in any other of his life, but he would not give the guards the satisfaction of knowing it. He kept his face to the ground and his footfall just behind the feet in front of him. He felt a blob of spit land in his hair; he clenched his jaws and ignored it. The poor fools who acted in such a way were every bit the victim he was.

When they arrived at the train station, animal wagons were provided. They were loaded into these wagons and transported to the port at Algiers, where they were paraded through the Place du Gouvernement. Again this was a warning. People of Algeria, take notice of our power.

The square was full of people. Faces twisted in hate. Voices raised in a rapturous rage. Mohand knew that the real source of that hate was the French, but those masters of manipulation gave that hate a focus: their own people. Criminalise them, chain them together and march them through the lives of a beleaguered people and you give them a chance to vent their frustrations. A successful diversion from their real problems.

* * *

Once the convicts arrived at the port, still chained like animals, they were taken in barges to a ship anchored a few miles out to sea.

Le Martinière, nicknamed the 'White Ship', had hailed from Ile de Ré in France. She had partly filled her hold with convicts in France, sailed across the Mediterranean to Algiers, and was now going to head through the strait of Gibraltar and across the Atlantic Ocean towards French Guiana.

The entire time he was being transported in the small barge to the ship, Mohand could do nothing but stare at the space between his feet. He was being taken away from his family. He would never see them again. He was going… His shoulders rose and fell with the force of his sobs. The fear that almost crippled him as he left the prison found a release.

'Cry all you like, boy. It will only get worse.' Mohand heard a voice so deep it almost scraped across his ear. He turned his head to the side and took notice for the first time of the man that he had been chained to, alongside Arab and Ali. Despite the man's hunched shape, Mohand could read strength. He looked at the man's hands. The knuckles were scraped and swollen.

'I…' Recognition was slow in coming. The last time he saw this man he was trying to throw a bottle of wine over the wall. 'You're the man I…'

'Stole from,' Zaydane said. 'No one steals from me.' His voice was thick with threat and Mohand felt fresh fear chill his bones. 'I won't kill you. At first,' said Zaydane. 'I haven't had a woman for some time. You'll do. I bribed a guard. I thought about your nice firm flesh all night last night.' He moved a hand to his crotch and slowly rubbed at his genitals. 'Soon, my boy. Soon.'

Mohand forced himself to look away and moved his vision towards Arab, who sat on a bench in front of him.

'Don't think he'll be able to help you. I'll slice him from his balls to his throat if he interferes,' said Zaydane.

As if aware that he was the focus of attention, Arab twisted his head round to look at his young cousin. He raised his eyebrows in question. Mohand reassured him with a similar movement. This was his fight. Although his time in prison so far had been peaceful, there was an ever-present promise of threat. He had come to understand that men in such close confines would always try to find a way to assert their power over others. So far, his youth, his brains and his personality had made others see him as a valuable ally rather than a threat.

These assets were no longer enough.

He had heard of older men taking on young men as lovers, forcing them with threat against their lives into becoming a *mome,* a passive member of a homosexual relationship.

Mohand's stomach churned, he forced air into his lungs. Adrenalin flooded his veins. He wiped his forehead and noticed the tremble in his hands.

Zaydane read the tremble and smiled. That smile was the trigger. Before his brain had registered the need to act, Mohand twisted in his seat and headbutted the older man full force on his nose.

'You little ...' Zaydane screamed and stood up.

Mohand turned to face the front and donned an expression of saintliness.

A guard took two strides towards them and clubbed the still-standing Zaydane on the back of his head with the butt of his rifle.

'Sit,' he commanded.

Zaydane slumped to his seat with a grunt, his eyes screwed tight against the pain. Minutes later he turned to Mohand with a leer tightening the muscles of his face.

'I like a boy with spirit. Just makes it all the more fun breaking you in, little boy.'

Mohand had never been a violent person. He'd never needed to be. Friends and family learned from early on that Mohand was a person to respect. He would treat everyone with honour, but it was known that if you were to push him too much he was bound to explode. And now he also had an outlet for all his fear and fury. Let Zaydane try, he'd regret it every day of his miserable life. He formed a smile. He found himself almost enjoying this side of his personality. If he got hurt, he got hurt. He'd do anything rather than give in to this excuse for a man.

'The price is too high for this piece of flesh, Zaydane. Cast your eyes elsewhere.'

Zaydane stared in to Mohand's eyes, read something there and reared back slightly. Mohand could read the man's uncertainty, but then a series of thoughts played across his features and he tried to re-assert his position. What he thought was an easy trick was now about something else entirely. Something that could make him even more of a danger to Mohand. Losing face.

* * *

Once onboard the ship, the men were unchained by the accompanying guards and directed towards their cells below. Rubbing wrists that were suddenly painful, Mohand prayed that Zaydane would not be placed in the same cell as him. If he was, there was little chance of him having an uneventful crossing, and a strong chance that he might get badly injured.

He forced himself to stop worrying, held his head high and determined that he would not be a victim. Arab would happily step in and fight this battle – it was something he would relish – but Mohand couldn't allow that to happen. The men around him were different now. He could sense it in the way they held themselves and in the way that they looked at each other, and if he wanted to hold his own among them, he would have to fight his own battles. It would take more than a bloody nose to put Zaydane off.

So pre-occupied was Mohand that he didn't take much heed of his surroundings. He noticed a narrow flight of iron steps. Then, in single file, they were made to step into a cage faced with heavy iron bars. The entrance into the cage was so small even the shortest man had to duck on the way through.

A guard stood at the entrance to the cage and counted each man in.

Then, with a clang of metal, the ring of keys on a chain and an easing of the pressure from the bodies around him, he realised he had reached his berth.

The hold had been divided into cages of iron, two hundred and fifty feet long, but only eight feet wide. The cages ran the length of the ship and had a corridor in the middle where the guards patrolled day and night.

The first thing that struck him was the smell. Vomit and excrement. Sweat and foul breath. Next was that the cell had already been half-full before they arrived. These new faces would be Frenchmen, Mohand judged, as the boat had already been to mainland France to pick up undesirables from there. While the rest of the new men with him looked around themselves, Mohand quickly read the situation. The cell's earlier inhabitants had organised themselves in small groups. Their hammocks were hanging from large hooks welded into the frame of the cell.

Looking around him, Mohand could see that there weren't enough hooks for all of the new arrivals. With a nod and a grunt to Arab and Ali, he took out the hammock from his haversack, moved to a collection of empty hooks, and hung up his hammock. Arab and Ali quickly followed suit.

Other men soon realised what was going on and copied them. No one wanted to be left sleeping on the floor. Mohand had realised what the implications of the horrible smells were. If anyone was sick, or the piss buckets spilled from the rocking of the boat, those men forced to lie on the floor would have a wretched time.

Voices were raised. Fights broke out. Hammocks were torn from their hooks. The old and the weak were left to bemoan their lack of power. Mohand, Arab and Ali stood firm in their triangle. They would not be beaten and they had found a corner where they could set up 'home' for the next couple of months. If someone tried to take on one of them, they had to face all three. Arab already had a fearsome reputation and by now everyone knew how Mohand had reacted to Zaydane. He had won a similar form of respect.

Having gained their own space, or stolen it from someone else, the caged men turned inwards and studied their fears. What would come of them? Would they survive the crossing? Some men groaned with fear, some wept openly, those lucky enough to be in position near a porthole crowded round the space for a last glimpse of their home.

Even had he been close enough to do so, Mohand wasn't sure he could have looked. He climbed into his hammock and fought back the feeling of hopelessness that threatened to engulf him. Zaydane's threats would have to be faced, and soon, but for now he could only mourn the loss of his family and home.

The ship's whistle sounded above their heads. The floor began to vibrate. The sound of despair from the caged men began to grow.

Mohand noticed little of this; he was thinking of his family and the pain they must be suffering. He vowed to consider that part of his life dead, for that was the only way he could survive with his spirit intact. He allowed himself the luxury of replaying the moment when he last set eyes on his family.

They were there in the crowd, just a few hundred metres from the prison gates. Something made him look up and, among the faces filled with hate, were the faces of stone of his family. Hadj Yahia, Dahmane, Amar, Hana Addidi, Saada and numerous cousins. All waiting to get their last glimpse of him, Ali and perhaps even Arab. As soon as they saw that he had spotted them, they started shouting his name.

He was not able to shout back, but he met each and every one of them eye to eye with a look that he hoped said everything. He tried to give more time to his father and Saada. As he moved closer to them, they seemed to fade before his eyes, grow watery and indistinct.

Only then did he realise that he was weeping. His limbs grew heavier, his chest tightened but all he could do was form one word over and over and over again. *Adieu.*

PART TWO

DEVIL'S ISLAND

ONE

The Crossing

As part of his education with the French, Mohand had been given Bible classes. A strong part of those classes was a description of the threat of eternal damnation: a place the Christians called Hell, where the heat would be unbearable, the pain unendurable and there would be no future other than a continuation of this.

The first night aboard ship was a taste of what that might be like.

They were enveloped in darkness so total that when Mohand held his hand before his face he could see nothing. When he stuck out his tongue, he could almost taste the blackness.

This was a darkness that certain men would take advantage of.

The vessel rolled and pitched in strong seas. Man after man succumbed to seasickness and vomited on to the floor. The latrine bucket was soon overflowing and excrement joined the bile on the floor. Mohand covered his face with his hat in a feeble attempt to counter the smell.

All along the ship, moans filled the air. Grunts and shouts assaulted his ears. Another fight sounded in the neighbouring cage. Fist on bone. A grunt and it was over. Men continued to fight each other. Power was the medal they sought. Some gave in for the hope of an easier life. Others fought for any meagre amount of status they could find.

Mohand lay in his hammock with his knees pulled up to his chin.

He felt a hand on his neck. From there it moved to his shoulder.

He slapped it away as if it was a giant spider.

'It's only me, you fucking idiot,' said Arab.

Mohand grunted.

'You okay?' Arab asked.

'Happy as a honey badger with his snout deep in the hive,' Mohand replied. To his own ears his voice sounded as if it was strung on a tremble.

Arab didn't appear to notice.

'Good for you, cousin.' Arab grunted a laugh. 'Try to get some sleep. I'll keep watch.'

'Ali?' Mohand asked into the dark.

'Leave me alone,' Ali replied. 'I was ...' Ali vomited on to the floor. After several minutes of heaving into the darkness he lay back into his hammock. 'If men were meant to sail on oceans ...' Whatever he was about to say next was lost as he began to retch once again.

Mohand was still staring into the space above his head when a weak morning light began to illuminate the ceiling of his cage. A pattern of holes, arranged in neat lines, could be seen in the metal. He craned his neck forward for a better look, wondering what they could possibly be for.

'Steam,' a voice sounded beside him.

He turned to his side to face the man who spoke.

'Henri Charriere,' the fellow offered with a nod.

'Mohand. You can call me Mohand.'

'Good. Keep the tough guy act going,' he grinned. 'And find yourself a weapon.'

Mohand sat up in his hammock. He looked down at the floor for a clean space to step into. He found none and stayed where he was.

'If any steam comes from those holes, it will be hot enough to scald the skin from your face.'

Mohand's face screwed up in amazement that men could think of such a thing to punish other men.

'There are many dangerous men in these cages. It's how they keep control of us.'

Mohand looked at the man for any guile in his words. He would trust no one until they earned it. But this man appeared to be no danger, indeed he looked almost relaxed.

'What do you know about Devil's Island?' Mohand asked.

'The *Bagne de Cayenne* has a dreadful reputation.'

A man behind Henri sat up and punched him on the arm. 'Don't be filling the boy's head with nonsense. He'll learn soon enough how bad it is.' This fellow then nodded at Mohand. 'Jean,' he said. 'And I've already had one stretch. I'm being sent back for good behaviour,' he finished with a grin.

Jean was a tall man and the sagging skin under his chin suggested he had, until fairly recently, been much broader. He assessed Mohand.

'Arab?'

'Berber.'

'Apologies, my young friend. You are young, aren't you? How long have you got?'

'Twenty years, plus doublage.'

A long, low whistle.

'My advice: stay away from the logging camps and you'll live to see the end of those years.'

He seemed almost jovial and Mohand could only stare at him as if he was another species. The three men continued to talk and, as the light strengthened about them, Mohand's night fears began to fade like a dream. There was something about the daylight and the normal tone of these men's voices that held his worries back, much like a campfire might push back the dark of a forest.

'The newspapers in France are full of this place.' The man named Henri was speaking again. 'It seems that men are always escaping. Each time, their name and story appear…'

'Yes, and what the newspapers don't report are the recaptures,' Jean interrupted, 'or the skeletons found in the jungle, or the shark-bitten corpses washed onto the shore.'

'Don't,' Henri grinned, 'you'll put me off my breakfast.'

Despite the stench, Mohand felt his stomach groan.

'Do we get breakfast?'

'Eggs Benedict,' Jean nodded somberly. 'Followed by a croissant from the best baker in Paris.'

'Prepare to go hungry, my young friend,' said Henri. 'Or hope that more men die during the voyage.'

'Shut up, Charriere. The boy has enough to worry about.' Jean glared at his friend and then turned to Mohand. 'This ship is run as a private business. The captain feeds us as little as he can get away with while maximising his profits.'

'We're also supposed to get some wine every day. But the guards make up a charge and confiscate it for their own use.' Henri spat on the floor. '*Cochons*.'

More men around them began to stir as the light grew. Up and down the cages, the hum of conversation filled the air. The men who had come over from France on the first part of the voyage were more relaxed. Their minds were already at work, shaping some sort of normality from the extraordinary situation they were in. Therefore, this was just another day on the voyage to hell. For the Algerians this was their first full day aboard ship and, to a man, they were on edge and wary of what to expect.

The thud of several booted feet caused conversation to stop. A guard stood before each cage with a basket of bread.

'You,' a guard shouted while pointing at Henri. 'Take this food to your cellmates. Any fighting over this and the steam will be turned on.'

Under watch of the guard, Henri took the bread and doled it out, making sure that plenty was given to Jean and Mohand, who tore a chunk off a long stick and handed it to Arab and Ali. Both of whom were by now as unmindful of the stench as he was and ate with gusto.

Much too soon the meal was over and the new men huddled in groups, watching where they placed their feet and wondering what would happen next.

'The guards will soon come for us and take us up on deck,' Henri said to Mohand. 'We get half an hour of fresh air while they clean the shit off the floor.'

This was a huge relief to Mohand. If this was the state of the floor after just one night, he was thinking they'd be up to their knees in vomit and excrement by the end of the journey.

'Right, bastards,' a shout erupted down the length of the cages, and a baton rattled against steel bars. 'Silence. Any man who speaks will get an hour in the hot cells.'

Mohand turned to Jean and Henri, his expression a question. *What's going on?*

Jean and Henri both shook their heads and mouthed, 'Quiet.'

A row of guards filled the corridor between the rows of cells. Each holding a rifle. The air was suddenly filled with threat and Mohand felt his legs weaken.

'Everybody face the portholes,' the same voice ordered. 'Don't speak. Don't move. Don't even turn your heads.'

Again Mohand looked at Jean and Henri. Again they both shook their heads and then moved over to face the wall that housed the porthole.

Mohand heard the sound of a key being pushed into a lock and turned. Then the sound of men walking. Another key was turned and more men were ushered from their cell. Feet sounded up the stairs and then silence once again descended.

Mohand was itching to turn round and see what was happening, but he forced himself to stare at a spot on the wall. An hour in the hot cell sounded like the last thing he might want. This cell was warm enough; he couldn't imagine one that was so hot it might be used as a form of punishment.

The next sound he heard was a spray of water. Some of it sprayed over the men beside him. He enjoyed the thought that he soon wouldn't have to watch where he placed his feet.

The men in the other cells were turned out and given their bout of fresh air and at last it was his turn. As Mohand walked out of the cell and along the corridor, he looked into the other cells, wondering where Zaydane was. He knew that the issue with this man was far from over and that he would have to be wary of when he might take his revenge. There was no sign of him.

Fresh air rushed at him as, blinking, he stepped on deck and into the full glare of the Mediterranean sun. He stood facing into the sun and breathed deeply. He stretched out his arms and savoured the feeling. It was only a matter of hours that he'd been below deck, yet how could he miss the air so much? He filled his lungs to bursting, and tasted salt in the air.

A shoulder jostled him into moving further up the deck.

'Move it, Saoudi,' a voice grumbled in his ear. He turned to face the bared teeth and unsmiling eyes of Zaydane. He quickly pulled his face into a neutral expression, but not before the older man read his surprise.

'We're in the same cage, Saoudi,' he leered. 'Isn't that convenient?'

The first thing that occurred to Mohand was the state of Zaydane's face. When he had butted him he had left him with the gift of bruising under each eye. The second was wonderment at how he had missed the fact that Zaydane was in the same cage. Why hadn't he sought revenge already? What game was he playing?

Then he realised how unsteady the older man was on his feet, how pale he was looking. Seasickness. The man had been too ill to attack him.

Arab noticed the interaction between the two men and stepped closer to his cousin.

'Know that if you challenge one of us, you challenge all three,' he said with menace.

Zaydane worked hard to maintain his tough-man stance, despite the weakness that a night of retching and nausea enforced upon him. 'You won't be there to protect him all the time, big man.'

With a gaiety that he didn't feel, Mohand placed an arm round the shoulders of his two cousins and guided them towards the side of the boat. 'This is too nice a day and too short a break to waste it on a walking dungheap.'

The three men then moved over to the side and sat facing the sea. They each looked into the depths and wondered how quickly would death salt their lungs if they fell into the water.

* * *

Such was the pattern of their first week at sea: long, desperate nights and long days broken with short breaks for food and half an hour of unsullied air and sunshine.

All the time, Mohand was watching and learning. He observed his fellow prisoners and how quickly they formed into their similar groups. Even the Frenchmen had their preferences among themselves. Parisians lumped themselves together, as did the men from Marseille. Arabs and Berbers also formed their own groups as did the men from other French colonies. One group formed their own class. These were the most dangerous men, the *fort-à-bras*. These men knew the French penal system with an intimacy only available to the long-standing convict. To a man, they were tattooed, carried themselves with a muscle-laden swagger and knew how to get the best contraband. They were the natural leaders in a system where strength was power, and they bullied, stole and murdered without compunction. Within days of being on board they had each picked themselves a younger man as a lover. These young men were at first courted with fruit and tobacco. Then with the offer of protection from other would-be rapists. Then if they still resisted they were forced at knifepoint to comply with the older man's wishes. This was the life that Zaydane had in mind for Mohand, though he determined he would fight it to his last breath.

He also observed the guards. They were a new breed of men from what he had experienced so far. Their job might be to enforce discipline, but they appeared to be every bit as reliant on the convicts as they were on them. The convicts needed the guards to improve their position, and the guards needed the convicts to line their pockets.

Jean explained this to Mohand.

'Many of these guards come from poor parts of France where they don't have two sous to rub together. They are every bit as capable as you or I of being cruel or kind. The blacks. They have the best reputations. They're rarely cruel just for the sake of it.'

Of course, the *fort-à-bras* were the first to understand the relationship between guard and prisoner, and they could often be found lingering near the cage wall and bartering with one of them.

* * *

One morning at the end of the first week, Mohand was taking full advantage of the sun and the breeze on deck. He had managed to get some sleep; Zaydane was still recovering from his seasickness and he was getting on with the business of living.

Under the watchful eye of a Senegalese man, he was chatting with Jean and Ali, finding something to laugh at in this desperate world they were now part of. Suddenly a young French guard ran up to them, pointing his revolver in their faces and shouting.

'I'll kill you. I'll kill you all,' he was shouting. 'How dare you mock Petit? He may be black but he's a better man than any of you.'

Even the black guard that they now knew to be named Petit appeared astounded at this outburst.

Before he knew it, Mohand had his nose inches from the Frenchman's.

'Go on shoot me. Shoot me. Better a bullet between my eyes than a lifetime in the *bagne*.'

The Frenchman took a step back. Petit moved closer to him and placed a hand on his arm.

'These men were simply enjoying the sunshine, Roger. There was no mention of my being black.'

The man called Roger placed his revolver in the holster at his hip and looking around him, struggled to regain his composure.

Mohand was uncaring of this and furious. 'You think you defend the black man against insult? You think this makes you more of a human being?'

Jean placed a warning hand on Mohand's shoulder, but he was too far gone.

'A Frenchman tries to establish his humanity. What a joke. Look around you, Roger. Your people are responsible for all of this…'

Before he could say any more Jean and Ali each grabbed an arm and pulled Mohand away. There were still a couple of minutes before their break was over, but they forced him below decks and back into the cage.

'You fucking idiot,' Jean raged at him.

'Mohand always was the one with the worst temper,' Ali chuckled.

'One day that temper of yours is going to get you killed, kid,' warned Jean.

* * *

The next morning at break, Mohand watched the guard approach him. He took a deep breath and vowed that whatever the Frenchman said he would face it.

'I apologise for my outburst yesterday,' he said. 'I saw you guys laughing… and I assumed…'

'It is forgotten… it never happened,' answered Mohand, sneaking a glance at Ali, who was standing at his side wearing a bemused expression. This was the last thing either of them expected.

For the first time Mohand looked at Roger. He was tall and thin; his adam's apple jutted forward above his collar like a chunk of rock he had failed to swallow. From his unlined skin and almost eager smile Mohand judged that he was probably only a couple of years older than he. And lonely.

'Is this your first time?' he asked.

'Yes,' Roger replied with a shrug, as if reluctant to admit to his naivety. 'You?'

Mohand laughed at the stupidity of this question and Roger quickly joined him, waving a hand in apology, and a friendship was sealed. From that day on Roger Hirault sought Mohand out at every break and the two young men found a commonality among their differences.

'I'm from Paris,' he told Mohand one day. 'I trained as a sous chef. Got married. Had two children.' He looked far into the horizon at this point, his eyes reading the past. He swallowed. 'There was a fire. I was at work.' He chewed on his bottom lip. 'They all died. My son, Andre, was only six months old.'

They stood in silence for a moment. Mohand wanted to speak, but what could he say?

'So,' Roger continued his story, 'I lost myself in a wine barrel for a few months, until one day I met a man in a café. He was the chief of staff on a six-month paid leave. He was recruiting for guards.' Roger made a face. 'I was living in a mental hell. Why not really go there and get paid?'

Life began to get easier for Mohand following his friendship with Roger. The guard loved to swap stories with the young prisoner and grew to respect his quick mind. As often as he could he would increase Mohand's rations, which of course he would share with Ali and Arab.

This attention didn't go unnoticed by the other prisoners, and Zaydane was always willing to say his piece.

'Fucked by a Frenchman once again, Saoudi? He's after your arse and you're too stupid to notice.'

Mohand made an insulting gesture with his hand. 'Go and do yourself, Zaydane.'

* * *

The captain of the boat used prisoners to do all the cleaning and maintenance. He had a bountiful supply of free labour, why not take full advantage? He would pick a few prisoners randomly and give them tasks to do. Roger recommended he enlist Mohand when he heard that he needed someone to work with the food distribution.

'You look too young to be here, my son,' the captain said when he approached him.

'Life is full of challenges,' he replied, feigning a convict's nonchalance.

'So you are a philosopher as well as speaking French, Arabic and Berber?'

'I am a good worker, captain.'

'I need a man like you. From now on you are to manage the food distribution to the prisoners. In return you can help yourself to the coffee in the kitchen.'

Once again, Mohand considered the advantages that an education had offered an *indigène* such as him.

'When do I start?'

TWO

In Self-Defence

Mohand's days were now filled with food quotas and distribution. He ate comparatively well and managed to sneak bigger portions to his cousins. His age was at first a barrier, but with the support of the captain and his own sense of fairness, he came to be respected among his team and among the larger groups of prisoners for his ability to appease the captain's need for profit while still feeding the men a reasonable amount of food. The men who worked with him were easy to control. They had a cosy number and they knew it. One word from him was enough to send them back to the cages, so he had little trouble.

The presence of threat never diminished throughout the voyage. It was always there like salt in the air, all it needed was someone to take offence, or someone to steal from the wrong man, a lover to look at another man the wrong way, and violence would erupt. But for the most part this section of the voyage was peaceful.

Zaydane had forced the affection of another young man, a Moroccan Arab called Hassan. Mohand read Hassan's haunted expression and was charged with guilt. Could he help? Should he help? It was true to say that the law of the jungle applied here and each man had to help himself. Hassan now had the shuffle and hang-dog expression of a victim and even if he did lose the attentions of Zaydane, some other *fort-à-bras* was bound to step in.

One morning, as they were leaving their cage for their exercise session, Mohand timed his steps so that they fell in with those of Hassan's.

As the Morrocan walked in front of him, Mohand could see a trace of a limp. The poor guy was being badly treated by Zaydane. A surge of guilt stirred in his gut.

He followed Hassan to a space on the deck.

'You okay?' he asked.

Hassan looked at him, searched his eyes for duplicity; found none and then shrugged.

'I'm alive.' He forced a smile into his answer and Mohand read of the man that this boy might become if given the chance. 'Just.'

Mohand wanted to place a friendly hand on his shoulder but worried that it might be mis-read. 'Zaydane is a bully. And like any bully he can be frightened off.'

'So that was you?' Hassan swung round and looked at Mohand properly for the first time. The two men stared, each taking the other's measure. Hassan was even-featured with a strong jawline, large brown eyes and plump lips. Mohand could understand why he had become a target. A pretty-boy like this one wouldn't last long without the worst kind of attention.

Hassan looked away first and screwed his eyes shut as if denying entry to a damaging thought. He crossed his arms and chewed the inside of his cheek. He looked away. Then back at Mohand. He seemed to shrink within himself.

'I wish I had your courage,' he said. His voice almost a whisper.

'It's not courage. I call it bloody-mindedness. I will be slave to no man. I'd rather be dead.'

Hassan considered Mohand's words. His mouth a thin line of regret and self-loathing.

'If I fight, he hurts me harder… I'd rather… live.' As he spoke, his eyes filled with tears.

Mohand looked away from Hassan out to the seemingly endless ocean, squinting his eyes against the sharp light of the sun. The boy was stuck and could see no way out other than death. Nothing he could say would reach through this fog of feeling and make a difference.

'If there's anything I can…' He stood up as he spoke and felt his words hanging between them like an empty promise. He knew that if Hassan did ask for help, there was nothing he could do. He was certain his own fight with Zaydane was unfinished and a strong part of him was relieved that Hassan was there to take the older man's attention away from him.

Acknowledging that harsh truth didn't stop the feeling of shame that pressed between Mohand's shoulder blades as he walked over to join his cousins.

* * *

Mohand vowed to put Hassan's troubles far from his mind and concentrate on his own issues. He was now able to let his guard down, but sleep was still a struggle. He flung himself into his work during the day, hoping that if he tired out his brain, sleep would be easier to achieve.

One evening, his tactic worked, but too soon he was dragged from sleep by a smiling Arab.

'How is everyone at home?' he asked.

'Eh?' Mohand rubbed at his eyes. 'Why did you wake me, you bastard? I was asleep. I was actually asleep.'

'At first you were talking to Hadj Yahia. Then you were having fun with your wife. Would you prefer I let the other men hear you having a wet dream?' Laughing, Arab stuck him in the ribs with a finger.

'Bastard,' replied Mohand. He lay back down and sought the release of his dreams. But he was awake now and sleep was as remote from him as the Djurdjura mountains of home. He remembered a fragment from just before Arab woke him. Saada's face below him, her eyes closed in pleasure. Her soft, hairless skin. Her hands on his back as he thrust.

Poor Saada. He wondered how she was coping. An Algerian's life was not easy, and she was far too young to be a widow. That was how she should think of herself. He was dead to her and his family.

In the dark, he wept and sought release in pleasant memories.

His wedding night. A trembling Saada parting her clothing to allow him access. His surprise at how quickly it was all over. Their whispers and giggles at the sounds from the other side of the curtain where Amar and Messaouda were learning the same lesson.

He felt his mouth shape a smile at the memory. Then the utter waste of it all clutched at his heart with fresh energy. And he wept some more.

* * *

The heat in the cages began to intensify. Jean informed Mohand that this was a sign they had entered the tropics. It was so unbearable that many men struggled to breathe. Even their morning break on deck did little to alleviate the discomfort and most of the men took to walking around naked apart from a small towel to preserve their decency.

Several times a day one of the guards would come down with a large hosepipe in his hands, pointing it towards the cages. Everyone would run towards the bars and the guard would open a jet of cooling water over them. This relief would last only minutes and too soon the cold water would heat on their hot skin and their bodies would be slick with sweat once again.

These conditions were perfect for disease to catch hold and a few of the older and weaker men were gripped by a fever. Friends would try to revive them with a cooling, wet cloth and by feeding them sips of fresh water.

One man died in Mohand's cage and he heard of others who couldn't cope with the conditions.

'Almost every day,' Jean said quietly into his ear as they felt the boat slow and heard a telltale splash, 'another poor bastard is fed to the sharks.'

The heat and the constant crowding of sweating men were turning many men's thoughts to freedom. A group of convicts beside Mohand spent every waking moment bent over a torn scrap of a map. Distances were measured, directions assessed and the names of rivers and towns memorised. Place names that at first sounded otherworldly became commonplace on everyone's lips: Venezuala, Orinoco, Paramaribo. Men were heard bragging that soon after they landed they would take the first chance to escape into the jungle. From there they would make it to Brazil and before you could finish the first verse of *Le Marseillaise*, they would be in Rio with a drink in one hand and a girl in the other.

Tempers were constantly ragged. No one had a peaceful tongue in their heads and scuffles seemed to break out with alarming regularity.

Mohand was aware of Zaydane's eyes boring into him more and more. Perhaps now that they were coming to the end of the journey, he might take the chance to settle matters. It seemed that every time he turned round, Zaydane was standing there watching him, waiting for an excuse to strike.

One evening, Arab took Mohand to one side and handed him a small implement.

'What is this?' Mohand asked, looking down at his hand. Arab had given him a spoon, but the handle had been sharpened until it had an edge like a blade.

'I can't fight this one for you, cousin. It's either you or him,' Arab said. 'If I...'

'I know,' Mohand interrupted, 'I'd be seen as an easy target for...' he tailed off. Mohand felt a charge of adrenalin. Fresh sweat burst out on his forehead. His heart beat hard against the cage of his ribs. He recognised the truth in what Arab was saying, but did he have it in himself to kill a man?

'I can't do this...' He made to hand the blade back to Arab.

'You have no choice, Mohand,' Arab answered, moving closer, his voice deep and harsh. 'He has some size on you, but you will be faster. He's been ill during the voyage, while you have been eating well. If the fight lasts more than a couple of minutes, you'll have an advantage.'

'I... I...' Mohand couldn't believe that Arab was discussing a fight to the death as casually as he might once have discussed the forthcoming harvest season. He slipped his blade into a pocket and hoped fervently that the moment might never come. With equal fervour he prayed that if it did, he would have it within himself to do what was required.

* * *

The days became even warmer. The water became contaminated. The captain had Mohand pour rum into it so that it was drinkable. As a result the men suffered from a light but continuous inebriation.

Half-drunk, covered in sweat, feeling like they were breathing through a wet sponge, the only release the men got was the twice-daily shower with the hose. Fights became more regular than at any time since the voyage began.

Just before dark one evening a loud cry came from the cage opposite to Mohand. Then there was a series of yells. Mohand was one of the first to the bars so see what was going on. Two Arabs were kicking and punching at each other. The other men in the cells began to cheer them on.

Something tugged at Mohand's mind. A sudden sense of danger. He turned and moved to the side quickly. His movement took someone by surprise and he saw a man fall at his feet.

Zaydane. He had taken advantage of the commotion elsewhere. Clearly he was thinking that while the guards were occupied with the other fight, he could move in.

Mohand kicked out, aiming for the head. Zaydane twisted out of the way and moved back onto his feet.

'Now you pay the price, Saoudi.' Zaydane's face was twisted with hate. He held something shiny in his left hand. A small blade.

As the two men circled each other the other prisoners lined up against the bars of the cage so as to obscure the vision of the guards. No one cheered this fight on. There was a sense that something more serious was at play here.

Zaydane lashed out. Mohand slipped to the side. Not fast enough. He felt something score across his arm.

Zaydane's smile at the sight of his blood was something he was sure he would never forget.

He reached into his pocket and pulled out his own blade, sending a prayer of thanks to Allah that Arab had the foresight to prepare him. Zaydane's eyes widened when he saw the knife. He didn't expect this. Taking advantage of the other man's momentary surprise, Mohand leaped forward. He slashed down with the knife and jumped back out of range. Now blood had been spilled on both sides.

The cage was eerily quiet now, save for his and his opponent's breathing. It was only a matter of time before the guards noticed something was going on. Mohand surprised himself by realising that he didn't want the fight to end. He was going to kill this bastard or die trying.

Zaydane made to move to one side. Mohand tried to counter it, but instead felt Zaydane's fist collide with his jaw.

He danced out of the older man's range, waiting for the blurring to clear, but Zaydane sensed the advantage and moved in, his weapon a cold sparkle in his fist. The blade was a lightning strike at his face. Mohand moved his arm up in time as defence. A hot tear in his forearm. A trickle of blood.

For a second the two men were closer than they'd been at any part of the fight so far. Ignoring the pain, Mohand butted Zaydane on the nose. Even before he had begun to move, his mind had sent the message to strike at this old wound. Zaydane staggered back, holding his nose and howling with fury. Mohand moved in.

He dropped his knife.

Everyone gasped.

But Mohand knew what he was doing. He didn't need a weapon. He was better than that. He jumped forward, grabbed Zaydane's head, butted him again. Kneed him in the gut.

The next few moments were a blur. He was all movement and power, fury and speed, knees and fists. Zaydane was on the floor. At last Mohand had a focus for all the anger that had been building up in him since the murder.

Mohand held Zaydane by each ear and slammed his head against the floor. He leaned forward and screamed something in the man's face. He wanted to tear his heart out. He wanted to break every bone in this man's body. His teeth clamped on to the man's ear. He didn't know what he was doing. He couldn't stop what he was doing. He closed his jaws tight and felt something like a piece of rubber fill his mouth, along with a taste of iron.

Rough hands were pulling at him.

Voices reached his ear.

Something clubbed him on the back of the head.

* * *

When Mohand came to, he was curled into a ball. His head hurt. His arms hurt. The big toe on his right foot felt like it was broken. His skin was burning. He felt like he'd been thrown against the sun. He'd never been hotter. He reached out and touched a burning metal plate.

He was in the hot room.

The fight came back to him in a rush. What had he done?

He remembered the taste in his mouth. He gagged. He was worse than an animal. Shame burned through him warmer than any furnace. This was what he was capable of? Just as well he was being taken to prison. Someone who could act like that had no place in society. Then the voice of sanity suggested he had no choice. He had to fight, and he had to fight with everything he could. Or die.

Until that moment he had no idea that the will to go on living burned so fiercely in him.

He had been tested. The other men would see this and realise that he was not a man to argue with.

All the same, the fierceness of his attack took him by surprise. To own such animal savagery scared him. Just what else was he capable of?

He faded out of consciousness again and, in a fevered dream, he felt the cool hand of Hana Addidi holding a wet rag and swabbing it on his forehead. She was often there with soothing words and a kind heart when he was a child.

Cool water splashed over him and he felt coarse hands pull him from the cell. With a guard on either side he was taken to the captain. His friend Roger Hirault stood by his side.

'I'm disappointed in you, Mohand,' the captain said. His eyes sparkled beneath the thick white bristle of his eyebrows. 'You should have used the knife and killed the bastard.'

Mohand looked up from his examination of the floor. He had been sure he was about to earn more punishment. It was not unusual for men caught fighting to be given a whipping.

'I... eh...'

'We know everything. Normally after a fight no one talks. Men who were close enough to be splattered in the blood of the dead often see nothing. Not wanting to be a grass often strikes men with blindness. But you and Zaydane?' The captain shook his head in disbelief. 'Men have been queuing up to tell us what happened.'

'We know he's been waiting to attack you since you arrived on board,' Roger joined in. 'And we've seen how you are with the other men. And how you work, Mohand. We know you are not the kind of man to start a fight.'

While he spoke, Mohand looked from the captain to Roger and then to the table in front of them. A jug of water sat in the middle.

'Zaydane is a killer, Mohand,' the captain said as he poured a glass. 'You should have finished him off. That one won't forget.'

For the moment Mohand was uncaring of any future threat Zaydane might pose. He worked his jaw and carefully opened his mouth. His lips were almost glued together. It felt like it was filled with sand. 'Sip it slowly,' said Roger, handing him the glass. 'And have a seat before you fall down.'

The room was silent apart from the glug of water down Mohand's throat.

'Now we're going to have to punish you,' said the captain, leaning forward and pulling the glass from his hand. 'We'll just give you two glasses of water when you really should have three.' His smile was broad. 'But when you go back to your cage, you've been treated terribly, haven't you?'

Mohand nodded.

'After all,' said the captain, 'we have a reputation to uphold.'

THREE

Land Ahead

Convicts crowded round the porthole, each desperate for a glimpse of what was to be their new home. After weeks at sea, land was at last visible and it was a land unlike any Mohand had seen so far in his short existence. He was used to the baked earth of the North African scrubland, or ranks upon ranks of olive or pine trees.

His new home was a riot of green. A solid bank of vegetation stopped short at the river's edge like an arrested gallop. Mangroves broke the wall of green, stretching into the water; palm trees and coconut trees stretched into the sky, away from the tall ferns that feathered the base of their trunks.

Parrots squawked as if drawing attention to their bright colours. They swooped close to the boat and even more quickly wheeled away as if frightened off by the smell of the confined humans.

Canoes filled with naked savages paddled alongside the ship. Men called down to the Indians and were rewarded with waves and smiles.

The three cousins stood shoulder to shoulder, looking with awe at their new environment.

'Look at the monkeys in those trees,' said Arab.

'And the colours of those birds,' exclaimed Mohand. Ali nodded and coughed. Mohand turned to assess his state of health. In only the last few days Ali had been taken ill with some form of fever, brought on no doubt by the insanitary conditions on board. He had appealed to Roger to have Ali taken on deck, where he might get some release from the foul smell of the cages. But Roger had shrugged helplessly. Now that they were closer to their destination, security was being tightened. This part of the voyage was apparently a danger point. Desperate men were known to have leapt overboard in past voyages, aiming to swim to shore.

Perhaps, prayed Mohand, when they get on to dry land that will be enough for Ali to recuperate.

As for Zaydane, there had been no sign of him since the fight. Roger whispered that he was still alive, but being kept in a solitary cell.

Hassan, Zaydane's *mome,* had quickly been picked up by another older man, and at every opportunity shot Mohand looks of utter hate. Mohand could only shrug. His actions had given Hassan the opportunity to get clear of just that kind of situation. He couldn't understand it. Perhaps Hassan was terrified and felt he needed the protection that a man like Zaydane could offer. Whatever it was, it was no longer his problem.

Ali's shoulders shook with barely suppressed coughs. His face was drawn and his skin an unearthly colour.

Dry land. Once they were on dry land his cousin would recover, he fervently hoped.

They were heading down the Maroni river to the administrative centre of the St Laurent penal colony, and as the ship was guided down the river Mohand drank in the view until the call came:

'Dress for landing.'

They had been all but naked for the last few weeks, but every man rushed to put on the uniforms they had been given by the authorities. They still had some sense of pride. There were crowds of people waiting to see them. It wouldn't do to walk into their new world, no matter how harsh it might be, wearing nothing but a rag of a towel around their waists.

Eventually the ship settled by the wharf. The whistle blew and they were all ushered out of the cages on to the deck. From there they were marched down the gangway on to the pier.

Although they were uncertain about the next phase in their lives, each man was relieved to be on land. The scent of the jungle replaced the stench of their fellow man and, with relief, they were each able to breathe deep the fresh tropical air.

Looking into the crowd that waited for them, it felt to Mohand that the entire town had come to welcome them. He was not wrong. Twice yearly this procession of the newly damned was the only entertainment the locals received.

The prisoners stood baking under the midday sun in the woollen suits they had been given before they departed Algeria. A cloth that was of course unsuited to the tropical sun.

The count was made – allowances given for the men who had perished during the journey – and the seven hundred remaining convicts were marched the length of the pier into the *bagne.*

As he walked, Mohand had Jean at his side explaining the sights he was faced with.

A group of black women sang and danced for them, shouted words of encouragement and laughed among themselves.

'Prostitutes, mainly,' explained Jean. 'There are also many Chinese people in this area. As soon as you can, get to know some of them. Very useful.' Mysteriously, he didn't explain exactly why they were useful, so Mohand determined he would find out at the earliest opportunity.

Mohand also noticed a good number of white men in the crowd. To a man, they were gaunt of face, barefoot and dressed in rags. Some wore frayed hats as shelter against the fierce sun.

'Who are they?' Mohand asked Jean.

'*Libérés,*' Jean answered with a glum expression. 'Men who have served their sentences and are now free to live in the colony itself. The irony is that life is so hard as a *libéré* they are often better off as a convict.'

Mohand could only stare open-mouthed at this explanation. How on earth could a man be better off as a convict?

'Such is the pain of doublage,' Jean offered by way of explanation. None the wiser, Mohand turned back to examine the poverty-stricken so-called freemen of this part of French Guiana and shuddered at the misery that haunted each and every face.

After they had marched along the pier they were turned to the left to face a huge wall. In the middle of the wall was a large, heavily guarded gate.

'Here we are,' said Jean. '*Le bagne.*'

Above the gate in huge lettering a sign read, '*Camp De La Transportation*'.

* * *

The convicts were guided through the gates and then into the main square. A group of other convicts approached them, carrying piles of clothing. They were ordered to strip off their old uniforms and put on the new ones of red and white stripes, which was made from a much thinner material.

Under the scorching heat, the men were spread out symmetrically across the whole courtyard. In front of them was a small, wooden platform bearing the tall, thin frame of the guillotine.

Mohand studied it and shuddered. There was no mistaking the simple menace of this tool. He then looked at the buildings around him. On each side of the courtyard were what appeared to be offices. They were too open to be useful as prison cells. Through an arch at the far side he could see other buildings of cream-coloured brick with red-tiled roofs.

Suddenly the guards shouted, 'Attention!' as three men walked through the arches dressed in white. The convicts stood like trained soldiers and watched the three men heading towards them. The man in the middle carried himself with authority, head high and arms swinging as if he was on parade. He walked up the stairs onto the wooden platform and stood beside the guillotine.

With narrowed eyes and a stern line to his mouth, he surveyed the men before him.

'I am the director of the penal administration here in French Guiana.' His voice carried loud and clear to the men before him. 'You have arrived at this very spot to pay for your crimes against France. You are all criminals and are not deserving of any mercy.' He paused and looked along the line of men as if judging their response. 'For those who behave, life will not be made unbearable. But for those who cause trouble we have excellent methods of punishment at our disposal.' As he said this, he placed one hand on the upright of the guillotine, and his message was not lost to any man before him. Even if you did not know what the contraption was, there was something about it that conveyed its own message of dread. 'I know that many of you will be planning to escape at the first opportunity – forget it. You may be given a great deal of freedom in the camps and in the town, but don't ever forget that the real guards here in French Guiana are the jungle and the sea.

'First attempt at escape adds two years in solitary confinement to your existing sentence. Second attempt adds five more years. Of course, more serious offences are dealt with in this fashion,' he said, eyeing the guillotine.

'Make the best of what we offer you and you will suffer less than you deserve.' Mohand read the tone of the man's voice and the threat that it promised. He felt himself shiver despite the heat.

FOUR

The Blockhaus

'Into the house, all of you. Go on! Get a move on!' guards shouted at the men, who were momentarily stunned by the power of that hanging blade.

Keeping as close as he could to Arab and Ali, Mohand followed a crowd of men towards a low building. Over the door was black lettering that read, '*Blockhaus*'.

This was a long room with two elevated platforms that ran almost its full length. There was a corridor in the middle for men who might want to walk to the Turkish toilet at the far end. The platforms were the communal bed for the men who were locked in here. A metal bar stretched from one end of the platform to the other. This was where the men would be chained as they slept.

Ali let out a slow sigh of concern.

Mohand turned to him and gripped his shoulder. 'We'll stick together and be fine.' His voice held a note of confidence that he didn't feel.

'Animals,' said Arab in a murmur. 'This is where you keep animals.'

High on the walls, a series of small, barred windows were set into the brick, to allow meagre light to filter darkness from the room.

The men filed in and quickly moved to claim their own spaces. Mohand recognised many of the men from the voyage. Some of whom he was pleased to see. Others, he would rather not. As with the ship, the *fort-à-bras* quickly set themselves up as leaders. They picked a space nearer the toilet and settled down to a game of cards with the uncaring attitude of experience. They knew that they could relax and take advantage of any other man in this room they chose.

Mohand was intrigued as to why they would set themselves down at the end of the room near the toilet. Jean, who had stuck close to the cousins, was happy to explain.

'First,' he grinned, 'they don't care about the smell. Second, they know that every man in here at some point will have to walk past them to go and do their business. If they see someone they like…' He tailed off, allowing his silence to carry his meaning. 'Men don't only go to the toilet for toilet purposes, you know.'

Mohand made a face. 'I'm not stupid.'

'I'm not talking about perversions here, Mohand. I'm talking valuables.'

Realisation hit Mohand. 'Of course. If you have a "plan", you have to fish it out of your arse at some point.'

'And these old cons can spot someone who's loaded with a "plan" from fifty paces.'

Looking down at the ranks of the scarred, tattooed, strong-armed desperados, Mohand could only feel sorry for any poor bastard who fell foul of them. 'I have nothing,' he said. 'And for the first time, I'm grateful of that fact.'

A long afternoon, when the men were locked into the *blockhaus*, was followed by a longer evening, and then a night that seemed to stretch into the next century.

Before the lights were switched off, a turnkey made sure all of the men were lying on a platform with their feet attached to the metal pole.

Jean had informed Mohand that these men were open to bribes. For a few sous, they would pretend to chain you to the pole, thereby giving you a little piece of freedom in the night. Other men would buy soap from the turnkey and use it during the hours of darkness to extract their foot from the lock. It was also possible to buy an ankle lock of a bigger size, Jean told him. Then the turnkey could lock you in without lying about it, and the lock would be so big that the convict could easily slip his foot from it.

Mohand had nothing, so he had to succumb to the lock and be chained up for the night. The lock meant that he was unable to change position as he slept. But even if he wanted to change, this would have been made even more difficult by the fact that men were pressing in on either side. So any movement was liable to send off a chain reaction of curses down the length of the room. The 'bed' was concrete. There were no mattresses to cushion your bones.

Only the dead could sleep here, thought Mohand. In those rare moments where sleep did claim him, he was soon awakened by Ali coughing.

Arab, however, slept like a man totally uncaring of his predicament. In the early hours of the morning Ali's coughing eased and an exhausted Mohand caught a couple of hours of sleep before the guards roused them with breakfast.

While the men were busy eating, Mohand took the opportunity to empty his bladder. He hadn't wanted to draw any attention to himself until he had a better measure of the men he was locked up with and what might happen to them all next.

He rounded the corner of the toilet and the sight before him was unlike any other he had ever seen.

A man lay stretched out on the floor, his frozen expression twisted into a shape of agony. A ragged line was cut across his throat. He was naked and had been, quite literally, butchered. His innards had been pulled out from the wall of his stomach and lay displayed on top of his groin like an obscene jelly. Blood coated his thighs like a dark, shiny cloth.

Mohand felt his stomach give and he vomited.

Just then, he heard a man approach him from behind. This man stumbled into him, cursed and then looked on the floor.

'Wonder what they got,' he murmured, and moved across to the trough where men were supposed to sit and shit.

Mohand was open-mouthed at the callousness of it all.

The new fellow looked at Mohand from his squat.

'Obviously he wouldn't give up his stuff and lost it the hard way.'

Mohand struggled to work out what exactly had happened. He had barely slept. Surely he would have heard something. A scream.

A scuffle. He remembered what Jean said about men retrieving their 'plans'. This guy must have been loaded and some other guy had come along with a knife to cut it out of him. Through his lower stomach. It was almost a mercy that they cut his throat first. He felt his gorge rise again.

'Get used to it, kid. This is no picnic.'

Mohand looked down at the ground, willing the nausea to cease. Until he noticed that he was standing with his bare feet in a puddle of congealed blood. He resisted the scream that rose in his throat. Instead he took a deep breath, walked to the wall and, turning his back to it, wiped his feet on the stone.

'You learn fast, kid.' The other man stood up and walked out of the privy.

The lessons for the day were not over for Mohand. After breakfast they were all ordered out of the *blockhaus* and back into the courtyard. Even the early morning sunshine and the song of the birds could do nothing to dispel the feeling of dread that sat heavy in Mohand's gut. He had witnessed many terrible things since he had been accused of Samson's murder, but this morning's events were beyond any of that. Did these men not value life? Was another man only a piece of meat that could be tossed aside? It seemed to Mohand that the authorities expected only the worst from these men. And the lower they set these expectations, the more men were willing to meet them.

Around him, men were speculating about the reasons for their being gathered in the courtyard. Another lecture from the dandy in the white suit? A chance to clear out the body of the murdered man in the toilet?

Minutes passed. The men grew restless, but were afraid to move due to all the guards surrounding them. Then Mohand noticed a man in a long, black cloak walking towards the platform where the guillotine stood. This man was a priest and he was carrying an open book that Mohand guessed to be a Bible. Behind him, two guards were pulling another man, who was a convict, judging by his dress. He wore the same uniform as the rest of the convicts. With one difference. The collar of his tunic had been ripped off. Mohand looked from the man to the guillotine and the reason for this became clear.

This man struggled to stay on his feet. The guards held an arm each and pulled him closer to the platform. The director walked behind them.

The convict started screaming.

'Bastards. Bastards.'

He turned his head and spat on each guard. One of them punched him in the gut. The other hit him with his baton on the back of the head. The convict fell forward on to his knees and the guards carried him the last few steps.

The assembled convicts facing this tableau quickly realised what was about to happen. To a man, they sank to their knees. Many started praying. This poor soul was being carried to his death. The thought occurred to Mohand that the prison authorities must have waited for the new shipment of convicts to arrive before carrying out this execution. A valuable lesson would be given here today.

Once on the platform, two other convicts arranged the condemned man onto a plank of wood. His body and arms were attached to the board by a broad leather strap. While the man was being arranged, the priest continued to read aloud from his holy book.

'In the name of the Father…'

Mohand caught the irony of this. Murder authorised by the state and given sanction by its church. Or was the priest there only to give peace to the condemned? Judging by the way the condemned man was behaving, this peace was lost on him. Even while he was being loaded into place below the blade, he continued to struggle against his bonds, throwing his head this way and that. His movements made the frame of the guillotine shake.

The prison director looked on with the stern expression of a schoolmaster. The man about to die was only part of the scenery. This was all about the lesson. He surveyed the crowd and appeared to take satisfaction in the looks of horror on the men before him.

He made a signal and a bell tolled.

'This man is to receive the ultimate punishment,' the director said, projecting his voice into the courtyard. 'Kill each other and, frankly, we don't care. Kill a guard, or a citizen, and you will be removed from this Earth. Your head will be cut from your neck while you still breathe, and your worthless carcass thrown to the sharks in the bay.'

'This …' He paused, as if looking for the right word. '… man tried to escape. He killed a guard and, with a friend, slipped into the jungle. He got lost. Starving and desperate, he then murdered his friend. Cooked and ate him.'

Mohand shook his head as if fighting to discard the images that the director's words had forced into his mind. He couldn't take much more of this horror.

'He was caught by a local tribe of Indians,' the director continued, with a note of satisfaction in his voice, 'and brought back. Today. In front of you all. He will die.'

The man on the plank let out a long, slow note of fear. A sound that chilled Mohand to the marrow.

The director nodded and another convict stepped forward. The condemned man's head was lined up below the blade and held in place by two half-moon-shaped pieces of wood.

Mohand thought of Arab and, despite everything he had gone through so far, felt at peace with his decision not to give him up to the courts. He would not wish this kind of treatment on anyone. Not even an enemy. He felt the slow burn of hate towards the French authorities tighten the muscles of his jaw.

The executioner must have shared the same sense of the dramatic as the director. He looked over the crowd as if revelling in his position of power. Then, after a few seconds posing, he stepped over to the wooden frame and released the blade. Mohand would never forget the sound of it hitting the man on the back of the neck. He looked away, but not before he saw the head fall into the basket and blood flow from the neck stump like wine from a burst barrel.

The executioner still had a part to play in proceedings. He leaned forward, put his hand into the basket and picked the head up by its ears. He raised it high for everyone to see and shouted, 'Justice is done.'

* * *

After the execution, the silent men were then ushered through to another space and lined up in front of another building. Above the door a sign read, '*Infirmary*'.

The men shuffled forward one at a time for a cursory examination. It took hours of standing under the force of the sun before the men were all attended to.

While they waited, speculation mounted as to what tasks they might be given.

'They say that every healthy man is sent out to the jungle to clear the forest.'

'You don't want to go there,' one man said. 'The guards beat you, they steal your food and your clothes and if you don't meet your quota they beat you again and lock you up without food.'

'There's a road-building project further down the coast.'

'Yeah, maybe you'll be able to take time off and go for a swim,' one wag countered. No one dared laugh out loud in case it drew the attention of the guards. A few of the men sniggered.

Mohand wanted to scream at them to shut up. Dread crouched in his stomach. He couldn't stand this speculation. He wanted to know what he was going to be faced with.

'Fools,' someone said quietly in his ear. 'These men won't last a second in the jungle.'

Mohand turned to the man who spoke.

'Larousse. Bertrand Larousse.' This man's eyes seemed to sit low on his face, his bottom lip hung down like a hammock fat with a giant worm. Mohand turned his gaze back to the end of the queue. There was something about the way the man was looking at him. As if he was working out how he could take advantage of him.

'But a man with money. His life can be made easy.'

'Well, I don't have a sous, Larousse. So go and spin your lies to someone else.'

'So young. So cynical.'

'So shut up and leave me alone,' Mohand hissed in his face.

At last it was Mohand's turn. A man in a white coat pulled at his arm and read the number tattooed there. He wrote this down on a ledger.

Next, he looked Mohand up and down with a thoughtful expression.

'Open your mouth,' he said and, leaning forward, looked down Mohand's throat. Then he tapped on his chest with two fingers.

'You're fine.' He finished by scribbling on Mohand's hand and shouted for the next prisoner.

After this check-up, Mohand was ushered out of the infirmary and into another queue. This queue led to a desk where a decision was to be made about his future. A man there noted his number and looked at the scribble on his hand from the doctor.

From this desk, prisoners would be assigned to different camps and activities. The deciding factor was health. Those who were physically fit were immediately sent out into the work camps, where the work could be anything from deforestation to the construction of roads. If you had enough money hidden about your person to bribe someone, you might land yourself something less onerous.

The man then looked at a file where a classification had been given by the prison in Algiers. He wrote something in the ledger and looked up at Mohand. He might have been ordering an expresso for all the interest he showed on his face.

'Deforestation in St Laurent.'

This was one of the worst activities available. Talk in the queues had all been about where you did not want to go; and this was top of the list. Apparently the conditions were horrific and the rumour was that seventy per cent of the men sent out there died within the first year with anything from malaria, to yellow fever, to falling victim to venomous creatures.

Outside in the square, Mohand met up with his cousins. Their faces were grim. It seemed that the authorities were keen that the men were split up. Arab was assigned to the camp in Kourou, near Cayenne.

'Bastards,' Arab swore under his breath. 'Ali is clearly sick, yet they are sending him out into the forests as well.'

Ali shrugged. 'I'll be fine, Arab. It will take more than a tiny mosquito to keep me down.'

That night, Ali's health continued to worsen. In the morning he could barely stir himself to eat his breakfast. Mohand looked with dread at the state of his cousin. His skin was pale and waxy, and he could see every bump and curve of his ribs as his chest rose and fell in his struggle for breath.

Mohand desperately tried to get the attention of the turnkey.

'My cousin needs a doctor,' he cried as he pulled on the man's sleeve. The turnkey slapped his hand away.

'What? You don't look after the sick here?'

The turnkey made a face of unconcern. 'You want a doctor, you pay.'

It took a moment before he realised what the man wanted.

He rushed back to Arab.

'Do we have any money?' he asked him.

'Nothing,' Arab answered, his voice weak with worry.

Mohand looked at the food he'd been given for his breakfast. Arab had eaten his, but he and Ali hadn't touched theirs.

He turned to the men beside him.

'Anyone want to buy our breakfast?'

Eager hands reached out for the food. Mohand pulled it out of reach.

'Money first.'

'I'll buy your coffee,' one man said.

'I'll take your bread,' said another.

They handed over some coin and Mohand rushed over to the turnkey.

'I have money now,' he said. 'Please get my cousin to the doctor.'

The turnkey was an older man, he held out his hand to take Mohand's pitiful amount of coin. Without looking down at it, he opened his mouth to speak. Mohand could see that he only had one tooth on the bottom row of his gums.

'Where are you from, boy?' he asked.

'A doctor? Please?' Mohand was certain his cousin would die if he wasn't removed from the oppressive heat and stench of the *blockhaus*. The turnkey just stood before him, waiting for an answer. 'Algeria. Near the Djurdjura mountains.'

'I thought I recognised the accent,' the old man said. 'I'm from Algiers. My father was a Frenchman. I murdered him.' He nodded as if this was the most just act in the history of mankind. 'He was a bastard.'

He walked away from Mohand towards the exit. Mohand could only stare at him.

'A doctor?' he shouted, unable to escape the strong feeling that he had just been fleeced.

FIVE

Out of the Woods

Arab and Mohand stood and watched while a pair of convicts arrived from the infirmary and loaded Ali onto a stretcher. In silence, they followed, until they were turned away at the door of the infirmary by a guard.

One of the convicts read their concern and turned to speak to them.

'Come back this evening and we will let you visit him.'

This kindness completely took Mohand by surprise. He had become so expectant of the worst behaviour man could come up with that such a small gesture almost unmanned him. He felt his eyes prickle with tears.

'Thank you.'

He and Arab walked back to their barracks, each deep in thought.

'He'll be alright, won't he?' Arab asked. He stopped walking and turned back to face the infirmary. His voice was thick with emotion. 'He'll be…'

Mohand could only stand there and shrug. 'It doesn't look…'

Arab looked deep into Mohand's eyes. 'I don't know how you can stand to be with me. I don't know if I could ever forgive you if you…' He slumped forward.

'We are each of us victims, Arab,' Mohand said and placed his hand on his cousin's shoulders. 'You acted the role you were given by the French.' He exhaled, worried by the change in his cousin. He,

Mohand, had come to rely on Arab's strength. The older man's ability just to get on with things had helped him when he felt he couldn't put one more foot in front of the other. This life was not one for men of a weak mental state.

'I have no…' Arab shook his head from side to side. 'How can I make this better? If Ali dies…' He bit his lip, closed his eyes and turned away.

Mohand moved closer and took Arab into his arms.

'Cousin, we are all we have. We are family.' The compassion he felt for Arab threatened to overwhelm him. He had to be strong. He had to endure this moment for the sake of them both. He searched his heart and mind for any feelings of resentment, any thoughts of revenge for the selfishness his cousin had displayed back in Algeria. With relief, he realised he had none, and he was able to speak truly.

'Arab,' he said into the other man's shoulder, as they continued to hold each other up, 'I forgive you.'

Arab sobbed and almost collapsed to his knees. Mohand felt him lurch and steadied him. Arab took a few deep breaths and fought to control his emotions. 'I don't know what to say, cousin. You make your father proud.' 'Now, you must make me proud and face whatever the French throw at you with courage and heart. We will endure.'

Eyes sparkling with emotion, his mouth shaped in a smile, Arab placed one hand on the curve of Mohand's cheek. 'What a man you have become.'

Pleased and embarrassed, Mohand brushed Arab's hand away. 'Right, let's stop standing here like a couple of old women. We need to go back to the barracks and spend the next couple of hours bitching about the French.'

Arab laughed loudly and shoulder to shoulder the two men walked off together.

* * *

That evening, they presented themselves to the guards at the infirmary and were given thirty minutes to spend with Ali. They sat beside his bed and talked of life back in Algeria. How, in the summers of their childhood, they would go swimming in the river outside the village. How stubborn Hadj Yahia could be when he reached an opinion. How much they each loved to go hunting in the mountains.

Ali was weak, but able to join in the conversation occasionally, and he managed a laugh when Arab relayed an incident involving his father, Hamadache. The subject then turned to the Great War and the experience Ali had there. At one point, Ali suddenly exclaimed, 'I should have just given Hadj Yahia that damned pension. Why didn't I give him the pension?'

Arab was taken aback. 'Brother, you …'

Mohand placed a hand on Ali's arm. 'It is over, Ali. There is no past. There is no future. There is only now. We must live with that in mind or we will never survive this.'

'Wise words, cousin,' said Ali. 'But revenge squats deep in the past and hunts in the future. That is where I must send my thoughts.'

Mohand shook his head. 'That is the path to madness, cousin.'

'Then madness here I come.' Exhausted with the effort of speaking, he slumped back down on to his pillow. He managed a smile before saying, 'It will just have to wait until I've had some sleep.'

* * *

Back at the barracks that night, after they were fed a thin soup and a chunk of bread, Arab and Mohand discussed the coming days. While Mohand was due to start working on the deforestation programme in St Laurent, Arab would be at Kourou, where the colony's main road-building project was based. His job would be to clear the route of trees and rocks or whatever the geography of the country required.

Neither man's challenge was an enviable one.

'I hear there are men who work here in town,' said Mohand. 'St Laurent has clean streets and smart gardens all worked on by the convicts.'

'Hey, another man told me that the better behaved cons get to work as houseboys for the guards and their wives. That would be an easy job, eh? Keep the house tidy, cook the meals, fuck the wife when the husband is away at work.' Arab grinned at the thought.

A fellow nearby overheard their conversation. 'You want to be careful with that.' His face was as long as a horse's when he spoke. 'A friend of mine did just that. Until the husband comes back from work, caught them at it, the wife shouts rape and the houseboy gets a bullet in his brain.' Mohand recognised the man from speaking to him earlier. He wanted nothing to do with this fellow, so he turned away.

'Hey, at least he died happy,' said Arab. 'How do I get myself a nice little job like that?'

'A couple of hundred francs,' the man said. 'Larousse. Bertrand Larousse.' He held a hand out for Arab to shake.

'And you can arrange this for me?'

'No, but I know a man who can. You have the money?'

Arab looked at Larousse, his face suddenly grim. 'If I had that amount of money and I admitted it now, I'd be found floating in the shit in the morning with my throat cut.' He caught the other man by the throat.

'What is your game, friend?'

'Hey, Arab. Relax,' said Mohand. This sudden turn to violence was more than he could take tonight. He'd had his fill of blood for the day.

Larousse was a picture of innocence. With Arab's hands still at his throat, he held his own out to the side. 'You're very suspicious, my friend. It was a simple question.'

'Nothing is ever simple in here, *friend*.' The emphasis Arab placed on this last word suggested that Larousse was anything but. 'If it was, where would a man find a couple of hundred francs?' He released Larousse, whose face was frozen with the same innocent look he'd been wearing since the conversation started.

'I know a man desperate to be relieved of such a large sum. He's definitely loaded and unable to rest for fear that it might be lost. It would be a kindness to help this man out, would it not? And if a certain fellow was willing to enter this enterprise with me, I'd be happy to split the proceeds… say, half and half?'

'You're full of shit, Larousse,' said Arab and turned away from the man.

* * *

Mohand slept relatively well that night. Again he dreamed of home, and again his dreams had given him time with Saada. He was finding that the more time he was spending with all these naked men during the day, the more he sought female company in his dreams.

His dream recalled a rare day in his marriage. Given the duties that they had, they rarely got any time away to get on with the business of being children. For although they were married, that was really what they were. One day towards the end of harvest season they had judged that most of the work had been done and Mohand suggested that, if they were to sneak away, no one would complain.

With Finette, his dog, at his heel and Saada holding his hand, he walked into the woods at the far side of Maillot. There was a little stream he knew well. It ran through a copse of pine trees and a series of rocks ran alongside it like the footpath of a giant. The air was sweet and the wind like a silk caress on the skin.

They'd chased each other across the steps and over the stream. A feast of tickling was the prize for the loser. Then they'd simply lay on the ground, each of them chewing on a stem of grass, savouring the fact that they'd nothing to do and a few hours to do it in.

Mohand grew guilty first. He wanted to go back to the house. Saada made a face at him. Why didn't they stay a little longer? He made to move off. She jumped on his back, like a cowboy might saddle a wild horse. He'd laughed, gently dislodged her and insisted they return in case they were needed.

When he woke the next morning, this dream lingered before his eyes like cobwebs. How he regretted not spending more time with Saada that day. Her little face, cheeks bunched in a grin. Expressing delight at the smallest thing.

Sighing deeply, he turned to the side to speak to Arab. The space where he normally slept was empty. Surely he hadn't been taken to Kourou already?

He felt a tap on his shoulder. He turned. It was Arab. His expression was unreadable.

'Wha…?'

'Breakfast, cousin.' He handed Mohand a tin mug full of coffee, sat down beside him and then offered him a chunk of bread. Suddenly realising how hungry he was, Mohand shoved a large piece of the bread in his mouth and chewed. A man slipped into place behind Arab. Larousse. He was also bearing coffee and bread.

'Thanks, Arab,' Mohand said and swallowed. 'Needed that. Now I need to go and take a piss.'

Chains rattled at the door. A turnkey entered.

'Prisoner 51240,' he shouted the length of the room. No one stirred.

'Prisoner 51240?'

All heads in the room searched for movement. Arab nudged Mohand.

'Is that not you?' he asked.

They both looked at the tattoo on his forearm. 51240.

What would the turnkey want with him? He stood up. Arab also climbed to his feet. He pulled his cousin into a hug and whispered in his ear.

'Go with Allah.'

Mohand stepped back from Arab, his mind struggling to articulate what has happening. There was a puzzle here and he just didn't have all the pieces.

Arab pushed him. 'Go.' He looked at Larousse, who nodded.

'What's happening?' asked Mohand, looking from one man to the other. 'I'm not leaving you, cousin.'

'For a clever man, you can be very stupid, Kaci.'

This use of his childhood name momentarily confused Mohand. He looked around himself as if seeing the *blockhaus* for the first time.

'Larousse robbed some poor Parisian. I caught him in the act and told him I'd let everyone know he was responsible.' Arab spoke in a rushed whisper and, as he spoke, he pushed Mohand towards the door. 'The bribe he paid me I gave to the guards.'

Mohand stopped walking and looked at his cousin. He opened his mouth to speak.

The guard shouted again. His voice sharp with irritation. 'Prisoner 512...'

'He's here,' shouted Arab. He faced Mohand. 'Now go.'

Mohand walked towards the turnkey, his thoughts careering from one place to another. At the door, he turned back to look at Arab. He was sitting in a crouch, bent over another chunk of bread. He waved Mohand away with irritation. Mohand was struck with the thought that he would never see him again.

Shaking his head, Mohand followed the turnkey to one of the administration offices. A man sat at a desk, his attention on a file before him. He pushed it to the side and picked up a scrap of paper.

'51240?' He looked round.

'Roger Hirault?' Mohand exclaimed.

'Mohand Saoudi,' he answered with a smile. 'If I'd known number 51240 was you, I wouldn't have asked for so much.' He stood up, the feet of his chair screeching against the wooden floor.

'Sorry?' Mohand felt as if he was out of step with the world this morning.

'A change of plan. You're being sent to the town garden detail. The jungle will just have to be cleared by someone else.' He smiled broadly. Another guard entered the room. 'Go with this man. He'll take you to your new quarters.'

Mohand turned to walk from the room. He heard the rustle of paper and felt something being slipped into the pocket of his tunic.

'If I'd known it was you …' Roger said quietly. 'You can have a little back.'

SIX

Little Paris

'Welcome to Little Paris,' the chief guard said to the line of men in front of him. 'St-Laurent-du-Maroni is nothing like Paris. Nonetheless, the charming colonial buildings you see around you have attracted this name.'

'Every time,' a fellow prisoner mumbled in Mohand's ear, 'every time we get a new man on this detail, Villiers goes through this little lecture.'

'You are all lucky men. Very lucky. Work hard on the jobs we give you and you have an easy life. Shirk away and do nothing and you will be sent back to the logging camps.' He looked along the lines of men, who were all wearing the traditional red and white stripes of the *bagnard,* with wide-brimmed straw hats to protect them from the sun.

'Saoudi. You will work with Simone for the day. He is a lazy good-for-nothing but at least he won't fill your ears full of crap. Go to it, men. And remember, when you hear the horn, get your skinny arses back here and we will escort you back to the *bagne.*'

With a nod of his head, he turned and walked away.

At this signal, all of the men dispersed and made off in separate directions. Some were accompanied by guards. Others simply walked away on their own.

'Don't hang about with your mouth wide open like that,' Simone said to Mohand. 'The insects are big in these parts.'

‘What is going on?’ Mohand asked. He was astonished. Used to violence, sickness and maltreatment of every kind imaginable, he’d walked a couple of hundred yards outside of the penitentiary and entered a different world.

‘This is a good number for everyone, guards and convicts alike,’ Simone said. ‘The guards can afford to be a lot more relaxed.’

Mohand looked around himself. The streets were long and wide. The buildings were immaculate, with small, white fences edging carefully manicured lawns. He looked at a building across the road. It had a row of large windows along the wall and all were open, with delicate looking cloth hanging inside them, waving in the breeze. The building had a narrow extension running its full length, with tables and chairs dotted here and there. At one, a man sat reading a newspaper. Another man approached him, carrying a tray and wearing a convict uniform. The convict poured the other man a drink from a pot on the tray, turned and went back inside.

‘This is… who is that man sitting there?’ he asked.

‘That is one of the guards. He is on the porch of a boarding house. The fellow who served him is a houseboy.’

‘This is…’

‘Where you want to stay, young man. Keep your nose clean and your dick in your pants, and you’ll do just fine.’

For the first time, Mohand looked at his new work companion. Simone had a touch of grey showing at the temples, a pair of wire-rimmed spectacles and the air of the professor about him.

‘Come,’ he said. ‘There is a little park at the end of this street. We are to trim the grass and clear the weeds.’ He smiled. ‘And we have all day to do it.’

‘Where have all the guards gone?’ Mohand asked. He was yet to move from the spot he was standing in when Villiers had addressed him.

‘A café? Fishing down by the river? To spend the afternoon with their creole mistresses? Your guess is as good as mine.’

‘And we just…’

‘We paint the houses, we tend the gardens and we trim the trees. We do all of this at a pace that can be described as leisurely. We do all this so that the authorities can pretend they have the perfect little colonial town, while ignoring the fact that they are working most of our fellow *bagnards* to death.'

Mohand slowly spun on the spot, taking in the vision as presented to him by Simone.

'I'm not joking about the insects, by the way.' Simone leaned forward and gently pushed Mohand's jaw shut. 'Let's go. We have an illusion to maintain.'

The two men walked together to the park at the top of the hill. This was an area about the size of a football field. A path ran through it, and another around it. The grass was neat. The borders held bushes of different sizes and with different colours of flowers. The whole place was very pleasing. Mohand could imagine the people who lived nearby coming here in an evening for a stroll, while the sun sank below the distant shores.

It was the first time he had seen a well-kept garden since his days of working at the town hall in Maillot.

Simone walked towards a tall bush, rummaged behind it and come out with a couple of sacks.

'You know what a weed is?' he asked, handing Mohand a sack.

'Any plant that has set its roots in a spot where it doesn't belong,' Mohand answered.

'Clever little bastard, aren't you?' He grinned. 'I think you and I are going to get along.'

* * *

The shop was nothing but a hut on the edge of St Laurent. Before he walked in the door, Mohand was able to judge that it was solidly built. This offered him some reassurance. If he was going to trade with this man, then he had to know his money was safe.

He need not have worried. The Chinese had built their reputation on hard work and honesty. They provided most, if not all, of the commerce along the length and breadth of the colony. If one of them should prove to be unworthy of trust, the entire race would be judged to be similarly tainted.

The man's name was Chin. He was very polite. He bowed a lot.

'Come in, come in,' Chin said, ushering him in the door. 'No stand outside. What we do is private.' Chin was a small man with a fat face and skin that was smooth and ageless.

Mohand's mind was full of questions. He wanted to know how these people had come to this place. How did they set themselves up as shopkeepers and traders? Did they make a profit from all of this misery and suffering, or were they as much a victim of the French oppression as he was?

Nothing of this reached his mouth. He simply stepped into the shop and stared around its walls. Goods were piled high around the room. There were no shelves, everything sat on the floor. There were boxes of fruit, cartons of cigarettes, bottles of some kind of alcohol.

'You like tafia? Make you very happy.' Chin followed his gaze and extolled the benefits of the local rum.

Mohand shook his head and continued his mental inventory. Dried herbs hung from the ceiling. On a small counter at the back of the hut, a small bowl sat with smoke rising from it.

'Helps with mosquito,' Chin said. 'You want help with mosquito?'

As he had walked to the shop, Mohand's mind had been filled with his purpose. He knew his idea was crazy. He knew it would never happen, but he also knew he had to prepare for it, just in case.

Twenty years had to come to an end. Then he would be faced with doublage. He had seen the *libérés* around the town. He didn't want to end up like them, starving and desperate.

'I want to save my money,' he told Chin.

Chin looked around him as if faces would appear from the wood panels of his hut. 'You want escape?'

'I want to save,' Mohand answered.

Chin looked him over with care. As he did so, a more calculating expression filled his face. Gone was the genial shopkeeper and in its place was a cannier creature.

'You very young. What you do to come here so young?'

This was a question Mohand was faced with every day. It depended on the questioner which answer he gave. He knew that the other convicts respected strength. He gave them the answer they were looking for. He killed a Frenchman in cold blood. For money. He added that the money, every last sous, had been recovered by the authorities. He kept his story brief and stuck to 'fact'. He knew that embellishments would only have the other cons laughing behind his back and judging everything he said as lies. So, he gave them a little and he gave them lies as close to the truth as he could make it.

With this little man in front of him, he knew that only the truth would do. So he told him.

Chin placed a hand on his shoulder. 'I can work with you. You good man.'

Feeling that he had passed some form of an audition, Mohand allowed himself to be guided towards a small stool at the side of the counter. Once seated, Chin poured him a small tumbler of tafia.

He threw it back and coughed as the liquid scored a trail down his throat and into his stomach.

Chin chuckled. 'Horrible stuff, eh?'

Mohand wiped tears from his eyes and smiled. And nodded. When he recovered, he outlined his plan and held out the two hundred francs he had been given by Roger.

'Money no good,' said Chin.

Mohand crossed his arms, 'My money is no good.'

'Gold better,' said Chin. 'I take your money. Turn to gold.' Here he chuckled. 'Like magic, eh?'

Mohand was confused. 'Money no good?' he asked and then mentally ticked himself off for mimicking the man's speech.

'Money burn. Gold stays forever.' Chin leaned forward, his eyes shining. 'Better you save in gold.' He nodded once as if he had just delivered incalculable wisdom. 'Money take space.' He motioned with his hands by his sides as if his pockets were bulging. 'Gold tiny. Can be hidden.' At this, he stuck the fingers of his left hand into his mouth and tugged. He held out his hand and in it was a small pebble of solid gold. 'See?'

Mohand understood. He handed him the notes. 'Every time I have some money, I will bring it to you and you can work your magic.' Both men grinned. 'I have twenty years to prepare.'

Mohand grew solemn. 'I need your help.'

Chin bowed as if grateful for Mohand's trust. 'I charge you for this help. We both help each other.' He moved to the back of the counter and pulled out a book. He looked at the tattoo on Mohand's forearm. He made some scribbles in the book. And nodded at Mohand.

Mohand had no idea how much gold his notes might be worth, but he felt in his gut that this man was absolutely trustworthy. He looked around the shop.

'I need some fruit and some cigarettes.' These were for Ali. He judged that some fruit could be eaten immediately, but if he bought too much, it would only rot. Whereas cigarettes could be stored under Ali's bed and then traded for fruit when his supply ran out.

The men bartered and Chin held out the items Mohand had bought. Then Chin scribbled some more in his ledger.

'You young man,' Chin chuckled and rubbed his thighs. The trader was gone and the amiable shopkeeper was back. He made a fist and held it before his stomach. 'You got horn. You need woman. I got plenty daughter. Clean daughter.'

His meaning was clear and Mohand had to admit that, now he was getting some sleep and some better food, he did indeed have 'horn'. However, he was not quite ready to go and lie with a woman who might have lain with another twenty convicts that day.

He stood up and shook his head. 'Another day,' he said.

Chin followed him out of the shop and at the door, he bowed. Mohand bowed back.

Chin nodded. 'I have good feeling about you, young fella. You be back plenty time.'

Mohand bowed again. 'I hope so, Monsieur Chin.'

* * *

That evening, after another day of working in the gardens of St Laurent, Mohand made his way to the infirmary. His face was familiar to the turnkey at the infirmary door and, for the payment of six cigarettes, he was allowed access.

Ali had rallied from his harsh cough, only to pick up another disease from the other patients in the ward. His immune system was so low, the doctor had told Mohand, that a condition which other men might recover from was proving difficult for Ali to shift.

'The fruit helps,' the doctor had smiled, and placed a hand on Mohand's shoulder. Kindness was a rare commodity in this place and he appreciated it greatly whenever it came.

Mohand sought out the doctor again before he went to sit by Ali's bed. His name was Raymond Vignon. He was from Marseille. He had joined the army to see the world and to cure the sick. He had seen enough of the world, he told Mohand with a smile, and his ambition to cure the sick had waned. Now, if he could make them die with less pain, that would make him happy.

He found the doctor taking a break at the far end of the infirmary. He was leaning against a doorway that led out into a small courtyard. He had a cigarette in his hand and squinted through the smoke to see Mohand.

'You bring gifts, I see,' he said.

'For Ali. He needs to build up his strength.'

Mohand studied the doctor as he stood in the doorway. Rays from the dying sun gave his skin a healthy tint, which was an improvement on the exhausted grey he normally sported. He was a good man and Mohand was grateful for every effort he made on the patients' behalf. With his silence he hoped that this message might get across. He knew that he, a convict, had no place to utter such words.

The doctor said nothing, accepted the appraisal and stared back at Mohand as if he was struggling with a decision. He chewed his lip.

'You know we have a difficult job here in St Laurent. The system never gives us enough equipment. We never have enough staff. The jungle breeds nothing but wild vegetation and disease. The convicts do nothing but harm each other and steal. Even the guards...' He shook his head. 'I want to help... with such limited resources we have to make difficult decisions. Who should be given medicine and who should be...' He bit off whatever he was going to say next.

'You didn't come here to listen to man who has privileges you can only dream of while you have nothing... but a box of perishable fruit.' He offered a sad smile of apology and placed a hand on Mohand's shoulder. 'Go see your cousin.'

'That's what I wanted to ask you about, doctor. Ali. Will he recover?' Mohand's face was flushed with concern.

'Go see your cousin.' Vignon repeated.

* * *

Mohand would never quite get used to the smell in the hospital. A mixture of excrement and creosote. The men were each given a tin at the end of the bed to use as a toilet. Many men suffered from dysentery and the tins were wholly inadequate for the task this presented. In an effort to keep the place clean, the floor was sprinkled with creosote once a week.

Holding his breath, Mohand made his way down the centre of the room to Ali's bed. The ward was full. Beds lined the walls, with enough space between them to allow the nursing staff to move.

The men in these beds suffered from varying degrees of illness and from various wounds. The first man on his right cut his foot out in the jungle. Infection was swiftly followed by gangrene and the only way the doctors could save his life was to cut his leg off just below the knee.

Another man lay shivering while malaria worked in his system. Beside him, a man lay dying from the effects of ankylostomiasis. On an earlier visit, curiosity about this man's condition had led Mohand to ask the doctor what had happened.

'You men are sent out into the jungle with no clothes and no shoes. What do you expect?' Vignon snorted. 'Ankylostomiasis comes from a parasite. It enters the body by drilling a small hole through the skin. And guess what? No shoes make the feet a great entry point for these little bastards. Once inside, the parasite makes its way to the gut where it matures to a point where it can live off the blood of its host. Your skin breaks out. Horrible, disfiguring lesions. And anaemia causes an exhaustion like you would never believe. Pray to whatever god you have, young man, that these little fuckers leave you alone.'

Ali held a hand up from his bed when he saw Mohand approach. This was the nearest he could offer as a wave. Mohand leaned over the bed and gave him a hug.

'Arab. Is he coming?' Ali whispered.

'No. He's been moved to another camp.' This was the greeting the two men went through each time Mohand visited. 'I brought you some fruit and some cigarettes.'

'Can I have a smoke?' Ali asked and then coughed. Mohand looked at the shape his cousin's body made under the thin sheet. Under the threadbare covering, he was like a line of sticks placed in the shape of a human skeleton. His once healthy cousin had withered to a pile of bones.

'You must eat, Ali,' Mohand begged. 'Please. Have a banana.'

Breath rattled in Ali's lungs. His mouth opened. Nothing came out. He tried again.

'Cigarette.'

Ali's face had shrunk so much that he appeared to be nothing but a huge pair of eyes, above the bristle of a nose and a mouth slashed across his tight skin. These eyes never left Mohand's. He struggled to hold their gaze. What did he read there? He was scared to admit it and looked away.

'I brought you some gifts,' he said and piled his offerings at the side of the bed next to Ali's belongings: a battered mess tin, torn trousers and a tunic, the wooden soled shoes all convicts were given, some fruit and a packet of cigarettes. This was all his cousin's life had come down to, thought Mohand, and he brought his eyes up to Ali's.

Still he was staring at him, and Mohand faced the truth of that gaze. His cousin had nothing left in him. He was dying. Mohand chewed on a sob. He swallowed. He would not let Ali see how he was feeling.

Ali's mouth opened slowly as if he was peeling each lip back from the other.

'Cigarette,' he repeated.

Mohand reached down. Picked one out, lit it and placed it in his cousin's mouth. It stuck there, unmoving. Ali didn't have the strength to inhale. The cigarette tumbled from his mouth and came to rest on the sheet at the side of his chin. Mohand plucked it away before it burned the thin cotton.

'Oh, Ali,' Mohand said, gripping his cousin's hand. He felt the coolness of a tear slide down the side of his nose. 'How can I make you better?'

Ali moved his head. From one side to the other.

'Can't.' His lips made a small smacking sound as he parted them to speak. 'Can't.'

Just then an attendant walked past. He was one of the convicts who was at the end of a long sentence and now in a position of trust. They were chosen for their ability to care for the sick and their willingness to deal with the dead.

'That one'll be feeding the sharks in the morning,' he said to no one in particular.

Mohand was on his feet and in the man's face. 'Shut up. Shut up. Shut up. How can you say such a thing? He can hear you, you bastard.' His shoulders fell to a slump. His anger passed as quickly as it arrived. This fellow had to face death every hour of every day. He was just dealing with it the best way he knew how.

He turned back to face Ali. His eyes were open and staring at the ceiling. His mouth slack.

While he had been arguing, his cousin had died.

He leaned over and pulled down the eyelids, before falling to his knees at the side of the bed. Holding Ali's hand, he allowed grief to take over.

He had no idea how long he was folded over the bed in that position. He only knew that his knees were protesting against the wooden floor, and the sheet was soaked with his tears.

He felt a hand at his shoulder. He looked up. Two attendants were standing there, ready to take the body to the morgue. Mohand stood up. There was nothing more he could do. Ali was no longer here. This was just a pile of skin and bones. They could do what they wanted with it.

One of the attendants motioned towards the meagre pile of Ali's worldly possessions. Mohand wondered what he meant.

Then it struck him that every man in this prison sought every advantage he could. It was the only way to survive. And in the quest for survival the rules of polite society were nothing but torn scraps of paper being used to clean the convicts' collective arse. One of the reasons an attendant in the hospital might be able to bear the suffering he witnessed every day was that he might get first pick at the possessions of a dead man, before the other hospital inmates began to loot the corpse.

This man had no need to ask his permission. This was his right.

* * *

Mohand stumbled from the infirmary, tears pouring from his eyes. He fell to his knees in the courtyard and gave full vent to his emotions. His gentle cousin was dead. Ali had been totally innocent of any wrongdoing and he, Mohand could have, should have spoken up. If he had, Ali would still be alive. He'd be on a hill outside the village, on the lower slopes of the Djurdjura, a rifle by his side and his eyes roaming his herd, making sure they were safe.

Instead, he was already cooling, being sown into a sack, waiting for the tide and a frenzy of hungry sharks.

If only he had spoken up. He was every bit as guilty as Arab in contributing to Ali's death and that guilt lodged on his shoulders, in his gut and wove its way through his system like a dark plaque.

* * *

The next day, he turned up for work as usual. He hadn't slept and was weary to the bone. He joined the line of men that would be escorted from the barracks and out into the town and waited for the march to another day's work. One of the guards called him over.

'Can't see that we'll get much use out of you today, Saoudi,' he said.

Mohand simply stood at attention under his gaze.

'My advice. Go find a bar. Get mad drunk. Fuck a prostitute and tomorrow is another day.'

Mohand's head was full of fog. He couldn't understand what the guard was trying to say.

'We know that your cousin died,' he said, not unkindly. 'You have the day off, you stupid piece of shit. Go and enjoy yourself.'

He looked round about him to see what the joke was. This was certainly a more relaxed attitude from any guard he had met so far.

'We have different standards in this detail,' the guard explained. 'The men working in this group have it very easy and we know you don't want to fuck that up. The price is too high. So… where are you going to go?' asked the guard.

He made straight for Chin's shop, asked for some money then marched into town, sat himself at the table of the nastiest café and worked hard at developing a taste for the local rum.

The café was a little shack at the side of the road on the way out of St Laurent. There were two tables outside the door, under the shade of a ragged tarpaulin that had been strung from the roof.

'Some rum,' Mohand ordered with a slap of his hand on a table.

'Are you old enough to drink?' A man leaned against the window ledge that acted as his bar counter. The tone of his voice suggested that he was having a little fun.

'I'm certainly old enough to kill,' Mohand answered. 'To drink? I don't know, but let's give it a damn good try, eh?'

'You look like a man who has had some bad news.'

'Is there any other kind, monsieur?'

The man barked a laugh. 'Michel Lacroix at your service. And it has been a very long time since anyone called me "monsieur".'

'Perhaps you ought to establish a better kind of customer, Michel.'

'Perhaps I should move to Paris on the next boat, set up shop on the Champs Élysées and serve free champagne and oysters to everyone who passes by?'

Mohand felt himself hang a smile on his face for the first time that day. 'Well, before you do, set me up with some tafia.'

The rum was fiery and tasteless. He demanded some more.

Six glasses later he still felt sober. Where was the release that alcohol was supposed to offer?

'More,' he ordered.

'Much as I am happy to take your money, young man, it doesn't appear that the rum is having the desired affect.'

'What would you recommend?'

'Sleep? Time?'

Mohand jumped to his feet. Staggered to the side and slumped to the ground.

'Or then again…' said Lacroix as he picked him up and carried him through to the back of the bar.

* * *

Some hours later, Mohand was nursing a mug of hot, black coffee and a headache that made it difficult to move.

'You have yourself a good little situation here, Lacroix,' said Mohand. 'How come you have this…?' He waved a hand in the air, but stopped when he realised it made his head worse. 'Most *libérés* barely have a pot to piss in.'

'An honest service. Men know they can trust me,' he said. While he was talking he reached under the table and pulled out a machete, which he dropped with a clang on to the table. 'And they know that I won't take any shit.'

Mohand sipped some more of his coffee. It revived him a little. He kept sipping till it was finished. He slid the cup across the table to Lacroix.

'Thank you.'

'Don't take this the wrong way, kid,' Lacroix said, standing up. He picked up the machete and slapped the width of the blade against the palm of his hand. 'This is not the kind of place for a bright, young fellow like you. Get the hell out and don't come back.

SEVEN

Temptation

Her name was Marie-Louise and she was the most beautiful creature Mohand had ever seen. She had long, lustrous black hair she was always playing with. Her hand would pick out a strand as she talked, then she'd slide her thumb and forefinger down its length before going back to the top of her head, picking another strand and going through the same process all over again. Mohand could watch her doing this in the same way some men might sit on their haunches staring out to sea.

She was a tiny woman, small-waisted with breasts and hips that swelled out on a promise, and she had a smile that never quite left her brown eyes. She was also the wife of one of the camp guards.

Mohand had been on garden detail for two months when he was approached by Villiers.

'You're a good kid, Saoudi.' He nodded as if he'd just reached a decision. 'Bright. Hard-working. Come with me.'

Mohand looked over at Simone, who was bent over a shrub, pulling off flowers whose time had come and gone. Simone continued his work, but he had of course heard the whole thing.

'I'll just give this to Simone.' Mohand picked up a sack full of weeds as he rose from his knees and walked over to the older man. As he dropped the sack at Simone's side, his eyes framed a question.

Simone shaped a faint shrug and mumbled, 'Just remember to keep it in your pants.'

As they walked, Villiers explained what was happening.

'Our last houseboy died. Marie-Louise was devastated. Refused to have another. She never could have a pet, not even back in Brittany.

'Twice a week I want you to come round and do our garden, tidy round the house. Do a good job and you might earn yourself some tips, okay?'

Villiers stretched into the sky beside him and Mohand looked up at him at the mention of money.

'Self-respect is very important to me, Monsieur Villiers. Of course I will do a good job.'

Villiers reached across and patted him on the shoulder. '*Bien.* Prove to me that I made the right choice.' The guard moved his hand to the base of Mohand's throat. His grip light, but the promise of threat clear. 'My wife is very beautiful. She is also very trusting.' A dark light shone in the Frenchman's eyes. 'Look at her the wrong way and I will cut your balls off.'

* * *

The house he led him to was the last in a row of cottages. White-washed walls, red-tiled roof and a riot of roses and azaleas in the garden. A palm tree towered over the house, offering shade. Mohand struggled with the idea that such a picture-perfect home was only minutes from the hell of the *blockhaus*. Keeping such thoughts from showing, he allowed Villiers to guide him up a small path to the cottage door.

The door was flung open and a small woman came bouncing out towards them.

'Marc, you angel. You remembered.' She reached up. He reached down and they kissed.

'You must be Monsieur Saoudi,' she beamed at him. Then she took him completely by surprise by leaning forward and kissing him on each cheek. He stood as if frozen. Sweat broke out on his forehead. Villiers was bound to draw his pistol and shoot them both on the spot.

Villiers stepped forward and, placing an arm over his wife's shoulders, he walked towards the house. Once inside he looked over his shoulder.

'Don't be shy, kid. C'mon in.'

Numb, he lifted his hat from his head, held it before his stomach and followed the couple. The room instantly reminded him of the Samson house back in Algeria. It had the same arrangement of furniture; two large soft chairs, a small low table and every surface held a square of lace as a stand for a vase of flowers.

Mohand felt a pang of loss and closed his eyes against the tears that threatened. The Villiers were oblivious to his reaction. They had arranged themselves on one of the large chairs, while Marie-Louise fussed over her husband.

'Can I get you a coffee, darling?'

'Have you read the paper?'

'Do you need something to eat?'

'For chrissake, Marie-Louise, calm down. It's just a houseboy.' He showed his wife a cold grin and Mohand felt the atmosphere change. There was something at play here and he had no idea what it might be. His convict sense of danger set his skin to prickle.

Marie-Louise stood up and took a step back from her husband. She swallowed and then offered her husband a smile laced with apology and appeasement.

Villiers jumped to his feet and pulled his wife towards him. His groin tight against her. His hand on her arse.

His message clear.

Then he smiled, warmth returning to his face, and he leaned forward to kiss his wife on the forehead. It all changed so quickly that Mohand thought the switch from affection to menace and back again was all in his imagination.

'Right. I have work to do. Saoudi. You do everything my wife tells you and remember when the bell goes…'

While studying the floor, Mohand nodded to show his understanding and Villiers was gone, leaving only an echo of chill to suggest he had once occupied space in the room.

Marie-Louise studied the door for a few seconds after it shut. Closed her eyes, set her shoulders and turned to face Mohand.

'I hope you are ready to work hard?' she asked with a tight smile, and Mohand read the shame and fear in her eyes. Shame that her husband would treat her so in front of another and fear because, for the briefest of moments, there had been a very real threat in the room. Mohand swallowed his pity for the woman and suddenly felt very vulnerable. Several what-ifs ran through his mind and he considered running for the door.

'Don't look so scared.' Marie-Louise sat down on the chair, composure regained. 'From time to time my husband forgets I am not a convict. That we come from a civilised part of the world.' She set her jaw. 'Come and sit with me and tell me all about yourself.'

Mohand stayed where he was.

'I am here to work, Madame Villiers. Show me what work you want me to do and I will get it done.'

'So serious, Monsieur Saoudi.'

'I am a convicted criminal, Madame Villiers, and I have been living in one of the worst prisons in the world. And now…' He motioned around himself with an open palm. 'Please forgive me if I don't join you on the chair. I would rather just go and do some work. If you are not happy with my efforts, you could just tell your husband that I am not suitable and I can go back to working in the town's garden detail.'

Marie-Louise stood up and walked towards Mohand. Her own fears had faded and she was wearing an expression that said, *if I have a difficult time, how must it be for this poor man in front of me?* '*Mon dieu*, you are trembling. What has happened to you that you are so scared?' She shook her head and gave him a look full of knowing. 'Stupid question, *non*?'

She stretched out a hand, pointing at the rear of the house. 'Come. There is work I want you to do in the back garden.' She offered a weak smile by way of apology and Mohand felt his heart give a little. 'I am so flighty sometimes. I mean you no harm.'

Mohand found himself nodding. She may be the wife of a guard. She may be free, but Marie-Louise was every bit the prisoner that he was.

'The garden.' She turned and strode through the room. 'I have a big job for you.'

* * *

Marie-Louise inhabited Mohand's thoughts the way ivy wreathes an old house. When the turnkey shouted, 'Breakfast,' to wake him from his dreams of her, his thoughts slid to the way she tilted her head when she was listening to him. When he was walking out of the camp into town, he would think of her small slender hands and imagine how they might stroke him. When he was working in the town gardens, he could smell her perfume sweetening the breeze. As he drifted off to sleep, she was there beside him with a whispered '*Bon nuit.*'

'You're doing that thing with your eyes again, Saoudi,' Simone said, nudging him with the handle of his paintbrush.

'Go and do yourself, old man,' Mohand answered.

They were standing at the corner of the main administration building, touching up the wood panelling with thick, glossy white paint. They'd been working together now on various projects for six months and Simone was the only man in French Guiana that he trusted, apart from Arab, of whom he had heard nothing since his transfer to Kourou. However, there was one thing he was not willing to trust with Simone: his feelings for Marie-Louise.

'You Berbers are so coarse. "Go and do yourself," indeed. And what should I use? Thirteen years of doing myself. I need a change. Can I use your hand?'

'You French are so limited in your imagination. Unless, of course, it involves human suffering. In any case, my hand is thick with calluses. Perhaps one of the town's blind prostitutes might do you a favour?'

'Cheeky pup,' Simone grinned.

The two men stopped talking and gave themselves to the rhythm of the brush. Dip. Slap. Slide. There was something soothing in the repetition and it allowed Mohand's thoughts to drift.

'Again with the eyes,' Simone mumbled.

'What do you mean?'

'I am older than you, Mohand. And a good deal wiser, I might add. All I'm saying is, be careful.'

Mohand pursed his lips and blew a dismissive sound. 'Don't know what you are talking about.'

He went back to his painting and started to worry. Does the old man suspect? Were his feelings for her so obvious?

'You wouldn't be the first convict to fall in love with a guard's wife, Mohand. And between you and me, you've picked the wrong guard.' The warning in Simone's tone caused Mohand to pause.

'The word is that Villiers is insanely jealous. His previous houseboy ended up face down in the river. The wife had a broken jaw.'

'No.'

Simone simply raised his eyebrows in answer.

Mohand's first thought was to dismiss his friend's fears. Compared to his fellow inmates, he was in a hugely fortunate position and he didn't want to think even for a moment that it might be threatened. Then he considered what he had witnessed and knew about Villiers. There had been that moment when he was introduced to Marie-Louise, but since then, nothing. The guard had said that the previous houseboy died. Could he have murdered him in a fit of jealousy?

Villiers had come home early on a few occasions, checked that Mohand was working and had a quiet word with his wife before heading back to whatever part of the prison he had been working in.

'I don't doubt you, young man,' Simone said and attacked another stretch of panelling with the brush. 'The wife, however...' He whistled. 'I've seen it all before. Many times. The husband has changed since he came to the colony. When he touches her, it's too firm. Almost painful. And once, he hits her. Then there're gifts and apologies until it happens again. The houseboy is quiet... timid almost. In the deepest part of her, she realises she has power over another human being. In other parts of her, she craves the touch of someone who looks at her like she's sixteen again... once again on the brink of womanhood.

'How am I doing so far, Saoudi?' Simone asked.

'You've read too many shit novels, old man,' he answered.

They went back to the rhythm of the brush for a few moments, both lost in their own thoughts.

'I've always wondered, Saoudi, why a Berber has a name like

Saoudi. Surely that's an Arabian name, no?'

Mohand smiled and then suffered a pang of homesickness as memory assailed him.

Noticing how his young companion's movement had changed, Simone apologised. 'If it's too painful, you don't need to tell me.'

'No. Not painful,' said Mohand. 'It's a good memory. A simpler, happier time.' And his father's voice filled his ears, and he was a young boy on the back of a donkey, begging his father for another story.

Mohand relived the moment as if it happened just yesterday. He could feel the slow sway of the donkey's gait, the dry air of Algeria and the warmth of his father's hand on his shoulder as he told the family legend.

'The story as my father told me was this. My great-great-grandfather, Mohamed OuMessaoud Zenouch, was one of five sons and when he first got married he and his wife struggled to have children. Being a filthy Parisian,' Mohand said, grinning and dodging his friend's weak punch aimed at his ear, 'you will not know that for a culture such as ours, a son is an assurance for old age. Poor Mohamed's wife died. His work was doubly difficult because he had poor eyesight and was all alone. He had to do to all the chores inside and outside by himself. He had to look after his land and his animals. His other brothers had their own problems. They had many grown-up children and not enough resources to go around. So one day they hatched a plan to get rid of their brother and take over his land.'

'Seriously?' asked Simone. 'They would kill their brother for his land?'

Mohand smiled. This was exactly the same question he had put to his father. 'These are the pressures the *colons* put on my people. They twisted our minds and had us fighting ourselves, so they could keep our country's wealth for themselves. Anyway. Stop asking questions. I'm telling you a story.' This time it was Mohand's turn to aim a wayward punch at Simone. 'The plan the brothers came up with was to sabotage his work. Make it look like an accident. It occurred to them that he would be high in the trees gathering leaves for his animals and wouldn't it be a terrible accident if he fell from a height and broke his neck?

'The animals loved the leaf from a very tall tree that grew well on his land. We call it *thasslent*. I don't know what the French word for this is. They judged the branch that he would be using next to get leaves for his animals and they sawed their way partly through this so that his weight would be enough for break the branch. And he would then fall to his death.

'Then they camouflaged the cut with mud, thinking that he wouldn't notice. However, that morning, while climbing up this tree, his hands landed on the mud, which was still wet. He cleaned it up, thinking it might make his climb on to the branch too slippy, and discovered the cut. He quickly realised what was going on and climbed down to safety.

'So not only was he alone, but on top of that his family wanted to kill him. For who else would do such a thing? He decided that life at home would be intolerable. He couldn't trust anyone. Why wait to see if they would make another attempt on his life, so a few days later, without a word to anyone, he packed his belongings on to the back of his horse and headed east.

'Some months later he found himself in Saudi Arabia, where he got some work and made a decent life for himself, but always he wondered about home. Then one day, a man came to him, saying that he was from Maillot, too. They talked well into the night, telling each other their stories, and this stranger tried to convince him to return. Family is everything to the Berber, he said. You must try and repair things with your people. But of course, he didn't want to go home. The other man argued and argued and eventually grew so frustrated that he threatened to kill Mohamed with his bare hands if he didn't go home. Hearing the argument, advice and the threats from this stranger, he decided the time was right. He should return home, but he would do so with a different name. Make it a completely fresh start. He dropped "Zenouch" and adopted "Saoudi" in honour of the country that gave him refuge and a new hope.'

***

The next day, Mohand was working at the Villiers' house, which gave him the chance to pretend for a few short hours that he was a human being again. As he walked, he smiled, an image bright in his mind of Marie-Louise curled up in her chair in the garden under the shade of the giant greenheart tree. A table set before her with a jug of chilled lemonade and two glasses.

They had found themselves in a rhythm where she would dole out just enough work to leave him a few minutes of rest before he returned to the prison. She would offer him a glass of something cold and they would chat, always separated by a safe distance.

Mohand came to treasure these moments. The novelty of being treated like a man was enough to take the edge off his fear. He knew that Villiers would be horrified if he were ever to witness these short moments of intimacy, but he re-assured himself that they were completely innocent of anything that could be charged against them, and surely that would be enough?

Marie-Louise was only a few years older than he and, he had come to realise, terribly lonely. Villiers should be happy that he was giving his wife an ear.

Mohand quickened his step. Today he would race through the chores so that he and Marie-Louise might have some time chatting under the shade of the tree, drinking ice-cold lemonade. Then his step slowed as a thought occurred to him. Was it his imagination, or did Marc Villiers look at him differently that morning at roll call?

An hour later, he was clipping branches from a large tree in her back garden. She was sitting on a low chair, wearing a light blue summer dress. He should have gone for a longer ladder, but he thought he could stretch just that little bit more. As he stretched, he turned his head to the side to look at how she had pulled her dress up just above her knee. The ladder tottered on one foot. He lost his balance and fell to the ground. As he fell, a branch scored a line across his ribs.

She heard him fall and came running to his aid. She pulled him into the kitchen and ordered him to remove his tunic so she could clean and dress his wound.

Once he was topless, she dipped a sponge in some water and gently swabbed at his side. His face was inches from hers. He could see the soft down on her chin, bleached to gold by the tropical sun. He followed the line of her face round to the swell of her lower lip.

She placed a hand on his hip so she could clean the end of his wound. This was the first time he had been touched by another human being since leaving Algeria, where the touch was not with the intention to harm. The skin on her hand was soft and warm. And electric.

With alarm, he felt himself respond. He closed his eyes and bit his lip, hoping the pain from this would cause his excitement to subside.

She made a little noise of recognition. 'Oh.'

He felt his face burn. Closed his eyes tight against his embarrassment and willed the insistence of his arousal to fade. So lost was he that it took a moment to realise that Marie-Louise had stopped moving. He opened his eyes to see that she was looking over his shoulder with alarm bright in her face and a scream frozen in her throat. Someone else was in the room.

'You little bastard,' Marc Villiers screamed. 'You little …' He was holding a gun in his hand. He was pointing it at Mohand. Looking at how his trousers jutted out with his arousal. His erection there, like an accusation.

Marie-Louise shrank against the sink. 'No, Marc, no.'

Villiers turned the gun to his wife. His face was white. His mouth a thin line of determination. 'Slut,' he shouted. 'Whore.'

'It was me,' shouted Mohand. He couldn't bear the thought of harm coming to Marie-Louise. 'I fell and cut myself...'

Villiers stepped towards him and crashed the barrel of the gun across his forehead. Mohand slumped to his knees. Blood obscured his vision. Fear jackhammered in his chest.

'Don't lie for her convict. I saw everything.' His eyes were red, bulging. Tears sliding down his cheek. 'She was loving it. She was begging for your little Algerian cock.'

'No. I … it was me.' Mohand fought against the pain in his head to speak out. Villiers lashed out again. This time with his foot.

'I love you, Marie-Louise,' said Villiers, his voice thick with self-loathing. 'What kind of fool am I?'

'Marc, there is nothing. This is nothing.' Marie-Louise was weeping too now.

'I don't want to hear your apologies, slut.' The gun was still pointing at Marie-Louise. Mohand needed to get it away from her. On to him.

'Shoot me, Villiers. Take me out into the garden and shoot me. No questions will be asked. You can say you caught me stealing. You can…'

'Shut up, convict.' Again he brought the gun down on Mohand's head.

'I should drag you down to the docks, Marie-Louise. Make you spread your legs for every criminal that comes off the next boat.' His voice quietened. He slumped onto a kitchen chair, looked down at the shirtless Mohand and across at his wife. She hadn't moved, hadn't dared. Terrified to provoke her husband into action.

'Marc. It's as Mohand says. Nothing happened. I love you. I'm sorry. I'm begging you to put the gun…'

'You called him Mohand.' Villier's voice was thick with a terrible truth of his own devising. They were clearly friends. More than friends.

He stood. Towered in front of them, his mind following the parade of his own fears and insecurities. His wife in love with a prisoner. The things he had seen and done since he arrived in the *bagne*. The things he had been made to do, until they became second nature. All of this passed across his face in seconds. Realisation hit Mohand. If you were the wrong personality, the *bagne* could be as hard on the guards as it was on the prisoners. It brutalised everyone and Villiers had just splashed hard, down at the bottom of his well of self-loathing.

His eyes clouded, he brought the gun up.

A shot rang out.

It was followed quickly by another.

EIGHT

Jungle Fever

Mohand was forced into consciousness by a vicious slap. Sensations assaulted him. Pain. He was in a chair, hands tied at his back and ankles secured to the leg of the chair. He was naked. Pain throbbed with every beat of his pulse on every part of his body.

This hurt was nothing. A beautiful woman he had begun to see as a friend was dead. He would never see his family again. He would rather they just killed him.

A man was standing over him, his hand drawn back as if prepare to strike another blow.

'Enough, Fournier,' a voice said. 'We will get nothing more from this prisoner.'

With a look of disappointment on his face, Fournier stepped back. The other man stepped into Mohand's vision. It was the director of the *bagne*.

'Will we, Prisoner 51240?'

Mohand shook his head and then nodded. Pain made him confused as to which response was required. The movement of his head caused some blood to drip from his nose onto his thigh.

'For the record, let me repeat what has gone on today. Marc Villiers shot his wife and then turned his gun on himself. You were working in the garden when you heard the shots. You immediately called for help, but both of the Villiers were dead before the medics arrived.'

The director stood up, dabbed the sweat from his forehead with a square of white cotton and then brushed his long fringe back from his eyes with his fingers. He nodded at Fournier. 'You may go.'

Fournier stayed where he was.

'Monsieur Fournier, the prisoner is bound and naked. He has also been beaten to exhaustion, do you seriously believe I am in any danger?'

Fournier grunted to show his reluctance and left the room.

The director pulled up a chair and sat facing Mohand.

'You are a very lucky man, 51240. My interest is in protecting the mindset of my guards. The collective ego would prefer a finding that describes a man whose mind has turned because of some jungle illness… to one where a man is driven to madness because his wife was fucking a prisoner.'

'But I didn't. We didn't...'

'Don't offend my intelligence, young man. I know what goes on in this camp. My problem –and your good fortune – is one of proof. If I could demonstrate that this lovely couple were killed by a prisoner then that would suit everyone and you would be lying prostrate before the guillotine. However, the proof is unquestionably clear that Villiers shot his wife and then turned the gun on himself.'

He leaned back on his chair and crossed his legs. He pursed his lips in thought.

'Madame Villiers was evidently a lonely woman. This camp has many lonely women and I am worried that others might fall prey to your… questionable charms. I can't legally kill you, 51240, but I can send you to a living death. It is for good reason that the *bagne* is called 'the dry guillotine'. You will be transferred to a logging camp in the morning, 51240.' He stood up and brushed some lint from his trousers. 'May God have mercy on your soul.'

* * *

The guards came for him in the morning and took him to join a dozen other men who were being sent out to the same camp. Mohand didn't bother to look at any of these men to see if he recognised anyone. What did it matter? He would surely be dead within a month.

In single file the men were escorted through the town of St Laurent. Mohand could barely lift one leg beyond the other he was so tired, but from somewhere he managed to find the strength to keep walking. Only when he passed a group of convicts working in one of the town gardens did he look up from his feet. There, in a corner, kneeling before some shrubs was his friend Simone. The older man looked along the line of prisoners being escorted. His eyes slid from Mohand and then back. From where he was standing, Mohand could judge the old man's reaction. His face was battered and swollen. He must look a sight.

Knowing that verbal acknowledgement would only get him on report, Simone lifted a hand in greeting. Mohand stretched his face almost into a smile and walked on, feeling certain that he would never see the old man again.

At the edge of town they joined a well-marked trail. Here at least, under a canopy of trees, there was some shelter from the sun. Birds squawked a continuous warning. Monkeys howled. Insects buzzed around them, looking for a landing spot on their skin.

The heat made it difficult to breathe. Sweat ran from every pore. And still they trudged through the forest.

From time to time, the guards gave the men leave to rest. Each time, Mohand walked to a spot away from the others. He wanted to be alone. He knew the other convicts would be aware of who he was, and he was determined not to give them any more reason to gossip about Marie-Louise.

A butterfly moved as if swimming through the moist air. It was a deep blue. Mohand looked around himself for the first time. Plants grew over plants, shedding blooms of vibrant hues. Birds hopped among the branches. He had never seen so many colours before. How could such a vivid place provide such torment?

They were soon back on their feet and on the march.

For most of the day they walked until, nearing exhaustion, they came across a clearing. Here, five small huts were built in a circle. The earth between them was bare and as hard-baked as the surface of a clay pot.

A small man, hunched over and shrunk by his endeavours, was

evidently the bookkeeper for the camp. He noted down the details of the new arrivals and told the men to make sure they had all their belongings as he was now going to take them to their barracks.

What belongings? All Mohand had was a hat, trousers, tunic, shoes and a battered tin mug.

He was shown into one of the huts and was able to pick a bunk for himself near the door. There were a dozen other men in the room when he walked in. No one stirred from whatever activity they were engaged in. Why would they want to? There was an excellent chance that some of them would die over the coming weeks, so why waste time making friends, it was less painful that way. He shrugged and sat down on the bare board that was to be his bed. From there he could look around him.

An oil lamp burned in the centre, spilling weak light over the men arranged on the two rows of bunks. Some were on their own, bent over butterfly nets, picking at sores on their feet or attempting to mend their clothing. Others were in groups playing with what looked to be a home-made sets of dominoes.

A bell clanged. Someone announced that everyone was present and the light was turned off.

Welcoming the darkness, Mohand lay back on his board, exhausted. Before he had done a moment's work, he was tired to the bone. He couldn't ever remember feeling this tired. How on earth would he feel tomorrow? And the day after?

Despite his tiredness, he could not sleep. Every time he closed his eyes, his brain filled with the image of Marie-Louise. Her head at that strange angle. Her beautiful black hair layered over the white cotton of the pillow. And the blood that bloomed like a giant flower from her chest.

How many more people would he see die? What had he done in his life that Allah could punish him so? Marie-Louise was so beautiful. How could someone like her die in such a way? He thought over all of the times he had visited her and all of the conversations he had had with her husband. Was there ever a time that he had given a hint, made any suggestion that would cause such jealousy? Had he unwittingly betrayed his lover?

While the other men snored, coughed and snuffled in their sleep, he continued to search for answers. None came.

He closed his eyes. Two minutes later, or so it felt, a loud voice ordered the men outside. The day had begun.

They were each given a half-pint of unsweetened coffee and a chunk of bread. As they ate, he noticed that some men were checking the condition of their feet and ankles.

One man saw him looking.

'Vampire bats,' the man explained.

'Excuse me?' Mohand was sure these creatures lived only in books.

'Its bite is painless, but they like to drink convict blood. Where they bite, the wound doesn't close. If you get an infection here, your leg swells, you die.'

After they had eaten, the men were taken out into the forest. They came across an area where trees had been felled. A series of knee-high stumps stood up from the forest floor.

Mohand was given an axe and told what was expected of him.

He had a quota to meet. He had to clear one cubic metre of trees per day. The trees that he cut down were to be stacked in the middle of the clearing, which was several hundred yards from the tree line.

At this instruction, Mohand looked at the trees and assessed his ability to chop them down. From there, he looked to where the trees had been stacked. He was to carry a tree all the way over there?

If you don't meet your quota, he was told, then your food ration is reduced and you spend the night in a punishment cell.

He looked around himself at the other men in his group. Many of them wore no shirt. Some were completely naked, apart from a wide-brimmed grass hat. No one wore any shoes.

Mohand felt the weight of the axe and then, gripping it in both hands, he swung it at the wood. He pulled it free and swung again. And again. After a few minutes of this, his hands were blistering and his skin was awash with sweat. He turned to watch the other men at work. The successful ones seemed to have a rhythm and an economy of movement that made the task easier. He attempted to match one man's movements and was pleasantly surprised to see bigger chips of wood flying and the mark on the trunk of the tree growing. Sweat poured freely from him now and insects clouded before his skin. He heard wood splinter and crack as the weight of the tree pulled it to the ground. Despite himself he felt a small surge of triumph. As directed, he pulled this log to the pile and then moved back to resume his chopping.

By the end of the day, Mohand's hands were raw and he wondered how he could ever hold an axe in his fingers again. But he knew he had no choice; no quota meant no food and a night in a punishment cell. That night, by the light of the oil lamp, he tore some strips from the legs of his trousers to act as a kind of bandage. He was very careful to wash them in the stream first as he was well aware of what might happen should infection set in.

As he worked on his trousers, he listened to the other men as they gossiped about events in the colony at large.

One man had heard of an escaped convict who had been returned by the Dutch in Surinam. This fellow had been a *libéré* who, tired of the thought of doublage and the lack of ability to make a decent living in the colony, had taken matters into his own hands. He had saved whatever meagre earnings he could and bought a small boat from one of the Chinese traders. He got stuck on the sand bars where the Maroni river emptied into the sea. By the time he was spotted by the authorities he was half-starved and fully insane from dehydration.

'They call that part of the Maroni the Frenchman's graveyard,' one man looked up from his dominoes to say.

'But he was Moroccan,' the storyteller said.

'Fucking idiot,' someone else butted in. 'What does it matter what his race was? The idiot got stuck.'

'Who are you calling a fucking idiot?'

'The fucking idiot who got stuck.'

The man who asked the question paused to work out if this answer was enough to mollify him. Every man there held his breath. Violence had broken out for less.

'I hear you should aim for Trinidad if you want to escape and stay free,' someone else added. Apparently escaping from these logging camps was not the issue. The guards could be fairly relaxed in their attitudes, knowing that the jungle and the sea did a far better job than they could. The jungle held any number of terrors – snakes, spiders, crocodiles, big cats – and even the sea itself was mysterious to most of these men. But still the convicts persisted in trying to escape from French Guiana.

'Brazil. Go for Brazil,' another said. 'A huge country. Easy to get lost.'

'Surinam used to be the best place until that bastard Coutancot ruined it,' an older man joined in. Every one stopped what they were doing to listen. This was the only entertainment they had and any story about escape and the dangers thereof would earn their immediate interest.

'It was back in '24. Before then, many men escaped to Surinam to work in the mines ran by the Americans. Coutancot had escaped years before and married a local girl. On one of his days off he went mad on a drinking spree. When he ran out of money, he demanded the shopkeeper give it to him for free. Of course, the fellow refused him, so Coutancot lifted a bottle from the shelf and broke it over the shopkeeper's head. Then, to disguise what he had done, he poured kerosene everywhere and set it alight. The shopkeeper and his wife and daughter were burned alive.'

Every man there gasped at the story. For most of them, their concern was not that an innocent family had been destroyed, but that the actions of this man had closed off Surinam as an escape destination.

That night as he drifted off to sleep, Mohand thought of escaping. Where would he go? How would he do it? Many of the stories he heard involved poorly dreamt-up schemes and examples of colossal stupidity, in his view. Why attempt to escape when you were poorly equipped, half-starved and you knew nothing about how to survive in the jungle?

One of the speaker's voices repeated itself in his mind. He was sure he recognised it, but the man himself appeared to be a stranger.

'Fucking idiot,' the voice echoed. Who was he? He shook his head. None of the men he had been working with had been known to him. They were all so skeletal, it was doubtful that even their mothers would recognise any one of them.

Just before sleep could claim him, a face added itself to the voice.

Zaydane.

NINE

Blue Morpho Butterflies

The jungle was filled with noise. Macaws and toucans advertised their presence, howler monkeys bellowed into the trees. It all made a welcome change to the curse and grunt of the convict.

Mohand had now been working in the jungle for nearly eighteen months and one of the first things he had learned was to finish his tree-clearing quota by mid-afternoon, as that would give him some time to try and make some money. The only way open to do that in this part of the jungle was to hunt for butterflies. The convicts caught them and sold them to the guards. The guards would then sell them on to collectors.

Eighteen months, he thought. Eighteen months in this festering heat. The guards complimented him. Most men didn't last a year before disease, malnutrition or the wildlife killed them. To last as long as he had must mean he was blessed, they said.

Not blessed, he replied. Cursed.

He tramped along, making his own path through the thick undergrowth, hacking at the vines and branches before him with every step. Fatigue was an ever-present and he hoped that the tiredness he was feeling would be compensated for by making a few sous with his captured butterflies. This money could then be used to buy extra food to add to the poor provisions he was given from the authorities.

A bird flew over head: a burst of red, blue, green and yellow. Mohand wondered what might have startled it. The forest was bulging with life, but thankfully the larger predators, like jaguars and snakes, tended to stay away from humans.

Before him, a wall of vegetation continued to make his progress difficult; lianas, vines and the many colours of fluted flowers behaved as if nature was bursting to show off its fecundity. The air was filled with the perfume of fruit and rotting vegetation. A sensory example of the life cycle, thought Mohand.

A flash of blue and his target was on a branch before him. The morpho.

One of the longer-serving prisoners had taught Mohand all he needed to know about this beautiful insect. Henri Laforge was an industrialist from Montpelier, sent to French Guiana for fraud and totally unprepared for the fact that the real love of his life owned a pair of iridescent blue wings. He passed much of his knowledge of the morpho butterfly on to Mohand before a combination of starvation, dehydration, blood poisoning and malaria had taken its inevitable toll.

'The juices of fermenting fruit can be used to trap them,' he told Mohand, standing in that curious arms-crossed posture of his. 'Of course, it is rare that any fruit gets to that stage in these parts, given the fact we are all insanely hungry.'

Mohand readied his net and prepared to pounce. He held his breath, stepped forward. And the creature promptly disappeared. He was ready for this. Laforge had warned him that the butterfly had a clever defence. The underside of its wing was coloured a dull brown. Perfect camouflage in the jungle. Any animal hunting for it would be on the lookout for the brightness of its wings. To hide, the butterfly simply closed its wings... and disappeared.

Trying to remember where he saw it last, Mohand launched his net.

He came up with nothing.

Something moved in the underbrush at his feet. He stepped back. Might be nothing. Might be a viper. There were times that a quick death was a welcome thought, but he'd much prefer it not to be from the venom of a snake. And there was so much of his flesh on display that any snake would have plenty of skin to target.

He looked down past the bumps of his ribcage, to the hollow of his stomach and the frayed rope that was holding up what was left of his trousers. Some of the other men had written to their families for money so that they could buy clothes. He had resisted until now, but with every passing day this was becoming an imperative. Others were resigned to working, living and sleeping in the jungle totally naked, but he was completely averse to that idea. Common decency and the last scrap of humanity he owned demanded that he wear something. He was not a savage.

You must think of me as being dead, he had told his father the last time they spoke. There had been letters from his family since he arrived, almost three years ago, but he had read none of them. Save that first one, which arrived just after Ali's death. Simply holding the paper that contained his father's words and thoughts was enough to fray any last thread of sanity he found himself clinging to, so each letter he received from then on had been set alight immediately. If he stored them somewhere, their presence would nag at him like an open sore that he would pick at and pick at, never moving on, never allowing him the mental space to cope.

That one letter was in French and written by Caid Mezaine. His father asked what he should do with Saada, his wife. Should they allow her to go back to her family or should she marry one of his brothers and remain a Saoudi?

Mohand's reply had been succinct.

'*Do what you want with my wife,*' he wrote. '*I am dead.*'

* * *

Mohand searched the canopy of trees above him and noted how weak the light was down here on the ground, so he moved through the tangle of roots and vines, towards the sound of water. If there was a creek, perhaps there might be a clearing allowing the sun's rays to reach the ground and provide somewhere for the butterflies to heat their wings. Again something sounded near him, but he ignored it. Most animals were spooked by humans. Only mosquitoes and ants would come and feast.

Minutes later, he was kneeling at the side of a creek. His reflection startled him. His face had shrunk, his skin was lined. He looked like a man in his middle years.

He plunged his hands into the water to disperse the disturbing image. Cupping them, he pulled fresh water up to his mouth. It was cool and delicious and revived his energies a little. He also sluiced water over his head and neck, hoping this would cool him.

Something caught his attention on the far bank. He lifted his head in time to see the long snout, sharp teeth and long body of a black caiman. These were the largest predators in the region and thought to be the cause of many a prisoner's disappearance. The animal stared at him as if measuring him as a mouthful. With both eyes on the beast, Mohand bent forward to scoop up some more. He judged that the animal would only come at him if he moved into the water.

As Mohand looked down again at the surface of the water, he caught sight of a shadow behind him reflected there. It was moving towards him at speed. By reflex, he threw himself to the side, rolled over and sprang to his feet.

A man tumbled into the water and was spluttering and splashing his way out.

Mohand recognised him as the man who had been sharing his hut for the last eighteen months. The same man who had threatened him on voyage across the Atlantic.

'So, Zaydane… you thought you would sneak up on me and try to finish the job you started on *Le Martinière*?'

Zaydane clambered up the bank of the creek, his face bright with fury. His chest heaved as he faced Mohand. He was completely naked, his dirty skin streaked with blood where branches cut him and insects bit him. His legs were so thin that his knees were the thickest part of them, and his hips jutted out like shelving. It was a wonder he was able to stand, thought Mohand, while realising that he must have presented a similar picture.

'I knew it was you from the moment you entered the camp,' Zaydane spat. 'But you are never on your own, always in the thick of the other men. This is the first time…'

'The first time you could sneak up on me. Only a coward attacks like that, Zaydane.'

The two men faced each other, both holding an axe, both realising that this time only one of them would walk away.

'What happened between us was a long time ago, Zaydane. I have no quarrel with you,' Mohand said, pretending to relax and allowing his axe to drop to the ground at his side. As he spoke, he looked over Zaydane's shoulder to see the long tail of the caiman slip under the water.

Zaydane stretched his lips in a snarl, displaying the stumps of his blackened teeth. 'You're the man who broke my nose and bit off half my ear. And you say we have no quarrel?' He jumped forward. Mohand moved back and the axe flashed past his face.

Mohand moved on to his toes and, avoiding the bulging root of a tree, he moved further out of range. 'We are not each other's enemy, Zaydane. If one of us kills the other, we are simply doing the Frenchman's job for him.'

'A job I would relish.' Zaydane jumped forward again, but landed badly on the same root Mohand had just avoided. He cursed as he stumbled back onto his feet.

'Why have you waited so long?' Mohand asked. 'We've been working here for years. I thought...' He moved slowly, circling back to where his axe was resting in the long grass.

'The right opportunity.' Zaydane moved into his next attack and Mohand raised his axe to block it. The blades sparked off each other. Their movements were slow and calculated. Neither of them had the speed, strength or energy they would have had the last time they fought. And after the initial surge of energy, both men were tiring. Mohand prayed that his energy resources would outlast those of his opponent.

Zaydane leaned down, picked up some loam and leaves, and threw them at Mohand's face. Under this cover, he slashed his weapon down. Mohand defended himself just in time. His axe met that of Zaydane's but the force of this strike broke the blade from its housing in the shaft. He stepped out of range and used his forearm to wipe the dirt from his face. He looked around himself; they had both turned full circle and once again he had his back to the creek. Except this time he was defenceless. He looked at the useless pieces of his axe at his feet and thought about picking up the blade. But without the handle it was unworkable. He had nothing left to fight with but his wits.

Zaydane noticed the weapon on the ground and smiled. His face was partly in shade. Sunlight touched his eyebrows and the long blade of his nose. His eyes and mouth looked like black holes. Mohand shuddered at the vision in front of him.

'We could be out here all night,' Mohand jeered, thinking he needed to make Zaydane even angrier. 'Just tell me where you aim to swing your axe the next time and I'll make sure I'm standing under it.'

'Bastard,' was Zaydane's concise answer before he lunged again.

Mohand moved just enough and Zaydane missed.

'Where's Hassan, your little Moroccan *mome*? Abandoned you for some man with half a brain and a bigger cock?' shouted Mohand. He took another step back towards the riverbank.

'Leave Hassan out of this, you bastard,' Zaydane swore. Both men's breathing was ragged now. Adrenalin and a severe lack of nourishment was not a good mix. Mohand's legs were trembling and barely able to hold him upright. He knew he did not have many chances left. Another step back. He allowed his fatigue to show and then exaggerated it, bending forward and placing a hand on each thigh.

Zaydane stepped closer, judged his moment and lunged. Mohand stepped forward inside the other man's reach and caught the handle of the axe on its way down to his head. He pushed up with every ounce of strength he possessed. The other man's breath was hot on his face and smelled of sickness. They would be locked in this embrace until someone weakened. Zaydane tried to aim a kick at Mohand's groin. He twisted his torso, lifted his knee and took the blow on his thigh.

As Zaydane fought to regain his footing, Mohand fell on to his back. As he fell, he pulled Zaydane on top of him, but just before the other man could land on top of him, he kicked up. The momentum of his movement was enough to send Zaydane sailing over his head. He rolled nearer the river's edge but managed to stop himself before he fell in the water. With a grin, he clambered to his feet.

'Clever move, young man. Very clever. But I still have the upper hand.' He hefted the axe in his right hand and laughed.

Then disappeared from view.

Fierce splashing and a scream filled the air. A sound that would haunt Mohand's dreams for life. Despite himself, he edged forward and was rewarded with a sight he hoped never to see again. The huge caiman had its teeth round Zaydane's waist and was working on its death roll. Round and round the huge beast rolled, just under the surface of the water. Zaydane's legs and arms were flung about like they belonged to a lifeless puppet.

* * *

Mohand woke the next morning on the plank in his barracks, frayed with guilt and haunted by a dream. In this dream he was kissing Saada. She smiled with an expression of love and forgiveness and then her skin lightened, her hair lengthened, and her face changed into the features of Marie-Louise. Her eyes were sparkling with tears, yet there was an acceptance there. A feeling of deserving whatever outcome might happen. Was yet to happen. Marie-Louise ran out of her bedroom door into a dark forest. The soles of her feet were as pale as silkworms against the deep green of the trees. She was pulled into the woods by Ali and Samson. Mohand chased them, lungs bursting, legs with the strength of paper, moving forward as if he was pulling a great weight. He reached a creek. He almost expected Zaydane to rear from its depths, but the pool was still. The surface as clear as a child's conscience. He leaned forward and in his reflection examined a face harassed with its own thoughts. Guilt stretched his skin, loosened his teeth until they dropped one by one into the water like blood-stained pebbles.

TEN

Word from Home

At the first opportunity, Mohand sent a letter through the director at St Laurent requesting that money be sent from his family. The letter was polite but distant, with no mention of life for Mohand in French Guiana. Approval was given and his family sent him two hundred francs, which he used to buy underwear and shoes that were better suited for the jungle. Along with the money came a letter that he couldn't bring himself to read.

My beloved son,

I send you news from home, by the hand of Caid Mezaine, whom you respect and love. I send you this news suspecting you will never read it. The last thing you said to me was that I should consider you as dead, and I can understand that this is the only way you can bear the pain of being apart from everyone you love. I also understand you will forgive a father who wants to reach out to his son one more time.

I miss you more than I can say, my son. I know this is not news you will want to hear, but nonetheless it is the truth. In my old age your name is seldom far from my lips. I am constantly being teased by the family – 'I am not Kaci,' someone will say, 'I am Dahmane,' or 'I am Amar.' Or worse, 'I am Saada.'

Saada has grown into a lovely young woman and a kind step-daughter. Her own father wanted her back. He had many suitors for her hand in marriage, but I preferred to keep her in the family. I wrote you a letter just after the ship sailed, asking for your permission to marry Saada to one of your brothers. The old ways are there for a reason and we should honour them. Your brothers did not find this so easy. It took strong words from Caid Mezaine to make them see that this was the only way. Dahmane would have surprised you. We persuaded him that this was the honourable thing to do and decided he should be the one to marry Saada, in order that we can keep your wife in the family as a reminder of you. This was not an easy decision for Dahmane. He loved his first wife.

As you can imagine there were complications after the marriage; after all, women can be difficult creatures, no? Messaouda left and went back to her brothers, leaving her daughters with Dahmane. This one was upset and kept riding his horse between the two homes. Eventually I bribed her family with a horse and its foal and Messaouda returned.

The house became more settled for a while, with always an undercurrent of tension. This did not last long, but not for happy reasons, for Messaouda became ill and died. Saada was a great comfort to Dahmane and he realised what a gift she was to the family.

Kaci, I grow tired now and Caid Mezaine has other duties he must attend to. I pray to Allah the money is of some help to you and I pray every day that you stay strong and true.

Your loving father.

* * *

Mohand never could quite get used to death and the many ways it came. Diseases too many to mention. Violence, random and as sudden as a caiman rearing from the water. A single bite from an insect or a bat became a swelling that turned flesh rotten.

In a part of the world that was plush with life, death skipped just behind, holding its tail, playing the great guessing game.

He forced himself to ignore the dead and the dying and to

concentrate on filling his lungs one breath at a time. To help in this quest to feel he was still a man, not an unappreciated beast of burden, he accepted the money he received from Algeria. The word 'home' hung in his mind as unpronounceable as the meaningless syllables that littered his ears when Monsieur Chin spoke.

* * *

The man in the next bunk was dying. His eyes were large in his thin face, and were dry with hopelessness. He stared straight ahead, barely registering Mohand's presence, but he knew if he moved, the fellow would panic at the thought of dying on his own.

'What is your name, friend?' Mohand asked. It was suddenly important that he should give witness to this man's passing.

'I have no name,' the man's voice grated with effort. 'I'll be just... another set of bones that will settle... into the earth in this godforsaken jungle.'

'You should sleep, friend,' Mohand sought to reassure him. 'The morning might bring...'

'Health?' The man managed a laugh that turned into a chest-rattling cough on the third note. 'Gold, frankincense and myrrh?' His head slipped to the side and for a moment Mohand thought he was dead, but he could see a slight movement in his chest. The man slept for around half an hour and just as Mohand was about to move back to his own bunk, he roused again as if given a charge of energy.

'Would you hear my confession, boy?' the man asked. Mohand had spent enough time around Christians to understand what he meant and he nodded while taking a hold of the man's hand.

'I had a choice once.' His eyes were focused somewhere in his past. 'Choice. It all comes down to choice, doesn't it? Have you ever made the wrong choice?' He didn't wait for Mohand to answer but continued speaking. 'I had to have her. She consumed me night and day. Except, she was married. I could have chosen to walk away. Instead I started a fight. Hoped this would show the woman what a hopeless case she'd married. The husband died and I ended up here.' He fell silent for so long that Mohand thought he had fallen asleep again. 'Do the right thing,' he said, gripping Mohand's hand with a force that took him by surprise. 'You always have a choice.'

'I had a choice too, you know,' Mohand said. As he spoke, he felt his face move into the shape of an ironic smile. 'A choice that brought me here. The right choice, and knowing that helps me deal ...'

'Shut the fuck up,' someone shouted from the other side of the barracks. 'Some of us need to get our beauty sleep.'

'There isn't enough hours in the month for you, Dede,' another man joined in and soon comments were flying back and forward.

Eventually the din died down and the men relaxed into sleep. Except for Mohand, who continued his watch until the man with no name gave up his last halting breath.

Being the first to notice, Mohand could loot the body of its belongings before anyone else stirred. He had a decent pair of trousers now that some money had arrived, but another pair would never go amiss. This fellow's trousers were knee-length and still bore the red stripe. Mohand turned to the other side and feigned sleep. Someone else could have them. This was not the kind of man he was. Stealing from the dead was something he could never quite bring himself to do.

The money, when it arrived, was desperately, fervently welcome. He had no idea how this would have affected the family as two hundred francs was a serious amount of cash. The letter that accompanied the money was a trial. He held it in his hands like it would contaminate. He guessed that it would start with the words, 'My beloved son'. It would be in French so that the authorities would allow it through. It would be written by Caid Mezaine and it would talk about events at home, the family. Saada would be mentioned with reluctance as he would not want to cause his son pain. Mohand did not wish to know what had happened to his wife.

He couldn't bring himself to read it.

He found a match and set the letter alight, watching as the flames ate hungrily at the paper.

Smoke stinging his eyes and charcoal stains on his fingertips were the temporary and last remaining elements of his father's words.

ELEVEN

The Morgue

It began with a high fever, alternating with chills. Mohand's muscles ached and whatever pathetic amount of food he was given was soon voided. Still he forced himself to move and to pick up his axe. Three years he had been working in the logging camps and each day he congratulated himself for surviving the last one.

He felt moisture at his eyes and his nose. He lifted a hand to wipe it away and noticed a long streak of blood on the back of his wrist. The march that morning through the jungle from the barracks to the work site was the longest walk Mohand ever experienced. He did not have enough power left to carry the weight of his body. Nevertheless, there was nothing he could do; he had to make the effort. The guards didn't bother with any of the men, as long as they were standing. A man needed to lose consciousness before receiving any help. By lunchtime he crumbled to the ground and could not move.

He was aware of a guard leaning over him, shouting, 'Get up you bastard.'

He was aware that the man was kicking him, but he could feel nothing. Then all of his senses closed down.

Realising that this convict was not shirking his duties after all, the guard in charge assigned two other convicts to carry him back to the infirmary.

* * *

Mohand rallied at one point and realised a doctor was leaning over him. The doctor prised open one of his eyelids while speaking to someone else.

'You see,' the doctor said, 'the white of the eye is no longer white. It is yellow. The disease attacks the liver and this jaundice is the result. Yellow fever.'

Mohand was aware of people around him, trying to force water down his throat. It was as if he was still of the world, but no longer a part of it. He was no longer in pain. Hunger was a remote memory. His body was shutting down, death was coming to claim him and his mind retreated to a dim corner where it could wait and see what the outcome might be.

He lost all sense of time passing. He lost the ability to control any part of his body. All he could do was wait and think. About his life. About his choices. He felt some relief that death would bring some form of liberation.

One moment when awareness did reach him was when nurses and doctors were talking around his bed.

'This guy's had it,' a doctor said. 'He's dead. Arrange for a transfer to the morgue.'

No, I am not dead, Mohand thought. I am still here. I am still here. No part of his body would obey his impulse to communicate his sudden desire to live.

I am here was a scream without sound that echoed, unheard, in the eternity of his mind.

* * *

Mohand was moved to a room full of dead bodies and dumped on the floor like a sack of potatoes. This was the space where the dead were stored until they could be loaded on to a boat and used as breakfast for the sharks.

* * *

The next morning, he was aware of movement around him. Two convicts had arrived and were loading the bodies on to a barrow. When they got to Mohand, one held his arms while the other grabbed his legs.

Reality stumbled towards him through the fog of his disease. He tried to speak. Not a sound issued from him. His jaw remained firmly closed.

He was picked up and sacking thrown around him.

I'm alive, he wanted to scream. *I'm alive.*

Again nothing happened.

He willed his hands to move. His eyes to open. He begged his lips to part. Everything was glued shut.

The men began to sew the rough material closed.

I'm alive.

One of the men paused in his sewing motions.

'What was that?' he asked.

His friend grunted and carried on sewing.

Help. I'm alive. Mohand willed some part of his body to move with a long silent scream of desperation.

Just as the men reached his head one of the men started.

'He moved. My god, he moved.'

'Shut up, you fool, and pick him up. We don't have all day,' his friend shouted at him and picked up the sacking.

'He's alive, you moron.'

'Don't be...'

'I'm telling you he's alive. I just saw his chest move.'

'That's because you wobble as you walk, moron.'

'Have you got a mirror?'

'Yes. It's in my pocket along with my shaving brush and my open razor.' There was a slapping sound and a note of outrage. 'Wait and I'll check my pockets. Or my vanity case. Of course I don't have a fucking mirror.'

'A piece of glass, then?'

'Oh for...' Mohand was dropped to the floor none too gently. He heard feet slapping the floor as they moved into the distance. Then they returned.

'Bugger me,' he heard someone say a few moments later. 'You're right. This one is still alive.'

As if this discovery gave the convicts fresh life, Mohand was rushed back through to the ward and placed gently in a clean bed. While they did so, the two convicts relayed to everyone within hearing distance just what had happened. They had witnessed a miracle in a room full of death and it almost more than they could bear.

A hand that was rough with calluses stroked his forehead and a voice choking with emotion sounded above him in a whisper.

'It's a miracle. A fucking miracle.'

TWELVE

The Eagle

A familiar face was hanging over his bed for a few moments before Mohand recognised who it was.

'Dr Vignon, is it time for my weekly check?' He sat up and knuckled the sleep from his eyes.

'Good morning, Mohand,' the doctor smiled. He put a hand on the sheet as if to pull it back. 'May I?'

'Of course.'

Dr Vignon listened to Mohand's chest, pushed his hands into his abdomen and peered into Mohand's eyes and, as he did so, made small satisfied sounds.

'It's amazing how some people can recover from yellow fever,' Vignon smiled and raised an eyebrow, 'when they are being fed proper food and not being worked to death in the jungle.'

'Is my doctor preaching sedition?' asked Mohand with a face full of mock horror.

'Just as well no one is listening, eh?' Vignon asked and sat on the bed. His face grew serious. 'You know I can't keep you here forever?' he said quietly.

Mohand nodded and acid flared in his gut. Another doctor would have prescribed him as ready for work again months ago, but Vignon had allowed him the time to recover fully. His weight was back up to the way it was when he arrived at the colony, thanks to being able to get some rest and real food. There had even been some fruit and vegetables in his meals. His strength was not quite there yet, but some more walking and perhaps some swimming would see him improve.

'I have asked that you be kept nearby for another month or so and given only light duties around the infirmary. Thereafter...' he let the rest of his sentence hang in the air.

'*Inshallah,*' Mohand said with more confidence than he really felt.

'I hope Allah has better plans for you now.' Vignon recognised Mohand's saying as the Muslim acceptance of Allah's will.

Allah's will is obscured to me, thought Mohand. Prayer brings no answers. Being near death brought me no answers.

'You had a cousin, didn't you?' The doctor's face was screwed up in the effort of trying to force a memory.

'Two,' answered Mohand. 'One died here. The other was sent to Kourou.'

'Kourou,' echoed Vignon. 'Hellish place.'

Mohand wondered what sort of hell it must be if it merited a special mention in this colony.

* * *

That weekend, Mohand was allowed to go into the town. Again, the guards recognised that he was not about to jeopardise what small freedoms he had and he was left very much to his own devices. At first, while he walked from the *bagne* and into town, his muscles were warmed through with contentment. He had faced the worst that the system could throw at him and he was still alive. And right there, right then, being alive felt good. He had strength, a full belly and the realisation that he had won a victory in the Frenchman's attempt to punish him.

Two more steps and this feeling all but abandoned him. He was still alive when so many others had died. Was this something to celebrate? Did they die so that he could live? Did Allah have a plan for him that he should be allowed to continue to breathe? He stopped walking and stared up into the empty dome of the sky. It was a blue so bright it dazzled and the sun was a howl that shone on into forever.

A void. No answers.

He kept walking, the occasional shriek of a bird and the slap of his shoe on the ground were the only noises he could hear. He had no plan, no activity that called him that day and, as he looked around himself, he realised he was heading in the direction of the bar ran by the *libéré* called Michel Lacroix. Like all the other convicts who managed to scrape together a few sous, along with some free time, there was nothing else to do except escape into the local rum.

'Tafia, my good man,' he said to Lacroix, who was leaning over the window ledge that passed for a bar.

Lacroix immediately lifted up a bottle and a small wooden tumbler. He poured a little out and handed it to Mohand. He made no attempt at conversation or to acknowledge that they had spoken briefly before. This suited Mohand perfectly, so he picked up his glass and moved across to a table under the canopy and sat down with his thoughts and his drink.

A few drinks later and he realised that he had gone over almost every conversation he had ever had with anyone he had ever loved and he was not coming out very well.

He had let everyone down. Again his mind turned to those who were dead and the question, why had he been spared?

The tafia didn't burn quite so much on the way down now and he ordered some more. As he leaned across the bar to order he spotted a calendar.

Lacroix examined him from under his thick, black eyebrows. 'Did I not tell you never to come back?'

Mohand ignored the question. 'You have a wonderful sense of the ironic, my friend. A calendar?'

'Some people like to count the days.' He gestured at the calendar. 'Others prefer to forget.' He shook the bottle of rum.

Mohand looked at the date and made a quick calculation.

'If my son had survived,' he thought aloud, 'he would be eight years old now.' He picked up his glass and downed the shot in one. 'Here's to forgetting.'

He had been here for four years. In this slice of hell, he had survived four years. And there was thirty-six to go. He shook his head and slumped forward onto the table. Hopelessness weighed down on his shoulders so hard that it forced his forehead on to the rough wood of the table. He could smell rum and timber and other more unsavoury notes coming from the wood, but he couldn't lift his head up. Just a few minutes ago he was grateful to be alive and here he was wishing he were dead.

'It could be worse,' Lacroix chuckled, standing over Mohand with a bottle in his hand.

'Yeah,' Mohand lifted his head up and offered a weak grin. 'I could be French.'

'I like you, kid,' the man said with a smile. 'But don't be going around saying that too much. Might not go down well with certain individuals.' As he said this he reached across with his left hand to scratch his right shoulder. His sleeve rode up exposing some skin and a tattoo in blue ink.

'We have a Berber custom,' Mohand said. 'To mark your body to remind you of an important event in your life. It's called *thimeshrats*. It can be a scar. It can be a tattoo.'

'We have a French Guiana custom. When you get bored out of your tits, get a tattoo.'

Mohand said nothing, he simply looked at the older man.

'So how does it work?' Lacroix asked, sitting down beside him.

'It's something that's there as a permanent reminder of what you've gone through. It reminds you that no matter the suffering you experienced, the mistakes you made … the choices you made … you survived and were stronger because of it.' He looked away from Lacroix as tears stung his eyes. Having reached some kind of control, he turned back to face the big man.

'You people talk about "forgive and forget". We know the first is possible. Forget? No. How can you learn?' He paused as if collecting his thoughts. As if wondering how much to say. 'Things happened. People betrayed me because of greed. A greed that they thought of as being a need. And because of that I ended up in this …' He swallowed. 'So *thimeshrats* for me means the past will not affect my future. I will learn, never speak of it again and move on.'

Lacroix said nothing for a moment, merely looking deep into Mohand's eyes.

'Spirit. Whatever spirit is, kid, you're full of it.' He poured some more rum into the glass. 'So what will you get done?'

'I want it on my chest …' Mohand sipped and thought. 'Something big and powerful. Regal.'

***

Fifteen minutes later, Mohand was in a shop where the owner could perform the service he was looking for.

A small man stepped towards him from his seat with his hand outstretched.

'Call me Anouk,' he announced, taking a firm grip of Mohand's hand. 'And what can I do for a presentable young man like you?' He was dressed in pale linen trousers that had obviously seen better days, but were spotless and pressed. His face was sharp, clean-shaven and his eyes scanned Mohand in judgement. He nodded once as if he was happy with what he saw.

'*Thimeshrats*,' said Mohand, wondering why he had said that. To his surprise the small man nodded again.

'I understand. You mark the event. You move on.' The little fellow peered into Mohand's face and at first he was discomfited by the attention. He was not used to such close scrutiny. Most people looked without really seeing, while this man was fully taking his measure.

Suddenly he gave a small bark.

'Strength. Authority.' He pursed his lips. 'And something that can rise above its troubles.'

Mohand couldn't help but smile. Despite himself, he was pleased at passing this little man's assessment.

'I was thinking of an eagle,' he said quietly.

'Exactly,' Anouk clapped his hands. 'Right across your chest.'

Mohand felt a surge of excitement. 'Exactly.'

Anouk bustled over to a table and placed a small pair of spectacles on his nose. Then he put on an apron and placed some paper and a pencil on the tabletop. Without another word he began to draw and several minutes later he held a drawing up for Mohand's inspection.

'You can have any colour as long as it's blue,' Anouk grinned.

'Fantastic.'

Several uncomfortable hours later and it was done.

Getting to his feet Mohand, walked across to a full-length mirror that sat in a corner. A thrill ran through him when he saw what the little maestro had achieved.

The head of the eagle was just under his neck, its sharp beak lined along his collarbone. Its powerful wings were folded back as if all it would take was a little thermal to give them flight. The body was lean and muscular, and the talons were sharp enough to tear the skin from just above Mohand's belly button.

It was perfect.

PART THREE

'WE LIVE AND HOPE'

ONE

Wind of Change

Just five minutes under the sun and Mohand was covered in a gloss of sweat. Standing with a group of around a dozen other convicts, he was wondering if he would ever get used to this humidity and heat.

Dr Vignon was true to his word and he was sent to work at an office that dealt with work that was required in the town of St Laurent. As he walked to where he had been directed, Mohand sent a silent prayer of thanks to Allah for the intervention of the good doctor. Not all of the French were bastards, he thought ruefully.

Outside of the office a group of around six men waited for instructions. They were all thin and weak as if they too had just recovered from some terrible illness. No one spoke or even acknowledged any of the others. As they waited for a guard to tell them what they were about to do, they were each lost in their own thoughts, possibly sending similar prayers to their god, thought Mohand. Each and every one of them would be grateful beyond measure that they were not being sent straight back out to the green and fertile hell they had just survived.

A pair of men shuffled over to stand beside Mohand, who looked up to see who had joined him.

'Are you not going to say hello to an old friend?'

'Simone.' Mohand's face creased into a wide smile. He stepped forward and hugged his friend. As he held him he could feel the other man's bones.

'What happened to you?' Mohand asked, looking his old friend up and down. Never a heavy man, he was clearly a good deal lighter than when Mohand last saw him.

Simone didn't answer immediately. He then held his arm to the side, indicating the man who was standing beside him.

'This is Hassan,' Simone said, looking at the ground for a moment as if making a decision. 'He is my *friend*.' His emphasis on the word friend gave it a special meaning that was not lost on Mohand.

He looked at the younger man at Simone's side and recognised him immediately. This was the man that Zaydane had preyed on after he had turned him down.

To a Berber, homosexuality was distasteful, but his time in the *bagne* was teaching Mohand that life was not quite so simple. There were very few women about and, if you were so inclined, the only real comfort available to you that did not come in a bottle or with the tag of prostitute, was from a fellow prisoner.

It was not a step that Mohand would ever willingly take, but he could see that Simone was content with his position and besides, who was he to judge?

Hassan was looking at Mohand with undisguised hostility. As if he would like nothing more than to tear out his heart with his bare hands. Mohand opened his mouth to speak; to challenge the young man's obvious dislike. After all, what had he ever done to harm him?

A guard arrived before he could say anything. Alongside the guard, a convict pushed a wheelbarrow containing several small leather sacs, with a length of pipe protruding from each of them.

'Each of these leather bags is filled with an insecticide. Your job is to spray this chemical on all plants in and around the camp.' He stopped for a moment and looked around the men, making sure he had everyone's attention. 'Do not touch this chemical with your bare hands; you need to have gloves on all the time.'

Mohand's immediate feeling was one of surprise. The authorities had done their very best to try and kill him and the men around him. Were they really now so solicitous of their health?

All of the men realised that a reaction was required so they all nodded their heads to show understanding. Then the guard continued. 'This chemical is to treat all plants against pests and diseases. Keep your skin away from the spray and you have an easy job ahead of you. Any questions?'

He looked around to see if anyone had anything to say. No one spoke. The guard then picked up one of the leather sacs.

'Let me show you how you use it,' he said while placing the sac under his right arm and holding the thin pipe out towards a small bush. He then lifted a smaller length of pipe, which Mohand hadn't noticed was attached, and blew into it. Then he pressed on the sac with the inside of his elbow and liquid spurted out from the sprayer.

While watching the demonstration Mohand immediately thought of the musical instruments used during parties back home in Algeria. He couldn't help himself. He clapped his hands and laughed.

'This is wonderful. I've never worked as a bagpipe player before.' He then said the same words in Arabic and Berber for the benefit of them all.

Everyone laughed.

When the guard heard him speak in perfect, unaccented French, he turned to face Mohand.

'How come you speak such good French?' He was obviously expecting a group of North African convicts to have only a limited grasp of the language.

'Of course I speak French,' Mohand answered with confidence.

'Do you mind if I test you?'

'Please, be my guest.'

The guard began with some basic questions about the colony, the vegetation and the tools they might use.

While wondering to himself how these questions constituted a test, Mohand answered easily.

The guard studied Mohand as he spoke.

'I think we could make better use of you than spraying plants.' He chewed on his bottom lip. 'Tomorrow, we will go along to the main offices and test you some more.' He then turned to the rest of the men. 'Right, convicts. You know what to do. Get on with it.'

As the men began their work, they all smiled at the picture they must have made, with instruments under their arm and a nozzle aimed at the vegetation. Simone and Hassan were working near Mohand so they managed to chat while they leisurely walked alongside the plants.

'That guard seems to have taken a shine to you, Saoudi,' said Simone. His smile showed that he was pleased for his friend.

'What happened to you … after I was sent away?' Mohand asked.

'They knew that you and I were friends,' Simone shrugged. 'So they took me for questioning.' Mohand recalled what his own 'questioning' consisted of and felt a pang of regret that this gentle little man should be treated in such a way because of his friendship with him.

'I'm sorry, Simone.'

'It's done, Mohand,' Simone answered. 'And forgotten. They were desperate to get to any truth other than the actual truth. They couldn't let it be known what actually happened. How would that be viewed back in France? Better that a convict rapes the wife and shoots the guard.' He offered Mohand a wicked smile. 'Besides, I knew nothing and couldn't give them what they wanted.' He paused and gave a small shiver as if the memory of a jungle illness was re-infecting him. 'So they sent me out to one of the camps… and that's where I met Hassan.' He looked across at the younger man, tenderness softening his features. 'He saved my life.'

'No…'

'You did, Hassan. I would not be standing here if you hadn't fed me through those long weeks of illness. Without you, I would have died in a ditch…' He broke off, his voice thick with emotion.

Mohand looked at Hassan with fresh eyes. There was more to him that he'd first thought. Although, he wasn't quite as thin as any of the other men, and this fact made Mohand wonder how Hassan himself had survived on half-portions.

'I hate to think of the sacrifices you made to get me food,' Simone found his voice again. 'Those guards…' he shuddered.

'These plants are done,' Hassan said and gestured further along the plant border with his 'bagpipe' nozzle. 'Let's move along there.'

Clearly he wasn't comfortable with the turn of the conversation and wanted to change the topic. Mohand was well aware of the currency of the jungle camps. When you had no money and no assets, there was only a limited way that you could earn food or money. Only a couple of the camps had access to butterflies to sell, which left your fists or other parts of your body in which to find favour with the other convicts or the guards.

Shaking his head, Mohand wondered again at the depths this place made men fall into. He looked up just as Hassan was reading his reaction. The other man's eyes narrowed with irritation.

'Listen,' said Mohand and held out a hand, 'your courage, I admire...' He paused, feeling that he wasn't explaining himself very well. 'Thank you. Simone is one of the few friends I have in this place. Without you, by all accounts he would be dead... so again, thank you.'

* * *

The next morning after breakfast, the guard who had tested Mohand took him to one side after giving the other convicts their instructions for the day.

'Come with me,' he said and ushered Mohand over to some admin offices. They entered a small room with six desks along the walls, clearly positioned in such a way that the men working there might catch a breeze from the open window.

The desks each had a chair and they were all occupied by three convicts and three guards.

'This one can speak fluent French as well as Arabic and Berber,' the guard said to the man at the first desk. 'I thought he could be of more use to the prison here, rather than spraying plants with poison.'

The man he spoke to stood up. He was tall, with a long face and a slight paunch that hung over his belt like an afterthought. In contrast, his limbs were stick-thin under his uniform.

This man unhooked a pair of spectacles from his ears and studied Mohand.

'You look rather young to be here,' he said.

'So everyone tells me.'

'Where did you learn to speak French?'

'I studied at school and gained *le certificat d'études*.'

The man pursed his lips. 'Did you work anywhere before you were sent here?'

'Yes, I was an assistant to the main accountant in our town in Algeria for a couple of years.'

'Ah... then you must be good with numbers, too?' A smile.

'Yes, I love working with numbers.'

'You speak excellent French.' He scratched at his jaw. 'You say you are good with numbers... young... fit. We could use you in our main depot where we stock all the prisons' merchandise.'

As he spoke, Mohand fought hard to contain his excitement. No more jungle. No more starvation portions. No more being worked into an early grave. He felt his legs tremble at the importance of what was happening here. He held his hands behind his back to hide them. He was sure they were shaking and he didn't want anyone to notice.

'I am here to serve my sentence.' He cleared his throat when he heard his voice tremble. 'I will do whatever the prison authorities want me to do, sir.'

'Excellent. In that case, from today you are assigned to work in the depot as an assistant.' He turned to the guard. 'Well done, Patrick. I'll prepare the way today. Take this fellow back to his work and then in the morning bring him over to the depot and get him started.'

Outside, the guard shook his hand and smiled. 'Well done, young man. You've just bought yourself a ticket to an easy sentence.'

For the first time, Mohand really looked at the guard who had worked this wonderful favour for him. So far he had been caught up in his world and hadn't bothered to properly acknowledge him. He was an older man, in his forties. He wore a thick moustache touched with grey and had a mellow cast to his eyes.

Mohand felt emotion build in his chest and clog up his throat. 'Thank you for... doing this. What... why?' He struggled to articulate what was going through his mind.

'I see all kinds of men in here, Saoudi,' the guard answered. 'Some of them undoubtedly deserve to be here. Some even deserved to be shot before they were led on to the boat, but some...' He put a hand on Mohand's shoulder. 'Some I can see straightaway have been sent here by mistake. You deserve to be in prison as much as I do.' He smiled. 'C'mon, let's get back to the bagpipes.'

* * *

The next morning, despite his lack of sleep, Mohand got up feeling great to be alive. He had hope in his life for the first time since this nightmare began. He could barely eat his breakfast of a baguette and coffee and waited impatiently for the guard to guide him to his new workstation.

He waited two minutes past the designated time. Five minutes. Ten minutes. He began to worry. Where was this guard? Maybe everything had changed. Maybe another guard had brought across another man who was better qualified than he was. Maybe the authorities didn't want any more convicts working in the offices. Maybe they wanted to send them all back out to the jungles to die.

He almost collapsed with relief when he saw the guard walking slowly towards him. A smile was hooked under his large moustache.

'Are you ready for your big day?'

Mohand nodded eagerly. 'I keep expecting someone to laugh and tell me this has all been a cruel joke.'

At the depot, Mohand was introduced to his new workstation. With a quiet 'thank you' to the guard called Patrick, he took his position in his new office. At the end of a working day that simply flew past, the three other convicts that worked there introduced themselves. For most of the day they had concentrated on their work while occasionally throwing glances his way. Now they had no option but to say something directly to Mohand.

A tall Arab called Jamil was the first to step forward. He nodded and offered his hand. His handshake was fleeting as if the touch of skin on skin was more than he could bear. The next man Mohand instantly recognised as being a Berber. From this man he expected at least a smile, but he simply went through the same actions as Jamil, mumbled that his name was Ahmed and stepped out of the way for the other man to introduce himself.

'Cesar,' he said with undisguised contempt on his face. 'Don't think you can come in here, little boy, and undo all the hard work we've done over the months and months we've been here.' He had blonde hair, an overly large nose and a face that was as lined as his prison uniform.

'Don't worry, Cesar,' Mohand said, offering a smile of friendship that he hoped included all three men. 'I have no intentions of putting anything at risk.' He could understand their uncertainty. Convicts in the prison guarded every advantage they managed to muster with their lives. Men in the *blockhaus* would quite literally kill for a position like this. Mohand was keen to allay their fears that he would tread on their toes. 'All I want is to stay out of the jungle and work hard.'

'That's exactly what we're worried about, cretin,' Jamil spat.

'Yes,' Ahmed decided he should add in his comment. 'We do enough to keep the guards happy. No more. Do you understand?'

Mohand understood perfectly.

'There's plenty of work? Yes? So what have you got to worry about?' With a smile he walked away from the men and returned to his barracks.

* * *

Very quickly, Mohand realised the importance of his office to the colony. From this depot the accounts were kept for all the prisons in the colony as well as the military bases. He and his fellow workers supplied all the furnishing, the equipment, the material, the laundry and sundry other requirements for prisons, military bases, railway stations, naval construction, field services and building construction for the whole of the French Guiana territory.

To the evident displeasure of his colleagues, Mohand picked up the work quickly and excelled. His quick mind could see all of the various elements of the organisation that was required, and he carried out his duties to a standard that delighted the officers and posed questions of the men who had been working there until now. Mohand repeated that he had no desire to put anyone's nose out of joint, but he had a standard of work he expected from himself, and pride in his ability to do a good job dictated that he should meet his own standards, not fall to those of his colleagues.

After a couple of weeks, he approached his boss with a request that took the older man by surprise.

'You want to work longer hours?' As ever when he was talking to the men under him, Xavier Deschamps unhooked his spectacles from his ears before speaking, giving the impression of great sobriety and contemplation. 'I don't think I have ever had a man ask me that.'

'I would rather carry on working here, sir, than go back to the barracks with all those foul, smelly men.' Mohand shrugged. It made perfect sense to him.

Outside the office, he was immediately set upon by Jamil, Ahmed and Cesar.

'What the fuck are you playing at, Saoudi?' demanded Cesar.

'Yes, why are you sucking up to the *colon*?' asked Ahmed, playing on the Berber connection.

He turned away from them and strode across a patch of baked earth towards his barracks.

'Talk to us, Saoudi,' Jamil ordered as the three men kept pace with him.

'Yes, talk to us,' Cesar pushed him.

This took Mohand by surprise and he stumbled. Righting himself, he turned on the Frenchman, no longer caring if anyone heard him.

'Don't push me, you lazy bastard.' He stepped in to Cesar's face. 'I work hard to forget this place. If my mind is on the number of uniforms that need to be sent to Cayenne then it's nowhere near the fact that I will never see my family again. If you don't get that then you are even more stupid than you look.'

The three men stared at him, a new respect shadowing their expressions. Mohand realised this and groaned inwardly. He should have known that despite the fact they were working in more humane conditions, the only thing that the other men understood was violence or the threat of violence. If that was what it took to get these guys off his case then that was what he would give them.

He allowed his anger to surface. 'And if you ever lay another finger on me, Cesar, I will break it like a twig.'

'Everything okay, gentlemen?'

The four men turned to face Deschamps, who was peering at them from behind his glasses.

'Everything is fine now, Monsieur Deschamps,' answered Mohand.

'See that it is, Saoudi. I will not countenance any fighting or bad feeling in my offices.' He moved his glare to take in the other three men. 'Is that understood?'

They all nodded. Each painfully aware of what was at risk.

* * *

Mohand dived into his work. Any spare moment he had, he would be found at his desk pouring over ledgers and accounts. Lunch hours, he found, were an unnecessary distraction and if he worked on until 9pm, he found that sleep came more easily and the days passed without his mind being pulled to his family and from there to feelings of hopelessness.

As a measure of his gratitude, Deschamps gave Mohand five centimes per month, which meant he was never short of cigarettes. Among his new tasks, he was given the responsibility for all ships that arrived at the quayside. These ships would hold cargo sent over from France to ensure the smooth running of the colony. The ship captains required a quick turnaround as they had several ports to call in on during their voyage. The less time they spent at the quay, the more profit they would make. Mohand saw an opportunity here and, as he had access to the ship timetables, he made sure he was one of the first people to welcome the crew. Before he walked over to the quay he also made sure he had a number of convicts to call on in order to unload the cargo. Each captain was more than happy to reward Mohand for his organisational abilities and he in turn passed on a share of this to the convicts who helped him.

All of this meant that Mohand was comparatively well compensated and he was given time off at weekends, which he spent mainly in bars with his friends, or swimming down at the convict's side of the beach. Simone and Hassan were among them and they were often found mumbling over a jug of rum into the early hours. During one such drinking spree, Simone had a word of warning for Mohand.

'Don't be too flash with your money, Mohand,' he whispered after Mohand had bought another jug of rum. He only ever called him Mohand when he was worried. When he finished speaking, he looked around the small café as if checking for potential assailants. As always, Hassan was at his side.

To Mohand's relief, after a few weeks of his company, Hassan had relaxed. He doubted they would ever be strong friends, but they had a common connection in Simone and this was enough to soften any acrimony Hassan might have felt for him.

The Moroccan smiled and finished off Simone's thought. 'There have been a few unfortunate events recently. There was that guy, that *libéré*, who was murdered.'

Mohand smiled at Hassan, thought about the *libéré* who had been attacked. 'What was that guy's name?'

Hassan shrugged. 'Whatever it was, he didn't have a sous to it once those bastards were finished with him.'

Just a few days before, news had reached them that a *libéré* had been murdered in a small farm just outside the town and every sous he had scraped together had been stolen, together with his crops and even his tools. This wasn't the first; apparently there had been a spate of such murders throughout the colony. Although life was relatively easy for Mohand, most of the convicts and indeed the *libérés* lived a hand-to-mouth existence. A situation that led to many desperate men taking what they needed without too much concern about the consequences.

Men like Mohand, who had managed to make life a little bit easier for themselves, were seen to be an easy target. Fingering the roll of notes in his pocket, Mohand was suddenly struck by the truth of this.

'Anyone tries to steal from me', he held up a fist, 'and the bastards will get more of a fight than they bargained for.'

'I'm terrified, Saoudi. You are safe from me,' said Simone with more than a hint of sarcasm. 'But keep in mind what the new regulations are.'

Mohand nodded. A few weeks before, in an effort to stem the increasing number of deaths in the camp, the authorities had placed a five-franc limit on the amount of cash a convict could carry on his person. To be in possession of more would lead to a report, at best, and possible confiscation.

He rubbed his eyes, not realising until now how tired he was. He should make his way to the Chinaman in the morning and put more into his account. He should also make his way back to his bunk for a good night's sleep.

'I'm dead on my feet. I'm going back to the barracks.' He placed a hand on Simone's shoulder and restrained him as his friend made to leave with him. 'No. You stay here with Hassan...'

'But...'

'I insist, Simone.' Mohand smiled at both men, aware that his smile faded as it was aimed at Hassan. There was just something about the man. However, he was fond of Simone and wanted to keep his friend happy. Everyone knew that the two men were lovers, but Mohand's presence gave them an air of legitimacy that prevented many of the unsavoury types from giving vent to their hatred of homosexuals. 'You two don't get much chance to talk when I'm around. Stay. Chat. Drink some more rum and I'll see you later.'

Hassan inclined his head and offered Mohand a small smile of appreciation, while Simone chased him from the bar with a barrage of insults that somehow managed to question his gender, his race and his genus.

Mohand began the short walk back to the barracks. The sky was studded with stars, the air warm and heavy with the perfume of the jungle: fertile loam, flowers and decay. Birds called warning. Night creatures under the cover of leaf and darkness waited to eat or be eaten.

He heard the noise of someone stumbling behind him. The warning that Simone delivered in the café shot into his mind. He turned round. A tall, thin figure was standing beside a large bush. Whoever he was, he all but merged into the darkness. There was a glint of teeth and a voice spoke.

'Give me your money or I'll stick you.' The voice was deep.

'If you want it, come and get it,' Mohand said, matching the voice's tone. Adrenalin sparked along his arms and down his legs. His heart beat like a drill in his chest. He was on his toes, ready to defend himself, or run if that was necessary. Whatever happened, this man was not getting his money easily.

The figure stepped out from the bush and into the moonlight. He was dressed in rags. Those patches of skin that were visible, were streaked with dirt.

'I said, give me your money, boy.' He took another step forward. His eyes were black spots under the overhang of his heavy brows.

'And I said come and get it,' Mohand answered, and wondered where this courage was coming from. This man was a good six inches taller than him. Something shone in the moonlight. And Mohand realised with a shock that the man was carrying a blade.

'Okay. I will.' The man moved forward again, but this time it was more of a shuffle.

'What kind of thief are you?' Mohand demanded. It occurred to him that this man was either too drunk or too tired to carry out his threats. 'I could be in another country by now.' His shock was fading but the adrenalin was still surging through his muscles. Tired this man may be, but he was still desperate. Mohand was ready for anything.

'A hungry one.'

'Come and get it.' Mohand took one step towards the man and then another, trying to judge his state of mind. Then, without conscious thought, he rushed him. The would-be assailant stepped back in alarm and fell over on to his back.

Mohand aimed a kick at the man's hand and with relief saw the knife skitter across the earth. He then moved closer and was about to aim another kick at the man's gut when he heard him make a noise. He expected a note of pain from the kick, but this... it sounded like the man was crying.

With astonishment he realised his would-be attacker was in tears.

Mohand's anger evaporated in a flash. He bent forward and reached out a hand. The man saw it and flinched.

'Here. Let me help you up onto your feet,' Mohand said while keeping his hand outstretched.

'You don't want to...'

'I want to help you up onto your feet ...'

'What, so you can stick me?'

'I don't want to stick you, idiot. I want to help you.'

Even in the weak light, Mohand could see that the man's expression was thick with confusion. He stood up and brushed the dirt from the seat of his trousers, which from where Mohand was standing, was a complete waste of time, but he thought it suggested some level of pride.

'What's your name?' Mohand asked.

'Armand,' he answered. 'And I'm terribly sorry I tried to rob you. I'm just so...'

'Desperate?'

Armand nodded.

'Stupid?'

He nodded again.

Mohand was suddenly overcome with empathy for this poor shadow of a man in front of him. From Armand's diction, he could tell he had once been a man of education. That he was reduced to a sorry attempt at mugging told Mohand almost everything he needed to know.

'Why don't we go to Lacroix's and I'll buy you a snack.'

Armand looked over at the lights shining into the dark from the bar and shook his head. 'Lacroix won't let me in.'

'He will if I show him the colour of my money.'

'No, young man. I've troubled you enough.' Armand looked in the other direction, deep into the woods. 'I'll... I'll just head...'

'What's your story, Armand?'

'I'm a buffoon. A clown that's lost his circus. A turtle that needs to crawl back into his shell.'

'When were you given your freedom?'

Armand looked into Mohand's eyes for the first time.

'The life of a *libéré* is harsh one,' Mohand said.

Armand hugged himself, rubbing his right shoulder with his left hand and read the empathy in Mohand's eyes. 'You're a strange one,' he said. 'I try to rob you and you stand there as if we just met at a cocktail party.'

'A party where the required clothing is a set of rags.'

The two men looked down at themselves and laughed.

'I was a teacher in Alsace.' Armand's mouth stretched into the line of a weak smile. 'My father was to gambling what Joan of Arc was to firewood. He owed the local hotshot a few francs. He set his men onto him. I was visiting and rushed to my father's help. One of the men sent to attack my father was unfortunate enough to fall onto the bread knife I was holding. Made a hell of a mess of the kitchen tiles. I was charged with his murder.'

'Tough story, my friend.'

'I've been free for two weeks.' Armand laughed at the word. 'Free. I was better off in prison. I was released into the wider community at eight in the morning. Given a pair of trousers and a hat. Warned to stay away from bread knives and told to report to the police twice a year.' He paused for dramatic effect. 'And officially notified that I was to live in French Guiana for the rest of my life and told I was forbidden to live in Cayenne for the next twenty.'

Mohand could say nothing. He couldn't fail to notice the irony. Here was a man who was technically free, yet he was at this point much worse off than he.

'There're no jobs?' Mohand asked, knowing the answer.

'And my family back in Alsace have sent me any cash father failed to lose on the cards...'

Mohand thought about the men he sometimes used down at the quayside to help him unload the boats. He explained to Armand how he might be able to help him.

Armand shook his head as if failing to understand how events had arrived at this point. 'I should try and rob someone every night.' He grinned and waved his knife grandly through the air.

'Yes, because you are so good at it,' Mohand laughed. He then felt in his pocket for a note, fished one out and pressed it into Armand's hand. 'An advance. Meet me at the dock tomorrow at ten.'

Armand simply stared at the piece of paper in his hand. When he lifted his head up, Mohand could see the tears that silvered his cheeks in the moonlight.

'I don't know...'

'Say nothing, Armand. Time to climb out of the gutter, my friend.' Mohand gripped Armand's shoulder for a moment. Released him and then turned and walked back to the barracks.

On his own now and surprised at the turn of events, he could still feel the alcohol in his system and as usual when his body was slowed with alcohol, his mind strayed to home. His Saada and her smile as bright as any of the stars overhead. His faithful brothers. His father, Hadj Yahia. Was he still alive? And Saada, if he had avoided jail, how many children would they now have? Would he be as good a father to his sons as Hadj Yahia was to him? The names his sons would have. Names of courage. Of hope.

As always his mind turned last to Hana Addidi. She was the one who would be suffering most from his absence. What mother could bear to know about the suffering of her child? He could write to her, he decided. Explain that, despite everything, he was coping. Then he remembered his decision to remain distant from his family. He couldn't allow himself such thoughts. He spat on the soil. Crazy, Mohand. That is the way to insanity.

TWO

Quartier Libre

Back in the office, Mohand continued to work hard in order to keep memories of home at bay. There were times when he missed his family so sharply that it was all he could do to lift himself from his bed. But he forced himself to go to work and so occupy his mind that the memories were swamped by lists, actions and the workings of the colony. The irony was that all of this hard work did not go unnoticed by the authorities and he became an even more valued member of their staff and to ensure his continued output, he was moved to the Free Quarter, where the guards were much more relaxed and where he was given a small cell to himself.

He managed to furnish this room with a bed, a real mattress and a small table where he could store his most prized possessions: his books. From the moment he had learned to read in the French schools, he always had loved the power of the written word and whenever he could he would lose himself in a story. He had managed to acquire half a dozen books and these he read one after the other, over and over again. His favourite was *The Man In The Iron Mask*. He could relate to the unfairness of it all and this afforded him the chance to address his own feelings towards his own incarceration. He may be living in the Free Quarter, but he was an imprisoned convict with a number tattooed on his wrist and nothing other than unconditional liberty would make that change.

He was now able to take more control of what was happening down at the docks and with this came more money. These were not huge sums, but over the months they would build up, until he could deposit it with Monsieur Chin as a tally of gold.

With some of this extra money he did what he could to help his fellow convicts. Late one evening after another sixteen-hour day, he realised that the patch of ground that he walked across from his office to his cell was untended. It was a plot of ground that was clearly ignored by the gardeners and was nothing but weeds. Perhaps it could be put to better use? He considered his own recovery from yellow fever and how fresh fruit and vegetables had helped. He also remembered that these simple foods were rare in this part of the colony. Why was that? This was rich fertile soil. Vegetation was in riot wherever he looked. Surely it would be a simple enough matter to grow some nourishing food.

That night he barely slept and at first light, he dressed, had his usual simple breakfast of bread spread thickly with butter and a mug of black coffee and then walked over to the office.

As usual, his boss was the first man there. Unable to contain the enthusiasm that had kept him awake all night, Mohand opened his mouth and a flurry of words filled the air.

Deschamps looked up from his papers with a smile on his face.

'What do you want to do with this land?'

'I could grow fruit and vegetables. The land is just going to waste anyway.' So caught up was he with the importance of this new project that Mohand thumped a hand down on the desk. Both men were startled by the sound of this. His boss recovered more quickly and chuckled at the force of Mohand's conviction. He instantly regretted his action and with a small smile of apology he took a step back.

'The land must be fertile. I could have a small market garden. I could grow all kinds of fruit and vegetables that could be used at the infirmary...'

'Okay, okay, okay,' Deschamps said and put a hand up. 'You've convinced me. As long as your work here doesn't suffer.' His expression grew mock-stern, for he knew that he could rely on Mohand to complete any task he set him. 'And as long as I get a share of any profits.'

Mohand could barely wait to get started on this and at the first opportunity he made a visit to Monsieur Chin and ordered seeds and new plants that he could use to start his venture. Any spare moment he had, even to the extent that on occasion he was forced to work in the dark, he tended his garden. So lush was the soil and so strong the strong sun, that his plants flourished and within weeks he was able to start supplying the hospital kitchens with nourishment for the sick convicts.

* * *

Following his recuperation from yellow fever, Mohand had often gone for a swim to help build up his strength. Whenever he could, he went swimming and after some time became very proficient, swimming for long hours and for long distances out into the ocean. Here, at least, he had an illusion of freedom. Out at sea he could pretend to be on his own.

Given that the weather was usually sunny, whenever the local people had some spare time they would also rush to the beach. This meant that after work hours and at weekends the beach could be very busy. The convicts were forbidden from mixing with the public, even those prisoners that were considered well-behaved. So Mohand was used to taking a spot at the far end of the beach, a good distance away from the crowd.

The sun was strong overhead, which made walking on the sand with bare feet a painful experience. When he was satisfied that he was suitably at a distance from the crowds, he stripped to his shorts and made himself a little camp with his shoes and his shirt.

He sat down on the sand and looked back along at the others, fighting back his feeling of resentment at their freedom. They were mostly camp guards, soldiers on leave and managers of the various elements of the colony. These men had the luxury of being able to relax with their wives and children. This was like a holiday spot for them, while he was nothing but a prisoner.

Still. He was in the fortunate position of being able to come here and enjoy the same space, while most of his fellow convicts were being worked into an early grave. He looked out to sea and noticed that it was calm.

His eyes were drawn to a dark cloud in the distance. There, the brightness of the day seemed to be swallowed up by a spell of bad weather. For a few minutes he stared at this cloud and tried to judge the direction of its movement. In that period it seemed to be moving closer to the beach. Even from here he could see that the cloud was almost as low as the sea and that waves were being formed by the weather it was producing.

He judged that given the speed that it was moving he might have another half hour before it struck the beach, so if he was going to go for a swim he should go now.

There was a large rock jutting out from the sea away to his left. He could swim until he was alongside it and then turn and come back to shore.

He paddled until the water was up to his waist and then kicked off into the sea. He loved that moment when he was powering through the water, just him and millions of gallons of this most basic element of life. After several minutes of swimming, he lifted his head, spat out a mouthful of salt water and treaded water. He looked out towards the bad weather and saw that it was moving faster than he realised. Even from here he could see that the wind was churning up the surface into large waves.

Turning back to shore, he felt that it would be much safer if he was on dry land until this patch of bad weather had passed them by.

He was soon on land and skipping over the hot sand towards the spot where he had stored his clothing. Sitting down, he could feel a stronger breeze than before. He looked out to sea and saw a bigger change even than he expected. The sky grew darker and as he looked along the beach he could see everyone leaving the water for the safety of dry land.

The wind was now whipping sand up into his face and the waves were hitting the shore in a rush. The change of weather had been so sudden that there had been no time for the authorities to place the red flags that were usually rolled out to warn of any hazards.

Mohand watched in amazement as the squall moved in. He

considered that he should probably just go back to barracks, but as other occupants rushed from the beach he enjoyed the fact that he might have this space to himself. He was safe. Why would he need to find shelter?

He noticed one family that hadn't moved. A woman stood up and with one hand placed at her forehead and one held over her heart, she appeared to be searching the water for someone.

THREE

New Trousers

The sea was becoming more violent by the minute. The waves were growing and crashing onto the shore. Coastguards were shouting and waving to the few stragglers still in the sea, urging them to come ashore.

Mohand stood up and moved towards the water's edge. Even from this distance he could see that whoever it was out there, they were stranded at the far end of the squall and struggling to come back. He looked back over towards the family and could see they all had their eyes trained out to sea, but no one was making any effort to help.

Without a moment's hesitation, Mohand jumped into the surging water and started swimming towards them. At one point he stopped swimming to assess his position relevant to the troubled swimmer. Looking around, he could see a small canoe being launched, but the coastguards and their little craft were having problems getting beyond the swell. The waves were so strong that their boat was continually being thrown back to shore.

Mohand tucked his head into a wave and fought its push with a kick. With all his strength he fought against the current. The distance to the victim didn't seem to be getting any shorter.

Again and again he splashed through the waves. Again and again fighting the power of the ocean. There was nothing but him and the elements and he would not give in.

At last he saw that he was getting closer. No wonder the woman on the beach was so worried, for the troubled swimmer was just a girl. This gave Mohand fresh strength and even more reason to save her. With a few more strokes he reached her.

'*Ne t'inquiete pas,*' he shouted over the roar of the wind and sea. She was so exhausted she barely had the strength to acknowledge. She opened her mouth to try and speak, but a wave washed over her. She came back up on the crest of the next wave, spluttering and choking. Mohand was picked up by another wave and crashed against her. He reached out and grabbed her arm. Panic gave her a little more strength. She thrashed her arms about and Mohand lost his grip on her.

He managed to swim behind her and pulled her towards him. As he did so, he held her under her armpits and brought the back of her head on to his shoulder.

'Don't worry,' he shouted into her ear. 'I've got you.'

She was now limp, a heavy weight in his arms.

Struggling to tread water, he looked back towards the shore and tried to judge the distance and the movement of the waves. He could see the coastguards still struggling to push the boat beyond the first breaking waves. Behind them a crowd gathered on the shore. They formed a chain along the front, watching the two swimmers being thrown up and down like a twig by the roiling sea.

Holding the girl's head, Mohand began to swim backwards. In this new position, he found it difficult to move any further. The sea was too strong. The girl was becoming heavier and heavier. The energy was draining from him.

A wave caught him in the face. He swallowed water. Spitting it back out, he fought for breath. The situation was becoming hopeless. How was he going to save himself now, let alone the girl?

The waves battered him. The wind howled in his ears. Spray filled his ears and his mouth. His eyes were stinging with salt.

His breath was ragged and forced. It felt that each time he opened his mouth to take a gulp of oxygen, only sea water filled his mouth.

He felt himself weaken. He shook his head, trying to shake water from his eyes. He fought against the next wave, anxious to stay above the surface, finding it more and more difficult to breathe. Battered by the wind and the waves, he became confused. He barely knew which way was up, never mind the direction of the shore.

His legs were weakening, he could barely hold on to the girl.

This was the end. He repeated a prayer over and over again.

'I witness that there is only one God and Mohamed is his prophet.'

Suddenly a giant wave come from nowhere and carried them both into the air. It flattened, and they were dropped in front of a large rock. Mohand somehow found the strength to kick forward and trusting that one hand was enough to keep hold of the girl he stretched his other out to try and get a grip on the rock. His fingers felt the slime of seaweed. He frantically wrapped this around his wrist, prayed that it would be anchored strong enough to the rock to hold him and prayed that another large wave wouldn't come and push them over the far side of the rock and away from safety. With all of his strength, he pushed the girl towards the rock. Seeing that she was close to being safe, she found some last reserves of strength and with one foot on Mohand's chest and a knee on his face she clambered to safety. He was bruised by her actions and pushed harder against the surface of the rock where he felt it tear at his skin. He barely felt the pain and now that he had a free hand he fought for a grip on the rock and pulled himself up out of the sea.

They both lay on their backs fighting to fill their lungs.

The girl was chanting, '*Merci, merci, merci.*'

Mohand sent a silent prayer of thanks to Allah and struggled up onto his knees to assess their situation afresh. They may be out of reach of the waves for the moment, but they were still some way off the shore.

He could see that the coastguards had eventually got beyond the first set of waves and were not far from them.

He waved to let them know that they were safe.

He shouted, 'A rope. We need a rope.'

Some minutes later they reached them, but couldn't come too close in case a wave lifted them on to the rocks. At least now the wind had died down a little and the situation was not quite as precarious.

A coastguard threw a rope to Mohand. He plucked it from the air and tied it around the girl's tiny waist. Her mouth made a small shape of panic. Her breathing, which had all but recovered, was becoming more and more ragged at the thought of going back into the sea.

'Trust me,' he said. 'This is almost over. I won't let you go.'

She opened her mouth and a tiny squeal was all she could allow.

He couldn't delay any further. Before panic could fully take a hold of her, he had to take the next step towards safety. He lifted her up and jumped back into the sea. She thrashed against him.

'*Calme toi,*' he shouted. 'They have the other end of the rope.'

In the water again, he could feel that the force of the waves had lessened, and the coastguards were able to pull the rope towards them. Once they were close to the canoe, one man reached over and pulled the girl on board.

There was no room for Mohand.

'Can you hold on to the side?' one of the men asked him.

He nodded, gripped the side of the boat and, as the men began to paddle, he sent a thousand prayers of thanks as he felt the craft move back to shore.

The journey back to the beach was relatively uneventful. Mohand initially worried that he wouldn't have the strength to hold his grip, but the closer the shore appeared, the more he was able to relax. As soon as he could, he stood up in the water and with more gratitude than he had ever felt, he made his way to the sand.

The canoe beached and was immediately surrounded. A man and woman were red-eyed and praising everyone for the safe delivery of their child. The father reached in to the boat and pulled the girl into his arms. The mother hovered over them both, tears of joy flooding her face.

People were crowding around the boat. Those at the back couldn't see what was happening and shouted anxiously, 'Is she alive?'

Someone close to the front shouted back, 'I think he saved her.'

'What a brave man!' a woman said.

'Did anyone see who he was?'

Mohand realised that the sheer numbers of people around them meant that few could see where, or even who, he was. Gratefully, he moved back to the area of the beach where he had stored his clothes. Without drying himself, he pulled his trousers and shirt on.

Now dressed, he headed back towards his barracks. Unfortunately, this meant he had to pass through the main part of the beach and with his head down he walked quickly.

Some people recognised him as the saviour of the young girl, and they congratulated him as he passed. He noticed that those who realised he was a convict held back their praise, unsure of how they should react. Mohand acknowledged no one and continued on his path. He was proud that he had saved the girl's life, but he knew that even if he saved one hundred of their daughters he would still be a convict. He would still be considered as the scum of their society.

* * *

Once in his cell, Mohand found a clean uniform and changed, but suddenly he was as exhausted as if he had spent a week clearing a spot in the jungle, and he collapsed onto the bed.

He closed his eyes and slept.

After what felt like mere moments, he heard a knock on the door. He lifted his head from the pillow, not sure who to expect. He was half-asleep, confused and had all but cast the incident from his mind.

Who would be knocking at his door, he wondered. A guard would just walk in. A fellow convict would hail him from the door.

A fist rapped at the door again. It's knocking almost polite. He stood up and opened it. A man he recognised as a fellow convict was pointing a finger at him.

'This is the convict, Saoudi,' he said to someone at his side.

Beside him was the couple he had last seen on the beach holding on to their daughter. Up close, Mohand could see that they were people who might be considered to be of some value by the society that had shunned him. They were tall, slim, clearly in rude health and dressed in expensive clothes.

Clinging on to her father's hand was the girl whose life he had saved. Mohand judged that she was about thirteen. She was smiling shyly at him from behind a long fringe of blonde hair.

'We don't know how to thank you for saving our daughter,' the man said. He held out a hand.

Mohand held his out and allowed the man to shake it.

'Don't mention it. It's nothing.'

The woman took a step forward and hugged him. Then, as if she was remembering herself, she stepped back beside her husband.

'Please. This is not nothing,' she said. 'Without you, our daughter would be dead.' At the thought of this she was suddenly overcome. She sniffed back her tears as her daughter tried to reassure her.

'Mama, don't cry. I'm here. I'm alive.'

The woman half-sobbed, half-laughed. 'Of course you are, darling.' She turned to Mohand. 'I don't know how to thank you, sir.'

Mohand stared at her, confused at the word 'sir'. Did she not realise he was a convict?

The man was studying Mohand's reaction.

'When everyone else was standing and staring', judging by the shadow of guilt that passed over his face he clearly included himself in this, 'you dived in to the sea and risked your own life. For someone you don't even know.'

Mohand looked him in the eye, feeling as if he had been noticed for the first time in a long time.

'Sir, I did not risk my life, since I am already dead,' he answered honestly. 'As to why I saved someone, I don't know,' he shrugged. 'I saw a human in need of my help and I offered it. Allah says that all lives are sacred.'

The man was stunned at Mohand's matter-of-fact attitude.

'Why did you not wait to be thanked?'

'I did not save the life of your daughter to be thanked, sir.'

The man narrowed his eyes and asked, 'Are you ashamed for what you did, or is your shame to do with your status as a convict?'

Mohand felt a brief flaring of irritation that the man had read him so well. 'Your daughter was safe, sir. That was thanks enough for me.'

The man bowed, as if he was impressed by Mohand's honesty and his dignity.

'Can we offer you anything as a gesture of thanks?'

Mohand opened his mouth to speak, but before he could answer, the man who brought them to his room asked, 'Do you know who these people are?'

'Forgive me.' Mohand nodded at the couple and decided to err on the side of caution. 'But should I?'

'This is Monsieur Lefevre. He is the prefect of Paris.'

At this, the man looked almost humbled. Mohand got the impression that normally such an introduction was a matter of course for him, but on this occasion it was almost as if he was desperately keen that Mohand was impressed by this title.

The convict who introduced him continued, this time turning to the mother of the child, 'His wife, Madame Lefevre, is the sister of the mayor of St Laurent's wife. They are visiting the colony on their holidays.'

Mohand blinked back his surprise at this news. Surely Allah had put these people in his path to help ease his time in this hellhole? His mind went wild with the possibilities. Maybe they could make his life in prison a little easier? Perhaps they could even have his sentence reduced. Who knew what influence this man might have?

Before Mohand could say anything, Monsieur Lefevre said, 'We would like you to come with us, as our guest, if you don't mind, please?'

'No problem,' answered Mohand with a shrug, while still mentally trying to come to terms with this development. 'I have nothing better to do.'

At this, the little girl jumped up and down and clapped her hands with delight. The adults all burst out laughing.

'My name is Valerie,' she said with a huge smile. 'What is yours?'

'My name is Mohand,' he answered and held out his hand as if in a grand gesture. '*Enchante.*' The girl took her hand in his and shook it. Her bones felt as delicate as eggshell against the work-scarred skin of his hands. And for the first time, Mohand was struck fully with the enormity of what he had achieved. He felt tears sting his eyes. If it weren't for him, this little girl would surely be dead instead of brightening the world with such a beautiful smile.

The girl sensed his emotion and moved closer. With no reservations or judgement whatsoever she hugged him.

‘Thank you, Mohand,’ she whispered. ‘Thank you.’

It was all Mohand could do not to give in the emotion that churned in his gut. For that brief moment, he was more than a number. He had value and this little girl could see that.

Outside his cell, Mohand could see that another couple was standing waiting. The woman was a darker, slightly younger version of the girl’s mother and the man was dressed in the kind of white cotton suit favoured by the local civilians.

‘Monsieur Le Maire and his wife,’ said the convict by way of introduction.

Both of them stepped forward and shook Mohand’s hand.

The mayor’s handshake was robust and heartily grateful. His wife leaned forward and kissed both of his cheeks.

‘You saved my favourite girl, Monsieur. How can I ever thank you?’

Mohand was fast becoming uncomfortable with all this attention. He mumbled something and waited to find out what was going to happen next.

‘*D’accord*, everyone. Let’s go,’ said the mayor and they walked in procession from the barracks.

* * *

They must have made a strange parade as they walked through St Laurent on their way to the mayor’s house. In front were Valerie and Mohand, with the two most important couples in the town just behind them. As they walked, Valerie issued a constant stream of chatter and, in his discomfort, Mohand couldn’t have been more grateful for it. The little girl had claimed his company as he was her saviour. Now that she was completely safe, she wanted to do nothing else but talk about how close she was to death.

‘And how scared were you, Mohand?’

‘I could hardly breathe when those waves kept crashing over me.’

‘Did you never feel like giving up and just going to sleep?’

Mohand laughed. ‘I don’t recommend you fall asleep in the ocean. You might find breathing a little too difficult. Not to mention the fact that your teddy bear would get soaked.’

Valerie giggled. 'I'm too old for a teddy bear, silly.'

At this point the parents lengthened their stride and stepped ahead of Mohand and Valerie, guiding them towards a shop. Somewhat mystified, Mohand followed them into what appeared to be a tailor's. Racks of suits and shirts and ties filled the walls. A large mirror stood in the far corner, reflecting back to him his own image. He looked away quickly. He didn't want to address the fact of his appearance at this moment. The washed-out cotton pyjamas he was wearing only encouraged thoughts of his unworthiness. Looking around himself in awe, Mohand thought that he must be the only prisoner in the history of the colony to have walked in here and been surrounded with all of these beautiful rich colours and cloths.

'Please don't be offended, Mohand. We would like you to have some handsome clothes.' Madame Lefevre smiled at him. 'You must be anxious to get out of that prison uniform.'

Mohand looked around himself, open-mouthed. He didn't see this coming. His first thought was that it would be wonderful to have nice cloth on his back, but then he thought, what would I do with a suit in prison?

'You are very kind, Madame Lefevre. Thank you, but I do not need any clothes.' This was clearly a lie as he had hardly any clothes to his name. The couple had been in his cell and they could have seen for themselves the full extent of his worldly possessions.

The prefect's wife turned to him.

'Are you not happy with what you just did for us?'

'Of course I am happy. But I only did what was right at the time. I felt it was my duty. If I did not try to save her, I would be feeling guilt for the rest of my life.'

The woman was clearly someone who was not used to being turned down. 'No, you have to take something.'

'In that case…' said Mohand, wondering how to deflect the attention elsewhere. He pointed at the mayor. 'I will take the trousers from your host, the mayor.'

The mayor was a good-looking man, with a head of thick black hair and a warm expression. He laughed. 'I can't give you my trousers. My wife bought me these for my birthday.'

'I already have trousers,' said Mohand with a comic expression. With each hand he held out the meagre cloth of his to the side.

Everyone laughed.

The two men clapped Mohand on the shoulder.

'I respect your wishes, Mohand,' said Monsieur Lefevre. His eyes were full of understanding and a fresh appreciation of the young man before him. His expression showed that he realised Mohand was trying to retain some form of dignity. He bowed somewhat formally.

'Another time, perhaps?'

Mohand nodded. This was an ideal solution. The gift was offered and accepted at some indeterminate time in the future. In this way, everyone would save face.

FOUR

Tea with the Mayor

At the mayor's residence, Mohand found that he was the guest of honour at a small party to celebrate the safe return of Valerie to her parents.

The residence was a grand home built in the colonial style, with large windows, wooden floors and swathes of linen. An army of servants stood at attention as they walked in and, with quiet efficiency, set about looking after the guests.

Each of them was handed a small glass of wine and as Mohand sipped at his glass he took the opportunity to look around himself.

Soft chairs in pale fabrics were positioned around the room he was standing in. Large tables of dark, rich wood leaned against the four walls and each table was topped with a lush display of flowers. So clean and tidy was everything around him that Mohand continually wiped his hands on his trousers.

On one wall a large oil painting of the bay of St-Laurent-du-Maroni was on display. Struggling to maintain some form of equilibrium, Mohand walked over to the painting and studied it.

He had never seen anything so beautiful. That man could make such a thing was a wonder to him.

'This was the scene where you were very effective today, Mohand.' He heard a woman's voice and turned to see the mayor's wife at his shoulder.

'This is very beautiful,' he said.

'Why thank you, Mohand.'

'My wife is a very talented painter, monsieur,' said the mayor, moving over to join them, a strong light of admiration in his eyes.

Mohand looked from the painting to the woman. He formed a small bow.

'Wonderful,' he said. He looked away from the woman back to the painting. Her frank gaze was making him feel a little uncomfortable. It had been a long time since he had last known the pleasures of a woman's body and he could feel himself respond.

'The colours...' He gave a little cough. 'How you achieved those colours...'

The mayor's wife touched his shoulder. 'Practice, Mohand. Just a little practice and anyone could do it.'

The mayor leaned forward and pecked his wife on the cheek. 'So modest, my love.' Then he turned to the small group of people and said, 'I believe that the food is now ready. If you would all follow me?'

He turned to face a set of double doors painted a bright white, opened them and walked through into another room set with a large table, groaning under the weight of food.

Plates of fruits, meat, fish and bread were arrayed in a dizzying display that brought an instant growling response from Mohand's belly.

A servant pulled back a chair for Mohand. Another set a napkin over his lap. Yet another filled a glass with water. This initially made Mohand deeply uncomfortable. He observed the servants as they quietly and efficiently worked around the room, ensuring that each plate and glass was full. It was all he could do not to jump up from his chair and join in serving the others. He felt that he should be working alongside the servants, some of whom were clearly ex-convicts. He caught a few glances from them, but in the main the servants treated him with the same deference they showed the other guests.

Valerie sat beside him, made sure that she had the lion's share of Mohand's attention, and she kept up the same stream of chat that she had started on the walk over.

It was like a dream. Mohand had never been treated this way. Back in Algeria, even with the Samsons he had never experienced this level of luxury. The two families were obviously devoted to the little girl, who was completely unspoiled by all of this attention. They were also clearly political animals and adept at making sure their guests were at ease.

They treated Mohand with respect. They asked questions about his background and his family life back in Algeria. At first, he was reluctant to answer but when it was clear they were being asked from a position of genuine interest, he relaxed and was happy to answer.

At one point a servant came in to the room and whispered something in the ear of the mayor. The two men left the room.

They returned moments later. The two wives asked what had happened.

'Nothing to concern you, ladies,' the mayor answered and smoothly changed the conversation.

Mohand puzzled on this for a moment and returned to the flow of the chatter. The evening passed quickly. The conversation barely paused and Mohand's wine glass was never allowed to empty.

Madame Lefevre tried to tell Valerie that it was long past her bedtime, but she was reluctant to leave Mohand's side. Only when her head was resting on the table did she allow her father to carry her to bed. Before she left the room she roused herself a little and quietly insisted that she give Mohand one last kiss.

After she pressed her lips against Mohand's cheek, he smiled. 'Pleasant dreams, *ma cherie*.'

Once the girl had been taken from the room, Mohand stood up from the table with wearied reluctance. The thought of leaving the comfort of this house and the affection in which he was clearly held was difficult for him to accept.

But what other choice did he have?

'I must go back to my room,' he said.

Just then, Monsieur Lefevre returned.

'Are you sure we can't give you something, Mohand? We owe you our daughter's life.' He pulled a wallet from his pocket and started to count out some money.

'Monsieur Lefevre, I can't accept your money. The fact that your daughter is alive is all the thanks that I need.

'Are you absolutely sure, Mohand?' asked the mayor.

'If you insist on giving me something, Monsieur Le Maire, I will take your trousers,' Mohand repeated his earlier request with a grin. Again everyone laughed.

Now that their formal behaviour had been softened by wine, both women hugged Mohand at the door and the men shook his hand warmly.

Then the two men insisted that they escort him back to his room. At the door to his cell, the prefect placed a hand on each of Mohand's shoulders and looked deep into his eyes. The emotion evident there sparked a response in Mohand. He coughed to disguise how he was feeling.

'You have no idea what you have done for us, Mohand,' Monsieur Lefevre said. He looked beyond the door and into Mohand's cell. 'I will find a way to make life a little easier for you in this place. It's the very least I could do.'

Mohand, realising he had protested enough throughout this evening, held his tongue. If good came from this, he would take it and thank Allah. If it didn't, he would endure. That was what he did.

When the men eventually said goodbye and left, Mohand felt their leaving with a heaviness that took him by surprise. He slumped onto his bed.

From all that kindness and luxury to this small and empty dark room. There was simply no comparison. Despite all of their good intentions and well wishing, the difference between them was a stark one. They held positions of privilege and wealth, while he was a convict in one of the worst prisons on earth.

He sat up, a little dizzy with all of the wine. A sudden longing for company, any company gripped him. He could go down to Lacroix's bar. Maybe Simone would be there. He hadn't spent time with him in a while. Maybe there would be some prostitutes hanging around willing to relieve some lonely man of a few coppers.

No. After spending time with those genteel sisters in such a beautiful home, the thought of rutting at the side of the road with a common whore was a good deal less than appealing. If it ever held any appeal for him, that is.

He stood up and walked the three steps to his door. He stepped out, sat against the wall, and looked up at the night sky. He thanked God once again for giving him the strength to save the little girl and for giving him the opportunity to meet such important people in his present situation.

He stood up and started walking. He was not sure of where he should go, only that he couldn't go back and sleep in that cell of his at the moment. He had to let the events of the day and the evening that followed wind down in his mind, or he would never find sleep.

Some minutes later he heard the low mumble of voices. One urgent, one moaning, both male.

His first thought was that someone was being attacked, but then he became aware that it was the noises of passion he could hear. Disgusted that he should almost be witness to two men having sex, he turned and walked in the other direction.

He continued for a good ten minutes until he found a low wall on which he could sit and collect his thoughts. The breeze was cooling on his neck, the insects for once weren't biting and the only noise he could hear was the lullaby of the tropical night animals.

The peace didn't last long. He heard a man moving towards him. Then the noise of a match flaring into flame, and a cigarette being lit.

'Oh, it's you, Saoudi. I almost didn't see you there.'

Mohand turned round to face the newcomer.

'Hassan. What are you doing out and about at this time of night?'

'Taking some air.' Hassan stepped closer, drawing deep from his cigarette. He then held the glowing ember towards Mohand, offering him a puff. With a smile Mohand reached out and accepted the gift. He breathed deep, filling his lungs with the tobacco smoke. Felt the hit of the drug and handed the cigarette back to Hassan.

He exhaled a mouthful of smoke. 'Thanks.'

The two men stood side by side in silence for several minutes. It was rare for them to be together without the presence of Simone and for the first time since the day with the weedkilling bagpipes, Mohand felt Hassan thrum with tension. He looked to the side and assessed the other man, who was studiously staring ahead into the darkness. The silence was like an itch. For the sake of Simone and continued smooth relations, he thought he should speak.

'Where's Simone?' asked Mohand.

Even in the dark Mohand could see the answering shrug. Hassan took a deep draw from the cigarette, the small light from the ember pulsing in the dark.

'You two fell out?'

'Sometimes I think men are worse than women,' Hassan answered and then looked over to study Mohand's expression. 'I have had women, you know. I've not always been... what you see here.' In the weak light, Hassan's features appeared softer, less burdened, and Mohand got a glimpse of the man he might have become if...

'Life hasn't been kind to you, Hassan.' The old guilt at how he had a role to play in Hassan's life in the *bagne* twisted at the muscle in his jaw.

'Luck is something that happens to other people, Saoudi.'

Mohand read so much into that small sentence and he realised with a start that any act of friendship from this man had been nothing but just an act.

'I thought we could become friends, Hassan. I thought...' Mohand shook his head. 'You don't like me, do you?' he asked.

Hassan drew another lung-full from his cigarette and exhaled noisily before he answered.

'I don't blame you for everything.'

'What in Allah's name is that supposed to mean?'

'I killed someone. I was angry. Furious. That was my mistake. Everything else...'

'You can't be serious,' said Mohand. He looked at Hassan, searched for some kind of humanity within his stare. 'All this time... the hours you and I have spent with Simone...' He paused again, swallowed down his irritation. 'I have come to love Simone as a friend. For his sake I am willing to pretend we are also friends.' He stopped speaking, allowing time for the other man to reciprocate.

Hassan cleared his nasal passages and hawked into the dirt. 'Yeah. That will work.'

Mohand bit down on the curses that were piling up behind his teeth. He exhaled and thought about the man standing beside him. How he had saved Simone in the jungle. What he had done to save Simone in the jungle.

The noises he heard earlier came back to him. The two men fucking at the side of the road. He wondered how Simone might feel about this now, in the relative safety of the camp.

'Simone. Does he know that you have other close friends?'

'What are you talking about?' Hassan demanded and then looked back over his shoulder at where he had come from and turned back to face Mohand. His face in a sneer.

'Not all of us can become heroes in order to earn some money, Saoudi.' He rattled some coins in his pocket, his meaning clear to Mohand.

'There must be some other way, Hassan. Surely you don't have to…'

'Shut up,' answered Hassan. 'How can you possibly know what I do and don't have to do? You don't have a clue, country boy.' He took another deep drag on his cigarette and studied Mohand's expression. Several thoughts flitted across his face before he looked away. He opened his mouth to speak and closed it again. He filled his lungs with smoke once more.

'You get it all so fucking easy, Saoudi, that you forget how difficult it is for everyone else.' He kicked at a stone. 'One day your blessed life will end and then you will know the pain I have suffered.' The expression on his face suggested he was the one who would make it happen.

FIVE

New Friends

The prefect was as good as his word and within days Mohand received an important promotion. He became the main man in charge of the whole depot, with the other convicts working under his authority.

His old boss was moved to another part of the administration and, without rancor and more than a little pleasure shining in his normally laconic expression, he showed Mohand to his new quarters. This was a room, not a cell, and it was actually outside the prison camp, just a few steps from his office.

The two men stood at the doorway to Mohand's new home; one smiling as if he had just won a prize and the other scratching his head in amazement that this had just happened to him.

'Monsieur Deschamps, I don't know what to say.'

'Say nothing, Mohand. You deserve everything that is happening to you today.' He patted him on the shoulder. Then he reached into his pocket and drew out a small card with some official-looking print on it.

'And this,' he said, handing the card to Mohand, 'is a grocery card. This allows you good meat every day from the butcher and a daily ration of bread from the baker.'

Mohand stared at it as if he had just been given the keys to unimaginable riches. Which to many prisoners, this simple piece of card would be.

* * *

The months passed by and Mohand worked hard in the office, drank moderately when he had time off, continued to grow his fruit and vegetables for the hospital and kept himself fit by swimming in the sea whenever he had the time. You never know, he laughed with Simone, he might manage to once again save the child of a visiting dignitary.

There was one difference, however and that was the introduction of a pair of hens. He kept them in a small enclosure within his garden and every day he had a pair of freshly laid eggs.

In his quieter moments he would realise that, in comparison with most of his fellow convicts, he was a fortunate man. He was not happy in prison – he was miserable, in fact – but he had managed to build himself a situation that gave him a small degree of contentment. Provided he kept out of the way of certain people and maintained a positive relationship with the authorities, there was no reason why things should change.

Of course his mind drifted regularly back to his family in Algeria, but he would quickly steer it on to safer ground. He knew that he had to accept that he would never see them again, or it would drive him insane. Reason told him that this was his home now and he had to keep himself busy, work hard and keep his nose clean.

Sometimes he wondered what had become of little Valerie. She would be back in Paris now, studying in school, teasing the boys and pleasing her proud parents.

* * *

One afternoon Mohand was lying on his bed in his room when he heard a knock. He sat up. Someone actually knocking on his door was unusual. The last time that happened… he jumped to his feet and walked over to open the door. As soon as the door opened, a young girl bounded into his arms. She kissed him on both cheeks and cried, 'My second father.'

Mohand was completely taken aback. It took a moment for him

to recognise her. She had grown taller and her hair was longer. He looked over the girl's shoulder and saw a man standing there.

'Valerie. It's you,' said Mohand. 'It's been such a long time.'

'I am fine, my second father,' she said, stepping back from him and recovering her composure. Her enthusiasm and pleasure at seeing Mohand again had overridden the behaviour that polite French society decreed should rule her movements.

'I am not your second father,' Mohand laughed while feeling unaccountably pleased that this girl should still hold him in such high regard.

'Off course you are, silly,' she grinned. 'Since you gave me my second life.' She paused and looked over her shoulder to introduce the man who was standing watching. The expression he was struggling to keep from his face was one of horror. That his charge should be so familiar with a convict was clearly breaking every rule he held dear. 'This is Matthieu. He is my chaperone for the day. We have come to invite you to a party at Monsieur Le Maire's residence.' She spoke formally, in the manner of one well trained in the niceties of French high society.

'When? Now?' asked Mohand.

Valerie nodded excitedly, once again a small girl.

Of course, Mohand was delighted to have this opportunity to escape his miserable life just for an evening.

'We should not keep the mayor waiting, let's go.'

* * *

When they entered the main salon in the mayor's house, Mohand was pleased to see that Valerie's mother and father were in attendance, along with a small number of other guests. A group of men sat chatting in one corner and a group of women in another. As soon as they saw Mohand, they all jumped to their feet.

The mayor held him warmly by the shoulder and introduced him to each of the guests, who were all the important personalities of the town, including the judge and his wife.

'Madame Le Maire,' Mohand smiled. He looked over a long table laden with food and gave a small bow. 'My stomach grumbles in anticipation.'

Save that there were more guests at this event, the evening passed in a similar way to the dinner party Mohand had attended the year before. The food and wine were plentiful and delicious, once again served by an army of waiters.

Again, Valerie demanded his full attention, but Mohand found her company easy and refreshing. She was a bright girl, displaying knowledge of a wide array of subjects and on more than one occasion, Mohand wished he had access to more information than the gossip of the other convicts so that he could offer her more of a conversation.

One man there intrigued Mohand. He sat at the far end of the table with his wife. Both of them had straight black hair, dark faces with delicate features, and were dressed in simple linen. The only adornment was a small dot of colour in the middle of the woman's forehead. When she spoke, her eyes were cast down to the table and she deferred to her husband. When he spoke, his words were insightful and chosen carefully and pitched beautifully in his soft voice; an accent that Mohand had never heard before.

Valerie noticed the direction of his attention.

'That is Judge Kathari and his wife,' she said quietly. 'He is from India. And he is in charge of all the judges in French Guiana.'

At this moment, aware that he was the subject of discussion, Kathari looked over at Mohand and gave a small nod.

Mohand couldn't have been more surprised had she said that he spent his winters in a red suit and delivered presents to all the Christian children in the world. A judge? His only experience of judges so far had been the man who had sent him here: Truck. The two men could hardly be more different.

This man wore a half-smile like it was part of his permanent mood and had an aura that suggested benign wisdom. Therefore, a judge from a different world compared to the court of the French *colons*.

Mohand nodded in return and thought that he would seek out this man at the earliest opportunity. Not to gain any favour, but for the simple realisation that he could be a friend.

He shook his head at the thought and dismissed it as quickly as it rose. He'd clearly been drinking too much of this delicious wine.

'What do you think the likelihood of war is, Mohand?' asked Valerie, breaking his train of thought.

'Darling,' interrupted Madame Lefavre, 'that is not a topic for debate at the dinner table.'

'*Pardon*, Mama.' Valerie coloured slightly and studied her plate.

'The girl is only repeating a question that is on the lips of each of her elders, my love,' Monsieur Lefavre said, defending his daughter. 'One would have hoped that Europe learned its lesson the last time, but Hitler's need for power knows no bounds.'

'And the father defends the daughter by continuing the conversation the mother would rather not hear,' his wife said and smiled primly. She may have shown displeasure at her husband's words, but her eyes showed real affection and for a moment Mohand felt a sharp pain in his gut that he would never again have such a relationship with a woman.

The prefect's wife nodded at Mohand's glass in an attempt to change the conversation. 'More wine, Mohand?' Her eyes searched his as if looking for something else. He coloured, thinking that his loneliness might be apparent to everyone sitting at the table. He coughed and then realised that some levity was required. 'Wine? But of course,' he said. And then, to much laughter, 'Provided it's not German.'

During a lull in the conversation, Mohand looked around the room and wondered about the nature of his relationship with these people and why they had continued to seek out his company. He was nothing but a criminal. What worth could he be to them? Did it amuse them to think that they had such a person in their midst? A convicted criminal no less. He remembered doing things as a child: running down a steep hill, climbing a tree, diving into water that was too deep. These actions were done by way of searching for danger, while knowing that someone was always on hand nearby to save him if things became too difficult. Was this how the French couples saw him? Were they using him to feel the presence of 'danger' while knowing they were perfectly safe?

But he remembered the light in Madame Lefavre's eyes as she looked at him during that moment when loneliness squeezed at his chest. Was there real affection there?

A voice interrupted his reverie. The mayor's wife was speaking to him, an expression of fondness illustrating her question.

'You had a wife back in Algeria, *non*? You must miss female company?'

'Please don't quiz the man, darling,' said the mayor.

His wife dismissed him with a wave of her hand.

'Forgive me for my clumsiness, Mohand. It's just that my sister and I were talking, and we wondered if it was not a marriage that you wanted?'

Mohand's jaw fell open. It must have been minutes before he felt able to speak.

'No, madame,' he coughed. 'I do not want marriage.'

'Are you sure you are not crazy? Did some guard beat you over the head?' She laughed at the idea of this as if it would never happen.

Mohand looked at the creature in front of him and realised she had no real idea of what life might be for him. Her husband had done a highly effective job of keeping the reality of this place from her. He looked around the room, at the furnishings, the large muslin-draped windows, out into the garden and down the path towards the town square. Her view of the world was so different from his they might as well be different species. He considered his history lessons and the story of *L'Autrichienne* herself – Marie Antonette – the ignorant young French queen/girl who said, 'Let them eat cake.' He should have felt anger at this, but he could only feel a deep sadness. None of this was her doing. She was simply playing a role she had been given.

He then felt that he should give this woman an idea of what he longed for most, but as he opened his mouth to speak, he found that he couldn't articulate it.

'What I want most in this world, you cannot offer. No one can.'

SIX

Closing the Bagne

On 2nd November, 1937, Mohand was called to the director's office. When he was handed the formal slip requesting his presence, he pushed it to the side and continued on with the tasks he was required to complete for that day. He had a ship due in at the port; an inventory to prepare for the goods due to replace those being removed from the hold. Important work that no one else could do with the same attention to detail as he.

He looked up from his work and glanced at the summons. He tutted to himself. 'What does he wants from me now? I wish they would leave me be.' He carried on working, delaying his visit to the director's office deliberately. On the whole he was a willing worker, but occasionally he found that, despite his best intentions, he would find small ways to keep the authorities waiting. A small rebellion as pointless as a teat on a bull. But a rebellion nonetheless.

Eventually, his conscience and a little curiousity got the better of him and when he arrived, the director was sitting behind his desk, his welcoming smile laced through with impatience.

'What kept you all this time? I have some good news for you; don't you want to hear it?'

'Sir, I was very busy,' replied Mohand with respect for the man's position. 'I have many tasks to perform, and,' he paused and offered a placatory smile, 'I did not know that it would be good news.'

The director stood up and held a hand out to Mohand.

'Because of your excellent conduct, it has been decided to reduce your sentence by one year.' His voice was loud and his tone thick with pride.

'Why, thank you,' Mohand took the hand and shook it. 'I don't know what to say.' He was sure his mixed feelings at this news would be obvious, but he wasn't sure how he wanted to react. He had been sentenced to doublage. That meant when his sentence was served, he would still have to remain in French Guiana for the remainder of his life. What would becoming a *libéré* one year earlier mean to him? What was a year's reduction of his sentence worth when he still was unable to get back home?

He looked at the pleasure shining in the director's eyes and realised that the man really thought the administration had done Mohand a great favour. Was he really so blind to the situation? Did he really not realise that this meant little to a man with doublage and perpetuity added on to the end of his sentence?

The director's expression was slipping from pleasure into mild confusion at his muted reaction and Mohand thought he ought to show a little more grace. After all, this man quite literally held his life in his hand. One word and he could be posted back to the jungle.

He offered a smile that would appear larger than the thought behind it. 'Sir, any good news is better than bad news. I welcome any clemency. Thank you.'

Reassured that Mohand agreed with his feelings about the development, the director's smile slid back into place. He handed Mohand the official slip.

'Congratulations, Monsieur Saoudi. This shows your fellow convicts that hard work will be rewarded.'

Walking towards his office and now freed from the need to appear agreeable to the situation, Mohand felt a scowl form on his face. The numbers ran through his mind. His twenty-year sentence had officially started in 1927, which meant he had to do nine more years in the camp as a convict and a further nineteen years outside for doublage. Then he would be 'free' but still unable to leave French Guiana. He felt his feet thunder on the wooden planks of the corridor.

'They can keep their clemency,' he muttered. This was a gesture that was completely without merit. The authorities made only themselves feel good with this small pardon. The next time he went to the toilet, Mohand thought, he should wipe his arse with the paper. That was how much it was worth to him.

* * *

Around a year later, Mohand was ordering goods for the prison from a catalogue. He was comparing the previous year's order with the current number of prisoners and then trying to formulate numbers for the upcoming year. This work was mind-numbing and after ten hours bent over a desk, he felt he deserved a break. One of the guards had left behind a local newspaper. He would make himself a coffee and read the paper for half an hour before going back to his work.

He leafed through the pages, enjoying the crackle of the paper as he turned to the next page. He treasured the written word and worshipped every medium it arrived in. As he read, he wondered if every local newspaper in the world contained similar news.

Some lady had won a flower arranging competition. The local soccer team had beaten a team from the other side of the country. Local personages of importance were mentioned as they arrived back in the colony after time away in Paris. Newborns were listed, as were deaths. Good job they don't mention the deaths out in the logging camps, he thought ruefully, or they would need the same amount of paper again.

His habit was to quickly leaf through the paper and mentally tick off pages that he wanted to come back to later and study. Having done so, he returned to page one and was immediately stunned. How did he miss this?

'La fermeture du bagne avait été décidée par le décret-loi de Daladier, le 17 Juin 1938'.

The French government had passed a law to close the *bagne.* He read the article over and over again. Could this be true? The *bagne* closed by legal decree? He read it again. There was no closure date given. How could they do this and not provide a date?

Hope flared in his chest. Then died as he considered what he knew about the French mindset. They were more than capable of passing a law and then ignoring it. They might not implement this particular law for years.

* * *

A few nights later this article was being discussed in detail down at the bar. Even Lacroix stopped serving to come over to the table and offer his cent's worth.

'Don't get your hopes too high, gentlemen. The French abolished slavery in 1818, but didn't get round to enforcing that until 1848.'

'Thirty fucking years?' someone at the back of the room shouted. 'I'm not waiting thirty fucking years.'

'What are you here for, Manceau?' his friend asked, leaning back on his chair.

'Murder. I killed the man who...'

'I could care less why you killed someone, you idiot. How much more of your sentence do you have?'

'Thirty years.'

Laughter boomed around the room. This was a welcome distraction from the nervous energy that flowed with the rum.

'The *bagne* could be closed soon,' a voice whispered in the corner. A voice hushed with awe.

'Not a chance,' someone else said.

'It's never going to happen,' yet another voice added. Then everyone clamoured to add their opinion. Every voice pessimistic.

Mohand couldn't stand the negativity in the space around him. He wanted to believe this was possible. He needed to believe it was possible. He picked up the paper and left the bar.

Walking back to his room, thoughts circled his mind. Excitement burned its energy down the length of his legs as he marched. If they closed the *bagne*, he thought, then doublage would automatically be cancelled. Even if they delayed the implementation until his projected liberation date of July 1946, he had only eight years left.

He turned his face to the night sky. The moon winked from behind a cloud.

'This means I will go back home to my family,' he whispered to the stars. 'Thank you, Allah, for giving me the strength to survive this hell. And making it possible to see my loved ones again.'

That night he could not get to sleep. His mind burned with possibilities as if liberation was just around the corner. The next morning, full of hope of returning home, he decided he should write to get news from the family.

In spite of himself, he was keen to know who of his family were still alive. In his own letter to them he deliberately failed to mention anything about his cousins. He was certain the authorities would have passed this information on and he had no wish to remind them of this loss.

A reply arrived within two months. Mohand held the letter for long moments before he could force himself to open it. He held the envelope to his nose, closed his eyes and sniffed at it as if it held the perfume of home. He was searching for pine trees, olives, figs, the dry heat of Algerian soil. All he got was paper, ink and the stale smell of a sea crossing.

He put the envelope down on the table and stared at it. He had asked for this, he should be able to open it. And yet...

He could fill in the blanks; everyone was well, they were all brimming with health and sending him hopes of the same.

And yet...

He knew.

And there it was at the end of the first sentence.

His father was dead.

The man he cared for more than anyone else on the planet had passed away. He stared at the floor until it became a grey, watery blur. It started with a sniff. Then a low keening sound. Before he knew it he was rocking back and forward, his knees pulled up to his chest.

His father was dead.

He howled. This was more pain that he could handle. Nothing compared to this.

A brief flash of awareness and he was at the bar. A jug of tafia on the table beside him and furtive expressions of concern from those around him.

The next morning when he woke up he could barely move his head. His limbs ached. His mouth felt as if it had been filled with sand while he slept. For the first time since his yellow fever, he took a day off sick.

Before he had even taken an inventory of the state his body, the thought had returned. His father was dead. He held a hand to his eyes. The tears flowed again. A part of him wondered how there could be so many tears. Would his eyes not dry out? Did he not expect this? His father would be an old man. No one lives forever.

His stomach twisted with pain.

How could he consider going back home? Algeria without his father was unthinkable.

He bit down on the emotion that threatened to swamp him once again. There was no point in going back home. There was no point in even writing home for more information.

He made his decision there and then. He would not think of home. He would not seek out news of home. Algeria and his family were dead to him. He would forget about them and concentrate on keeping busy for as many hours as he could. This was the only way he could stay sane.

* * *

Life settled into a pattern of work and sleep, with the odd hour at Lacroix's bar. Work at the depot became more of a challenge as the war in Europe began and then started to bite. The German U-boats were patrolling the Atlantic, which meant very few supply ships could come through from France and her colonies on that side of the world. Everything the colony needed had to be sourced elsewhere. Which of course led to regular headaches for Mohand and his colleagues.

Which in turn meant a whole new level of austerity for the convicts. Men working in the jungle camps, who were already starving for the want of a few crumbs, had even less to eat.

Fragments of war news filtered through to the colony. A few men managed to locate the odd radio and would spend their evenings clustered around it. From there the rumours would spread.

The first one that Mohand learned of was that the Germans had overrun France. This led to subsequent rumours. What need would the Germans have of the *bagne*? Surely they would close such an institution down?

They had set up a new government. That was the first time the term 'Vichy' was heard on the colony, but it was one that was to prove unpopular for the prisoners.

The new government wanted their own people to run outlying properties and colonies. Men in power in the French Guiana were suddenly ousted from their positions and replaced with those who were loyal to the new Vichy government.

One evening at the bar, Mohand was debating this with Simone and Lacroix.

'So, there's a war on in Europe,' Lacroix shrugged. 'That's a million miles away. Or it might as well be.'

'Yes,' Simone agreed. 'What impact does it have on the colony? Look around you. Nobody gives a shit.'

The other two men did as Simone suggested. Around the room men were huddled over their jugs of tafia in various states of inebriation. A pair of them snagged Mohand's attention. He hadn't seen them here before. They looked related to each other. They also looked like Berbers and, sadly, they wore the rags and haunted expressions common to the *libéré*.

'See,' said Simone, misreading the look on Mohand's face. 'They're more interested in who is sleeping with which guard's wife or what the going rate for a bribe is.'

Mohand set his thoughts about the strangers to one side for the moment and shook his head. He, for one, was worried. He could already see the impact the war was having on supplies.

'The Third Reich has ambitions that should worry us all,' said Mohand.

Simone made a dismissive sound. 'They want to take over the old country? Let them. They should start with Paris. Parisians are degenerates.'

'Are you not from Paris?' asked Lacroix.

'I rest my case, your honour,' Simone answered with a grin.

Mohand studied his friend's face. He couldn't believe he was so relaxed about this. 'There is a lot to worry about, my friend, but at least I hear that Paris is safe.'

'Oh,' Simone said, leaning forward. He knew that Mohand had friends in high places, friends that would provide a good source of intelligence. Most of the men he spoke with he would listen to and then add a ladle of salt to their words. Mohand's words tended to have a strong ring of truth.

'The Vichy government have reached an agreement with the Boche. They will not bomb Paris. They may borrow a few of her treasures, but they will leave her architecture intact.'

Simone sat back in his chair and made a dismissive sound through his lips. 'Paris is like a whore, protecting her face while pulling up her skirts and spreading her legs.' He scratched the side of his face and thought for a moment. 'What should we be worried about, then?'

'The first worry is the level of supplies we're receiving. The colony has been lazy over the years, relying on France. Now that she is less able to send us goods, I am worried that a lot of men are going to starve. The *libérés* will find it harder to get work. They too will starve. Not good, my friend.'

'Any more messages of doom, Monsieur Saoudi?' Simone tried to add some levity to the conversation with a smile that held only half the humour he intended.

Mohand thought with dread about what he had heard was happening in Europe. The Germans were rounding up all of the Jews in France. What was then happening was unclear. Speculation was rife and none of it pleasant. 'If the Germans win this war, Simone,' he said, 'they are talking about rounding up all the Jews in Europe and placing them in death camps.'

At the mention of Europe's Jewish population being in danger, Simone was suddenly on edge. His parents were both Catholic, but his mother's mother was a Jew, born in a small community in Georgia. Her parents had fled the region following a pogrom in which most of the men had been slaughtered by Cossacks. They arrived in Paris after long months of travel and worked hard to integrate with the local population.

'Death camps,' Simone thought aloud. 'Surely they wouldn't dare?' Although his words conveyed doubt, his expression showed that he could well believe it.

Mohand considered the Jewish population back in Algeria, most of whom were living easily beside their Muslim neighbours and adding a good deal to the country. 'And if they are starting to kill off the Jews, what use will they have for Berbers?'

Simone took a long drink from his glass. And belched dramatically. 'There, my friend, your worries should cease. The world has long held a fear of my family's religion. Germany's hunger for the blood of my ancestors has a long and troubled history. Jews have travelled the world. Everywhere they put down some roots, they flourish. Some say, like weeds. Through a combination of hard work and good brains', at this, he tapped the side of his head, 'they succeed. More often than not, they succeed even while the other communities around them fail. Then the rumours start. The Jews eat their young and pray to strange gods. They are the source of all our problems, the larger community argues. It would be better for everyone if they died. In Georgia, they would whip themselves into a frenzy so that the only thing to do would be to go out and maim or murder a few Jews. In the dead of night, they would ride into a Jewish village with their swords and cut down anyone in their reach. Men, women or children. If it carried the tag of "Jew" then its neck should be met with a sword. Some of the stories my grandmother used to tell me...' He stopped and looked into Mohand's eyes, his own giving hints of the horrors brought to life as they dripped from his grandmother's tongue.

Mohand shuddered and thought about his own people's struggles with a different oppressor. One group acted through fear and suspicion. The other through greed. Which was worse? In any case, mankind, it seemed, found it very difficult to ignore its worst urges.

He stood up, bid Simone goodnight and on the way out of the bar found himself walking towards the pair of Berbers.

'Do I know you?' he asked the men in their own language. He was surprised that he had switched to his old language without thought, and after so long without speaking it the words felt rough on his tongue.

As he had walked over, the two men looked at him with suspicion. They had both leaned forward, hands on the table, looking as if they were ready to spring. When they heard the Berber words, the suspicion softened on their expressions.

'I am from Maillot in Algeria,' said Mohand.

Both men smiled broadly. One said, 'I am Arezki and this is my brother, Aissa. We're from Oued Amezour.' They both stood up at the same time and moved to embrace Mohand.

They spoke one over the other. Each anxious to hear the other's story. Mohand felt his chest was about to burst. Conflicting emotions piled up one on top of the other. Joy that he should meet men with whom he shared a culture. Sorrow that these men should be in the same position as him; possibly a worse situation, judging by the shabbiness of their cloth.

'Oued Amezour?' Mohand wondered. 'That is just... what... forty kilometres from Maillot, and yet we meet here... Incredible.'

'You look as if prison has been less... of a challenge,' Aissa, the younger one, said. Mohand looked at him, judging the tenor of this comment. He was aware that many men were jealous of his position in the colony. Most of them lost this when they saw that he used this position to help those around them. However, Mohand was satisfied that Aissa was merely stating a fact and not voicing a criticism. He was skinny, but not skeletal as many of the men around him were. He placed a hand on Aissa's shoulder.

'My hell is a little cooler than yours, Aissa,' he said. 'I was lucky to find a way to work with the system to make things a little easier. But make no mistake, this is still hell.'

As the conversation went on, Mohand watched the men and observed how similar they were. How they smiled at the same thing, finished each other's sentences. Mohand envied them their closeness, but at the same time he wanted to distance himself from it. Life here was difficult but it would be unbearable if you had that relationship with someone and then lost it.

Memories of home crowded him. Scenes of Maillot jostled for attention. The chatter and rough humour in the evenings when the men sat on the carpet outside the house as the day cooled. Picking figs from the trees during the harvest. The many versions of couscous Hanna Addidi would serve him after a long, hard day.

Before he realised it, he was slowly rocking back and forward in his chair. A tear forming a slow slide down his cheek.

The two men looked at him, clearly alarmed at his actions.

'Are you ... ?' one asked.

'We didn't mean to ...' the other tried to join in.

'Home ...' Mohand closed his eyes tight. He could feel the sting as he fought the tears. 'I miss it every day.'

'We apologise ...' began Arezki, at a loss as to what to do when faced with Mohand's pain.

Mohand shook his head wordlessly. He fought for control, surprised at his own response. Perhaps he was still grieving for his father.

'Fine,' he managed to say. 'I'm fine. It was just ... your voices ... the Berber ... so difficult.'

Both men looked at him, empathy widening their eyes.

'We understand,' Arezki offered.

Mohand bought some tafia and they chatted for an hour or so about their stories since they had come to French Guiana. Before he returned to his room, he promised the men that they would all meet again.

SEVEN

Accusations

Captain Sancarve was an officer Mohand had come across in the prison from time to time. He was a tall, slim man with the archetypal French profile and one of the fairest men he had met since entering the French penal system.

'Captain.' Mohand stood up from behind his desk when the man entered his office. 'What can I do for you?'

'A glass of water would be welcome, Saoudi,' Sancarve replied while mopping at his brow with a square of cotton. 'A man could die in this heat.' This statement had Mohand immediately on alert. His finely tuned danger alert system was prickling down his spine. Sancarve was a man who never allowed nature to impact on his appearance. While other men around him might have brows dripping or the usual telltale patches of sweat on their uniforms, he was always scrupulously clean. Even now as he dabbed his forehead his skin looked as cool as if he were standing in a mountain breeze.

Mohand immediately fetched the captain a glass of water and placed it before him. Sancarve drained it in one gulp.

'Most pleasant,' he said, 'thank you.' Sancarve may have been one of the fairest men Mohand had met, but he was also one of the most humourless. Even now, when he was on unofficial business, his eyes had all but slipped halfway down his cheeks and he wore the expression of someone waiting for the world to end.

'Is there anything else I can offer the good captain while he is here?' Mohand asked while his mind was working on the possibilities for the man's visit.

'There are times when I have a very difficult job to do, Monsieur Saoudi. Complaints are made. Complaints about black marketeers. Even against good men like yourself, and I have to investigate. There are even times when I have to do this secretly, when I know that I am wasting my time.' As he spoke, his eyes bored into Mohand's.

With his heart tightening in his chest, Mohand's mind worked on the importance of what Sancarve was saying.

Someone had made complaints about him. Those complaints must have been so serious that Sancarve felt the need to warn him. And if they involved the black market and the individual was found to be guilty, there was only one way for that to end. Under the guillotine.

The authorities took that sort of crime very seriously, because it meant the thieves were stealing in great quantities from the prison authority and the colony itself.

Despite knowing that he was as innocent as a baby, Mohand felt anxiety build. His eyes smarted. Sweat burst out on his palms. He rubbed them on his trousers, under the table. Slowly. He wouldn't want Sancarve to read the gesture and then read too much into it.

'I'm sure a man like you would have nothing to worry about.' Sancarve's mouth twitched in his approximation of a smile. 'Time will serve its function, Saoudi. The truth will reveal itself and we can go back to worrying about what the Boche will do to the mother country.'

He left the room as abruptly as he arrived. The only sign of his passing was an empty glass.

* * *

Over the next few days and weeks more complaints arrived with the prison authorities. Other guards that had come to know and trust Mohand let the situation be known to him in similar ways to Captain Sancarve. In these letters the accusers alleged that Mohand was selling materials from the depot on the black market.

These were allegations that could cost Mohand his life.

Having contacts of his own, Mohand did what he could to find out where the accusations had come from. From his various sources, he found that Hassan had set the ball rolling. There were other accusers:

French convicts who were insulted that a man who was not of French stock had achieved a position of responsibility. Again, it was Sancarve who highlighted this to him, in his own fashion.

He paid another visit the next time he was 'thirsty'. He spoke in the tone of someone who was discussing the weather. 'Some men feel that French blood is superior. In that, they are no better than the Germans. This means they might take any opportunity that arises to... get rid of someone who doesn't meet their view of what is correct. These men are blind fools, Saoudi. They are to be pitied.'

* * *

One evening, a chief of the brigade of *gendarmerie* came to visit Mohand in his room. He was one of the guests Mohand had been introduced to at the mayor's party. The chief was a man of ruddy complexion and booming voice, who was simply known as 'The Chief'.

Mohand had been resting on his bed after another long hard day when he heard a knock at his door. He opened it to find the chief standing there in full uniform. Mohand's first thought was that he had come to arrest him and he managed – just – to stay on his feet.

'Don't worry, Mohand,' the chief said, placing a hand on his shoulder. 'I am here unofficially.'

'If you are here to tell me that there have been complaints...'

'I am here to tell you that there have been complaints which have resulted in my placing someone within your staff to observe you.'

'But...' Mohand began to speak. He was stung that someone who he believed held him in trust would go to such lengths to find out if he was guilty of such a crime.

'I have no choice, Mohand. This is the normal process when complaints like these are made. Oh, we know that things go missing and to an extent we turn a blind eye. However, when complaints are made on this scale...'

'I assure you, Chief, that I am doing nothing illegal. Nothing.'

'These guys are after your head, Mohand. But as you say, you have done nothing wrong. The truth of that will surface and they will lose.'

He offered Mohand a smile of support. 'If you need me for anything, don't hesitate to call on me."

The services that Mohand's department provided were under the army control. They needed to get to the bottom of these allegations. Mohand understood that they had to act on any suspicion, whether that suspicion came from someone's imagination or not. There were other areas of concern. Because Mohand didn't sleep in the camp like all other prisoners, it would be easy for someone in his position to take advantage of the situation and make a great deal of money for himself.

Knowing this, and being able to present a logical argument as to why that might be the case, did not make it easier for him. People who had trusted him to do a good job were being let down by the simple fact that he was under a cloud of suspicion.

* * *

They came for him an hour before first light. The door was all but torn from its hinges and two men pulled him from his bed.

Heart spiked with adrenalin, legs weak with fear, Mohand attempted to speak to his captors. All that came out of his dry mouth was a weak, half-formed question.

'What the...?'

In the dim of dawn's light he could see that the men in his room were all guards.

'What is...?'

Again fear snatched the words from his mouth. Aware that he was only wearing a pair of undershorts, he looked towards the chair beside his bed for his prison uniform. One of the guards read his head movement.

'You won't need them where we're going,' he said. Mohand recognised the voice immediately. Fournier.

His feeling of fear increased.

'*Allons-y*,' Fournier commanded and the two men holding him marched him from the room.

He was pushed into a cell, stripped of his shorts and tied to a chair.

Fournier punched for maximum effect with minimum effort. The soft tissue of the ears, nose and mouth were his targets.

Mohand clenched his whole body against the pain. What was going on? Why was he being treated like this?

No one answered his questions. No one spoke as he grunted against the pain.

After what felt like hours, the beating stopped. A cold bucket of water was thrown over him and he was taken to another cell. Before the door was closed on him he tried to speak through his swollen lips.

'Please tell me...'

'Quiet, scum,' Fournier shouted. 'No talking allowed here.'

'But I...'

A fist sparked pain on his temple, he was thrown back into the tiny room and the door crashed shut behind him, leaving him in darkness.

He crawled along the wall until he came to a corner and there he squatted, trying to make sense of what was happening and fighting to contain his fear.

He was trembling. Every inch of him was shaking as if he had some terrible fever.

This was not the first time he had been in this situation, he told himself, and he would come out of this alive and well as he had before. The words limped across his mind with little conviction. All of his worst fears crowded him. He would be kept in solitary confinement for years, going slowly insane; he would be sent back out to the jungle to die; the guillotine was being erected at that very moment, just waiting for that sweet spot on his neck.

Gradually the light began to grow and Mohand was able to make out the detail of his cell. From his crouch he was able to pick out the wooden bench, which was surely to be his bed. The only other item in his cell was a small bucket.

Not sure which part of him was in most pain, he straightened his legs and, with a loud groan, moved over to the bench and sat down. What had happened? From being given warnings by some of the most important men in the colony, he was being beaten and locked up in a cold cell. The complaints against him must have risen to a level the authorities felt they could not ignore.

Was there evidence against him? How could there be, he had done nothing wrong.

His mind looped back to his long years in the jungle. Could he survive another term there if that was where he was sent? He almost preferred the guillotine.

But wouldn't that be a cruel trick? After years in hell he receives the punishment he had worked so hard for others to avoid.

He heard footsteps. Pails scraped against concrete as other inmates pushed their toilet buckets to their cell doors to be emptied.

Then nothing but hush.

He placed his feet on the bench and hugged his knees. Something he hadn't thought about in years came back to him. Mezaine's comment about Joseph. He tracked his own story against that of the prophet. The comparisons were there. Both of them betrayed by family, both of them found a way to overcome. Both were imprisoned, and Joseph had found a way to safety and security. Might he also be able to recover once again from an impossible situation?

He heard a cough and a groan from another part of the prison and then silence again reclaimed the corridors. He shuddered. It was a silence thick with fear.

He heard the soft, confused sounds of someone crying. It came from his left. Footsteps and a gruff voice ordered quiet. Or else.

More feet sounded on concrete. Wordlessly, a convict was working his way down the row of cells delivering what Mohand guessed might be food. He counted the number of times doors creaked open and tin was slid across the ground.

A small insert at the bottom of his door opened and a chunk of bread and a cup of water were pushed through.

He waited until the door was closed before moving over to collect his food. As if some part of him did not want anyone to see how desperate he was. Or how quickly his dignity had fled. It took minutes to finish, only aware when the first chunk of bread hit his stomach of just how hungry he was.

Good. They were not about to starve him.

Bad. They wanted him to be alive when they made an example of him. Which was surely what they would want to do.

From his crouch on the bench he held his hands out in front of him. He was no longer cold but still they shook. He considered what the viewpoint might be of the authorities. They have a convict who has been allowed into a position of trust. This convict is given control over a large part of their budget and has been given a big role in the smooth running of this part of the colony. Then this convict betrays their trust. He makes them all look the worst kind of idiots. They would be harsh in their judgement. What else could they do?

After long hours the weak light faded and the dark took over.

* * *

Fournier came for him again. The punch connected before the first question reached his ear.

'What have you done with the money?'

Mohand spat blood from his mouth before answering.

'What money?'

Fournier punched him again.

'There's only...'

Punch.

'...one way this will end.'

Punch.

Fournier grabbed Mohand's hair and brought his face to his, making sure he had eye contact.

'The guillotine.'

Punch.

Pain was everything. Mohand gulped for breath, fighting down the panic that surged within him.

He was lost. Surely he wasn't coming back from this. He closed his eyes.

'Villiers was a friend of mine.' Fournier had expended so much effort he was sweating. He slapped Mohand's face hard, waiting till he opened his eyes. 'I don't give a fuck about any money. I've been waiting for a chance to do this again for a very long time.'

He punched Mohand in the gut.

Breath exploded from him. He doubled over.

'You're mine now, Saoudi. I'm going to make you wish you'd never been born.'

Mohand was on his knees, his eyes screwed shut. Fear tore the wind from his lungs. He felt Fournier reach for him again and he leaned back, pushed against the floor and tried to get as far away from this maniac as he could.

In two steps Fournier caught him and pushed him against the wall.

'Marie-Louise Villiers was one of the loveliest women I ever met. Until you got your hands on her, you ugly son of a whore.'

There was a rasp to Fournier's voice that suggested a darkness the man was only just allowing himself access to. Despite himself, Mohand looked up into the other man's eyes and then he shrank from what he saw there.

The big man's face was in his. His breath hot and foul on his cheek. His tongue rasped down the side of his face.

Fournier smiled. 'So that's what fear tastes like.'

Without another word, he turned and left.

* * *

Mohand wasn't aware how long he had been in the cell. His toilet pail was collected. Meals were delivered. The dark weakened and then grew. Such was the pattern of time as he fought to control his fears.

There was barely a night when he had slept from dusk to dawn. He knew he was innocent of any wrongdoing, but if the authorities had been desperate to find him guilty they would have found some way of doing so.

Hour after hour, he lay on his bench worrying about what the next day might bring. Would some 'evidence' turn up? Would one of his 'trusted' colleagues fabricate some lie and testify against him? When he did sleep, he often woke up in a cold sweat just before the blade plunged through his bare neck.

Two questions ran through his mind in a continuous loop: when would Fournier come back? Would he want to finish the job once and for all?

* * *

They released him as suddenly as they arrested him. The door was opened and a guard stood on the other side bearing Mohand's prison uniform. He held the clothing towards him.

'You might want to give yourself a wash before you put these on,' the guard said.

Mohand stood up. His feet were stuck to the floor as his mind sought to make sense of what was happening.

'C'mon, convict. I don't have all fucking day,' the guard barked. 'I'd be just as happy to close the cell door again.'

A confused shuffle led Mohand to the door. He held a hand out to take his uniform.

'Back to work, prisoner. You have a job to do,' the guard said. He wrinkled his nose with disgust as Mohand drew nearer. 'But before you do, give yourself a wash.'

Back at his room, everything was just as it was when he had left all those... days? weeks? hours ago? He had no way of knowing just how long he had been away. His bed and chair sat in the same position he had left them. The blanket was scrunched up at the foot of the bed as if he had just left the room to visit the toilet.

He filled his small sink with cold water and worked to wash away the stench of the cell. With a small sliver of soap he tried to work up a lather to release the grime and the odour that had built up. As he scrubbed, he examined himself in the small, cracked mirror on the wall. It was so small that all he could see was his face.

He tried to remember the young man who had arrived in the prison all those years ago. Had he aged much since? He couldn't remember if his cheekbones had been that prominent, or if the skin under his eyes had been so dark.

Who are you? he asked himself. How will you survive if the authorities decide to punish you again? His spirit quailed at the thought. Fear rose in him, dark and unfathomable. He looked away, uncomfortable with what he saw.

* * *

In the office, everyone greeted him as if he had been away for moments. He sat at his desk, teeth grinding against a strong feeling of injustice. A feeling that warred with relief. There had been no explanation, no apology. He had simply been released and returned to his duties.

He stared at the papers in front of him. How can they treat people like this, he raged inwardly. He aimed a pen at some paper. His mind suggested numbers he should annotate. His body could not obey. He had been stripped naked, caged, beaten and given starvation rations and then the door was unlocked with the instruction to go back to work.

He should complain. He should go to the director's office and let them know how he felt. He should sit down, shut up and get on with his work or they could throw him back in a cell and this time never let him go.

Habits formed in the long years of self-preservation took over and he examined the papers in front of him and began to write.

* * *

A few weeks later Mohand received a familiar visitor. With a degree of trepidation, he watched Captain Sancarve as he drank from his cup.

'Ahhh,' Sancarve sighed after a sip. He closed his eyes. 'I needed that. Shame you have no cognac on you.' Mohand nodded, his mind elsewhere.

'You do have cognac?' Sancarve misread his action.

'Sorry, no,' answered Mohand. 'I don't store alcohol in the office. It would only get stolen. Excuse me, Captain, perhaps you might explain why...'

'Oh, yes...' Sancarve studied Mohand's face and read the tension there. 'Excuse me, Monsieur Saoudi. If I may...' He placed his cup on the desk. 'I am aware that there have been some investigations and that a... mutual, ah, acquaintance has been involved. Because my visit is unofficial, I have to be indirect...'

Mohand thought to himself that if the captain wasn't a good deal more direct in the next couple of seconds, he might stick a foot up his well-tailored backside.

'Our findings have found that the individual investigated was honest and trustworthy and should never', here his expression changed from his usual hangdog look to one of empathy, 'have been placed under such strain.'

Sancarve then went on to explain the results of the investigation into Mohand's affairs.

'There were a lot of papers to go through,' was as close as anyone came to offering an apology. They found nothing in the office. In his room, they found some butter. The director was not happy about the butter.

'The prison clerks don't have butter and Mr Saoudi allows himself butter,' he had apparently said.

There was, however, one issue they decided should be upheld. Mohand's chickens. For many years he kept chickens in his backyard as a source of fresh eggs. After the director's search, there was nothing else they could find worth to report back to the authorities.

'The chickens,' said Sancarve. 'The chickens have to go.'

Mohand simply shook his head. It was ludicrous. He stifled an impulse to laugh. After all of the mental anguish and the physical abuse he had suffered, all they could say was that he should have his chickens confiscated.

His mind returned to the source of all of this: Hassan. It must have been Hassan.

How far would he go?

One more attempt by Hassan, and Mohand didn't know how he might react. An action formed in the heat of the moment would result in only one thing: a dead Hassan and the guillotine for Mohand. No, that would not be a suitable outcome.

If he was going to deal with Hassan, it would have to be planned and executed with care.

EIGHT

A Burial at Sea

Mohand looked at the calendar on his desk. It read 16th March. He had an order to complete before the twentieth, but other camps in the region were not answering his requests.

Everyone was suffering from the effects of the war. France still struggled to send goods over from the other side of the Atlantic and other contacts at this side of the ocean were now less forthcoming. Mohand rubbed at his eyes and worried. Food supplies were becoming dangerously low and in a place where more men starved than managed to eat, this was potentially disastrous.

He had met with Armand, the would-be mugger, over at Lacroix's just the night before and couldn't help but notice that his friend was displaying the swollen stomach typical of the malnourished.

'How are you managing?' he asked.

'Tsk,' Armand dismissed him. 'Don't you be worrying about me, my friend. Armand will always rise to the top. Like scum in a swamp.'

'Nice thought, Armand,' Mohand said and grinned. 'I prefer oil on water.'

'You, my friend, have class. I...' he looked down at the dirty rags that just about preserved his modesty, 'I have nothing.' The grin he wore to answer Mohand's was weak and lopsided.

Mohand rested a hand on Armand's shoulder. He himself was

struggling to get enough food, but he would get whatever he could for Armand.

'Be at my office tomorrow morning, eh?'

Armand's head moved jerkily from side to side, as if he was holding a debate with himself. Pride versus need.

He managed to nod. Need won.

'I'll see if I can scare up a pair of trousers. We don't want people to be looking at that sad little penis of yours.'

* * *

Mohand roused his thoughts when there was a brief knock at the door and a messenger from the director's office entered the room. A young guard, David Faber, held forward a summons.

Walking towards the director's office, Mohand's mind was full of queries. It was rare to receive such a summons and, in his experience, it was never something worthwhile. Did he do anything wrong in his work? Had the complaints started up again?

So it was that when he entered the director's office, he was in a state of apprehension. This was not helped by the director's expression. He looked like a man who was about to deliver bad news.

'Please, Saoudi,' the director said, pointing to a chair, 'sit down.'

Even as he placed his backside over the seat and started to sit down, Mohand was praying to Allah that he was safe. Holding his hands on his lap, he fought to control his nerves.

Director Ramirez was not a man to waste any time, so without delay he told Mohand the reason why he had been summoned.

'I am very sorry to inform you that your cousin Arab is seriously ill and has been delivered to the hospital in Cayenne this morning.'

Mohand struggled to take the words in. They didn't make any sense. Arab was indestructible. 'Surely there must be some mistake?' He didn't realise that he had spoken these words out loud until Ramirez replied.

'There is no mistake, Saoudi. I have the notice here on my desk.' He pointed a long finger at an ordinary slip of paper before him.

'But...'

'You have been a good servant to the colony all these years, Saoudi. You deserve our respect, so if you want to see him before he dies, I can arrange this.'

'Yes,' Mohand managed to say as his throat tightened. 'That would be...' Aware that the director was staring at him, Mohand gathered his thoughts together. 'Sir, I would appreciate this opportunity to say goodbye.'

By around lunchtime Mohand found himself in the camp at Cayenne. He had an official authorisation and they were informed of his arrival. The guards at the hospital were brisk and uncaring; this was one more bag of meat and bones about to be fed to the sharks and they would like to get on with their day's work.

One guard took Mohand to a small ward where Arab lay under a threadbare sheet. The smell of dying men, creosote and excrement hit Mohand like a fist. He held a finger under his nose and forced breath in through his mouth until he was able to cope. He looked over at his cousin and was immediately transported back to the time he spent with Ali just before he died.

If he hadn't already known why he was here, and therefore what the bundle on the bed might be, he would have thought the cloth covering the body was nothing more than a collection of rags, so slight was the pile.

Mohand crouched at the side of the bed. He spoke softly. 'Cousin.'

Arab turned his head to face Mohand. A movement that surprised him. The man on the bed had been so still he thought he was asleep. Or worse.

'You came,' Arab said in a dry whisper. 'I hoped you would. Before I died.' This was Arab. This was the man whose actions led to him living all of his adult life in this waking hell.

'Cousin, hush.' Mohand paused, words caught in a lump in his throat. A man he had known his whole life was about to die. His last link to home was about to be severed. 'Save your energy.'

Arab's eyes met his. They spoke of regret, pain and guilt. Guilt so heavy it was squeezing the last drop of air from his lungs. His lips parted slowly as if held together by weak gum. A word escaped. Released on an exhalation.

'Sorry.'

'Hush,' Mohand said again and reached for Arab's hand. His skin was cool. Dry. Mohand leaned forward until his forehead was resting on the back of Arab's hand. He allowed the release of his grief and wept.

He felt a hand rest lightly on the back of his head. The benediction of a dying man.

'Don't... deserve...' Mohand heard him say and then the hand slid off to the side as if the energy needed to keep it there was too much.

Mohand leaned back and noted that Arab's eyes were closed. Was this the moment? He could see that his chest was rising and falling in a slow rhythm. Death may have been imminent but it wasn't going to happen right away. He had more time to spend with his cousin.

He recalled the time he spent with Ali near his end and, although he was sure that Arab was sleeping, he talked of the things they had spoken about then. Words of the past vibrated in his throat and hummed in his ear. He didn't get many opportunities to speak Berber and he relished this connection to family and his past. He spoke of mountains and rivers and olive groves and dry heat. Speaking until fatigue worked his voice to a whisper and then released him into sleep.

* * *

A voice startled him. Deep and strong.

'It's time.'

Mohand sat up and looked at the orderly who had spoken. The message delivered with a practical note. What was left unsaid was, 'We need to clear the bed for the next patient.'

With an almost scientific detachment, Mohand studied the face of the corpse. He had done all his crying the previous night while his cousin still breathed. This was a different Arab. His face was lined and had shrunk. Mohand could read the pain and misery in those lines that radiated around his eyes and from around his mouth. Arab's skin was grey. His hair was white. Life in the camp had leeched all colour from him.

Mohand searched his heart and his conscience and knew that he could feel no anger towards the man who once made this shell of skin and bones live and work and breathe. The suffering caused by the colonial French changed everything. It brought greed, jealousy, hate and numerous dangerous qualities with it.

They engineered a situation where their lives were one big struggle. Arab would have never been driven to behave in such a manner if they hadn't been so poor.

Mohand traced the line of Arab's nose with his eyes and prayed that Allah might be lenient with him.

He shuffled alongside the body on his knees until he was by Arab's head and finished by reading some verses from the Koran. He stood up and nodded at the orderly.

'It's time.'

* * *

From the morgue, the body was taken by a small carriage drawn by a donkey to the pier. One of the guards gestured that Mohand could accompany them out to sea. It seemed to Mohand that it would be fitting if someone who knew Arab in life would be present to witness his burial at sea, so he climbed down the ladder to the boat.

He didn't think beyond that until the first fin broke the surface of the sea. Within moments of rowing out into deeper water, there were three fins circling the boat in long slow circles. Mohand was acutely aware that the only thing separating him from a row of sharp teeth was the wooden panels of the boat. He watched the convicts rowing the boat and noted how calm and everyday this whole situation was for them. He took his cue from them and relaxed.

The men stopped rowing at the same instant, as if they had communicated telepathically. Together they wrestled the body of Arab to the side of the boat. Before they tipped it over the side, one of the men turned to Mohand.

'Any last words for your friend?' he asked.

Full realisation of what was about to happen struck Mohand like a sledgehammer. His cousin's corpse was about to be thrown to a group of hungry sharks. He gave himself a shake. When you climbed into the boat, what did you think was about to happen?

Horrified, he could only shake his head and turn away from the sight. Just before he turned, he saw a grey snout raise itself from the waves. A single eye stared with cold hunger.

He closed his eyes and sent a prayer heavenward and fought to ignore the furious splashing. Bile rose in his throat. His stomach heaved and before he knew it he was leaning over the side of the boat emptying his breakfast into the waves.

The other men laughed at his distress. They had been on countless such voyages. It meant nothing to them. For them, this held all the routine of feeding an exhibit at a zoo.

The splashes behind him seemed to grow in volume.

Row, guards, row. He sent a silent command to the other men in the boat. The noise was horrific and conjured images in his mind that were unbearable. In desperation to distract himself from what was happening mere feet away, he turned his mind to prayer.

Praise be to Allah that his cousin would be forgiven his sins. As the noise from the water started to fade, Mohand's thought was that surely here on Earth Arab had received full punishment.

NINE

The Judge and the Gold Dust

The pain he felt at thoughts from home never lessened for Mohand. For a few months after meeting the two Berber brothers from Oued Amezour, he found himself avoiding their company. On the occasions when he was free to go down to the bar, he would scan the crowd from the safety of the door. If he saw the brothers before they saw him, he would turn and go elsewhere. As he walked away, he would tell himself that the next time he saw them he would sit and talk with them. It would be nice to hear the old tongue.

Eventually he realised that he was being stupid and that knowing the brothers might actually make his time here less painful, rather than more so, he began to seek them out and allowed himself to relax in their company.

When he managed to find some wine, he would even invite the brothers to his room and cook them a meal on his small stove. The delight that they showed on these occasions made Mohand feel guilt that he had gone through months avoiding them.

As *libérés* their time in French Guiana was difficult. When he could, Mohand would give them some work on the docks, but he already had a number of regulars that he couldn't let down. The brothers' position was difficult but so was that of any number of men in the prison.

The two men did what they could to survive. Whether that meant working on someone's garden or resorting to petty theft, that's what they would do.

One Sunday morning, Mohand was awakened by Aissa knocking on his door. When he opened it, he saw Aissa standing there. The sun was bright in the background, hiding Aissa's features in the glare. Even so, Mohand could tell from his posture that something was terribly wrong.

'Aissa, what's wrong?' Mohand asked and pulled the man into his room. Aissa spun in the small space, at a loss as to what he should do. He sat on the chair. Then he stood up. His face was twisted with fear. His breathing coming in ragged gulps. Mohand's first thought was that something was wrong with Arezki.

'Is everything okay? Where is your brother?' he asked.

Aissa took a deep breath. He held his hands before him as if trying to stop them from shaking. 'Arezki has been arrested this morning. Suspected of murder.' He sat back down on the chair. 'I don't know what to do.' He held his head in his hands and began to weep.

Mohand poured a tumbler of wine for the man and told him to drink it down and then give him more specifics.

The two brothers had been playing cards with some men. One of them was a bad loser. A man that Mohand might know. At this Aissa scratched his head.

'His name is... could it be... Hassan?'

Mohand was not surprised that Hassan was close by when there was trouble.

'Could be,' he nodded.

'There was a fight. I don't know who the men were. They just asked us to join in the card game. We thought... Arezki thought we might get lucky.' He stopped talking and wrung his hands some more. A shrug. 'We could always do with some money. Anyway, one of the men didn't get back up, and Arezki tried to help him to his feet. The man who did it ran into the jungle. The guards came and they took Arezki away with them.' At this he began to cry again. 'These other men must have been friends of the man who fled. They told the guard that Arezki... your friend Hassan was one of the loudest.'

Mohand's jaw tightened. His nails were digging into his palms. Hassan. Why had he suddenly taken against him? Did he really blame him for the split with Simone?

He would know who the brothers were. He would know that if

something happened to them that he, Mohand would be hurt by it. Was he really that petty? Whatever was going on in the man's mind, Mohand couldn't allow bad things to happen to his friends. He had few enough of those.

One day, he and Hassan would have a reckoning and he hoped it would be one day soon. In the meantime, he had a friend to save and he would do whatever was in his power to do. Even if it meant putting himself in danger.

Mohand sat down on a chair and rubbed his face with his hands. What he was about to do could get him into serious trouble. He might lose every privilege he had worked for and possibly be sent back out to the logging camps. He took a deep breath and held his hands out. They were shaking. However, he really had no choice; he had to do what he could to save a fellow Berber.

He knew that this went against everything he had learned since he came to the colony, but he couldn't ignore the urgency that told him he must do something about this situation.

He had come to this prison so that his cousin wouldn't face the guillotine. The thought of another friend in such danger made him sick. He couldn't, wouldn't allow anyone else to suffer like this.

Aware of the tremble in his voice, he gave Aissa some instructions.

'This is what I want you to do. Go and get me some gold dust and don't let anyone know about it. Once I have the gold, I will take some action. For now, don't worry about anything.'

In the colony, gold dust was collected and sold mainly to Chinese shops. Most of the convicts knew where to get the gold dust cheaply if they could find the money. And although the brothers were poor, Mohand knew they would have a secret stash, which they would be saving for an emergency. Surely this was one such situation. He had the gold himself, but by his measure if he was going to take a huge risk, then the person he was helping had to be equally committed.

The fear faded from Aissa's face as he listened to Mohand speak. It was clear he had absolute faith in his friend. Mohand stood and wiped his hands on his trousers. Aissa jumped to his feet and, leaning forward, he kissed Mohand on each cheek.

'Thank you. Thank you,' he said and then ran from the room.

***

A day later, Aissa arrived at the office while Mohand was working. His presence was announced by one of the convicts employed as a guard. Mohand stood up from behind his desk and walked to the door. As he did so, he looked back over his shoulder and asked his deputy to keep an eye on things in his absence.

With a confidence he did not feel, he walked Aissa to his room. Once the door was closed behind them, Aissa pulled a white cloth from his pocket. He unfolded it on the bed.

'Here is the gold dust you asked for.' He took a step back from it as if it might infect him. 'Is this enough?

Mohand nodded and offered Aissa a tentative smile. This was enough. Enough to try and bribe someone. Enough to get him locked up if he was found and charged. He nodded again, leaned forward and tidied up the gold.

'You can go now,' he said to Aissa. 'And don't worry about anything. I will get back to you once I have an update. The two men hugged each other and Aissa left the room.

With Aissa gone from the room, Mohand once again considered what he was about to do. Thanks to the mayor's party, he had met a few important people. One of whom had become his friend: the Indian judge, Kathari. On more than one occasion he had been invited to the judge's home, where they would sit and sip from cups of tea and chat about the world they had each found themselves in. Despite his prominent position, the judge still felt himself to be an outcast and he felt a form of freedom in Mohand's company that he couldn't achieve with anyone else.

Before Mohand could persuade himself of the folly of his action, he placed the folded white cotton into a pocket and left his room to start the short fifteen-minute walk to the judge's house.

He had a large, beautiful house in a quiet corner of the town, between the beach and the town square. Mohand had deliberately chosen to go at this time because he knew that Judge Kathari would not be at home. He had huge respect for the man, but was unsure of how he would react to the request he was about to put to him. No, it was far better that he speak to the judge's wife, Ameena. She was grateful to Mohand for the friendship he offered her husband and was clearly fond of him. She would provide a good sounding board for his request, meaning that his question would find the judge's ears without placing either man in an awkward situation. Normally, Mohand would not use his friendships to achieve any favours, but this was a drastic situation. To help his fellow Berber in such a desperate time, he would do anything.

When he arrived at their front door, the sun beat on his head remorselessly. As did the voice in his mind that ordered him to go back and not to do what he was about to. For reasons he could not explain to himself, he was locked into this course of action. He knew better than to bribe a camp official. He knew how much trouble this could get him into, but he had to do this. He had to make absolutely sure that his Berber friend did not face the guillotine.

He looked around to see if anyone was watching. He tidied himself and took a couple of deep breaths then knocked on the door. He was expecting a servant to answer the door and was surprised when the judge's wife opened the door herself.

'Mohand', her face brightened when she recognised him, 'what a lovely surprise. Come in, it's been too long since we last saw you.' She gave him a small hug and invited him into her home.

The house was cool and bright. Richly coloured fabrics were everywhere, giving the house a vivid, yet welcome feel.

'Please, Mohand, come this way. We will have tea and you can tell me all of your news.' Ameena spoke brightly, conveying none of the curiousity that must have been scratching at her mind.

They sat in tall armchairs in the main salon. Over coffee and pastries they spoke for a time about life in the colony, the war and all sorts of other things.

'Why don't we see so much of you these days, Mohand? My husband does so enjoy chatting with you,' she said in a mock scolding voice. Her face then folded with concern. 'This is not the kind of visit you made in the past, Mohand. You knew my husband would be at work...' Her expression sharpened and she leaned forward. 'You want my husband to do something for you. But something you are unwilling to approach him about.'

For the first time since meeting this couple, Mohand got a glimpse of the quick mind behind those large, bright eyes. As a dutiful wife, she clearly deferred to her husband in public, but Mohand was now sure that in private this woman was quite a force behind her husband's decisions.

The gold lurking in his pocket, light as it was, weighed heavily against his leg. Should he go ahead with his plan? What if she threw him out? She could have him thrown into solitary confinement. While his mind worked, he held his hands before him on his lap, afraid that if he held them out she would see them shaking.

'Mohand', her voice was low, concerned, 'is there something we can help you with?'

He met and held her gaze for a moment, while the debate continued in his mind.

'Well, what is it? Are you going to keep me in suspense?'

Mohand took a deep breath and told Ameena the story of the two brothers. 'I am convinced that Arezki has been arrested by mistake. I know him very well and I can give you my word that he is innocent. He was pointed out as the only suspect by a man who will do anything to harm me and the people I care about.'

As soon as he finished talking, he put one hand in his pocket to pull out the gold. He leaned forward, opened her hand and put the white cloth full of gold dust on it.

She shook her head slowly. By the expression on her face she was clearly aware of the ramifications of this action and equally aware of how things were made to happen in this colony.

Fear burned in Mohand's chest. He could only take narrow breaths.

'No, Mohand, I will not take this from a friend,' she said at last. 'My husband will help and see that justice is done.' She refused to take the gold. While she was trying to push the cloth back to him, he turned around and walked out of the room. By the time he reached the door, he was running.

'Mohand, come back. Mohand...' she shouted. Mohand ignored her and kept running. He reached the corner without looking back once. He ran as fast as he could in the direction of Lacroix's café.

When he entered the bar, he was struggling to catch his breath.

Lacroix simply shrugged, as if he saw this kind of behaviour everyday and carried on rinsing out the rum tumblers in a barrel of rainwater.

Mohand sat down and with a shaky voice ordered a jug of tafia.

'Anything else, my friend?' asked Lacroix as he leaned over with a jug and a tumbler. He filled the tumbler and continued. 'Some kerosene and a match, perhaps?'

'What?' Mohand looked up at the larger man confused.

'You look shit scared, my friend. Douse yourself in kerosene. Light it with a match and it's all over. Meanwhile, we get the bonus of a nice fire to keep us warm.'

'Shut up, Lacroix.'

The big man went back to his work with a chuckle.

With trembling fingers, Mohand took a grip of the tumbler. He had just attempted to corrupt an official of the colony. This action could earn him, at best, another five years onto his sentence or, at worst, a trip to the guillotine. This wasn't just any official; this was the head of the judiciary in this colony. If word ever got out, Judge Kathari would have no option but to protect his reputation and that of his wife. He held the tumbler to his mouth and tipped it back.

He was not worried about Ameena or the judge. He was more worried that he had been seen leaving their house at such an unusual time. If this were to get out, the couple would be forced to come up with a viable reason. They were an honourable pair and would not find it easy to lie.

That evening, he was sick. He attempted to eat, but everything he put in his stomach forced itself back out. His fear turned into a strong fever. He spent the whole night wrapped in his thin cotton sheets, shivering. He could not throw the fear from his mind or the crazy thoughts it encouraged. He would be caught. The couple would be disgraced. Someone would say they were having an affair and, to save his wife's reputation, Judge Kathari would be forced to say what actually happened. As soon as this was known, Mohand would be marched to the guillotine.

Dark thought after dark thought crowded his mind and clawed at his conscience.

The next day was interminably long. Distracted, he could achieve nothing and drew worried glances from his office staff. He counted each minute as it wound its way round the large clock on the far wall. The news would come soon. The *gendarmes* would come for him any second.

The day passed without incident and Mohand spent the night in much the same position as he had the one before. The next day passed in the same pattern. One of his office workers worked up the courage to ask him what was wrong and, for his trouble, received an order to carry out one of the least popular jobs in the office.

The next day was exactly the same. Uneasiness fluttered in his chest every time someone spoke to him. Each time someone with a uniform walked towards him, it was all he could do not to hold his hands forward, waiting for a set of manacles to be locked onto his wrists.

On the third day, he saw Aissa walking towards him from afar. Immediately, his mind threw up the worst possible outcome, until he got closer and Mohand could see a large smile on his face.

When he reached Mohand, Aissa embraced him and kissed him on the cheeks many more times than usual. During this performance, his voice was high with joy.

'He was freed this morning, Mohand. He was freed.'

Mohand held Aissa by the shoulders. 'Good, I am glad,' he said. Relief washed over him. If he hadn't a good hold of Aissa, he was sure that his legs would have given out and he would have crumpled to the floor.

'I don't know how to thank you for saving my brother.' A tear washed its way down Aissa's face.

'Your thanks are enough, my brother,' said Mohand.

'The judge is a wonderful man. I didn't know that these people could be so...' He searched for a word.

'Tell me, what happened,' asked Mohand.

'Arezki was freed this morning. Just before his release was announced, the judge came to see me. He said that he was a man of reason and if my brother was arrested unjustly, we should not worry. Then without another word, he returned the gold dust and left the room.'

TEN

A Letter

A guard was handing letters around the office. As usual, Mohand ignored him, his face aimed at his papers. He became aware that the guard had stopped in front of him. Mohand looked up.

With a smile David Faber held forward a small brown square of folded paper.

'It has your name on it,' Faber stated as if he was talking to a child. 'It's a letter from your home.'

Mohand simply stared at him. Home. He didn't have a home.

'You're from Algeria, aren't you?'

Obeying a neural impulse he wasn't aware of, Mohand managed to hold out a hand. A letter from home. He felt his legs weaken. He didn't know if he could open it. He had spent all this time constructing a protective barrier against thoughts of home and family and it was shattered in seconds.

'Oh, and the director wants to see you in his office,' said the guard, patting Mohand on the shoulder. 'Now.'

The guard was about five hundred yards away before Mohand moved. He simply stared at the envelope. Then he read it. Strangely, it was not addressed to him but to the director of the prison.

Should he find a match and burn it? Could he read it? Or destroy it. His mind presented opposing arguments. His gut roiled. Reminders of home were nothing but a quick route to the sanitarium or a short hop into the dark maw of the jungle.

However... his heart longed for words from his homeland.

After this long silence from Algeria, his heart and a burning curiosity were too strong to resist. Before he knew it, he was pulling the letter from the inside of the envelope.

He started reading.

...we hunger for news of our sons. The world is a difficult place now but we would take strength knowing that our three menfolk still draw breath under the same sun...

The letter was penned in the careful script of Caid Mezaine, who surely must be nearly one hundred years old. Its contents, rather than pleasing him, worried him. The family had written to the prison authorities desperate for information. They didn't know that Arab and Ali were dead. His gut twisted at the impact this news might have on his family back home.

He could not and would not be the one to tell them.

By the time he arrived at the director's office, a cold anger burned in his stomach.

'Did you read the letter from home?' the director asked.

'Yes.' Mohand paused. Anger would get him nowhere. He took a deep calming breath. 'I am surprised to hear that they have never been informed of the deaths of Ali and Arab.'

The director chose to ignore the tone of Mohand's inquiry. 'Do you want me to inform them?'

'Of course I do. This should be the responsibility of the authorities.' By now Mohand was completely uncaring of how he might be perceived.

The director nodded as if considering the idea for the first time. 'You are right, convict, your family should have been informed of this. I will correct this omission. In the meantime, I want you to start writing home. I can't have families writing to me demanding news of our prisoners.' He studied Mohand from the other side of the desk. 'Is this too much to ask?'

Mohand laughed, taken aback by the director's request.

'Sir, it's been a long time since I wrote home. I have no idea what to say.'

He looked Mohand in the eyes and said, 'Just write anything that comes to your mind.'

Mohand stepped back from the director's desk, his mind working on the thought. What would he say? What on earth would they want to know about his experience in the prison? He thought about the great excitement that would surely take hold of everyone when they crowded around Caid Mezaine, waiting for him to give voice to the script on the page. He imagined eager smiling faces. Old and young alike, holding their breath.

Who was he to deny them this moment of happiness?

'I will write a letter today.'

As he walked back to his office, his mind was crowded with words that he might say. Sentences jostled for his attention and each of them were quickly dismissed. Everything that suggested itself to him was summarily dismissed. It all seemed so small. So meaningless. So ineffective. He wanted to communicate with them, but what did he want to say?

Should he talk about the actions of his day? Would they want to know about the few real friends he had? The monotony of his world, the small amount of privilege he had earned and how quickly it might be taken away from him would be difficult to articulate on the page.

Once in his office, he pulled a crisp piece of white paper from a drawer and placed it on the desk before him. The clean space before him was daunting. How to best fill it? He quickly scratched the date on the top right hand corner, like an act of defiance, before he lost his courage.

Should he mention the fact that the *bagne* had been ruled illegal and a law passed to ensure its closure? All these months after hearing this news and still they were no closer to being released. The French seem to have a singular talent at ignoring their own laws.

With pen poised to write, he stopped. What was the point? He was surely going to die in this cursed place. But still, he was determined he should write something.

After all this deliberation he placed a pen on the page and wrote without thought, allowing his sub-conscious mind to decide what he should communicate. When he lifted the pen, there were five words in the middle of the page.

On vit et on espère

He spoke the words out loud – 'We live and hope' – and folded the page. His words were apt. That was the only thing that could clearly explain how he felt. All he had was hope. He went on waking in the morning, working one leg before the other into his prison-issue uniform and pouring all of his energy into his work while hoping that at some time in the future he might have a life that would not be dictated to him by the rhythm and needs of such an establishment.

With a delicate touch, he placed the paper inside an envelope as if he hoped his attention and love would filter from the paper into the hearts and minds of the people who read and heard his message.

Once the envelope was addressed, he dropped it in the prison letterbox. Before he let it go, he almost plucked it back out. For the briefest of moments he examined his motivation. He hoped fervently that the family did not decide to reply. He did not want to read any news from home. He did not want to know how they were suffering, as they would surely be, during this period of worldwide conflict. He would only feel worse knowing there was nothing he could offer by way of assistance.

Again he determined that this was the last time he would ever write home. And the last time he would ever open a letter sent from home. He bit down on his lower lip and choked back on a tear. It was better for him to forget that he had a family or a past. There was only now, this moment that he must endure.

There could be nothing else.

ELEVEN

Thoughts of Freedom

It was spring of 1945 and thanks to stolen moments with a radio, Mohand was aware that the Soviets had pushed the Germans before them, from the Vistula in Poland to the Oder River in Germany. Rumour grew on rumour. Ears were buzzing every night down at Lacroix's bar, as the *libérés* and prisoners alike fed their hunger for supposition, guesswork and hope.

Hope lit in every man's chest with every passing day. The war was being won by the Allies. Those who stood for freedom were coming out on top and surely that energy would carry through to the French administration.

'The French will surely come to their senses and close this place once and for all.' That was the opinion that Mohand heard voiced every day. The mood among the convicts was as positive as Mohand had ever experienced it. Gossip and guesses were never good enough for him. He had to hear it from a reliable source, so he visited his Chinese friend with a view to buying a radio. Ownership of such an item would have led to a serious reprimand so he hid the radio in a under a loose board in his room. Mohand would sit in his room after an evening with his few friends at the bar and, with his small second-hand radio pressed to his ear, listen to news bulletin after news bulletin about the war as it raged all over the globe.

Months later and the war was still being fought. Freedom was less certain, but hope still burned in hearts of the *bagnards*.

With his radio, Mohand learned on 12th April that the American president, Roosevelt, died. Mussolini was killed by Italian partisans on 28th April and two days later Hitler shot himself.

In May of that year, it was announced that the Germans had surrendered. That night, the celebrations at Lacroix's bar were loud, with many of the men spending their last few sous on a jug of tafia.

Mohand thought that this must spell the end of the war, and surely the end of the war would mean the French would eventually close the *bagne*?

He gathered his meager belongings on top of his bed. Two pairs of trousers, a shirt and some socks. They were clean and still in good shape, with only a few holes in the fabric where the seams had worn over time. He found some needle and thread and worked into the small hours over a number of evenings to repair them. If freedom was coming, he wanted to look his best.

Despite the surrender of the Germans, the Japanese continued fighting. Hope was dampened by Japan's refusal to capitulate. News then filtered through of events at Hiroshima and Nagasaki.

The men stumbled over the thought of that for days. Two full cities had been wiped from the face of the Earth. The idea that a bomb possessed enough energy to snub out all those lives and to cause so much destruction was beyond their comprehension.

Eventually, Mohand heard that on 2nd September, 1945, Japan had surrendered.

Lacroix's bar was crowded that night. Men jostled for elbow room in the small space. Tafia was ordered by the jug. Every mouth gripped a cigarette. Voices were raised with hope and expectation. The end of the war could surely mean only one thing?

Cigarette smoke hung in the air like the ghosts of those who had failed to combat the dangers of the *bagne* while men talked about friends who had died.

Mohand was leaning over his wooden tumbler, elbows resting on the table, watching his friends as they drank. He tried to remember both Armand and Simone as they were when he first came across them. Studying them, it appeared that Armand had had the hardest time. He was all bone and gristle, his cheeks sunken due to constant hunger and a lack of teeth. However, the change in Simone was more profound. Sure, in a health comparison with Armand, he would win, but there was a haunted acceptance in the slant of his shoulders and the tremor of his occasional smile.

How about his own appearance? He had aged as well, would his family recognise him?

Mohand considered Simone's muted reaction to the news. When did this happen? When did his friend become so beaten up by this place that he all but gave in?

He felt irritation rise. He reached across and gripped Simone's forearm.

'Freedom. It's so close I can smell it,' Mohand said.

'Your nose is too near your arse, my friend,' Simone answered and took a quick sip of his drink.

'You don't believe that the end of the war will bring freedom for all of us?' Mohand could feel any concern at his friend's demeanor vanish from his mind. He wanted this dream of hope so much he couldn't bear it that his friend didn't agree with him.

'I believe in what I have in front of me, Mohand.' He picked up his tumbler and offered it to the air in front of him. 'I believe in this shot of tafia.' He pulled at his left cheek.

'I believe in the dry and droopy skin on my face. I believe I will die in this place.' He patted Armand on the shoulder. 'I also believe that Armand's penis has withered to the size of a button from lack of use.'

'Hey…' Armand protested. 'I'm just sitting here minding my own business.' He paused a beat and then offered a toothless grin. 'But you are right, it is withered.'

'This is shit,' Mohand said, jumping to his feet. No one was as surprised as he at how quickly his anger had risen. 'Look at you…' he pointed at Simone. 'You've all but given in.'

'C'mon, Mohand,' Armand said, reaching up and tugging at his sleeve. 'Have a seat. Let's not have anger among friends.'

'Friends, pah. Friends would not...' Hot with irritation, he pulled his arm from Armand's grip. 'Give up and the French have won.' He turned away, but not before he caught the wounded look on Armand's face. But his anger demanded more fuel and would not allow him to seek conciliation yet.

'Look at this.' Mohand jerked his shirt open with such force a button popped off. 'This eagle is free and one day so will I be.'

Armand studied the eagle tattoo as if he had never seen it before. Simone's eyes slid off Mohand's chest on to the floor.

'Freedom is an illusion, my friend,' Simone said. 'No one is free. Look at the guards, the *libérés,* even the indigenous people of this shithole. We are all prisoners of one kind or another.' His eyes now drilled into Mohand's. His pupils were large black dots of hopelessness. 'You'd think after all these years here a clever man like yourself would have learned that particular lesson.' He laughed. A quick sharp note that sounded more like a bark. He drained his tumbler.

'You are crazy if…' Mohand began.

'No. You are the crazy one.' Simone jumped to his feet. They were now face to face, glaring at each other. Simone pushed a hand in to his pocket and pulled out a coin. He placed it on his palm and displayed one side and then the other.

'Heads or tails. Hope and despair. Two sides of the same coin, Mohand. And you continually change from one state to the other. That, my friend is crazy. To stay sane in this place, you need to kick hope into the corner and ignore it. Better still fling it into the latrine and piss on it.'

Mohand would not allow himself to hear the truth in Simone's voice and the words that he had often thought and said himself. To retain some sort of sanity in this place, a man needed to forget that he had any chance of another life. The luxury of a dream was the quickest route to an unhinged mind. He knew this. He had told himself this on numerous occasions. However, today, he would not, could not, listen to this reasoning. He would be free.

'No one, least of all a man's best friend, should pour piss on his dreams,' he said and then turned to leave the room.

'Mohand. Simone. You two are friends. Don't argue like this.'

Mohand could hear Armand's words follow him as he walked outside. He could almost see the pain in the little man's expression as he tried to bring conciliation to his friends. But he was having none of it.

Anger burned in his chest and tightened the line of his jaw. So focused was he on this, that he didn't hear the song of the insects or feel the heat and moisture of the humid air. It was only when he almost tripped over a man's foot that he realised he had company.

'What the…' He stumbled back a pace or two, righting himself. 'Armand, what are you…?' He looked into the other man's face through the gloom of the evening. He had a familiar outline, the same soul-less smile.

'Hassan, what the hell are you playing at?' he asked. Hassan's chest was rising and falling as if he had run to be in this position.

'So, you have fallen out with your friends?'

Before he knew it, Mohand's fingers were around the other man's throat.

'Don't test me. Not tonight, or I swear by the *thimeshrats* I will tear your throat out and leave your sorry carcass for the insects.' He pushed Hassan away from him before he did any harm and stalked off into the night, looking for a degree of peace that he knew would evade him until his feet were on Algerian soil once more.

TWELVE

Welcome News

The night of Mohand's argument with Simone was quickly forgotten. The next day the two men hugged each other and laughed at themselves.

'Here,' grinned Simone, pretending to fumble at the waist of his trousers. 'Let me piss on that dream of yours one more time.'

Mohand gripped his friend on the shoulder. 'And I will take that coin of yours and shove it up your arse.' Both men collapsed on each other, laughter ringing in the air like a shower of new pennies.

Armand simply stood by watching them, completely at a loss as to how the same words issued in anger could cause such offence and yet here they were laughing like a pair of village idiots.

'You should have seen your face,' giggled Simone. 'The way you pulled back your shirt...' and off they went again.

Mohand read the look of confusion on Armand's face. He patted him on the back. With his other, he reached across and gripped Simone's shoulder. Affection for the older man caught in his throat.

'This man...' He coughed, releasing the knot of emotion. 'I love like a brother. And you should know, Armand, that the day a man can't laugh at himself is the day he should run into the jungle and jump into the mouth of the first caiman he sees.'

'Right,' Armand nodded, unconvinced but, unable to avoid the contagion of his friends' good humour, he joined in.

***

Some days later, Mohand arrived at Lacroix's bar after twelve hours bent over a desk to find Simone standing at the front door. His hair had been cut and combed. His face was clean-shaven. A smile hung warily on his cheeks.

'I heard this morning,' he said, shuffling his feet nervously. To Mohand, he looked like he was about to jump out of his skin. And yet he was holding back for fear of upsetting his friend. 'My sentence is over. I'm a free man.'

'Allah be praised.' Mohand rushed to him and gathered him in a hug. Then he kissed him on both cheeks.

'Simone, I couldn't be happier for you.' He felt like his grin would split his face in half.

'You're not...' Simone looked at him, his expression torn between joy and concern.

'Jealous? You were worried I might be jealous?'

Simone nodded.

'This gift to you costs me nothing, Simone. Why would I be jealous?' Mohand asked.

'I never thought this day would come, Mohand.' Simone's eyes shone with tears. 'I thought I would die in this place. I was convinced of it.'

Inside the bar, Lacroix set up the jug and the tumblers. 'Bugger me,' he said when he heard Simone's news. 'I might be doing a roaring trade at the moment, but I'm losing one of my best customers.'

'You'll just have to go back to France and make an honest living, Lacroix.'

'I can never go back to France, Saoudi,' Lacroix replied. The light in his eyes dimmed for a moment, darkened by a moment of memory. 'Besides, some of you poor bastards will never be able to leave this place and you'll need somewhere to drown your sorrows.' The smile was back in place.

He turned and walked over to a group at a neighbouring table. Mohand watched his retreating back and felt shame that, despite all the time he had spent in this bar, he had never thought to hear the man's story.

'...Are you not listening, Mohand?' Simone was tugging at his sleeve.

'Sorry, I was thinking of you in Paris, pimping yourself under the Eiffel Tower.'

'Ha,' laughed Simone. 'I can't imagine any self-respecting woman wanting to pay to go with this bag of bones.'

'I thought you were...'

'A pederast? No, Mohand. Some of us just needed comfort and a human touch and were less choosy than others where they found it.'

'So. You were saying while I rudely imagined you in Paris?'

'Right. Paris. I'll be there very soon, my friend.'

'Seriously? Soon?' Mohand was astonished. Although the authorities were giving Simone his freedom, there was still the practicality of how he might return home. There would be no return voyage paid for by the penal colony. If freemen wanted to go home, they had to find the ways and means on their own.

Mohand had heard of charitable organisations that had stepped in to help some of the men return to Europe. As this thought entered his mind, Simone mentioned one of them.

'The Salvation Army has arranged passage for me on a boat that leaves next week.'

'Next week?' Mohand fought to hide his feeling of disappointment. He was going to lose his friend so soon?

Simone nodded fiercely. 'It seems I am just such a Christian gentleman who is deserving of their help and... who am I to say no?'

'Fantastic news, Simone.' Mohand turned away from his friend to allow him a moment to arrange his features into an expression of happiness. He was going to miss Simone terribly but he couldn't let this spoil the man's moment. 'Another jug, Lacroix.'

'But you haven't finished that one yet, Saoudi,' bounced back the big man's reply.

'And your point is?' demanded Mohand.

The evening passed in a fog of smoke and tafia. A crowd gathered round their table and Simone, more animated than normal, took centre stage. He spoke of his life in Paris before he had been sent to French Guiana.

'I was innocent, of course,' he said, to much laughter. 'After all, there are no guilty men in a prison such as this.'

While his friend regaled them all with tall tales of his youth, Mohand studied him and considered the man he might have become had he not been sent across the ocean to such a place. He seemed brighter, sharper, clearer. There was more of him somehow, and only now that home was just a week away was he allowing the real Simone to the surface.

'Right, you bunch of reprobates, time you were all crawling into whatever ditch you call home,' roared Lacroix. 'I need to tidy up and get my beauty sleep.'

A few men grumbled. It was too early for the night to be over, they thought. But no one argued. Lacroix was too big and too handy with his thick stick.

The men stumbled out into the dark, humid air. As a crowd, they walked in the direction of their accommodation. Simone was so drunk he was walking one step forward, one step back and then one step to the side.

Mohand was also affected by the alcohol but not to such a great degree as his friend. They fell behind the larger group while he tried to help Simone travel in the direction of his cell.

Although there was not much of him, he was a dead weight as Mohand tried to steer him along the dark path. He was tempted to leave him to sleep it off at the side of the road, but he let this thought pass. This was the man's party night. He should wake safe in his own bunk, not covered in insect bites at the side of the road. He was bound to have a monster of a headache. Let that be all that he suffers on this night of all night.

'You are a good friend, Mohand,' Simone mumbled. 'I've never really told you that I love you, have I? He took a half-step to the side. 'You never judged me. You just… you were my friend. A good friend.'

'I know, Simone.' Mohand was warmed by his friend's admission. He tried to deflect it. 'Someone other than me would just leave your drunken carcass at the side of the road.'

'Drunken carcass. Drunken carcass. Drunken carcass,' Simone stumbled over the sibilant note at the end of the phrase. 'S'easy for you to say.'

Mohand laughed at his friend. He'd never seen him quite so drunk.

He heard another note of laughter coming from the near distance, further along the path. At first he thought it was the larger group of men they had been with earlier. Then he realised the sound was moving closer to them.

Mohand peered through the darkness trying to work out who it was.

'Armand? Is that you, Armand?'

'And here we are yet again,' a familiar voice said. Hassan.

'What do you want?' Mohand felt his head clear as adrenalin surged through him. His convict sixth sense was instantly on full alert.

'This is how you celebrate your freedom, Saoudi. How ordinary.' As the man talked, he moved closer.

'What are you talking about, you halfwit. It's Simone who's been freed.'

'He doesn't even know,' the man laughed and moved closer. 'How delicious.'

'Hassan, what the hell are you talking about?' Mohand demanded.

'I salute you who are about to die,' Hassan said, his voice hard. He moved another step closer and Mohand could see that his arm was outstretched. Just then a cloud cleared from the moon and its silver light shone on an implement that Hassan was pointing in his direction.

Jutting from the clench of his fist was the long, silver barrel of a gun.

THIRTEEN

Fight and Flight

'Harrrummm,' sang Simone and held a clumsy hand to his forehead. 'I salute you,' he repeated. He tried to click his heels together, the result of which didn't please him, judging by the way he then stared at his feet. 'Dust. Need concrete. Shoes would be good, too.' He giggled, completely oblivious to the danger they were in.

While Simone mumbled, Mohand dared not take his eyes off Hassan and the gun.

'Where did you get the toy, Hassan?' Mohand asked. He chose his words carefully. He didn't want to alert Simone to the truth of the matter; drunk as he was, he might do something stupid. He also thought that the word 'toy' might irritate Hassan. Mohand had learned by now that the man who kept his cool in a fight was usually the one who won.

'From the same source that I found out about your freedom.'

'Free,' sang Simone as he performed a little drunken dance. 'I'm free.' He waved his arms in the air and danced towards Hassan. Mohand's heart lurched until he saw Simone dancing back and away.

'A very important man told me, Mohand. He then fell asleep... and I managed to get my hands on his... toy.' Hassan raised his eyebrows. 'I can't bear the thought of you being free. I can't bear the thought of you doing anything while I'm in this hell.'

'Hassan...' Mohand took a step closer.

'Don't move any closer. Do you realise how much I hate you, Saoudi? Before you die, you need to realise how much I hate you.' His hand shook as he spoke.

Heart hammering at his chest, Mohand thought frantically about what he should do. How could he get out of this situation alive? He needed to get the gun off Hassan. He needed to get in close before he had time to pull the trigger. One thing was for sure, he wouldn't let Hassan kill him without putting up a fight.

'If it wasn't for you, I wouldn't be in this hell.' With his free hand, Hassan knocked on the side of his head, his expression wild with self-loathing. It was clear that the hell he referred to was not the *bagne*. 'You fought off Zaydane on *Le Martinière* and he turned to me. The things that man made me do.' Saliva sprayed from Hassan's mouth. 'But then he protected me. Other men, more dangerous men, wanted me and Zaydane fought them off... and you killed him.'

'That's not true, Hassan. He fell into the creek. A caiman got him.'

'The only thing I know is that the two of you went into the jungle and only one of you ever came back. And from that moment on I was anybody's.' Hassan had control of his emotions now and the gun was trained at Mohand's chest.

Simone continued to perform his little dance, backwards and forwards. He picked up the odd word from the other men's conversation and sang it repeatedly. As he watched him move, Mohand realised that there was a purpose to the seemingly random movements of the older man. Wherever his dance took him, it appeared that he never moved in front of the gun, but each time he moved away from Hassan and moved back, he was closer to the object of danger. Perhaps he wasn't as drunk as he was making out.

Mohand had sobered immediately at the sight of the gun.

'Anybody's and everybody's until Simone came along.' Hassan's eyes shifted from Mohand's face to Simone's and a brief look of affection flitted across his eyes. 'But I never stopped hating you. You were the golden boy. Everything you touched worked out well, yet before I met Simone I was...' He fought to control himself. 'It all comes down to you, Saoudi.'

As he was speaking, the arm holding the gun had drooped until the weapon was pointing at the earth. His eyes dark with the heat of his resentment, he again lifted the gun and pointed it at Mohand's chest.

'It's such a happy coincidence that I get to kill you just before you become a free man.' He smiled and delayed the moment of his gratification.

This gave Simone his chance. He danced in closer to Hassan and made a grab for the gun.

'Run, Mohand, run!' Simone shouted.

Mohand had no such intention. Hassan fought to re-train the gun on Mohand while Simone clung on to his arms, pushing them towards the earth. Mohand jumped in closer to Hassan and aimed a punch at his chin. He felt his knuckle connect and aimed another one. Hassan managed to duck and the punch sailed past his ear.

Both Simone and Hassan now had their hands on the gun. Mohand had to get it away. He too placed his hands on Hassan's and, when he was close enough, butted his nose with his forehead.

Hassan grunted. The pain and the surprise of it was enough for him to lose his grip on the weapon. Simone failed to track the movement and he too lost his grip on the gun. A small thud sounded as it fell to the ground.

'Shit, shit, shit.' Simone fell to his knees. 'I've lost the gun.'

'Doesn't matter,' said Hassan, blinking against the pain that flared across his face. 'I'll kill the bastard with my bare hands.'

'You're welcome to try,' said Mohand, facing off to his adversary.

Another thing that Mohand had learned during his years as a convict was to get in fast, cause maximum damage and then get back out again. Mohand leaped towards him and aimed a punch at his nose. He felt it connect. Before Hassan could shrug off the pain he let out another. He aimed for Hassan's gut. The man took it and threw a punch of his own.

He caught Mohand on the side of the head. The impact stunned and slowed Mohand's movements for a moment. This allowed Hassan to get in a few more punches of his own. Mohand was surprised by the other man's strength. He looked like nothing but a collection of bones, yet he was giving as good as he got.

Mohand's breathing was now ragged. His head hurt. His knuckles hurt. He was struggling to hold up his arms. The long night of drinking was beginning to take its toll. He had to finish this off quickly.

He could still hear Simone scrabbling about in the dark for the gun and judging by his grunts of frustration he was getting nowhere.

Getting the strength from somewhere, Mohand threw a punch at Hassan's gut. Then another one. He was rewarded with a satisfying groan and the sound of air being expelled from the other man's lungs.

'I can't find the fucking gun,' Simone cried. Mohand turned to where his friend was rooting about in the undergrowth by the side of the path.

This moment was distraction enough for Hassan. He had his hands around Mohand's throat. His breath hot and foul on Mohand's cheek.

Hassan brought his head forward with a sharp crash onto Mohand's nose. He felt the shock burst across his face and the blood spill metallic on his lip and down his chin. The pain must have been almost as bad for Hassan as the two men reeled apart.

They stood facing each other, struggling for breath, adrenalin trembling through their limbs, each trying to clear the pain from their heads. Hassan recovered first. His kick caught Mohand in the gut, and he fell forward. He tried to get up. Hassan wouldn't give him the space. Kicks and punches rained down on his back.

From the ground, Mohand kicked out so that his heel crunched into Hassan's shin. He howled with the pain. Pushing up, Mohand came to his feet and launched himself afresh at Hassan.

Both men fell to the ground with Mohand on top. He clawed at the other man's face, his eyes. Hassan did his best to throw him off, but Mohand was desperate. He could feel himself tire even more. He *had* to end this.

From his position, Mohand straddled Hassan and hammered punches down on the other man's face. One after another he aimed at Hassan's nose. He became an automaton. All he could do was form a fist and punch. He was completely unaware that the other man's struggles had all but ceased.

He felt Simone tugging at his shoulder.

'Enough, Mohand. Can't you tell he's had enough?'

'No. Never.' Mohand grabbed Hassan by the throat and began to squeeze.

'Go on, Saoudi. Finish me...'

Mohand's grip tightened. Hassan's eyes bulged. His heels scuffed at the earth as he fought for oxygen.

'Enough, Mohand, please,' Simone begged him.

'It's never enough, Simone. This man will not be happy until I am dead. It's either him or me.'

'It doesn't have to be that way, Mohand. You're better than that. You came here an innocent man. You must leave the same way. If you don't, the system has won.'

Gasping for breath, Mohand allowed Simone to pull him off. His friend's words reached him through his anger. Simone was right. He was better than that. He had struggled all these years to retain his sense of self. He could not give in to the de-humanising process now. He stood up and leaning forward with his hands just above his knees, he fought to control his breath. As he did so he was able to see his handiwork.

Even in the moonlight he could see that Hassan's face was a mass of bruising and blood.

'You're lucky, Hassan. If I kill you, I'm just as bad as every man who has abused you. Worse in fact.' As he spoke, Mohand felt a strong surge of pity for the man. Perhaps he was right. If he hadn't fought off Zaydane, perhaps Hassan's lot would have turned out differently.

He dismissed this thought as he remembered the row of *fort-à-bras* on the boat and how they surveyed the younger, weaker men as nothing but prey. If Zaydane hadn't got his hands on him, someone else would have. Hassan had 'victim' stamped on his forehead the second the authorities tattooed his convict number on his forearm.

'We could have been friends, Hassan.' He looked down at the younger man.

Hassan cleared his mouth of blood and spat his response on to the earth. 'Spare me your pity.'

'C'mon. Let's go,' said Simone, pulling at Mohand's shirt. 'The fight is over. Hassan has learned his lesson.'

With a last look at his prostrate enemy, Mohand allowed himself to be guided back down the path in the direction of his accommodation. He hoped that this was the last he had heard of Hassan, but he somehow doubted it. The man was intent on making him suffer and he doubted that he would ever stop.

As he trudged along the path, Mohand thought about how he could put Hassan out of reach. He still had friends in high places. He could surely use them. All he had to do was find out where Hassan had stolen the gun from and make it known to the right people. Such a crime could not go unpunished and Hassan would be sent to a more secure situation, where he would no longer pose a threat.

So deep in thought and so dim with fatigue was he that Mohand was slow to react to what happened next.

There was the sound of running feet from behind. Simone turned, shouted something and then stepped towards the danger, his arm extended.

'No,' Simone shouted.

A gun fired. Simone collapsed on the ground.

'No,' screamed Hassan.

Mohand fell to his knees and gathered Simone in his arms.

Simone coughed a ribbon of blood from his mouth down his chin. Mohand pulled his friend to him. Rocked with him in his arms. 'Hang on, Simone. We'll get help.' He looked up at Hassan, who was standing above them, his mouth open in a tortured, silent scream.

Hassan forced a breath into his lungs and gave a low moan. 'No, no, no.' The gun tumbled from his fingers and with one last groan, he turned and fled into the darkness.

'Hang on, Simone. Hang on. We'll patch you up, my friend. You'll soon be as good as new,' said Mohand as he rocked back and forth. While the words tumbled from his mind, he recoiled at the horror of it all.

Another country. Another gunshot. Another friend dying in his arms.

Not again. This couldn't be happening again.

'It's too late, my friend. He got me good.' Simone mumbled and coughed again. Blood burst from his mouth.

'Please don't die, Simone. Please don't die,' begged Mohand. It was happening again. Another Frenchman was dying in his arms.

'I told you, didn't I? '

An image of Simone at the bar. His eyes heavy. His words… *I believe I will die in this place.*

He coughed once more. The light in his eyes dimmed and his head slumped to the side.

It was over.

FOURTEEN

An Offer and a Refusal

The report from the gun had brought people running. Lacroix was first on the scene, followed by Armand. While Armand wept, Lacroix took charge.

The first thing he did was to slap Armand across the face. Hard. Stunned, the other man could only hold his face and stare at Lacroix.

'I need you to be calm, Armand. Nod if you are feeling calm.'

Armand nodded.

'*Bien*. Now, take Mohand back to the bar. He's still a prisoner. He can't afford to be involved in the death of another man when a gun has been used. Understand?'

Armand was still holding his cheek and nodding.

'Armand,' Lacroix placed a large paw on his shoulder, 'you need to help your friend here. Do you understand me?'

'I understand you,' Armand croaked. His expression showed that he did indeed understand. The murder of a convict was neither here nor there. It was part of life in the *bagne*, but it would not go unpunished. A few months in solitary. However, on this occasion, a gun had been used. Nothing worried the authorities more than a *bagnard* with a gun. A murder like this would receive the full weight of their displeasure and a short trip up the stairs of the guillotine.

'Mohand, tell me who did this,' Lacroix said, peering down into his face. Mohand simply stared into Lacroix's eyes.

'He shot him. He tried to kill me. He missed me and Simone…'

'Who did it, Saoudi? Tell me who it was.'

'His aim was crap. He got Simone. It was me that was meant…'

Lacroix shook Mohand. 'Saoudi. Tell me. Quick.' He looked up and looked into the distance. He could hear the sound of many running feet. The guards were on their way.

'He knew,' Mohand said to no one in particular. 'He knew he would die here.'

'I have a good idea who did it, anyway,' Lacroix said with a grim certainty. 'Armand, take Mohand. In the back room I have a clean pair of trousers. Get him changed and let him sleep on my bed. Do not leave him.' He raised his eyebrows in warning. 'Do not put your thieving hands on any of my rum. Now go. Go.'

Mohand allowed Armand to guide him back to the bar, where Armand did as Lacroix ordered.

Meanwhile, Lacroix waited over the body for the guards to arrive. Mohand worried that the big man might be in trouble, but Lacroix was well known and trusted by the guards. He had saved them a lot of trouble over the years and his word was good.

* * *

The authorities had no trouble in piecing together the course of events. The hapless guard who had been Hassan's lover was forced to admit his part in the killing. Explaining away the fact of a missing gun was not an easy task. He was given twenty lashes for his stupidity and the call went out that Hassan should be brought to justice.

He was never found.

Like many others before him, he simply disappeared into the jungle. Mohand tried to harden his heart to Hassan. The man had meant him harm from almost the first moment they met. And yet he couldn't bring himself to hate him. If Allah had given Hassan more courage and Mohand less, the situation could have well been switched.

Hassan had been a victim every bit as much as he had and he couldn't allow himself to sit in judgement of the other man's actions. Would he have behaved as Hassan did if he had been given the same experience? Being used as a slave to satisfy another man's sexual depravity was not something Mohand could ever have dealt with. He would rather have died. He couldn't know how that sort of treatment could have changed him.

Time and time again, Mohand was brought back to that night. The fight. The gun. Simone dying in his arms. Was there something he could have done differently? Could he have averted the tragedy if he had behaved in a different way? Should he have killed Hassan while he had his fingers round his throat?

That scene played itself in his mind over and over. Each time, Mohand tried to ignore Simone's words. He was not better than that. He should have killed the bastard when he had the chance. But each time the memory played itself in his mind, he could not bring himself to tighten his grip. He simply did not have it in him to end another man's life.

The *bagne* would not brutalise him.

Another part of the night repeated in his mind. Hassan had mentioned several times that he was a free man. He, Mohand. He had not once said anything to Simone. What did that mean? Hassan had proven himself resourceful over the years at finding out information and yet, on this occasion, he had got it all wrong. Or had he?

Did Hassan know something?

Mohand gave himself a shake. He was a prisoner. It was not his lot to be freed just yet. He couldn't allow himself to think otherwise.

Until the afternoon of 25th September, 1945, when he encountered a florid-faced and excited David Faber. The young guard and he had become friendly over the years, never passing the opportunity to chat.

'Did you hear the news?' David asked while crossing the street.

'What news is this?' Mohand asked, his heart pounding. From the other man's expression, this news was big and it concerned him.

'No. Don't tell me you don't know?' David's smile was huge.

'David, if you don't tell me now, I swear, guard or not, I will punch you.'

'You are a free man, I just heard it an hour ago.'

Mohand's legs weakened. He would have fallen had Faber not held out a hand to steady him.

'It's true. I just heard at the office. They've given you some time off your sentence for good behaviour. Mohand, you're free.'

'I'm...' Mohand could hardly issue the word. 'How...?' He wanted to believe David. But why was he finding out in such a way? 'Shouldn't I be called in to the director's...?'

'Come with me, Saoudi.' Faber placed an arm across his shoulder. 'This is clearly a shock.'

The two men walked to the small cottage where Faber and his wife lived. As he walked in the door, he shouted for her.

'Mohand has been freed, Claire. But he doesn't believe me.'

Claire was a small woman, with long dark hair. She and Mohand had met perhaps once or twice, but nevertheless she was caught up in her husband's excitement and she drew Mohand into a quick hug.

'Congratulations, Mohand.'

Mohand simply stood there. Hands by his sides. Face drained of colour.

'Please, Claire, fetch the man a strong drink. We need to bring the tan back to his cheeks.'

She brought him a small glass full of rum.

Mohand poured it down his throat without pausing for breath. It warmed his belly and clarified his thoughts. He turned to David.

'Swear on the life of your children that what you tell me is true.'

'Mohand, I swear on the lives of my sons, Jacques and Jean-Paul, that I heard this morning that you are a free man.'

'I'm free.' Mohand could feel the sting of tears. 'I'm really free?'

David nodded. Claire dabbed at her eyes.

'Mohand, you are a free man.'

Mohand let out a roar. 'I'm free.'

Then the emotion swamped him. He fell to his knees, his shoulders heaving, his lungs unable to take in enough oxygen.

The noise brought the two boys running.

'*Maman*, why is the man crying?' one of them asked.

Mohand smiled through the tears and stood up. 'Young man, your father has just given me the best news of my life.' He turned and embraced David. Then his wife. Now everyone was laughing. The boys joined in, not sure why they were doing so, simply caught up in the moment.

* * *

The next morning, Mohand woke up to a beautiful day with bright sunshine. He jumped to his feet the moment he was awake. He felt as giddy and excited as a child on his birthday. In fact, he thought to himself, he would celebrate every day from this one as if it was his birthday.

The events of his life played over and over in his mind. His thoughts were like a monkey swinging this way and that among the trees. An image of Zaydane would be replaced with an image of a bright and happy future. A memory of Arab's sunken face would switch to the smiles of his brothers on his return to Algeria.

Algeria.

Maillot.

Would his family have forgotten him? Would they want to see him? He slumped down on to his bed. So many years had passed. Would they still care? Surely he would be nothing but a stranger? Why disturb them from the pattern they would have worked into their lives?

Bending over his little sink, he showered using a small cup to pour the water over his body. He shaved and then prepared his usual breakfast of coffee and a piece of well-buttered bread. He savoured every mouthful. His first breakfast as a free man. He then smoked a couple of cigarettes.

This is my day, he thought, and I will make sure I remember it.

The clothes he had prepared for this moment all those weeks ago were pulled from the box under his bed. He cleaned his shoes and pulled on a pair of new socks.

Once dressed, he appraised himself on the small piece of broken mirror that hung over his sink. Yes, he looked handsome, if a little worn, but not at all like a convict, and what's more he was still young enough to enjoy the freedom and the rest of his life.

He lit another cigarette, put on a new hat that he had set aside with his clothes for just such an occasion and walked out to the street.

For the first time in almost twenty years he did not look like a convict. To the contrary, he felt that he could be mistaken for a wealthy businessman. He headed towards the town with his head high, proud to have made it. Pride was not normally an attitude he would allow himself to foster, but he could not help feeling proud of himself on that day. He had taken everything the system could throw at him and he had survived intact. He was still the same man who had been thrown into that jail cell all those years ago. The brutality, the deprivation and the despair had not taken a hold of him.

He was an honourable man.

He was Kaci Mohand Saoudi.

* * *

He reached the bar at around 11am. Even at this early hour, it was full. Apparently a few others had found out about their freedom the same day as he, and they had gathered to celebrate.

Lacroix spotted him as soon as he walked in the room. He walked towards him, arms wide.

'If I am not mistaken, this is a certain Monsieur Saoudi. A free man?' He boomed.

'How did you … ?'

Lacroix tapped his hat with a fat finger. 'You don't normally dress like this, Mohand.' He grinned. 'So, have I guessed correctly?'

Mohand nodded, feeling his eyes smarting with tears.

Lacroix gathered him into a hug, his big arms squeezing the air from his lungs.

'My god, Lacroix,' Mohand stretched to tap the giant on the side of the head, 'if you don't let me go in the next five seconds, I won't live long enough to enjoy my freedom,' he grunted.

'Ah, quit grumbling, Saoudi. You Berbers are all the same.' He smiled and released his friend. 'I assume a jug of my finest would be in order?'

Mohand bowed. 'You would assume correctly, my good man.'

The next few hours passed in a blur of handshakes, gossip and rum. Smoke filled the small room as if everyone was trying to get through as many cigarettes as they could before they ran out.

Gripped by the bonhomie in the room, Mohand was surfing

along on the feeling of good humour until a thought sobered him: what if this was only a hoax? After all, he still had not received official notification.

He stood up, the feet of his chair squealing against the rough planks of the floor, and without a word he left the bar and headed towards the camp.

When he reached the office, one of the few remaining convicts looked up from his paperwork. Judging from his dolorous expression, he was yet to hear the good news.

'*Mon dieu*,' he remarked, 'Saoudi takes the morning off. Is there something wrong? Have you some strange illness?'

'Very funny, Pascal,' Mohand replied. He looked around the office. 'Where is everyone?'

'Suffering from whatever ailed you until moments ago.' Pascal shrugged and went back to his papers. 'Oh, almost forgot. The director wants to see you in his office.'

'The director?' asked Mohand. He sat down. This was it. He was about to be given his official release. He tried to stand. His legs wouldn't obey his command.

'You're looking very smart today.' Pascal scratched at his cheek with his pen. 'Is it your birthday?'

Mohand grunted. His mind was in the office with the director. This must be it. His stomach turned over on itself. He wiped sweaty palms on his trousers.

'Are you going to see the director or not?' Pascal asked.

'He can wait,' Mohand answered. 'I am little bit busy at the moment.'

'If you don't mind me saying, my friend, you are acting somewhat strange this morning.' Pascal looked over. He nibbled at the end of his pen.

'I need a cigarette,' Mohand answered and left the room. In the corridor, he lit up and inhaled deeply. I should go, he thought. I should go now.

'Saoudi.' Pascal stuck his head out of the door. 'Is everything okay?'

Mohand stretched forward, brought the other man's head closer to his and kissed him on the forehead.

'What the ... ?' Pascal complained.

Mohand grinned. 'Everything is fine. Couldn't be better.' He handed Pascal his cigarette and turned in the direction of the main man's office.

When he got there, he paused for a couple of beats in front of the door. If this is only a dream, wake up now, Saoudi, he told himself.

He knocked on the door.

'*Entrez*,' sounded from the inside.

Mohand opened the door and slid inside the room, eyes downcast and feeling as nervous as a novice thief. The director's attention was firmly on the papers in front of him. He continued to write while Mohand stood fidgeting before him.

The director eventually moved his eyes from his work to the man before him. He peered over the top of his glasses.

'You are smart today, Monsieur Saoudi. What's up? Are you in a hurry to go back home?'

Mohand could not contain the smile or the hot wash of relief that rushed through him. With these words, the truth had been confirmed.

'Of course, what do you think? I have been waiting for this day for a very long time.'

'Please. Sit.' The director motioned towards a chair.

Unable to contain his excitement, Mohand blurted out, 'Thank you, sir. This is the best day of my life.'

The director stood up and pushed his hands into his pockets. He studied Mohand's face for a moment, his own expression unreadable.

'What are you going to do now?' he asked.

'I'll rest for a few days and perhaps go and visit some friends in Cayenne.'

'And then what?'

Mohand leaned forward, sure from the director's expression that he had something in mind. 'I'm thinking of getting a job to afford the ticket back home.' He paused. 'I have a family back home.'

The director smiled. 'You have been a valuable resource to the colony, Mohand. You could stay here and work for us.' He held his hands out as if he was paying Mohand the highest compliment he could offer. 'You will be the first prisoner ever to do that.'

Mohand was so stunned he forgot for a moment that he was addressing a man who held the power of life and death over him.

'You've lost me there. You want me to stay in a place where I have been imprisoned?'

The director laughed. He sat down and leaned forward on to his elbows.

'We never considered you as a prisoner, Mohand.'

Mohand thought about this. There was some truth in what the man said. Apart from the hell of the first few years and the more recent investigation, his prison experience had been much smoother than most of his counterparts. He mellowed his tone and replied.

'Sir, I understand what you are saying. And I thank you for your respect. However, I woke up every day with a number tattooed on my arm...' at this, he presented his arm and rolled back his sleeve in order to display the ink that was worn into his skin, 'and the worry that one wrong step could see me back in the jungle. You may not have treated me like a convict, but I surely feel like one.'

The director's mouth hung open for a moment. He had clearly not considered that this might be Mohand's reaction. He truly believed that he would get Mohand to work inside the prison again.

'You will be well paid. You will have proper working hours with time off at the weekend...' He paused and read from Mohand's expression that he was of the firm opinion this was not going to happen.

'Sir, I appreciate the offer, but I have to go back home. I would like to work long enough to earn enough to pay for my passage... but as far as staying in the colony', Mohand felt he had to say something that would make this man understand him, 'I would never lose that feeling of being something... something less than human.'

The director nodded. He took a deep breath and sat back in his chair. 'Okay.' He placed his hands before him on the desk as he considered what he should do next. 'Given the service you have offered me over the years, I must respect your wishes. I will send you to the office in charge of the accounts of all prisons. There you will find no convicts and you will choose the room you like.' He nodded and smiled. ‘We will provide you with all you need to start this next phase of your life.’ He held his hands out wide. ‘Who knows, you might like this good life and decide to stay.’

They shook hands.

‘Oh, before I forget, you need to sign your release form.’

With his pulse thundering in his ears, Mohand read, signed and dated the document. It was Wednesday 26th September, 1945, at 3pm. Exactly eighteen years and eighty-five days since he was torn from his loved ones.

FIFTEEN

Paid Work

Mohand had only three days of rest, during which he visited Cayenne with the permission of the prison authorities. Here he looked for some old friends, including Dr Vignon.

The doctor was delighted to see him.

'You look good, Mohand. News of your freedom suits you.' His expression was brightened with a huge smile.

'You look good too, my friend,' Mohand said and asked Allah's forgiveness for the lie. His old friend was thin and worn down with his constant battle against death and disease over the years.

Vignon took him to his cramped office and together they shared a glass of cognac.

'I can only afford one glass,' Vignon shrugged.

'Do you have no plans to return home?' asked Mohand.

'Where would I go? What would I do?' Vignon replied. 'This is my life, Mohand. Here with the sick and the dying.' His smile was one of acceptance. 'The men need me.'

Mohand could only nod, his throat thick with emotion. He was humbled that such a man could devote his life to help people that his countrymen had decided should die.

The two men spoke for a few hours, both delaying the moment when they would have to say goodbye. They were saved from this indecision by an orderly peering in through the door.

'Doctor, we need you at …'

'I'll just be with you,' Vignon said. Both men stood up. They hugged.
'Not bad for a Frenchman,' said Mohand with a smile and left.

* * *

On 30th September, 1945, Mohand visited his new office, which was located at the far end of the town, away from the prison camp. Once he was aware of this, some of his reservations melted away. He was still unsure of working for the authorities, but the location of his new workplace helped to assuage his concerns.

This was a means to an end, he kept telling himself. He was doing this out of choice. And he was being paid good money that would help him return home. Along with the money that he had saved over the years with Monsieur Chin, he might even have enough to set himself up in a little business when he got back to Maillot.

His reservations shrunk even further when he was taken to his new accommodation. He had a room very close to the town centre. His room had space for a bed, a table and chair and a small trunk for his belongings. The curtained window looked out onto a small courtyard that was bursting with flowers. The room even had a shower. This was a luxury he had never experienced in his life. He felt like a little boy opening his first Christmas present. This was a new world for him and one he could easily get attached to.

The next day, he reported early for work. His new boss shook him warmly by the hand.

'Louis Bonnet at your service.' He was a tall, slim man with a brush of dark, untidy hair and a pair of ears that would not have looked out of place on a baby elephant. 'Delighted to have you on board. You come with a very strong recommendation, Monsieur Saoudi.'

Astounded at such a warm reception, Mohand could only nod his thanks.

He was shown around the office, introduced to the men he would be working with and had his duties explained to him. Each of the three men he would now be working with stood up to shake his hand.

'Hi, I'm Bruno.'

'Didier.'

'Serge, and I am the brains of the outfit, as you will come to see. The other two are merely waiting out their retirement.' Didier and Bruno, who both looked like they were mere months past their first shave, simply laughed at their colleague and called him a rude name.

The rest of his first day passed in an atmosphere of good humour and hard work. Everything was done with maximum courtesy and respect. At one point he almost told the men to stop being so pleasant. He felt unworthy of this manner of treatment.

He fought down this emotion with all his energy. He was a free man. This was how free men talked to each other.

The job was more or less similar to what he was doing before and he slipped into his work pattern as if he had been working there for most of his life. Within a week, he knew the ins and outs of the job, knew his way around the building and could remember most of the names of his workmates.

His new colleagues were a sociable group and he quickly opened up to them. In turn, they took to him and invited him to every function available and even to their homes.

* * *

On New Year's Eve, 1945, Mohand was surprised when his manager awarded him a promotion. That evening, he was invited to attend the New Year celebration for the first time in his life. He was surrounded mainly by French people, and he managed to integrate seamlessly with them. This, however, became like a worm that buried itself into his conscience. He was so comfortable in his new job and new environment that he feared going back home.

He could have a good life here: he had friends, he was earning decent money and he was in a position of respect. What would he have if he returned home? Would his family even want him?

His guilty conscience was troubled even more when fresh news arrived from Algeria. This letter was written in a different hand than normal. From this, he assumed that his old friend Caid Mezaine had died. As he read, he wondered who had penned this letter. Whoever it was, they didn't share the same delicate penmanship of Mezaine.

Instead, it was like a series of scratches across the paper; the words were so poorly chosen that he struggled to make sense of them.

In essence, what he managed to learn was that the war had only made things more difficult for the *indigènes*. The world was in bad shape and the French were taking whatever they could from the fields of Algeria to feed her population in France. This left the Algerians with what amounted to famine conditions.

Also, the *colons* were up to their usual tricks. Dahmane had been charged with theft and sent to prison.

This meant that the family was under the stewardship of Amar, who was half-blind and weakened by years of illness and deprivation. As to his wife, Saada, Mohand still had no idea what his family had done with her.

After a few sleepless nights, he came to his senses; his place was with his people, to help them during this time of need. Nonetheless, he worried that they might not want him. After all, the family land would have been split between Dahmane and Amar, and he was nothing but a stranger to them now. Why bother having him back when they could split the land between only two of them?

Lying awake, staring at the ceiling, he came up with an idea that would prove whether his family still wanted him. If they were able and, more importantly, willing to send him some money, then he could be certain of his place within his tribe. He had no wish for land or money, nor did he wish to upset anyone. All he wanted to know was that he still had their love.

He jumped from his bed, turned on the light switch and sat at the chair by the table. He addressed his letter to Amar.

My dearest brother, I write with good news. After all these years as a prisoner of the French, I have been given my freedom.

I am anxious to return home to you all, but I may have to wait years before I can earn enough to afford the passage.

I hate to ask this of you, particularly during these hardest of times, but if you are in a position to send me some money I will be able to return home sooner.

Your humble servant and loving brother,
Kaci.

Addressing himself as Kaci so automatically came as something of a shock. For so long he had thought of himself as Mohand, the convict. Now he was about to return home, he had slipped so easily into his old self.

The wait for a reply was agonising. Having decided what his course of action should be, he was impatient to return to Algerian soil.

At last he held the reply in his hand. With trepidation he opened it and when he realised what the response was, his eyes filled with tears. So much so that he could barely read the letter to the end.

It was written in the same poor French as the last one and in the same scratchy style.

Kaci,

The news of your early release has filled us with joy. Every one of the neighbours came to celebrate with us. Sadly, Dahmane was unable to join us for the celebrations as he is in El Harrach prison in Algiers. Our neighbour, Ou Rabah, was murdered. You remember him? A good man. Why he was killed we don't know, but the enemy pointed the finger at our family and Dahmane and four cousins were sent to prison.

Mohand bit his lips at this news, feeling his moment of happiness wither. Would this ever end? He knew Dahmane would be innocent; that this was simply another way the French kept the *indigènes* fighting among themselves. To make it less likely they would turn on their oppressors.

But good news. You are coming home. Your dear mother, she told us. With her last breath, she said you would be coming home and to make you promise that the first thing you do is to visit her grave. We wanted to tell her she was a crazy woman. But you can't speak to the dying like that.

But Allah be praised, she was right.

Dearest Hana Addidi. Mohand held a hand to his lips and felt his throat tighten with emotion. He would never see her again. He braced himself to read the rest of the letter, in case there was any more bad news.

There is nothing so important than you come back to your family. These difficult times mean we are struggling, but we have sold our last two bulls to help you.

Please forgive us the little this brings. It is all we have.

Your loving brother and faithful servant,

Amar

The letter contained what would have been a fortune to his family: fifty francs. He held it in his hands as if it would turn to dust at the merest touch of his skin.

He cried. Tears slid down his cheeks. Dahmane was in prison. Poor weak Amar was in charge of the family's affairs. His mother was dead.

Such news.

Dear Hana Addidi was dead. The woman who looked after him better than her own children. He recalled her smile. The love in her eyes every time she looked his way. She was dead. Of course she was. Few Algerians lived deep into old age.

He cried some more. And promised. Mouthing the words, he sent a silent message to his dead stepmother. He would visit her grave as soon as he arrived home.

Mohand plucked out the fifty-franc note. He understood how difficult it would have been for his family to spare this money. Emotion swamped him anew. He knew then that the family was desperate for his return, and from that moment onwards, his impatience increased, he wanted to be with them as soon as possible.

* * *

When Mohand heard that the first civilians' boat had arrived, he started getting ready for travelling. He had to raise an application to ask for permission to leave the colony. In those days, the entire region was still under the control of the French military, and so an official pass from the army was needed in order to travel between the islands or away from the area.

At the earliest opportunity following the reply from his family, Mohand submitted his application. Give it a week, he was told. Perhaps two, and he would have the permission he sought.

His boss, Louis Bonnet, and the rest of his colleagues did not want to see him go. From the moment he heard of Mohand's plans, Louis tried at every opportunity to change his mind.

One Friday night, everyone was at Louis' house for some drinks. Once they were sure he had drank enough wine to soften his mood, Louis and Serge had a word with him.

'Mohand, what can we do to make you stay?'

'I'm flattered, Louis. Really I am. But I must go back to my family.'

'Do you have a wife? Children?' asked Serge.

'My son died,' answered Mohand. 'My wife…' He shrugged.

'That's what you need,' said Louis. 'The love of a good woman.'

'I'm sure my family could arrange one of those within days of my return,' said Mohand. If that was even necessary, he thought to himself. Perhaps his Saada was still waiting for him?

'Please think about staying, Mohand. We need someone like you to keep us right.'

This was something Mohand didn't expect and he was immensely flattered. Until only weeks ago he was the lowest of the low. He was nothing but a convict, and now these men were practically begging him to stay.

* * *

Weeks later, his travel pass had still not arrived. Surely this was a simple request, he thought to himself. It should have taken no more than a week to come through and here he was almost a month later and still no sign of it.

He spent the next week like someone walking on hot sand. He couldn't concentrate, couldn't settle, and jumped from one task to the next before the first was finished. At the end of the week, there was still no word and he made contact with an old friend: Captain Sancarve.

Two days later he was summoned to the captain's office.

'Coffee, Monsieur Saoudi?' Sancarve asked, his bearing every bit as militaristic as Mohand remembered it to be. As usual, despite the heat and humidity, the captain was immaculately presented.

'Yes please, Captain.' Mohand knew better to rush the man and allowed the coffee to be poured and pleasantries to be exchanged.

'Your application', Sancarve changed the subject as abruptly as a bluebottle might change the pattern of its flight, 'has been removed from the bottom drawer and placed at the top of the pile.' His mouth moved into a shape that might have been a smile on anyone else. 'I don't hold with such underhand tricks, Monsieur Saoudi. You have been a good friend to this administration and you should be treated as such.'

'Thank you, Captain,' Mohand said, his mind in a whirl. 'Underhand tricks? Who would try to keep me…?' As he uttered the words, the answer came to him.

'The military were quietly requested, by Monsieur Bonnet, to postpone or perhaps even ignore your request for a travel permit. Now that this has come to my attention, I shall see that it is expedited with haste.'

Bonnet.

His boss had conspired to keep him here against his will? How could he? He thought of the man as his friend. It was all he could do to stay in the chair and not run straight to the office and strangle Bonnet with his bare hands.

As if he could read Mohand's mind, Captain Sancarve said, 'I have known men to be murdered for less in this place. You have your freedom, Monsieur Saoudi, ensure that whatever you do, that situation does not change.'

'I appreciate your counsel, Captain, and I appreciate your help.' Mohand stood up. 'You are a good man, Captain. The *bagne* is a better place for you being here.'

The captain's face twitched in a smile and Mohand could have sworn that he almost looked pleased.

Next morning, Mohand walked straight into Bonnet's office. He hoped that a night sitting quietly in his room would ensure he would stay calm, but at the sight of Bonnet, he lost his temper.

Before he knew it, he had Bonnet's shirt bunched in his hand and the man pushed up against the wall. When he heard the commotion, Serge ran into the room, quickly followed by Bruno.

'How could you treat me like that, Louis?' Mohand shouted. 'I thought you were my friend.

'Calm down, Mohand,' shouted Serge. 'You could get into serious trouble for this behaviour.'

'You all have family here that you see whenever you want. You think I don't have one, or maybe you don't want me to have one?'

'Louis, what is the man talking about?' asked Serge. 'Mohand must have good reason to go on like a madman.' He tried to add a joking tone to his voice, hoping that this would calm Mohand down.

'Go on, Louis, tell him.' Mohand pushed Louis against the wall one more time.

Louis stared at the far wall. He wasn't able to look either man in the eye.

'I'm sorry, Mohand. I'm really sorry.' His eyes broke contact with the wall and met Mohand's for a moment, before sliding away in shame.

With this apology and the man's lack of fight, Mohand's anger quickly dissipated. He sat down, his legs giving way at the realisation of what he had just done. Such an action could have led him back to solitary confinement. But he was still determined to get an answer.

'I'm sorry I lost my temper like that, Louis,' he said. 'But you have no idea what this means to me.'

Feeling that he owed the man an explanation, he told Louis about the Berber people; how family loyalty meant everything and how his family needed him in Algeria during one of the worst famines in the country's history.

'Also, I am a proud man who has been reduced to nothing but a slave. I am categorised with thieves, rapists and murderers, and you would have me stay in a place that I am reminded of this every day?'

'Mohand, I had no idea.' Louis was eventually able to meet his eyes. 'How could we have behaved so selfishly?' He shook his head slowly.

'We?' asked Mohand.

'You don't think that the military would hold back someone's application purely on my say-so, do you?'

Mohand read into this that the request to retain him in the colony came from the very highest quarters: the director's hand had been in this.

'You are that rare beast, Mohand,' said Louis. 'Someone who is irreplaceable. You can deal with the French. You can deal with the Arabs. You know the system inside out… you will be a difficult man to do without.'

'Nonetheless, Louis, I am needed at home,' Mohand said, shaking his head.

* * *

His pass secured, Mohand organised his passage on the next available sailing. And then began the task of saying goodbye to everyone he knew.

His work colleagues organised a party in his honour. Some notable people in the community were invited, including Judge Kathari and his wife. Even Sancarve and his wife turned up for a few hours.

Lacroix appeared for about five minutes, with Armand by his side.

'I have a bar to run,' the big man said as he drew him into a hug.

Armand kissed him on both cheeks and said, 'I'll never forget you, Mohand.'

Lacroix ushered him out. 'Before he embarrasses everyone.'

Mohand laughed at his friend's gruff comment, relieved that it checked his own emotion.

As he did not want to take presents on such a long journey, his friends collected money for him instead. Queuing up to speak to him at the end of the night, they all wished him well in his new life and apologised for their attempts to keep him on at the *bagne*.

The party went on until the early morning and Louis, Bruno, Didier and Serge were the last to leave. Louis was the last to say goodbye. He was very drunk, very apologetic and very emotional.

'I know we have only known you for a few months, Mohand, but we will miss you terribly.' He fought back a sob. 'You are a good man, Mohand. One of the best.'

Amazed at this outburst, Mohand could only let his mouth hang open.

'C'mon, Louis,' said Serge, leading his boss away. 'You never know, Mohand might come back for a visit one day.'

'You will?' Louis made a comical full-circle turn to ask.

'No,' answered Mohand with a smile. 'Not even if they promised a free trip, twenty wives and a bottomless cask of wine.'

The next day, he went to town. He first visited the Chinese shop to pick up his savings. He was amazed when he saw what Monsieur Chin had done with the gold dust he had saved over the years. It was now a leather pouch full of jewellery and would be worth a small fortune once he was back in Algeria.

Then he did his shopping for the journey. Monsieur Chin advised him to buy several boxes of cigarettes as they were a lot cheaper in French Guiana than they were in France. He could also sell them en route in Marseille for a substantial profit, he was assured. Mohand also bought some food for the journey because it was cheaper on land than buying it on the boat. Besides, the civilian boat he was sailing on was not going directly to Europe as it had several ports to stop at before crossing the Atlantic Ocean, so Mohand had to prepare thoroughly for so much time spent on board. On top of that, he bought a few other things for home. In all, he had something like two huge cases and a big bag to carry with him.

* * *

For his last night in St Laurent, Mohand booked a room in a guest-house near to the port. He wanted some time on his own to contemplate the next part of his life, and he wanted to have a short journey in the morning.

All night long he expected a sharp burst of knocking on his door and an army of soldiers to burst into his room. Every time he looked out of the window, it was with the full expectancy that someone would be watching him, waiting for him to come out so that they could then tell him it had all been a horrible joke.

At first light, he got out of the softest bed he had ever slept in, washed, shaved and dressed and then carried his luggage down to the embarkation point.

He looked at his watch. It was only 6am. His instructions had been to be here for 8.30am.

An old *libéré* was slumped in a corner, nursing a bottle of water like it was a cure for all of the world's problems. Mohand gave him ten francs to watch over his luggage, which the fellow accepted greedily.

Morning was Mohand's favourite time of the day. At this hour, while the world remained under the fog of sleep, there was still a promise of better things to come before the heat from the sun began to evaporate it.

The sky was wearing a pink blush, the morning bright with the cries of gulls and parrots as Mohand walked a short way into town. The air was already warm off the river to the left of him, the soft light shining on the white walls of the ranks of buildings that stood to attention before him.

Here and there, gardeners took advantage of the relative cool to water the trees and the grass. Plants burst in a tangle of colour wherever he looked: roses, bougainvillea and azaleas.

If he had just arrived here off a boat, he would have been forgiven for thinking he had landed in a tropical paradise. How deceptive appearances can be, he thought.

It wasn't all a living work of art. There was another reality here, a darker reality: the tang of urine and the musk of unwashed bodies of the *libérés* who had nowhere to go.

Then there was the blood of thousands of men who had been brought here by the administration and worked into an early grave.

He tried to remember the young man who had been escorted off *Le Martinière* all those years ago. At that point he had already experienced some of the worst than mankind could offer, but had he learned anything?

He had learned that evil does not wear a specific skin colour, or own a designated nationality. He had been witness to some of the best that man could do and the very worst that he was capable of.

He had written a note to his family some time ago. It contained only a few words. *On vit et on espère.* We live and hope. Yet hope had been his enemy. He had never allowed himself the luxury of hope. But now he was going home.

He thought of his loved ones. A family much depleted. They needed him. He thought of Saada, his wife. She was so young when he was imprisoned. How much would she have changed? Would she be there waiting for him?

He cursed himself for a fool. His words to his family all those years ago came back to him in a rush. I am dead, he had said. Consider me as dead, for I will never return.

The Berber way meant that she had to be kept as part of the family. That meant she should have married one of his brothers. Would either of them welcome such an arrangement? Did they have a choice?

He saw her smile. Her large, beautiful eyes. He heard the song of her laughter and his throat tightened. What had happened to his wife?

Patience, he counseled himself. Patience. The important thing was that he was free. He was going home.

He searched the sky. Watched a white-tipped dove as it swooped and soared on thermals across the sky, he felt his chest swell with the realisation that he had survived. He was still his father's son. With courage and acceptance, and by concentrating on the simple act of placing one foot in front of the other, he had won the long and hard battle for his own soul.

Now, standing at the pier's edge, he looked down at the water as it lapped at the wooden struts. From there, he lifted his eyes to the far distance. The sun was growing in strength. The sky was clear, apart from a stretch of cloud touching the horizon, curved and slender like the wing of a giant hawk.

Somewhere across that vast distance, a family waited for its son to return.

SIXTEEN

The Man in the White Suit

The sky arched overhead. A cloudless blue so bright it hurt his eyes. Mohand had forgotten how much brighter it could be at home. How much drier the air was as it filled his lungs.

Weeks of travel. Boats of many sizes. Ports almost too many to count and this final train. He was almost home.

His stomach churned. His eyes moistened. His hands trembled.

Home.

He took a breath. And another. And asked himself why he was so nervous. He was almost there.

What if the French were waiting for him and he had to finish the remainder of his sentence here in Algeria? He'd lost count of the times on this trip that he had encountered a French uniform and quailed. A prisoner mentality was all he'd known for years. He had a fear of the authorities that he was sure would never leave him. But each time he felt it, he fought it. They would not win. But still, each time, certainty sliced his gut: he was about to be placed in handcuffs and delivered to the nearest prison.

He breathed again and willed his trembling to stop.

He had left home as a boy and now he was a man. A very different man to the one he might have grown into had he stayed.

He pulled back his sleeve and looked down at the tattoo on his forearm and noted how stubbornly the ink still clung to his skin. He laughed in recognition at the silliness of this thought. Did he imagine the numbers would fade when he crossed the ocean?

With his index finger, he traced the numbers 51240. How deep did that ink run, he wondered. He had been conditioned over the years and had formed the thought processes of a convict. He remembered how uncomfortable he had felt when the men he worked with treated him as an equal. That was an attitude he would have to learn to overcome if he was to make a success of his new life. Did the ink run through layers of skin and muscle to taint his psyche?

That he could not allow. Would not allow.

He had endured everything the system had thrown at him and he had wandered from the maze of suffering with his spirit intact.

He closed his eyes and allowed this thought to seep into every inch of him.

The train chuffed along the line. He craned his neck to see out of the window. In the distance, a vista he recognised. A shoulder of mountain, the Djurdjura.

Almost there. And joy sang its song in his heart.

This part of the journey was the shortest, but felt like it was taking much longer. A variety of boats had carried him from French Guiana to a number of Caribbean ports, before he eventually caught a ship bound for Marseille. There, Monsieur Chin's recommendation to buy cigarettes for sale had proved to be a wise one. He spent three nights in town before the next ship would carry him across the Mediterranean to Algiers and he made full use of that time, selling the cigarettes at the market for a handsome profit.

Near the port, he had happened across a tailor's shop. A dummy in the window wore a white suit and Mohand was gripped by an idea.

It was clear from the moment he stepped inside the building that the owner dismissed him as yet another *bagnard*. The man took in his cheap, dirty clothes at a glance. His tone was sharp, his greeting perfunctory.

'Good day. How may I be of service?' he said, with a sub-text of, *Please just leave and save us all the embarrassment of me turning you away*.

Mohand peeled some notes from his plump pile. Normally, he would never consider being so showy with his funds, but this was an altogether different situation. 'How much for the suit in the window?'

Immediately, the owner's demeanour changed. 'Monsieur Bisset at your service.'

'The white suit. I would like to try it on,' said Mohand.

'It is very expensive,' said Bisset with a shake of his head. 'The best cloth from Paris.'

'Monsieur Bisset, I am no fool from the provinces.' Mohand stood strong, feet planted, shoulders wide. He had dealt with enough suppliers over the years to know how to present himself in the best way possible. 'Please don't insult us both. Give me a fair price or I will take my business elsewhere.'

Bisset shrugged and named a price while trying to disguise his surprise at the turn of the conversation. Mohand halved it.

'*Mon dieu*, you are taking food from the mouth of my babies.' Bisset reduced the sum.

Mohand thought that the man looked old enough to have grandchildren. He named a figure in between the two numbers.

'*D'accord*.'

'Do any required alterations by tomorrow.' Mohand spotted a hat behind the counter. 'And throw in a hat and I'll give you another ten francs.'

'Done.'

That afternoon he had booked his seat on the boat for Algiers and sent a telegram home informing them of his arrival date and asking them to book him the best room in the best hotel of Algiers in his name.

* * *

It was the morning of Friday 17th August, 1946, when Mohand saw the low line of his motherland fill the horizon. At first light, he had climbed to the deck and stayed there till well past noon, watching Algeria grow in the distance. Each moment was one to savour.

Then the dazzling white buildings that filled the crescent-shaped bay of Algiers had hoved into view and Mohand's heart pounded harder.

Before disembarking, he changed into his new, white suit and donned his hat. He had a message to convey. He would step on to his motherland's soil a free man. A man unbroken by all he had gone through.

People jostled for position, shuffled forward with their luggage, impatient to see family and friends. For Mohand, what did one more minute here or there matter? He had waited years for this moment, so he waited patiently and followed the crowd through the passport control gates.

Once his papers had been stamped, he walked through the gates and paused. He was on home soil. He was actually standing in Algeria. His eyes filled with tears. He could feel his bottom lip tremble. He sank to his knees and, leaning forward, kissed the ground.

Home, he thought, as a tear spilled to land on the earth.

* * *

Smoking had become a strong habit while he was in the prison colony, and Mohand now had a large Havana cigar he had been saving for this moment. He pulled it from his pocket and lit it. He took a deep puff. Expanded his chest. Now he was ready to go home.

The port building had two exit doors. He chose the one on the left and walked through into a large waiting area. The first face his eyes lit on was his cousin, Mohand Ameziane, who so strongly resembled his father that he couldn't fail to recognise him. This man was only a child when he had been transported; now he was an adult. That simple fact brought it sharply back to Mohand just how long he had been away. The years away were long and slow in his memory, but here they sped up with physical, visible proof.

His cousin was holding a large piece of card with the word '*Saoudi*' written on it. His eyes hadn't settled on Mohand in his keen search, moving quickly past.

Didn't he recognise him? Had he changed that much?

Then he remembered the suit. The hat, the cigar. He would be expecting a beaten wretch of a man, not someone who was tall, well-built and with an air of prosperity about him. With a smile, Mohand realised that at this moment he must look more like Al Capone than a released convict.

He walked towards the younger man and stood in front of him to disturb his view. But still his cousin didn't look at him, moving to the side and straining his vision to find his returning relative.

Mohand addressed him like a stranger. 'Excuse me. Where are you from, son?'

His cousin moved his eyes from his search and faced the man before him, thinking he was lost and looking for information. 'From Maillot, sir.'

'Which family in Maillot, if you don't mind me asking?'

Eyes still searching, his cousin replied, 'The Saoudi family.'

'You are the son of whom, exactly?'

The man before him grew confused. Who was this man? He looked Mohand up and down. He read the younger man's eyes. This was a rich *colon* in front of him; why was he asking these questions?

'Why, have you been in Maillot? Do you know the Saoudi family?'

Mohand smiled. 'You must be Mohand Ameziane.'

A beat.

'I don't know you …'

Mohand thought his face would split, so broad was his smile. 'I am the man you are waiting for.'

A moment of recognition and the two men were kissing and hugging each other and crying.

'Forgive me, Vava Mohand. I wouldn't have recognised you if you hadn't spoken to me.'

'I knew you straightaway,' said Mohand. 'After all this time.' He shook his head. 'You have grown into a fine young man.' Could do with a good feed, thought Mohand. And some decent clothes. These things remained unsaid. The world was a difficult place for the *indigènes*, but perhaps he could do something about that.

Ameziane blushed, delighted that a man such as this would be so complimentary. He paused and remembered where he was. 'We are booked into a hotel just five minutes from here and more members of the family will join us. Your brother Amar will arrive on a train shortly. He will be waiting for you.'

'Wonderful.' Mohand gave Ameziane another hug, almost squeezing the last drop of air from his lungs. 'This is the best day of my life.'

By the time they arrived at the hotel, those relatives travelling from Maillot had arrived. There were five men standing in the room when he opened the door. He scanned them all quickly, looking for Amar, trying to remember the boy and imagining what the years might have done to him. They were a ragged, poor bunch. All of them wearing huge smiles.

He couldn't work out which one of them was Amar until he noticed the glass eye. His brother looked much older than he should have. Thin and worn with decades of worry. They walked towards each other. Arms out. Mohand couldn't stem the flow of tears.

'My brother,' he cried and held him close. The other men stood around waiting their turn to greet him. 'I don't think I've ever been happier than I am at this moment.' He felt like he was discovering his family for the first time. He stepped back to have a closer look at his brother. At the lined, darkened skin, the withered cheeks, the surprisingly long and unkempt beard. In truth, he was surprised that the hotel had allowed such a bedraggled creature inside one of its rooms. This is what colonialisation has done to my people, he thought. He swallowed the flare of anger, determined that nothing could spoil this moment. To hide his true feelings, he laughed and gently tugged at his brother's beard.

'When I left, he was a boy, and now he is hairy like a monkey.'

* * *

'We have one thing we need to do before we go home,' Mohand announced. 'I have to see Dahmane.'

They arrived at the prison gates around 11am. The guard looked at them quizzically. Seven *indigènes*. All of them unkempt except for this one man in the white suit and speaking perfect French.

'No visits on a Saturday,' said the guard.

Mohand explained his situation politely and asked if he could speak to the director. Normally, the guard would have laughed off this request, but something about Mohand made him reconsider. Minutes later the director was at the gate. Again Mohand explained his situation.

' ... so after twenty years in Devil's Island, I would dearly love to see my brother.'

'This is a special occasion,' the director said, once Mohand had stopped speaking. 'I think we can make an exception today.' A pass was quickly written up for all seven of them and they were guided into a small room and asked to wait.

Inside the room, Kaci could not stand still. He paced the four corners. Rubbing his hands as he walked. Dahmane had been the closest person to him on the planet. After eighteen years' absence what would he look like? Would he have aged like Amar? How would he be handling the pressures of life in prison?

Eventually, a door opened and a guard entered. Dahmane followed. He stood in the doorway, paused for a beat, then took a tentative step toward the group of men facing him. He scanned the faces. Recognised Amar. But an expression of confusion formed on his face when he looked at Mohand.

Mohand feasted his eyes on his brother. His lined face. A body less muscular. Still wearing a long moustache. A tear ran down his cheek.

'Don't you know me, brother?'

Dahmane's mouth fell open. 'Mohand?' He walked towards his brother, arms wide. Emotion robbed him of strength. He stumbled. Mohand stepped forward to catch him and they were in each other's arms. They stood in a hug, gripping each other for long minutes. Weeping, laughing ... grounding themselves in the moment and the truth of Mohand's homecoming.

Then Dahmane murmured, 'Now that you are back, I can die in peace.'

Mohand answered, 'Nobody is dying. And no-one has anything to worry about any more. I am home to look after the family.'

* * *

And now here he was, on a train and minutes away from Maillot, wearing his suit. He checked his palms were clean and then ran them carefully over his thighs, down to the knees. Then he squared his hat. He wanted to make a good impression.

The steam engine on this train was interminably slow. Mohand willed it closer to the station. The patience that had served him so well on his eight-month journey home almost betraying him at the last.

Calme-toi, he told himself. What are a few more moments?

The engineer sounded his horn. They were close to the station. Mohand stood up and looked out of the window.

All he could see was people.

Hundreds of them.

Would Saada be among them? His heart beat faster. He cursed himself again for a fool. Whatever the family had decided, he would have to live with it.

It was clear that people had come from all around the region to welcome him home. In the field behind the station he could see lots of mules, horses and donkeys.

Just before the train stopped, Mohand walked to the end compartment. While people were waiting for him at the front end, he descended from the back. The family members who had travelled with him, let him walk ahead.

Walking towards the waiting crowd in this way meant he could watch them. Many, he knew, would be there out of curiosity. Some of them, the important ones, would be waiting out of love.

As he walked, he examined the excited faces. Mouths open in anticipation. Eyes searching for the man of the hour. Then a shout went up: 'There. He is there.'

Then a clamour. Cheering. Drumming feet. Hands touching him, tugging at his jacket. Wet faces pressed against his. So many faces. Smiles. His name being spoken: here, in a whisper; there, in a shout. All voices reverent. Thankful.

'*El hamdou Allah,*' were the words he heard over and over again.

Then a horse was brought forward. It was three kilometres from the railway station to Maillot itself. The great man should not be allowed to walk. With gratitude to the horse's owner, Mohand climbed on its back and began the last leg of his journey accompanied by a crowd.

His first stop, he insisted, was to visit the families of the men who didn't make it back: Arab and Ali. At Arab's house, he kissed all of his cousin's children, embraced his wife and said, 'I am very sorry that Arab didn't come home. We must forget the past and embrace the future.' He took in their gaunt, lined faces, bellies swollen with malnutrition and their threadbare clothing. A sight, he noted with sadness, that was prevalent wherever he looked. This post-war period wasn't being kind to his people. 'Whatever I can do to help you, I will,' he said.

He repeated this performance at Ali's former home, and was then determined to make good on his promise to visit the grave of his stepmother, Hana Addidi.

By now, the crowd had thinned and only close family remained. Amar was on a donkey to his right. They chatted as their home drew near. Mohand looked over and, not for the first time, took in his ragged condition. His weak frame, his impressive beard and moustache. He smiled at his brother.

Amar's pleasure was clear to see; his answering smile shrunk the cares from his lined face. Moved, Mohand waited until his brother was closer. He leaned over and drew him into a hug and whispered in his ear. 'You have nothing to fear now, brother.'

He drew away from him and considered his next question.

'Saada. My wife. What became of her?' he asked and braced himself for the answer. Amar's expression was one of puzzlement. 'You don't know? Dad wrote and told you. Years ago.'

Mohand made a face of apology. 'I didn't read … couldn't read all of the letters.'

'Dahmane,' Amar answered.

Mohand swallowed. Nodded. Looked away to the far hills. Bit his lip. That one word was enough of an answer. It made complete sense. The old ways were there for a reason.

'I hope he makes her happy,' he said, while thinking that would be difficult when Dahmane was in a prison cell. Poor Saada. Both of her husbands had fallen foul of the French penal system.

When they arrived at the low building that was Mohand's childhood home, he jumped from the horse. He looked around him, taking in the spread of hills on the distance, the light scrub, low trees, the dry earth. He breathed deep, aware of the earth through the soles of his shoes, feeling his connection with the place.

He turned to Amar. 'Where are they buried, brother?' He would deal with the emotions concerning his wife another time. He had goodbyes to say.

'Over there.' Amar pointed to the far end of the field behind the house, knowing exactly who his brother was talking about.

There in the earth, side by side, lay his father and the woman who cared for him more than anyone else, Hana Addidi. Two graves. No signs. Only dirt and one modest stone each, in the Muslim tradition.

'Do you mind if I … ?' Mohand asked.

Amar shook his head in understanding and stepped back towards the house.

In between the graves, Mohand slumped to his knees. He leaned towards Hana's burial mound first and offered a silent prayer to Allah. He considered all of the pain his decision to remain silent had caused his family. No one would have suffered more than this woman, with the kindest heart and warmest embrace. He closed his eyes and allowed the tears to flow.

He could see her there in his mind's eye. Her toothy grin. That way she had of telling him she loved him, without words and with the smallest of gestures.

He allowed the emotions to swamp him and somehow three words escaped the morass of emotion in his mind and slipped past the tremble of his lips.

'Hana, I'm back.'

EPILOGUE

Bashir's Story

I was on my way to my father's funeral.

The plane landed in Algiers at around 12pm in the harsh, dry heat of 31st August, 1991. A heat ardent enough to dry the tears from my face, had I been crying as I exited the plane. I was travelling light and, on autopilot, I walked past the customs officers carrying my small duffel bag containing toiletries and a change of clothes.

My wife had packed it in Boston and placed it in my hand while my three boys – aged ten, five and two – were quiet for once, holding themselves statue-still. They knew Daddy was sad. They knew it was something about Papa, but sensing the adults' need for silence, they hadn't asked.

Outside the airport, a crowd of Algerians waited for their loved ones. Shouted names and laughter clamoured around my ears. People rushed to returning relatives. Backs were patted, shoulders gripped, cheeks kissed.

Before me stood my cousin Abdenour, wearing the universal uniform of T-shirt and jeans. Sunglasses were pushed high on his head and a cigarette was being worked in his mouth.

'I wish it were happier circumstances, cousin,' he said, squeezing my shoulder and kissing me on the cheek. I returned his kiss and patted his arm. Tried a weak smile.

Our village was 142 kilometres from Algiers and I spent most of the journey in silence, like a facsimile of a human, my thoughts closed even to myself. I simply stared at the heat haze in the distance as Abdenour drove at high speed along the empty roads while chatting incessantly.

At one point I interrupted.

'Did he suffer?' I asked.

'He never complained,' he answered.

No surprises there.

I looked around me. Traffic was light. For long minutes, it seemed like we were the only people on the road.

'Where is everyone?' I asked.

'It's the heat,' answered Abdenour. 'Drives everyone indoors.'

'The heat,' I repeated, thinking about the force that slammed into me when I exited the plane. 'I'd forgotten about the heat.'

'America has made you soft, cousin,' laughed Abdenour.

The thought hit me again. Squeezed at my heart. I was on my way to my father's funeral.

My dad was dead.

Someone else was making me move. I wanted to stop travelling any closer to the event I had flown across an ocean for. I needed time to process the information. To assimilate this new dread fact. But time was not on my side. Ritual had to be observed and it ran on its own clock.

Eventually – it could have been minutes or days – we reached Maillot. Abdenour turned into the dusty road that led to my father's house. Both sides of the track were lined with cars and people.

This threw me from my mental malaise.

'All of these people ...' I managed to say.

'For Vava Mohand,' Abdenour said, pride evident in his voice. He was related to this great man and he was proud that people had come from many miles around to pay their respects.

People also assembled in front of our gates. Mainly men. The women would be gathered inside the house, under shelter from the strong sunshine.

Abdenour parked the car. I stepped out into the heat. Faces crowded me. Hands pressed my shoulders. Deep voices praised me for rushing to my father's side. Everyone knew the distance I had travelled and remarked that it demonstrated great love and respect. I accepted their words but internally thought, how could I not?

News reached the house of my arrival and all of the Saoudi menfolk gathered around me; my brothers, uncles and cousins. Each of them greeted me with hugs, and sorrow made their voices gruff.

My uncle Dahmane stood apart. He appeared lost, gaunt with grief. His eyes dimmed, his face slack with the depth of his loss.

I was guided towards the big garages built on to the side of the house, where even more people waited. The space here had been emptied, cleaned and lined with chairs. In the middle of the garage, my dad was laid on a table.

As was the custom, his body was covered with clean, white sheets. Only his face could be seen. By his head stood the imam, reading from the Koran.

How can we be in mourning? I wanted to say. He's here, right here. How can he be gone, if he is right here?

My feet were locked on to the earth. My limbs leaden. I studied the shape under the cloth. This is my father? I looked at the people around me, their faces lengthened in grief. Then back at my father, his face waxed in death. His features seemed different. It was clearly him. But it wasn't. Where was the vitality, the colossus that had strode through my life? I refused to accept that he could be diminished by death.

My body belonged to someone else. This other person reached out for Papa, desperate for contact one last time… one last hug. Before I reached him, I felt the heat from someone's hand on my shoulder.

'The body has been washed and made ready for burial,' my uncle said kindly, reminding me that contact was not allowed.

I stood by my father's head and closed my eyes in prayer. It was true. Mohand Saoudi was dead.

After just thirty minutes with him, my uncle said, 'It is time for his burial.'

'Already?'

Of course, they were in a hurry to prevent the body from decomposing in the heat.

As was our custom, a grave had been dug at the top of the back garden. This was fitting. My father's favourite spot. From here, you could look in one direction over the village, and turn to the other and see in the distance the great Djuradjura mountains. Dad had loved his garden. It was to my shame that I struggled to name more than a few of the trees, bushes or flowers that scented this small corner of home. Dad had spent most of his days since retirement among these plants, creating a sanctuary from the upheaval that politicians continued to foist onto Algeria's present. Given everything that he had suffered, who would know more than he how nature could soothe?

Past, present and the future were here in this garden, and as my father's meat and bones would be claimed by the soil, one of the last links to the events of yesterday would be lost.

Algeria's history is a long and bloody one. The recent past – my father's lifetime – was no exception. Perhaps his life was a demonstration of this fact, his life story reflected the torrid and tormented era of colonialsation by the French, and our country's painful attempt to break free.

More people should know what happened to him. He was only one innocent in a long history of colonial abuse and yet... I should tell the world his story, I thought. Again it occurred to me that we should demand an apology from the French government.

* * *

By late afternoon, the sun was still baking the earth. Four men carried the body on a stretcher. In procession, the Saoudi menfolk walked slowly up the length of the garden to my father's final destination. The garden was full of people – they even hung over the fence that bordered it – but they were all silent in their love and support.

So many people, so little sound, I thought. I could hear every footfall as I stepped over grass. Eventually someone spoke.

'Oh Saoudis, who do you have now to fill the shoes of this great man?'

Silence shouldered this voice aside as if it had never spoken.

Although I appreciated the sentiment, we didn't need anyone to spell out what had been lost.

Papa was lowered into the hole and covered with stones and soil.

Chins on chests, everyone prayed. While I searched for the words to say goodbye to my father, I tried to ignore the nagging feeling of guilt that prodded me like a finger between my ribs ... I had not been by his side to witness his last painful breath. How could I call myself son to this man?

From somewhere a breeze cooled my exposed neck. I looked over at the branches of a tree. Nothing stirred and yet the breeze persisted.

Silence reclaimed us as we walked back down to the house, where my mum and sister waited.

Mum took me in her arms as if I was once again a child and all of the emotion that I had stored up behind my numb facade was released. As if she knew exactly what I needed, she guided me to a room where I could be alone with my grief.

On a bed, I curled into the shape of a foetus and allowed sorrow to take me. For hours I lay there while my pillow grew wet and salty with tears. How does one measure grief? Do you count the tears? Do you measure the energy that seeps from your bones, while you lie as limp as a shroud?

'You pick the flowers as a reminder of the beauty in life and you mourn until the flowers wither and die,' a voice sounded in my mind. 'Then you go on with the act of living. There is no other choice.'

Had I heard my dad say this? It sounded like something he would have said. My mind was a melange of images past and present. My father alive. Then a jumble of the faces that lined the outside of the house, the garage, the garden and our neighbours' land. How many had there been? Thousands? Is that how you measure grief?

I picked at the frame of my father's memory. What do I remember of him? Memories bleed and snap into broken chunks of jigsaw. Here, a grin. There, a bark of warning. The constant plume of cigarette smoke. Teeth marks in thick butter spread on a baguette. The spread of the eagle tattoo across his chest.

So much and so little.

He left French Guiana in the 1940s and I wasn't born until later in the next decade. What happened during those years? A jigsaw incomplete. What filled the gaps?

I imagine him on that last day in French Guiana and wonder at how he must have felt. The emotions that would have been rioting in his mind: anticipation, fear, apprehension, joy, self-doubt. He came home to a nation still struggling under the yoke of the French, a family desperate for a leader and a wife he didn't know, who was no longer his.

Events once again forced him to leave Algeria and it was only when I was six that I was to meet him for the first time.

More gaps in my knowledge of the man. What happened to him then? Allah clearly didn't believe this particular man had suffered enough and offered him more difficulties to learn from.

So many gaps.

I see him in his office behind his large oak desk. The desktop has neat piles of papers arranged at intervals. A stubby cup stained with coffee is within reach. A cigarette neatly balanced on the edge of an ashtray sends a thin ribbon of smoke towards the ceiling.

All of those people out there had come to see him. What would he have made of that? Doubtless he would have shrugged, drawn on a cigarette and exhaled a comment along with the smoke, thinking them mad.

He didn't look for thanks or appreciation. If he could help, he did. If a few words could assist someone to make sense of their life, then what was the cost to him?

I hear him again.

'Then you go on with the act of living. There is no other choice.'

Who among us, when faced with the events of his life, would have had the courage and determination to go on with the act of living?

I wonder at his life and his legacy. His name still carries a powerful charge in the Kabylie. People remember with awe that he kept silent rather than issue the words that would have his cousin sent to the guillotine. They remember that he endured years of hard labour without complaint. That he lived with deep respect towards his culture. That he considered all to be his children.

My mind strayed again and again to that last visit. We had a passage of the moon together. A month where he waited each morning for me to wake up, a strong coffee on the table in front of him and a smile on his weathered face. He was an early riser and when he tired of waiting for me he would walk up and down the main corridor of the house, knocking his stick off the walls and coughing.

'What are we doing today, son?' he would ask when I stumbled through to the kitchen, swabbing sleep from my eyes.

I sat beside him, my hand ready for the coffee that I knew my mum was bringing to me, and shrugged. 'How about we go for a drive?'

'A drive would be good,' he nodded and smiled. 'I must go and pay a visit to...' A different name formed on his lips each day. We had a large extended family and, as an important man in the region, he had many, many friends. He also had many people calling on his time and wisdom.

We spent many hours visiting his parcels of land just outside the town. There, we wandered through his olive groves and lines of orange trees, and he would pause occasionally to stroke a leaf or squeeze some low-hanging fruit. As we walked, his low voice filled my ears with words heavy with wisdom, much like the trees bursting with fruit.

We both knew that the visit to the friends was an excuse. Even if no one asked for his time, we would have gone to the car and driven; we simply wanted to spend as much time in each other's company as was possible before the demands on my time forced me to leave. We had many years to make up for and although I didn't know it at the time, we had little time remaining to us.

I can't remember when I first learned that my father was sent to Devil's Island in French Guiana for murder. However, knowledge and understanding are as wide apart as the ocean that separated my father from his family in Algeria for the long years of his incarceration.

This book is my attempt to bring understanding to that knowledge. It is my attempt to demonstrate the evils of colonialism, and it is a campaign bound in a novel to ask the French authorities for an apology for the treatment meted out to my dad.

Most important of all, it's a son's effort to really know his father.

Acknowledgements

MICHAEL J MALONE

I would like to thank Bashir Saoudi and the Saoudi family for granting me the privilege of writing their father's amazing story.

Also, many thanks to Elizabeth Garrett for the gift of space and time in her writers' retreat in Aberdeenshire, where much of this book was written.

BASHIR SAOUDI

First I would like to thank my mother for the persistence she maintained for many years until she persuaded my father to allow me to interview him. I thank her, too, for giving me an insight to his personality and helping me to get to know him better.

I would like to thank Nana Messaouda, who, despite her old age (98), remembered so many details from the day she married my father's brother Amar. She was the source of all the missing information that my father did not share with me himself.

Also many thanks to my cousin Brahim, who introduced me to an old friend of my father's during our time in Bezit. As it turned out, my father had left with this friend many secrets when they went out hunting together. Sharing these secrets filled in many missing pieces of this story.

I'd like to thank my brother Chérif in Paris, for all his support: for getting the taped interview written down, and for introducing me to his friends David Applefield and John Calder who believed in the story and encouraged us to publish it.

Thanks are also due to my elder brother, Tahar – the closest to our father – for his contributions in describing my father's day-to-day habits and foibles and for sharing some of his thoughts.

I'm grateful to my ex-wife, Michelle Barnes, who lived with my father for a while, and who put up with my crazy ambition to bring this story into the world. I also thank her for giving me the dearest three sons, Tamlan, Lias and Nathan, with whom I have discussed many aspects of this story on a regular basis.

I also would like to thank Dominique, a former French teacher in Algeria, with whom I worked on this project for two years until the complexity and depth of this story prohibited more. Her drive to help get my father's story written was an inspiration to me.

Many thanks to my friend William McLymont for believing in the project and for encouraging me to find a way to communicate my father's experiences to the world.

I would like to thank many friends at work in CSR for reading and commenting on the initial drafts, as well as my cousins Lamine, Djallel and Karima for helping to find so much information from different members of our family.

Finally my deepest thanks are due to Michael Malone, who has managed to make my dream of thirty years into a reality. His eye for detail, his patience and his storytelling ability have all helped to make this book everything we hoped for.

Bashir Saoudi with his mother; Kaci Mohand Saoudi.

About the authors

Michael J Malone is a Scottish author and poet, born and brought up in the heart of Burns' country, leading him into a career in the book world. He is the author of two crime novels and a non-fiction book, *Carnegie's Call,* and has had more than 150 poems published in the UK literary press. He wrote this book in collaboration with **Bashir Saoudi**, a semiconductor engineer in Cambridge whose life's dream is to see his father's incredible story brought to a public audience before he retires to Algeria.

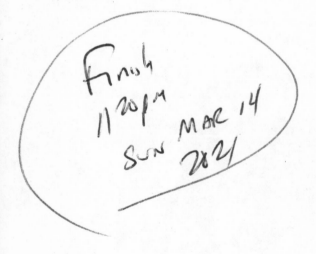